JETTY MAN

D1456341

Jetty Man

G.W. Reynolds III   11-9-18

This is a work of fiction. While, as in all fiction, the literary perceptions and insights are based on experience, all names, characters, places and incidents are either products of the author's imagination or are used fictitiously. No reference to any real person is intended or should be inferred.

High-Pitched Hum Publishing

www.highpitchedhum.net

ISBN: 978-0-9792780-3-7

Dedication

In memory of my
good friend Jean Gilmer,
my uncle, the real Bobby Merritt,
and Mr. John King, a master storyteller.

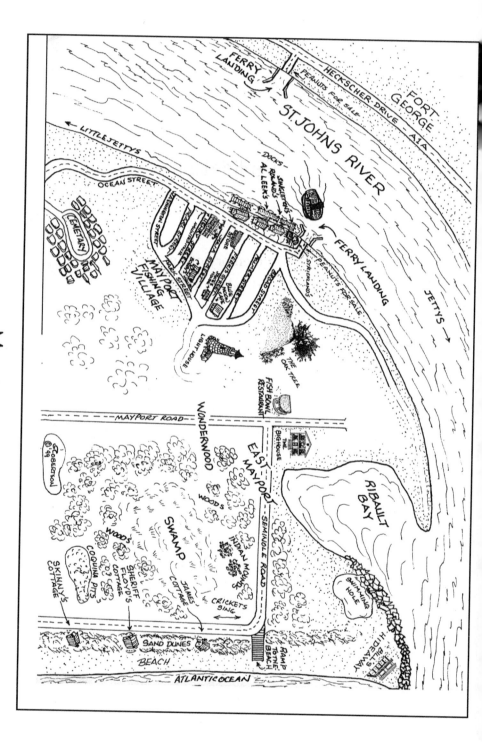

MAYPORT

HIGH-PITCHED HUM

CHATTAHOOCHEE

PRELUDE

AS THE FLORIDA SUN DISAPPEARS FROM THE HORIZON, THE PATIENTS OF THE Chattahoochee Mental Hospital sense that their pleasant day in the courtyard will soon end. The sight of three young men dressed in white reinforces the fact that the time has come for all patients to go back to their rooms for the night. The patients are distributed throughout the grassy courtyard area in groups. In one corner of the yard there are five patients sitting together along the side of a small wading pool. Three are barefoot with their pants rolled up to their knees, however none have their feet in the water. It seems the evening breeze has cooled the water, and the sun is no longer giving the patients a need to splash the heat away. To the left of the pool, two patients are walking together. One is a rather small man; the other is quite large. After about every five steps, the smaller man bends down and picks up an acorn and hurls it at his large companion. The large target only tries to dodge the acorn bullet; he doesn't return his partner's fire. It seems that he rather enjoys being the target. About twenty yards to the right of the wading pool there is a large oak tree that stands as a shield for the wheelchair patients during the heat of the hot summer days. On one side of the tree are three wheelchair patients sitting together. Two of the three are arguing over who has the best set of teeth, while the third sleeps. On the other side of the tree is a single wheelchair occupied by a man in his thirties. His broad shoulders and strong muscular arms don't seem to fit the chariot of the handicapped that he sits in. His facial features are handsome, and the sun has already darkened his easily tanned skin. The young men in white are beginning to round up the many patients and head them in the direction of the main hospital building. One of the young men passes the lone patient. He stops and walks back to where he sits.

"Time's about up for today, sir," says the young man.

The patient looks up but doesn't smile or speak.

"I'll leave you 'til last like before, sir. I know how much you like bein' out here. Even though you don't say it," continues the young man, "I can just tell you'd rather be out here in the cool evening than anywhere else."

The patient still doesn't speak.

The young man then walks away. He soon returns, pushing another patient in another chariot. There is a small transistor radio hanging from the moving chair, and there is a soft voice coming from the small black box.

This is your local yokel from WACO, everybody's favorite station, playing all your favorite tunes. You ask....and....we play. And don't forget, folks, all the proceeds from this station go to helping our neighbors over at the Chattahoochee Mental Hospital, a great Florida institution dedicated to helping mankind.

The sound from the radio fades as the chair is pushed up a ramp and between a set of swinging doors. The silent patient watches a group of other patients walk by as a squirrel chatters out a "good night" to all in the yard. Two more chariots, pushed by the men in white, catch the silent one's eye as they, too, are taken up the ramp and through the set of doors. He closes his eyes and takes a deep breath of the evening air. His long moment is soon interrupted by the nice young man as he passes with one more wheelchair patient.

"This is the last one, sir. So you'll be next. I wish you could stay out longer, but you know the rules."

The silent one again watches the young man and the chair take the path up the ramp. Then the patient's eyes widen at the sound of a familiar noise. It's the hum of a north Florida mosquito, and it passes his ear. Then the courtyard squirrel hollers again, and the thought of a dead squirrel flashes in the patient's head. His thoughts are broken by that familiar hum again. It becomes louder as it nears his ear, and then it fades as the insect flies by. Then the small visitor lands on his hand. The patient looks down and watches the mosquito hunt for a tender spot to settle. A warm evening breeze touches his face, causing the silent one to breathe deeply again, driving the bloodthirsty visitor away.

The time of the evening, the warm breeze, and the familiar sounds all seem to ignite a small flame in a dark and forgotten section of his mind. His thoughts are shaky and broken, but they bring to his ears a voice from the past.

CHAPTER ONE

"PEA—NUTS! PEA—NUTS! BOILED AND ROASTED. TAKE YA PICK. GET YOUR peanuts—fresh today."

A young, dark-haired boy ran to the window of his grandfather's house and peered through the torn screen.

"Daddy Bob! Daddy Bob! Tom Green's a-comin'."

An old man with long white hair joined the boy at the window, laying his hand on his head.

"You always act surprised, Jason. Tom Green comes by every night 'bout this time. Why you gotta act so silly all the time? Act your age, boy." He spoke gruffly, but ruffled the boy's hair. The boy looked up at his grandfather. He didn't seem to notice the reprimand.

"Can we get some? Can we, Daddy Bob? We ain't had none two nights runnin'. Can we, huh? Please, Daddy Bob!" The old man shook his head at his grandson's needless excitement.

"Please, Daddy Bob," begged Jason, tugging at his big hand. His grandfather held back a smile, but the boy's silly face and drawn-out "please" made him laugh. The old man reached into the pocket of his overalls, pulled out a handful of change, picked out a dime, and handed it to Jason.

"Okay, boy, run and get me one of each. Stop actin' silly."

Jason grinned broadly as he moved his eyebrows up and down. He snatched the dime and ran out onto the front porch. As he pushed the screen door open, he sidestepped two rotten boards that were directly in the path as he stepped onto the porch. It was just natural for Jason to dodge that obstacle. Past the two boards, he looked back at the window, where his grandfather was still standing.

"Them boiled ones is for me, ain't they? I just love them boiled ones."

Daddy Bob only shook his head.

"Ain't they?" Jason asked again.

"They might be, boy," Daddy Bob agreed. "They might be. It just depends on how you act tonight. Just you calm down. I never seen a boy ask so many questions before. You gotta calm down, and I mean it. Quit doin' your eyes like that."

Jason didn't appear to pay any attention to the old man's words. He turned and stared intently down the road in front of the house. He could see the small black man, Tom Green, coming into sight. Tom Green was carrying two baskets, one on each arm, and Jason knew what they contained.

"Tom Green! Tom Green! Over here," yelled Jason, waving frantically. He watched the peanut man walk past the one big oak tree that stood near the road. He watched him work his way over the uneven red brick walkway from the road to the steps of the porch. Weeds and grass grew between the bricks, raising some out of place. Many of the red squares were broken, cracked, or missing. Dozens of holes and gaps marked the once neatly formed walkway. With careful steps, the small man moved closer to the porch. Jason leaned against one of the three large white pillars that held up the balconies over the porch. Three of the same type of pillars supported the roof of the balcony.

Tom Green's black skin, darkened to its deepest tint by the summer sun, shone in the evening sun. His white-rimmed black eyes were most noticeable. Jason knew why he had a large scar on his left cheek and a hole in the top of his left ear. Stories around the little town of East Mayport had it that both the hole and the scar had been inflicted upon him, as a child, by his owner. He and his mother had been slaves at Kingsley's plantation. Supposedly, the hole had come about as a result of having had his ear nailed to a door as a punishment. The scar had been made by a lady who had hit him in the face with a ring of keys. People said Tom's mother had died at the hands of her slave master. It was hard to tell Tom's age. He could have been old enough to have been a slave as a child.

The young boy jumped off the porch to greet the peanut salesman.

"Good evenin', Bob Merritt's grandson," Tom said with a wide white smile. "Is we doin' business tonight, suh?"

"We is, Tom Green." Jason grinned. "We truly is. One of each, please. Here's my dime."

Jason held out the dime. Tom Green was quick to take the small, shiny coin. Jason liked the way he and Tom Green conducted their peanut business. It all seemed so important. Tom Green always took the time to play the game. Jason knew that it was only a game, yet he always looked forward to their dealings.

"That's one of each, ya say?" teased Tom, as he dropped the dime into a small change purse.

"Is they guaranteed fresh, Tom Green?" asked Jason.

"They is, Mr. Jason, they is."

As Tom talked to him, Jason saw that the black man was looking beyond him toward the house. Jason turned as his grandfather pushed the screen door open and walked out onto the porch. Bob Merritt was an above-average man in build and size, but his once handsome features had been marked by age and hard work. He looked tall as a giant as he stood on the porch above Jason and the small black man. He was clean-shaven. His hairless face contrasted with his shoulder-length white hair. A full head of hair was strange for a man of his age; yet Bob Merritt took great pride in his thick white crown. He combed it straight back in the tradition of the old westerners, Bill Cody and Wild Bill Hickok. The hair on his arms added a darker shadow to his already tanned skin. Deep, wide crow's-feet in the corner of each eye hardened his look. Young Jason never understood the silence that followed his Daddy Bob. Seemed folks always waited for Bob Merritt to speak first. One might call it fear. Sometimes fear and respect went hand in hand. Tom Green waited respectfully, but Jason didn't.

"I got 'em, Daddy Bob. One of each, like you said. Look!" Jason held the bags up to his grandfather's face as he sat down. "And they is guaranteed fresh." He gestured toward Tom Green.

"That's good, boy. Now get back up here on the porch," ordered Daddy Bob.

Jason gazed back at Tom Green as he walked reluctantly up the steps past his grandfather. Then Daddy Bob looked down at Tom Green.

"Evenin', Tom Green," he said.

"Evenin', Bob Merritt," replied Tom.

Jason thought that maybe everybody played a game with the peanut man, even Daddy Bob.

"I hope this night finds you and yours well, suh," continued Tom.

"I thank ya, Tom. We're all fine here."

"And the boy, suh," asked Tom, "How is the boy?"

Jason looked at his grandfather. Tom Green's question had triggered the thought of a dead squirrel.

"He's doin' better now," said Daddy Bob, as he smiled at Jason. "He knows that the way you handle your fear makes you a man." He paused, staring straight ahead. There was a long silence. The crickets were beginning to fill the evening with their sound. "He did go through an awful thing last year. We most likely never will know how bad it was. Four days alone in those woods is an awful thing for a young'n to go through. Any young'n."

Tom Green slowly nodded his head in agreement. "It was a sure blessin' y'all was able to find him like ya did. Yes, suh, sure a blessin'. Them woods is deep. It was a miracle, that's what it was, a holy miracle." Tom looked up as if to thank God. "The Lord was smilin' on y'all on that day."

"The Lord—" Bob interrupted impatiently. "Maybe so, but those two big black buzzards circling in the sky didn't hurt matters any."

"He do work in many strange ways, Bob Merritt," continued Tom. "Yes, suh, many strange ways."

"Maybe so," Bob said, "but a man does what he has to do. I reckon nothin' could have stopped me from findin' that boy. Nothin'." A look of pride, fading into anger, came over Bob Merritt's face.

As they talked, the sound of a shotgun blast rang in Jason's ears. He was lying on his back, eyeing the peanuts. He barely listened to their words.

"Why would the Lord make a little boy go through so much pain, Tom Green? Why?" Tom Green looked away from Bob.

"And why would the Lord even think of takin' the boy from us? Can you answer that?"

Tom was surprised at the questions. "I can't say, suh. I just don't know. But He didn't take the child, suh. He didn't."

"But maybe He would have if we hadn't searched for so long."

"Maybe the Lord knew what kinda man was doin' the lookin', suh." Tom fingered his hat thoughtfully.

Bob seemed to ignore the black man's words. "And now the poor boy's nights is filled with nightmares. He wakes up sweatin' and hollerin'. It's a damn shame, and there ain't no reason for it. He don't pay no mind to nobody or nothin' most of the time. If you do get his attention, he ruins it by actin' silly. I just don't know. But we workin' on it."

"Don't give up, suh. The Lord will smile on y'all again." Tom smiled his great white smile.

Bob stared at the small black man. After a while he said, "And you, Tom Green, why would a man like you be so deep in religion? After the way you was treated as a child. Don't you ever ask why the Lord would let somethin' like that happen to a small boy?" Bob was taunting him.

"I tries not to think about the hard times too much, suh. They is gone now, and I reckon He had a reason for the way I was to spend my life. I like to think that if there was to be any hell for me, that I has already seen it and now it's behind me."

Still taunting, Bob continued, "And your mama, Tom Green. What about the way the Lord let 'em do your mama?"

Tom's eyes filled with tears at Bob Merritt's question. The thought of his mother cut sharply into his heart. He took a deep breath. Even after all those years he could see her beautiful face.

"My mama, suh, died because it was the Lord's way of freein' her from all her pain. That, too, was a blessin'. Ain't it a nice evenin', suh?" With Tom's change in thought, Bob didn't pursue his question.

The smell of fresh peanuts was everywhere. Jason, hardly able to wait to get into one of the bags, sat down in the porch swing. He hoped that the conversation would soon end. He could hear them discussing some future yardwork that his grandfather wanted Tom to do. Tom Green sold peanuts in the evening and usually found odd jobs during the day. Every now and then Bob Merritt gave Tom a small job.

Jason rubbed his nose on one of the peanut bags and then on his shirt sleeve. He looked around the porch and then down at the gray wooden floor. He lay down on his stomach and began to count the strips of wood, rubbing his fingers along each rib on the swing. His number game soon ended. His eye caught the sight of a palmetto roach as it climbed up one of the white porch pillars. He watched the shiny insect slowly make its way to the top of the pillar. Large pieces of peeling paint blocked the insect's movements when it tried to crawl onto the wooden slats above the pillar. Jason rested his chin on his hand and stuck his tongue out at the motionless insect. After one more ugly face from Jason, the black crawler disappeared into one of the wide cracks in the ceiling of the porch. Jason smiled to himself and, looking around, made another face. He hoped to drive off any other intruders that might be on his porch.

The small town of East Mayport is located about a mile from the shore of the Atlantic Ocean on the northeast coast of Florida. Jason always lived here with his mother and his grandparents. He knew that their two-story white frame house was the largest in the East Mayport area. It was well known to the people of the county as the

"Big House." He loved both the front and the back porches with the upstairs balconies over each. He liked to walk on the balconies surrounded by picket-fence-type railings.

Remnants of a stately look were visible; but age, lack of upkeep, and many beatings by the weather had taken their toll on the Big House. The once white outside had been dulled. The paint was cracked and blistered. The house was located about thirty yards from the road. It had a red brick walkway from the road to the steps of the front porch. The backyard was rather large. Three fig trees were located in one corner. A dog pen, full of bird dogs and shaded by a chinaberry tree, was in the other corner. There was an outhouse in the middle of the yard, near the edge of the woods. It was flanked to the right by a peach tree that didn't bear much fruit. It did bear limbs that could become handy switches. They put those thin red stripes on a child's legs when he was whipped. That peach tree had given up many of its thin branches to the mothers of the area so they could discipline bad children.

There was a small creek that ran past the dog pen and a huge wooded and swampy area directly behind it. There were many paths and trails throughout the wooded area. These were often used by Bob Merritt and his friends when they hunted. There were many thick underbrush sections filled with briars, wild vines, and many varieties of bushes. In the middle of the woods there was a large swamp that bred moccasins, stinkbugs, and those mosquitoes that sometimes ruined Jason's evenings on the porch. Squirrels were plentiful during the day; raccoons, opossums, and small armadillos roamed during the night.

About fifty yards to the left of the Big House, located farther from the road, was Ray Klim's house. It was smaller than the Big House but a good size compared to others. Oak and pine trees filled the yard, causing an early darkness. Grass was sparse because it lacked sunshine and was covered by fallen pine needles. The next house was located about three hundred yards to the left of Ray Klim's house. To the right of the Big House there was a small coquina brick building that was once a store and a catchall for junk. It was full of old tools, yard equipment, old furniture, and hundreds of used items that had lost their usefulness. The small store was empty except for a number of boxes filled with old clothes. Fleas inhabited the boxes in the dark corners. The fleas were there mainly because of the many cats that found shelter in the old building from time to time. Old clothes boxes served as soft, warm places to give birth to litters of tiger-striped tomcats that plagued the woods area. Everybody said that when the Widow Harper passed on, she left her collection of cats to roam free, multiply, and fill the earth.

Jason glanced toward the road and spotted a number of lightning bugs as they flashed their green lights near the big oak tree. His eyes followed one of the lights as it moved up into the top of the tree. He lost sight of the green glow every now and then as it flashed on and off and moved in and out of the hanging moss. The large tree was coated with the hanging growth. It seemed to shroud the oak as a shield against the night. As Jason watched his flashing friend, the thought of a woods fire flickering popped into his head. Then he saw a dead squirrel. The sun passed in the sky. The shotgun blast rang out once more.

Jason struggled to bring himself back to the reality of the porch. He went over to touch his Daddy Bob's white hair as his heart raced in his chest. With his hand on Daddy Bob, he cleared his mind of the strange flashes. Touching Daddy Bob always brought a relieved, safe feeling over the young boy. As Tom Green and Daddy Bob continued to talk, Jason became occupied with the first mosquito of the evening. It landed on his arm and quickly began to hunt with its long, needlelike nose. Jason held his arm completely still, letting the insect settle itself. The mosquito penetrated Jason's skin. He squinted his eyes but remained motionless. He felt the familiar sting and tickle at the same time as the creature began to fill its small body with the boy's blood. Jason knew that the discomfort would soon end. He allowed the evening's first bloodsucker to continue without disturbing it. It was fun to watch a mosquito try to fly after satisfying its hunger. Jason allowed the creature three chances to fly after it was filled. After the third chance, Jason would end the insect's life with the push of his thumb, leaving a small stain of his own blood where it had last landed. He only allowed one pest to fill up each night for fear of losing too much blood. Suddenly, Jason's mosquito ritual was interrupted by Daddy Bob. He changed the rules and quickly slapped the insect before giving it the usual three chances to get away.

"You gonna let them nuts just sit there, boy?"

Jason spit on his hand and quickly wiped the blood off his arm. His grandfather was walking toward the swing. He could also see Tom Green sauntering down the road in search of peanut customers.

"Good night, Tom Green," Jason yelled.

Tom Green didn't turn around to look back, but he did lift one arm and called back to Jason. Tom Green's voice faded as he moved on down the road, calling, "Pea—nuts.... Yes, suh, Mr. Jason, good night."

Daddy Bob sat down in the swing.

"Do I get one of those bags, boy?" asked Daddy Bob.

"Yes, suh. You want the roasted, right?"

"Right, boy."

Jason smiled and handed the bag of roasted nuts to his grandfather. He crawled into his lap, and they began to crack and eat nuts as they swung. Jason thought that the roasted nuts were noisy. They seemed to holler "Crackle!" with each of Daddy Bob's bites. His boiled ones only whispered "Squish" as he sank his teeth into each one. Each time Daddy Bob ate one, Jason did the same. Jason played another game. He wanted to finish his bag at the same time as Daddy Bob. He had to hurry a few times to make sure they stayed even. It wasn't long before Jason had finished eating. To his surprise, Daddy Bob hadn't finished. Jason watched as his grandfather reached into his bag again and again for another peanut. Jason's disappointment was too great to remain silent.

"Daddy Bob, your bag had lots more than mine. Tom Green sure ain't no good counter. We was supposed to finish at the same time, remember?"

"Stop carryin' on, boy. I don't ever know what you're talkin' 'bout. You come up with the silliest things sometimes. I just don't understand ya, boy. I just don't."

Jason, shamed, hung his head. His grandfather reached into the bag for one last nut and then crumpled the bag and put it down beside him on the swing.

Jason looked up. "You finished now, Daddy Bob?"

"That's all she wrote, boy."

"We'll have to tell Tom Green to count better next time, huh?"

"Count what, boy?"

"Them peanuts."

"You still talkin' 'bout them nuts, boy? I don't understand ya. I just don't understand ya." He shook his head. "You ain't never satisfied. You got the ones you wanted and you still ain't satisfied."

Jason studied Daddy Bob's words for a few seconds and forgot them. He slipped off Daddy Bob's lap onto the porch.

"Four's a lot, ain't it, Daddy Bob?"

Daddy Bob sighed with a shake of his head, leaned back in the swing, and didn't answer Jason's question. Jason quickly realized that there would be no response. He climbed back into the swing and leaned back as he thought to himself, "Four's a lot; I know it is." The two remained silent. Jason thought about how he hated the way that the old porch swing cracked and squeaked as they swung back and forth. He wondered why Daddy Bob never noticed the awful noise that the swing made. He also hated the high-pitched hum of those north Florida mosquitoes. They sometimes ruined a nice evening on the front porch. He hoped that soon his grandfather would light up his pipe. He knew that the pests would leave then. Daddy Bob shifted, causing the swing to crack even more, and then closed his eyes. Jason edged over to place his head on his grandfather's knee. The instant Jason closed his eyes, a picture of a bobcat carrying a dead squirrel popped into his head. He ignored the brain flash and opened his eyes quickly. He peeked at his grandfather to see if the old man was falling asleep. He knew his Daddy Bob had a habit of nodding off every now and then, when night stole over the porch. He thought of the many times Daddy Bob had fallen asleep, even when he was telling him something of grave importance. Jason became afraid.

He was losing his companion. He knew he must break the silence. He was reluctant at first. The thought of sitting alone overshadowed the possible consequences.

"Daddy Bob."

Without opening his eyes, Daddy Bob answered, "What is it, boy?"

"Daddy Bob, do you really think Mr. Ray has a devil in him?"

Daddy Bob opened his eyes at the mention of his friend, Ray Klim.

"No, boy, you just been listenin' to too much of the crazy talk that's been goin' on around here lately."

"Well, Gramma said he did."

"Well, your gramma's wrong, boy. Ain't nobody got no devil in 'em, nobody. An' you remember that."

Daddy Bob appeared to think to himself for a few seconds. "Now, don't get me wrong, boy. There's a lot of bad and evil folks in this here world, but Ray Klim ain't one of 'em."

"Daddy Bob, why is it so hot now at night?"

" 'Cause it's July, boy. That means heat rash and mosquito bites."

"Where do all the mosquitoes come from?"

"From the swamp. An' you stop askin' all these questions. That's all you seem to do lately is ask questions. A boy your age shouldn't ask so many questions. It just ain't good for ya."

Jason thought for a second. "Why ain't it good for me?" he asked.

Daddy Bob shook his head and cuffed the little boy's head affectionately. "'Cause I said it ain't, that's why. Now you hush up."

Jason turned his head as the screen door squeaked. His mother walked out of the house onto the porch swinging a rag at the mosquitoes.

"Some of these damn things are as big as your hand," she said.

Daddy Bob's eyes widened. "Mary C., why have you gotta talk like that in front of the boy?"

"Oh, Daddy, Jason don't pay no mind to nothin'. Most of the time he's in another world. He don't even know what's real and what ain't."

"Well, that's what you say, but he sure hears all that devil talk of you and your mother's. Y'all oughta stop all that bad talk."

As they argued, the thought of a shotgun blast kept roaring in Jason's head.

Jason's mother was twenty-six. He thought that she was most beautiful. She had dark skin, deep brown eyes, and long black hair. She had the look of an Indian. Her face was still childlike, but her eyes and body were that of a mature woman. During their hot summer months, she wore tight cutoff jeans with a shirt that was tied in front, exposing her midriff. She seldom wore shoes. All this made her look like a teenager. A few loose buttons on her shirt always revealed the cleavage between her breasts. She had very muscular legs. Her thighs and calves showed the strength of an athlete.

Jason got off the swing and ran to his mother.

"Mama, don't Mr. Ray have a devil in 'em?"

Before Jason's mother could answer, his grandmother came out onto the porch and took over the conversation, as usual.

"He sure does, boy. And you had better be sure and stay clear of him," she stated firmly.

Daddy Bob sat up in the swing and glared at his aging wife.

"You crazy old buzzard," he said, "why you gonna fill the boy with all that hard talk? If it was up to you and Mary C., he'd never get well. Even now his nights are filled with nightmares about his father. Now you're just gonna add to the problem. After what he went through last year, it seems you wouldn't want him to go through no more." Bob Merritt was angry.

Shotgun blasts rang in Jason's head. He held on to his mother's hand.

Wanting the last word as she usually did, Jason's grandmother fired back at Daddy Bob, "He's old enough to know about the evils of the world. And it's our duty to teach him. And it's a sin you sayin' we don't want him well, a sin, I tell ya."

Jason could see the anger rising in his grandfather as he insisted, "Ray Klim ain't got no devil in him and you know it. He's just sick and he needs help. If there's a sin, it's in what you're sayin'."

The old lady interrupted again. "He's sick with the devil. He's got evil in his eyes, and he has those evil fits. You know how those fits do him. I know evil when I see it, and it walks with Ray Klim."

The thought of Daddy Bob and Ray Klim wrestling on the ground flashed into Jason's head.

Daddy Bob looked at Jason's mother.

"And what about you, girl? You see evil in Ray Klim?"

Jason's mother looked away from Daddy Bob and didn't answer his question.

"You know why your mama ain't talkin', boy?"

Jason looked up at his mother and then over at his grandfather. His Daddy Bob seemed to be waiting for an answer. He didn't know what to say. It seemed that his mother had completely ignored the question. She continued to look away from them. Jason thought that it was strange that his mother didn't answer. "Will it make Daddy Bob mad?"

"She ain't sayin' nothin', boy, because before her and your daddy was married—God rest his soul—she had another good-lookin' man that she used to laugh and dance with. But she seems to forget the good things."

Daddy Bob sat back in the swing, and the foursome on the porch remained silent. Jason's mother was still looking away from the others. She pushed his hand away. Daddy Bob lighted up his pipe. Jason was afraid. His grandfather's face seemed to glow in the dark when he held the match up to light the pipe. It reminded him of the devil. He closed his eyes, trying to shake the ugly thoughts from his head. Closing his eyes only added to his fears. When he did, he heard a voice within him say, "You gotta help me, boy."

Jason's grandmother's voice broke into his thoughts.

"He was a good man, but that was before the devil took him.

And that was before them evil fits started."

Daddy Bob took his pipe out of his mouth. "You make me mad sometimes, woman. Ray Klim is a sick man. There ain't no evil, an' no fits caused by the devil, an' no devil inside 'im. He's just sick; and when he drowns his sickness in that hard liquor, it just makes things worse. We oughta try to help 'im."

"Uh-huh. Like you did last week? You almost got yourself killed by that thing you call sickness. Have you forgotten that he almost stuck that ax in your face?" Gramma said.

"I haven't forgotten anything, woman. You're the one with the short memory," Bob's voice rose angrily.

"And what is that supposed to mean, Mr. Defender of Evil?" She stood with her hands on her hips.

"It means, my aging wife, that you've forgotten that Ray Klim is the man that helped you when you got that fishbone stuck in that throat of yours. That could have very well ended your life. It just seems to me you oughta have better feelin's for a man like that."

Jason's grandmother never changed her expression after her husband's reminder. "He ain't the same man, I tell ya. He ain't the same. He's gonna kill somebody durin' one of those fits one day, and it will probably be you since you're the only one that spends any time with him." She toddled over to sit down heavily in an old rocker. "Or it will be poor Eve as she tries to fight that devil one night. I don't know how she can live like that, but you'll see I'm right—you'll see. Then we'll all be sorry we didn't do something about it."

Daddy Bob looked down at Jason. He was lying on the floor, legs crossed, staring at the ceiling.

"Your Mr. Ray Klim," he said, "was a strong and good-lookin' man one time, boy, but some kinda sickness took his strength and handsome looks. He'll never hurt ya, boy, and don't you ever be afraid of him. He's a good man."

Jason could feel the power in his grandfather's words, and the women must have felt it, too, because neither spoke.

During the silence, Mary C. drifted away with her own thoughts. She remembered how, on her sixteenth birthday, she gave herself to Ray Klim for the first time. Her feelings were never sad or guilty when she thought of those meetings with Ray. They were a happy part of her life. She smiled to herself to think that after ten years she still got butterflies in her stomach when she thought about Ray. There had been others since Ray, but that first time with him was still special. Nobody had made her feel as good as Ray did then. He had made her feel like a lady, and she always liked feeling like a lady. She frowned as she remembered that Jason's father, J.P., hadn't made her feel like a lady. She reassured herself that J.P. had been a good man, but he did fall short of the man that was in Ray Klim.

Thoughts of her wedding night with J.P. broke through the thoughts about Ray. She remembered J.P.'s anger when he realized he had not been the first to share her body. She had been ignorant about sex. She didn't know that he would know about her past experiences when he made love to her. Since she had had a number of affairs in her youth, she truly had no idea there was any change in her. Naturally, she denied his claims. He only laughed and called her a child. He had never touched her sexually before that wedding night. It wasn't his way.

"I'm seventeen and more woman than you can handle," she had sneered. Her vicious remark hurt and angered J.P. to his limit. He slapped her across the face, knocking her down on the bed.

Her long black hair gave her the look of a wild lioness. Her young, firm body ignited the anger within J.P. There were no tears in her eyes as she stared in anger after the slap.

"Was it Ray Klim?" he asked through clenched teeth.

"Was what Ray Klim?"

"You really don't understand, do ya? You've got a child's mind in that beautiful head of yours."

She turned her head away and didn't answer.

"You should have told me before. What kinda woman are you? You know how much I love you."

Again she didn't answer, but she could feel that his anger was easing.

"What does a woman like you want?"

She turned her head toward him, and her eyes answered his question. J.P.'s love for her always weakened his thoughts of anger. He scanned her naked body from neck to toes with lustful eyes. Her physical attraction had always been too great for him, and his only thoughts had been of taking her on that night. Mary C. licked her top lip as a small tantalizing gesture. She took a deep breath and stretched her arms over her head, allowing her body to beckon him in silence. She smiled as he fell onto her body.

"He was a fool," she thought to herself.

After a few minutes of silence, except for the porch swing and those high-pitched hums, Jason's mother went into the house. Jason's grandmother spoke again.

"Why you wanna bring up the past and make her feel bad?" she asked, glaring at her husband.

Daddy Bob took his pipe out of his mouth. "Because what y'all sayin' ain't right. She knows it and you know it."

"I don't know no such thing," she argued, "and if you don't stop messin' with Ray, you gonna get hurt by that evil you call sickness."

Daddy Bob closed his eyes and sat back in the swing.

"I ain't gonna talk no more about it," he said, "and keep them awful thoughts of yours away from the boy. He'll be havin' more dreams, and it'll be your fault."

Thoughts of a dead squirrel flashed in Jason's head, and a loud shotgun blast, then another. Jason blinked his eyes to fight the thoughts. As the porch debaters continued, a man's limp arms were being tied to the headboard of a bed in the house next door.

The man's eyes were closed, and he moaned as a woman tied his arms and legs to the bed. The woman wiped the hair and sweat out of her eyes with the back of her hand as she continued to work. The man pulled one of his legs free, making her job harder. She cursed him in a harsh and raspy voice.

"You bastard! You ain't gonna get away tonight. You ain't

gonna vomit in my livin' room, and you ain't gonna break nothin'. You can fight and twist all you want. If you holler, I'm gonna shove somethin' in that big ugly mouth of yours. I'm sick of this crap, and I ain't gonna take no more of it." She worked at the knots around him, making sure he was tied tightly. The man tried to speak but only managed a weak whisper.

"Please, Eve, I'm sick, I tell ya." The woman moved her face almost eye-to-eye with the man, but his eyes stayed closed.

"You're sick with liquor, you son-of-a-bitch; and I hate your guts. I hope you rot."

His eyes stayed closed. He tried to speak again. "I ain't drunk nothin', I swear. Eve, please help me. I fell 'cause I got dizzy. Help me, please. My insides is on fire."

Eve's hard voice interrupted. "A man deals with the devil, he oughta get used to burnin'." Satisfied that he was done, she slammed the door as she left the room. The man continued to mumble.

"Please, Eve, please—help me." He called and called, but there were no ears to hear but his own.

The woman walked on down a long, dark hallway and stopped at a small, dimly lit room on her left. She peered into the room to see an old man sleeping. His mouth had dropped open wide as he slept. He snored with a nasal whine. She watched him sleep for a few seconds, her eyes filling with tears, and then softly closed the door and walked away from the room. She walked into another bedroom, where she splashed her face with water from a white porcelain basin. After drying her face and hands on a ragged towel, she pushed her long, black hair back out of her eyes and stared at herself in a small mirror. Light from a candle added a shadow around her deep black eyes. She continued to stare at herself as she unbuttoned her worn and stained ruffled blouse. She rubbed her neck with a wet rag. Then she reached into her open blouse to wash her breasts. She rolled her head back and shook out her hair as the water cooled her skin.

"Oh, Lord, it's hot," she whispered aloud to herself.

She decided to undress and to wash her body all over. She continued to admire her full woman's figure in the small looking-glass.

She stretched and turned her profile this way and that way to reassure herself of her beauty. She yawned as she washed under each arm. Throwing the rag back into the basin, she fell down across the bed, chilling her warm body on the cool sheet. She began to fall into a half sleep. A coughing sound echoed down the hall, but it only disturbed her for a moment. Her breathing became heavy and slow as sleep overtook her. Suddenly, the sound of her name brought her out of deep slumber.

"Eve."

Startled, she opened her eyes and stared at the bedroom ceiling.

"Eve."

Awake, she turned toward the sound of the voice and saw the figure of a man standing in the bedroom doorway.

"I told you not to come to my room," she said flatly.

"I know, but I want you," said the figure.

"You crazy fool. Of all nights. You've got other things to do. Keep your mind on that. First things first."

She pulled the sheet over her body and turned her back to him.

"I said I want you."

She didn't answer.

"I said I want you. . .and don't call me crazy."

He passed through the doorway and walked to the side of the bed.

CHAPTER TWO

On Jason's porch, his grandmother was fanning herself. Daddy Bob was surrounded by a cloud of smoke. His mother came out of the house and flopped down beside him. Jason was beginning to yawn. He realized that he must not be seen. If the others saw that he was falling asleep, he would surely be sent to bed. He started a battle with eyes that just wouldn't stay open. His eyes closed, and his head nodded forward. The sudden nod brought his senses back, and he continued his struggle. His fight was interrupted by an unexpected noise. This time, when he opened his eyes, all his family on the porch was looking toward Ray Klim's house. His grandmother was the first to speak.

"What was that? Did y'all hear that?"

Daddy Bob stood up. "Hush, woman, and listen."

"What is it, Daddy Bob?" Jason ran to his grandfather's side.

"Hush, boy. It ain't nothin'."

Daddy Bob's answer angered Jason's grandmother.

"Nothin'! You call an evil noise like that nothin'? It came from Ray Klim's house, and so you call it nothin'."

Daddy Bob's eyes narrowed and he shook his head.

"Woman, you know how on a still night like this noises carry for miles. That could have been a bobcat or some other animal ten miles away. All that devil talk has got you thinkin' every sound is evil."

That bobcat carrying a dead squirrel popped into Jason's head. He shook it away.

"Well, it wasn't, and it came from next door, and it was an evil noise. Oh God, I don't know how that poor Eve can live with that man. He'll kill her one night and we'll all be sorry," she droned.

"Don't start that killin' talk in front of the boy. You don't seem to think before you open that mouth of yours. It's late, and we're all tired, and I'm about ready for bed." Daddy Bob stretched his long arms.

Jason, wide-awake now, thought of how nice it would be to sleep in the safety of his mother's bed. He didn't dare ask, because he knew Daddy Bob would be mad if he acted afraid. He remembered that Daddy Bob always said, "It's how you handle fear that makes you a man."

Jason's grandmother continued, "I don't know how she does it. Poor Eve has to fight with the devil at night and take care of that old man during the day. He must be getting on to ninety-five. She's always cleanin' up after him. He messes and wets hisself. It must be awful," the old woman grumbled.

"That old man just happens to be Eve's daddy. It's her duty to care for him." Bob Merritt was exasperated.

"Yeah, but when does duty end? He's been a cripple for years now. Nobody over there ever helps her at all. She does all the house-work and takes care of that old man. It'll be a blessin' when the old man's gone," the old woman prattled.

"That's an ugly thing to say, woman. I never thought I'd hear somethin' like that from you." He felt like hitting her.

"Well, it's true, and you know it," she replied, rocking faster now.

"Well, nothin'! I just hope that somebody takes care of me when I can't go no more. And you'll be glad when somebody helps you live longer, too. You just wanna be contrary to whatever I say." He returned to sit in the swing.

Jason's grandparents were at last silent. His mother began to think to herself again: "Poor Eve, my ass. I hate her. She deserves all she gets. I hope he does kill her one night. She turned him into a shell of a man. It's a sin. If he's sick, it's because of her."

Out loud she said, "And that brother of Ray's, that Charlie, he ain't no help or no good. He just stays out all night with those women of his, gets into fights, and eats up all the food in Eve's house. There's a lot of evil in that house. She oughta run his ass off. She hates him, I know."

"There ain't much you don't know, is there, woman?" added Daddy Bob.

"You mean to say you think I'm wrong about Charlie, too? You defend 'em all, don't ya?" Gramma was still trying to provoke him.

"No, woman. I'll admit he's a mean one all right. There wasn't many around here who could handle him when he was a young'n, and now that he's a full-growed man, I don't know of anybody that can stand up to him. The only ones that try are fellas that ain't from around here, and they just don't know no better. But believe me, they'll learn fast if they come up against that Charlie Klim."

"He's just crazy," interrupted his wife.

"Crazy, yeah, but crazy mixed with meanness. His strength is just too much for a normal man. You never know what a man like Charlie Klim is gonna do next. I ain't never been scared of much, but that boy gives me a funny feelin'. I don't like being' round him at all," Daddy Bob admitted.

"Well, somebody should have put him away after that young girl was raped and killed. We all know it was that crazy Charlie."

"Now, woman, we don't know no such thing. There weren't no proof that Charlie Klim did that awful thing," Bob retorted.

"He's always roamin' the beach, and all he thinks about is gettin' women. They shoulda hung him and he wouldn't be walkin' around waitin' to hurt somebody else. She was such a pretty child, too," Gramma shook her head slowly as she rocked.

"She was a looker all right, but she was more a woman than she was a child. She had even been dancin' at the Fish Bowl a few times before it happened. We forget sometimes how fast these young'ns grow. They is men and women before ya know it."

Mary C. decided to join in the discussion. "The way she flipped that butt of hers around every man in town, she was just askin' for somebody to take her. And somebody did."

"You hush up, girl. That's awful."

"Mary C. is right, woman," added Daddy Bob. "Sometimes folks don't know the whole story. That little thing bounced around in front of them older men until things just went too far, and it's a shame, but she most likely brung it on herself."

"I hope her poor mama never hears y'all talkin' like that; we been friends of the English family for years."

"Now, we just talkin' family talk; it ain't goin' no other place, but other folks know the truth, too, so we just statin' facts. Sometimes folks don't know the whole story. And as far as it's bein' Charlie Klim, I wouldn't put nothin' past that one. Nothin'. But it wasn't proved, so I'll never say it was him." Daddy Bob settled back in the swing.

"Well, somebody will cut him down a notch or two one of these days. Then he'll be sorry for all his wildness," Mary C. offered.

"Maybe so," continued Daddy Bob, "but I can't see it happenin'. I just can't. He's the meanest I know of, and he's gettin' known in other places, too. Folks is stayin' clear of that boy. They's stayin' clear."

"You could get him, Daddy Bob," Jason blurted out.

Daddy Bob smiled. He had forgotten the boy.

"Maybe in my day, boy, but my day is long gone now. Old man like me would be bringin' sure sorrow and misery on hisself if he was to go eye-to-eye with a man like Charlie Klim."

"Well, my daddy could have if he'd been here." Jason couldn't give up.

Daddy Bob smiled again.

"Maybe so, boy, maybe so. Them daddies can do lotsa stuff sometimes."

"Daddy Bob, what does rape mean?"

"Hush, boy, you ain't suppose to be listenin' to us talk."

Jason leaned back in the swing. At the mention of Jason's father, the porch foursome became silent again.

Trees filled with squirrels flashed in Jason's head. Then the old familiar shotgun blast. Somehow, this time the trees were empty, the squirrels were dead on the ground and the sun passed in the sky. Jason returned to the porch as he fought his way through the mixed and crazy images. He noticed that his grandmother seemed to be in prayer while his Daddy Bob and his mother were both in deep thought. They all sat in silence for a moment, and then Daddy Bob spoke.

"Yeah, I never will forget that time we was all at the Fish Bowl and that crazy Charlie Klim fought them three men from Saint Augustine. It was really somethin'. He didn't want nobody to help either. He kept swingin' them big sledgehammer arms of his until they was beggin' him to stop. His face was fire red. I'll never forget it. His eyes looked glassy and wet, kinda like they was full of tears that needed to come out. Each time he'd throw one of those big fists of his, he'd give out a grunt, like maybe he was in pain after each lick. If the bartender hadn't shoved that double-barreled baby in his face, he'd a most likely kilt them fellas. He seemed to enjoy it all as it went on. And it was all over some woman. A pretty woman, too. And the really crazy thing is that the woman was with them Saint Augustine fellas to start with. She had even tried to stop the fight once, but Charlie broke her nose with one of those wild punches. I tell ya, it was a sight to see. She ran out onto the beach hollerin', 'He done broke my nose! My face! My face! He done broke my nose!' It got kinda funny there at the end. We all tried not to laugh, but it was hard." Daddy Bob relayed all this solemnly.

"Well, I think it sounds awful," said Mary C. "That poor woman."

Daddy Bob scrutinized Mary C. after this comment. "If a woman puts herself in that kinda situation, she's gotta know what to expect. She had been starin' at Charlie and flirtin' for a good while—even while she was dancin' with one of them other fellas. She had one of them low-cut dresses on that shows all ya got. She wiggled around, makin' sure everybody saw her. Charlie danced with her one time, and then I reckon he wanted her to leave with him. She seemed to change her feelin's about him and he got mad. That's when all the hoo-doo started. Boy, it was somethin'. We don't need them Saint

Augustine folks 'round here anyway."

With that, Daddy Bob and Mary C. drifted back to their own thoughts.

Mary C. remembered her first run-in with Charlie Klim. She thought about that night—not long after she had married J.P.—when they had been walking on the beach and had come upon Charlie sitting near the sand dunes. Charlie only stared at them as they neared him, so J.P. spoke first.

"Evenin', Charlie."

Charlie only nodded and stared at Mary C.

"Evenin', Charlie," added Mary C.

Charlie nodded again and continued to stare. He looked her over, lingering on every curve. And as usual, Mary C. wasn't hiding much. Then he gave another nod, giving his approval.

"You got a lot of woman there, J.P., a lot of woman."

"Thank ya, Charlie, I'm kinda proud of her myself." J.P. smiled proudly at Mary C. Then J.P., sensing Charlie's thoughts, tried to change the subject. "What ya doin out here tonight by yourself, anyway?"

"Oh, I just finished layin' some woman I picked up at the Fish Bowl up here in the sand dunes. I didn't like it too much. So I was just sittin' here thinkin'."

Charlie's rough words didn't surprise J.P. because Charlie always made those shocking statements. He always said whatever was on his mind. People who knew him had learned to expect it.

"You ain't sick, are ya?"

"No, I ain't sick. What you mean, sick?"

The word sick seemed to anger Charlie somewhat.

"Oh, nothin'. I just thought maybe we could help ya. That's all." J.P. walked away several yards.

"Well, I don't need no help. Unless you can get me a good piece of ass. That's what I need. That bitch wasn't even near bein' a woman. She cried through the whole damn thing. She cried. Like a damn baby. That bitch cried. Ain't that some shit?" Charlie seemed to be building up more anger with thoughts of his earlier sexual let-down. He continued, "Yeah, a good piece of ass is just what the doctor ordered." Charlie smiled, but he could see that the others didn't appreciate his little joke. "How long y'all been hitched up?"

"We got married, oh . . . about a month ago," answered J.P.

"A month, huh? Things oughta be gettin' right 'bout now. Yes, suh, things must be gettin' good."

"Things are nice, Charlie, if that's what you mean."

Charlie smiled. "You know what I mean. Did ya take her before ya married her?"

"Men don't talk about such things," replied J.P. "I ain't that way."

"In other words, ya didn't, did ya? 'Cause you ain't that way, huh?" Charlie threw his head back and laughed out loud. "I'll bet ol' brother Ray popped that thing long before you even got close, boy. It wouldn't surprise me if he still tapped it off every now and then. Ya didn't know that brother of mine was a lover, did ya, boy? No, suh, I sure wouldn't let that pretty little ass of hers out of my sight if she was mine."

"Well, I already know all about Ray. And she ain't yours. So you can stop tryin' to start trouble." J.P. began to walk away.

"How'd ya like it when that thing of yours slid in easy that first night? Or did she moan a little so you'd think it was hurtin'? I'll bet y'all did some hollerin' that night. And has she called ya Ray yet while y'all was gettin' it on? Or maybe you ain't done it yet cause you ain't that way." Charlie threw his head back and laughed again.

Mary C., sensing that a fight was short in coming, interrupted. "He's just drunk, J.P. Let's go home. I'm gettin' cold."

Charlie looked at Mary C. "I got somethin' in my jeans that'll warm ya right up, girl. You can pretend I'm Ray, me bein' in the family and all."

Charlie's crude statements had become too much for J.P. to ignore. He ran up to Charlie and hit him in the mouth, knocking him over and rolling him in the sand. J.P. was surprised when Charlie jumped to his feet and smiled.

"You ain't nothin', boy," he said, "and when I finish with you,

I'm gonna take that woman of yours an' get just what the doctor ordered."

Then Charlie ran at J.P., swinging those huge arms. Charlie was so fast that it looked as if J.P. wasn't even trying to defend himself. After Charlie landed about three or four hard licks in the general area of J.P.'s head, the weaker J.P. was lying facedown in the sand. Charlie wasted no time, and jumped on J.P.'s back, pushing his face into the sand. Mary C. began to scream.

"Don't kill him, please! I'll do anything you want, just don't kill him."

Charlie looked up at Mary C. and smiled.

"Okay, girl. I don't know why ya want him, but okay"

He then moved away from J.P., leaving Mary C.'s beaten husband still facedown in the sand.

"So . . . " he said, "you gonna do anything I say, are ya?"

She didn't answer.

"Well, girl, I'm gonna tell ya . . . "

Charlie paused and walked over to Mary C. Her insides quivered as he reached out and put his hand behind her head. He pulled her head toward him until they were face-to-face. He kissed her roughly. She tried not to cry or respond to his touch. Charlie stepped back from her and smiled that crazy smile Mary C. was learning to hate.

"You ain't scared, are ya?" Mary C. only stared at him. Charlie returned the stare for a few seconds, but they were interrupted by a painful moan from J.P. They both looked down to see J.P. roll over onto his back. They looked at each other, but this time Charlie was quick to break the stare.

"Go to your man, girl."

Mary C. looked at Charlie as if she didn't understand.

"I said, go to your man. Now, do it before I change my mind."

Mary C. moved quickly past Charlie and knelt next to J.P. Then she looked back at Charlie.

"He ain't gonna die, girl. So don't worry yourself. But he ain't gonna hit Charlie Klim no more, either, is he?"

Mary C. was surprised and relieved when Charlie began to walk away. She looked down at her husband and then back at Charlie as he moved on down the beach. Charlie walked about twenty yards away from his victims, looked back, and yelled: "I'm gonna have ya one day, girl, but I'm gonna wait 'til you want it, too." His voice faded as he walked on down the beach. "Yes, suh, Miss Mary C., 'til you want it, too." Charlie began to sing as he disappeared into the night.

Mary C. remembered how, as she helped her husband to walk from the beach, she could hear Charlie singing up in the sand dunes, as if he were watching her as she struggled with her beaten J.P.

While Mary C. was thinking back, Daddy Bob recalled his first run-in with Charlie Klim. Bob had been fishing on the jetties for about an hour. In that short length of time, he had a stringer filled with nine sheepheads, all over three pounds, and two red bass, both over five pounds. He had truly found a productive spot on the big rocks. The ritual for catching the beauties was to throw out your line, lean back against a large rock for comfort, and then pull in a whopper. It was all easy enough, and Bob Merritt had no complaints. It was windy that day, and Bob was the only one fishing off the rocks. He remembered how he had been startled when he turned to see Charlie Klim standing on one of the large rocks behind him. Charlie only stared at first, and Bob stared back. Charlie had on an old pair of dungarees with holes in both knees and no shirt or shoes. At nineteen, he had developed into a bear of a man. The sun made his nut-brown chest shine. Bob remembered that he had thought even the rocks weren't as hard as that young boy. To stand there and stare at each other seemed needless to Bob. He turned away and began to bait his line again. He bent down, shading himself with one of the large rocks for a few seconds. Standing up, he looked back to where Charlie had been seen. He was gone. Bob thought to himself as a strange feeling came over him. "That boy's crazy, and he likes scarin' folks. You never know what crazy people gonna do. You just don't know." Charlie's disappearance ended Bob's relaxed feeling. He now felt that he had to be on his guard against whatever was on Charlie's mind. He had decided that the best thing to do was to desert his fish

find and take his catch home. He pulled in his cane pole and turned
to where he had his stringer of fish hanging in the water. Once again
he was startled as he turned by the presence of Charlie Klim. He
was standing there holding Bob's string of beauties. Bob again found
himself looking into Charlie's wild eyes.

"I don't want no trouble with ya, boy. What you doin' sneakin'
around these rocks? Put my fish down!"

Charlie only stared and gave no response to the question. He did,
however, give one of his rare, disquieting smiles.

"You take pleasure in scarin' folks, don't ya, boy? Pure pleasure.
I said put my fish down."

Charlie stopped smiling and looked at the fish, then at Bob.

"You know," Charlie said, "I've been hearin' about what a man
you was ever since I was little. But I ain't never been able to see it
like the others around here. I just ain't been able to see it. You're just
an old man and that's all. You ain't no more, and you ain't nothin'
special. And I ain't never been afraid of ya."

Bob remained glued, eye-to-eye, to Charlie as he continued.

"I remember the time you made me get out of your backyard.
You said I was crazy and to stay away from your place. You remember that, Bob Merritt?"

"I remember, boy. But do you remember that you had already
kilt three of my chickens with that slingshot before I was able to stop
ya?"

Charlie smiled and slung the stringer of fish into the water. Bob
made no move in Charlie's direction. He never changed his facial
expression.

"Stay off these rocks, old man, or I'll do you the same way."

Then Charlie jumped down behind a group of rocks out of Bob's
sight. Bob waited for a minute or so to see if Charlie had any more surprises. After a short wait, watching the rocks cautiously, Bob climbed
up one of the largest rocks so he could see better. As he stood up,
he saw Charlie walking down the beach in the direction of the Fish
Bowl.

Mary C.'s mother, feeling the need to add her two cents, broke into both Bob's and Mary C.'s thoughts about Charlie Klim.

"That Fish Bowl breeds nothin' but trouble. They oughta let it fall into the ocean."

Daddy Bob shook his head. "You just talkin' to be talkin', woman. I ain't never seen no trouble in there unless Charlie's around, so you can't blame the place for that. It's a nice place for a man to have a drink with his friends. As a matter of fact, we danced for the first time right there; and I know you ain't forgot that."

His words brought a smile to his wife's face for the first time that evening.

"You always bring up the past, you crazy ol' fool. Them days is gone. As old as we're gettin', we just gotta live from day to day."

Daddy Bob smiled and winked at Jason. Jason didn't understand the happy gesture, but he sure liked to see his Daddy Bob smile.

Once again the foursome was silent, and they all drifted with their own thoughts.

Mary C. began to think of her second encounter with Charlie Klim.

"Charlie's a pig," she thought, "but he's a handsome pig."

She smiled within and remembered the time when she had had her big encounter with "the handsome pig." It was the time she was digging on the old Indian mounds looking for arrowheads. She had gone into the woods to be alone to think about what she would do next. J.P. had only been dead for a few months, and her life was mixed up and confused. She had only been digging for a few minutes when Charlie came up on her. She hadn't heard him.

"Hey, Mary C.," he said, "find anything?"

She remembered being startled at first. She had always been afraid of Charlie because of all the bad talk of all his evil ways that was heard around town. That night on the beach was always on her mind. But he was big, strong, and good-looking; and it was hard not to be attracted to him. Charlie looked like Ray in some ways, but talk of Ray was always kind and gentle. Nobody ever seemed to have any bad words to say about Ray. Charlie was younger, but he was the bigger and stronger of the two.

"You wanna help me dig for arrowheads?" she asked.

"Shit, no. Who the hell cares about any old damn arrowheads? I'd rather just sit here and watch you dig. You got such good moves about ya."

As usual, Mary C. was revealing her sensuous womanhood with every move. Each time she bent over to search in the dirt, Charlie would give a low moan of satisfaction; and every now and then he would make a crude comment. Mary C. tried to ignore him, but he made it difficult.

"You got a mess a good meat on ya, too, girl."

She kept digging and didn't look up.

"Is that brother of mine gettin' any of that good stuff like he used to, or you savin' it for somebody to take it?" Mary C. looked up angrily at Charlie's grin, and then she looked down again.

"If he ain't, it sure is a waste, I'll tell ya that. But I'll be willin' to bet you're teachin' him a few things at that. Now that good ol' J.P. is gone, maybe you can get Ray back from Eve. She's a bitch all right, but she's a woman. I don't think you're holdin' enough to take him away from her."

Charlie made a noise deep down in his throat as Mary C. bent down once more, causing the cheeks of her butt to pop out of her cutoff jeans. She stood up quickly.

"Oh, please do that again. That was worth comin' out here for."

She turned away from him so she couldn't see his gestures.

"What's wrong with you, anyway? You sound like an old hog rootin'. You act so crazy."

Charlie smiled. "We can do some rootin' if that's what's on your mind. But don't say I'm crazy."

"You had better leave me alone, Charlie Klim, if you know what's good for you. And quit talkin' so nasty."

"Now, Mary C., I ain't done one thing to you, now have I? So why you wanna be so hard on me for? And stop actin' like you don't like that kinda talk. You love it and you know it."

Mary C. stared at Charlie as he continued.

"Besides, I ain't never been scared of that ol' daddy of yours, if that's what you're thinkin'. You always mention your daddy when things don't go your way, but he don't matter to me none. And that J.P., he's dead and gone; so he ain't worryin' nobody. Anyway, he couldn't stop me if he was here. If I wanted ya, I'd just take ya. But you ain't my type; and besides, I don't want nothin' that belongs to Ray. You hear me? Nothin'. And you'll always be his."

Mary C., now feeling insulted, blasted out at Charlie. "I don't belong to nobody! And what's wrong with me, anyway? Why ain't I your type? You ain't nothin' special, Charlie Klim. You say I ain't your type 'cause you can't have me."

Mary C. didn't understand why she had said what she had. It had been said, and she couldn't do anything about it.

Charlie leaned back against a tree and didn't answer.

"I asked you a question, Charlie Klim, and a lady expects an answer when she asks a gentleman a question."

Charlie laughed out loud at the raising of Mary C.'s tail feathers.

"You're the crazy one, girl. You're really somethin'. I ain't much of a gentleman, as we both know. I have this feelin' that you ain't much of a lady, so you don't need no answer. Besides, it ain't somethin' you just come right out and talk about. It's what folks call a hush-hush subject. One of them delicate matters."

Mary C.'s eyes were ablaze when she spoke. "Boy, that's funny. You always say things you ain't supposed to anyway. So why is this so different? Or is it that you ain't got no reason?"

Charlie nodded and smiled again.

"You know, Mary C., maybe it is somethin' you should know at that."

Then he paused as if thinking of a way to say what he had to say. "Boy, that honeysuckle sure smells good."

"You stop tryin' to change my thoughts, Charlie Klim; and you tell me."

"You do like honeysuckle, don't ya?"

"Yeah, I like it. So what?"

"Well, I just wanted you to know that I got some honey you can suckle if you want to."

Charlie laughed out loud at his little joke. Mary C. had to hold back a smile herself.

"Well, I don't want to, and I don't think that's very funny either."

"Yeah, you do. And stop actin' so high and mighty. You're just like me and you ain't no more."

Mary C. looked away after his put-down.

"Okay," he said, "I'll tell ya, but remember you wanted to know; so don't get all mad after you hear it."

Mary C., now intent on his words, nodded in agreement and looked wide-eyed at Charlie, waiting for his criticism.

"Well, it's like this. I hear tell . . . " Charlie paused.

"You hear tell what? You better tell me, Charlie Klim."

"I hear tell," he continued, "that your tits is too soft."

"What!" she screamed, grabbing her breasts with both hands. "They're what?"

"Too soft!" Charlie's words cut deep. "A man likes to have firmness in his hands when he holds a woman."

"Who told you that?" she demanded. "You tell me."

"I just heard, that's all. Maybe it was a mistake. Maybe it was just a rumor that was started by somebody that don't like ya. Is there anybody that maybe tried to mess with ya, and you didn't let 'im?"

"Maybe," she said.

"That's probably it then. Just a rumor. People will tell tales, you know."

"Do you think they're too soft?" she asked.

Charlie smiled. "Now, you know that I can't answer a question like that. But you ain't no teenager no more, girl; so maybe age is gettin' to ya."

Mary C. walked over to Charlie, took a deep breath, and stood with her hands on her hips and her chest out.

"Well?"

Charlie looked up at her as she stood there over him.

"Sure, I can see, but sometimes things look better than what they really are, you know?"

"Do you want to touch me and see for yourself?"

"Don't think so." Charlie smiled.

Mary C.'s eyes widened again.

"Well, would you just touch me and give me your opinion? Or are you afraid you might be wrong?"

"If you want my opinion, I'll help you out; but remember you wanted me to."

"I know. I know. I'm not gonna get mad."

"Well, come bend down here near me so we can get this done."

Mary C. bent down, bringing her breasts within Charlie's reach. He reached up with his right hand and touched her left breast.

"May I squeeze a little?" he asked rather properly.

She nodded her permission.

He began to squeeze her gently at first. After only a few easy touches, he stopped. He did not remove his hand; he only stopped squeezing. His hand remained on her.

Mary C. watched him intently as he brought his left hand up to cover her right breast. He touched her as he had done with his other hand. First a gentle touch and then a firm squeeze. He now had both hands on her. He began to squeeze both sides, gently at first and then roughly. The feeling was pleasant to Mary C., but she was more interested in the decision soon to be reached by her examiner. Charlie began to squeeze harder, pushing them toward each other, causing them to brush into each other. Charlie's strokes became uncomfortable, and Mary C. tried to pull away. With her first pull, she realized that even if she was able to pull away from his strong hold, there was a strong possibility that she would leave some of her behind.

"You're hurtin' me. Stop."

Charlie stopped his movements and let go. He grasped her shirt. Mary C., glad the squeeze was over, tried to pull away again, only to find that her shirt had been caught by one of Charlie's powerful hands.

"You act like you don't like it," he said.

"I don't!"

"Now, that's crap and you know it. You been dyin' to get in my pants ever since that night on the beach, so don't hand me that 'I don't' shit."

Charlie then reached up with his other hand and grabbed the waist of her jeans. With one strong yank, he pulled her off her feet and down on top of him.

"What the hell you doin?" she cried out.

"I decided that while I was checkin' out your firmness, I'd check out the rest of ya, too. Then I can give you a complete firsthand report. Oh, and don't forget that honey's all yours, so feel free to suckle."

Charlie laughed as they wrestled for a few seconds on the ground. Then Charlie sat on her, with his butt on her stomach and his knees on each side of her. He held her arms down over her head on the ground. She looked up into his wild eyes. He smiled, and she began to shake her head from side to side.

"Don't you kiss me, Charlie Klim," she ordered.

"Boy, you're somethin', ain't ya? Hell, I don't care if I kiss you or not. Kissin's just a waste of time, anyway. It just gets in the way of the real action. You need some good action, too, 'cause I'll bet that ol' mama of yours has had you locked up in that house mournin' for weeks now. So you oughta be gettin' ripe just about now. So if you'd start thinkin' about how much you're gonna enjoy this, we could get things under way without all this talk."

A cold chill ran through Mary C.'s body; and she realized she wasn't going to get away from Charlie's hold. Charlie then shifted his body forward so his legs would hold her arms down and he could free his hands. Mary C. stopped talking because it was hard enough to breathe with his weight on her chest, much less talk. With his hands now free, he took off his shirt. His stomach muscles rippled. His chest was rock solid. The veins in his arms bulged out because of the muscles underneath them. Mary C. swallowed and found herself no longer fighting to get away. Charlie also sensed her lack of struggle. He untied her shirt in front and opened it, exposing the cause of her downfall. Charlie smiled. "Girl, you sure gotta mess a good skin on ya. You gonna be glad you went diggin' today."

Then Charlie pressed his chest against hers. Mary C. remembered the great amount of heat she had felt when their skin touched. It was something she had never felt before. She remembered how after feeling the heat, Charlie began to moan and groan and thrash her around on the ground. She couldn't remember when he had taken her pants off, but she saw them on a pile of leaves. The more Charlie rolled, pushed, and pulled, the more excited she became. Charlie added a few words every now and then to help add to her excitement.

"Try not to holler, girl, when I start pumpin' your eyes out, ya hear?"

Charlie seemed to enjoy his crude words; and the more Mary C. struggled underneath him, the wilder he became.

"You got a good feel to ya, girl. A good feel."

Even in her uncomfortable position on the ground, Mary C. felt more pure physical excitement than ever before. She stared up at the sky and let herself go. But Charlie's movements stopped. She opened her eyes and he was staring at her with that smile on his face.

"You want me, girl?"

That night on the beach ran through her mind, and Charlie's words rang out in her head, "'Til you want me, girl."

"You say you want me, girl, and I'll satisfy your need. But you say it."

Mary C. closed her eyes and tried not to answer, but the throbbing inside was too great.

"I want you," she whispered.

"I can't hear you, girl."

"I want you!" she screamed as she reached down to touch him.

Mary C. kept her eyes closed so she wouldn't have to watch the look on his face after he had won the battle. All she wanted now was her needed physical satisfaction. She thought of the pain she felt when he finally took her completely, but she didn't know if the pain was from him or the rough foreplay she had taken. He began to pound her like a wild animal, making his noises with every stroke. She felt tears forming in her eyes, and then more of Charlie's words rang out in her head: "She cried through the whole thing. Do you believe that? She cried like a baby." With those thoughts, Mary C. fought back the tears, wanting to match up to what Charlie Klim considered to be a woman. Then, as fast as it had started, it ended; and without lingering, Charlie gave out one last loud grunt and rolled off her. His unexpected exit embarrassed Mary C. and added to her discomfort. She could feel leaves and moss underneath her. She felt leaves and twigs in her hair. The muscles in her arms and legs ached, and she had three bite marks on the lower part of her stomach. She looked up into the trees above her. The sunlight was the only movement she saw as it flickered between the moving leaves and branches. There were no birds or squirrels to be seen, and she thought that perhaps their wild act had driven all the animals away. Then, out of the corner of her eye, she saw Charlie moving around trying to find his clothes. She thought how odd it was to make love and never kiss. Charlie hadn't kissed her through their entire tumble. Then Charlie threw her her jeans and shirt. Then, as usual, he smiled and broke the silence.

"Don't worry, Mary C., you got good tits."

She hated to but she had to smile at his clever methods of seduction.

"You ain't much good, are ya, Charlie Klim?"

"No, ma'am, but I never claimed to be. You know, Mary C., you're what I call a pleasure unit. You'd make any man so very happy."

Mary C. realized that in his own crude way Charlie was trying to compliment her.

"Maybe," he said, "we can dig for arrowheads again sometime."

"Maybe," she said.

Charlie began to walk away, but after only a few steps, he turned and gave Mary C. one more of those smiles.

"You know, Mary C.," he said, "you could sure get red bugs in some funny places if you keep sittin' on that Spanish moss."

Mary C. smiled to herself at the thought of that first wild meeting with Charlie Klim, but the thoughts and smile were interrupted by her father as he brought her back to the reality of the porch.

"What you grinnin' at, girl? Sometimes I don't know which one of you is the craziest, you or your mama. I tell ya, sometimes I just don't know. We're all goin' to bed now. Come on, boy."

Mary C. looked at Jason. "Good night, son."

Jason beamed at his mother's kind words. "Good night, Mama. I love you."

Jason hugged his mother as he passed her. Her sweet smell, which always brought him pleasure, touched his small nose. He lingered in her arms, anticipating his Daddy Bob's deep voice. It wasn't long before the awaited came.

"Okay, boy, let's get to bed now."

On his grandfather's command, Jason pushed himself away from the comfort of his mother's arms and went into the house. As Jason entered his room, he heard his mother say, "I'm gonna stay up for a while." He heard his grandfather say to his grandmother, "You had best hush all that evil talk. Ask the Lord to forgive you for your thoughts."

Chapter Three

The window in Jason's bedroom faced Ray Klim's house. He sat on the edge of his bed. Many of the things said on the porch began to run through his mind. He tried to picture Ray Klim as a man with handsome features, like his Daddy Bob had said, but it wasn't easy. Jason had only known Ray Klim as a man with dark, sunken eyes, a thin face marked by scars, and a toothless grin. Jason shivered inside at the thought of Ray Klim's eyes. Then the thought of the devil flashed into his head. Jason quickly jumped from his bed and knelt on the floor to pray. "Now I lay me down to sleep, I pray the Lord my soul to keep. If I should die before I wake, I pray the Lord my soul to take. God bless Mama and Daddy Bob and Gramma." He paused. "And Tom Green. Amen."

He jumped back into bed and thought of Ray Klim again. He remembered Daddy Bob saying that Ray had gotten one of his scars from fighting with his brother Charlie when they were just boys. The other scars were from Ray falling and hitting his face on things when he was drunk. Jason knew that Ray Klim must drink all the time, because his grandmother always talked about it. He thought that Ray Klim's toothless grin was due to the same falls he had taken while being drunk. The sight of Ray Klim's sunken eyes once again sent chills through Jason's body. He hid his face against his pillow. "Please, Jesus," he prayed, "stop the things in my head, and please get that devil out of Mr. Ray."

Jason pushed his head deep into the pillow and tried to think of more pleasant things. He thought of how good his mother smelled. Then he saw her face and smile. "I love my mama," he thought to himself.

Then a voice in his head cut into his pleasant moment.

"Jason, you get away from that door."

Jason pushed his head deeper into the pillow. "I hate Sheriff Floyd," he thought. "He's fat and ugly. He fights with my mama."

Jason's thoughts were again interrupted by voices within him. His grandmother's words, "fits of evil," echoed in his head. The words reminded him of the night, not long ago, when he witnessed one of Ray's "fits of evil."

It had been just before the summer had begun. Jason's mother was not there that night, and Jason remembered that Daddy Bob came in after dark. Daddy Bob came to the front door and asked Jason where his grandmother was. Jason told him that she had gone into the kitchen to clean up. Then Daddy Bob went back outside for a few seconds and came back in, followed by Ray Klim. Jason remembered being startled when he first saw Ray. They both went upstairs quickly, and Jason followed close behind his grandfather. They went into a small room in which were kept a few pieces of old furniture. Ray Klim laid down on an old sofa and closed his eyes for a second. Daddy Bob shoved a few things around so they could have more room, and then he turned to Ray.

"I'm goin' down now. I'll get back up in a little while. Will you be all right?"

Jason watched Ray.

"If I can just rest, maybe it'll pass this time. I don't wanna cause you trouble. I just need to rest some."

"Don't you be worryin' 'bout bein' trouble. You ain't no trouble at all. I know you'd do the same for me. And that's a fact. So there ain't no trouble."

Ray nodded his head and closed his eyes again.

Jason stared at his grandfather's sick friend. He became so

intent on his stare that he didn't realize that he had been left alone with the sick one. Daddy Bob had left the room and started downstairs. Jason watched Ray Klim for a few seconds and turned to talk to his loved one. He was gone. Jason's heart raced as a small amount of panic overtook him. He looked back at Ray Klim. Ray seemed to be asleep. Jason could stand alone no longer. He raced down the stairs. Daddy Bob had almost reached the bottom of the stairs when Jason went past him in a run. His grandfather grabbed him as he passed.

"Stop makin' all that noise, boy! You want your gramma to hear us? You gotta be quiet. Now hush. And don't say nothin' 'bout Ray bein' up there, you hear? We gotta keep it a secret for a while."

"Yes, suh." With Jason's answer, they both turned toward the living room, where they ran into Gramma.

"What the hell's goin' on, Bob Merritt? I heard what you told the boy."

"Nothin', woman. Nothin' at all."

"You don't go up into that old room for nothin'. Now what you up to?"

"I ain't gotta stand here and answer your stupid questions. Now you get out of my way."

Jason was surprised as his Daddy Bob pushed his way past his grandmother. He walked into the kitchen. Jason and his gramma followed.

"Bob Merritt," she shouted, "you stop actin' this way! You tell me what's goin' on! What you got yourself into this time? I have a right to know what's happenin' in my house."

"Shut up, woman. You're just carryin' on so. I got Ray Klim up there. He's sick and I'm gonna help him."

"Ray Klim, is it? You gonna start bringin' that kinda trouble home again? I thought we was finished with that. You're a fool, Bob Merritt, a fool. You'd bring the devil himself if he asked ya for help. A fool, that's what you are."

"Don't act so crazy, woman. Ray Klim's just a man, and he happens to be a good friend. He's done a lot in the past for us."

"Folks do change, ya know. When the devil takes 'em, they change. I don't want no part of it, ya hear? No part."

"Woman, you the one askin' all the questions. Now you don't want nothin' to do with it. You're the crazy one."

"And what you gonna do if he has one of those fits of his again? You tell me that, Bob Merritt. What you gonna do then? He'll probably kill us all."

Jason's eyes widened at the word kill. He looked at his grandfather, awaiting his reply.

"I'm gonna help him get through it, that's what. And you stop that killin' talk. The boy don't need to hear that."

"Bob Merritt, you know with that full moon out there that he's gonna have one. That's why he come here. He knows he's gonna have one, too. The moon makes a lot of crazy things happen."

"Woman, if he does have one, it won't be 'cause of that moon out there. It'll be 'cause of his sickness, and it just happens that the moon is full. And that's a fact."

"Well, you think what you want, Bob Merritt. But the devil works best under a full moon."

At the mention of the devil, Jason moved closer to his grandfather.

"What's wrong with you, woman? You always gotta say things to scare the boy. If Ray does have a fit, I'm gonna be there to help too. So shut that mouth of yours and say some prayers of yours that we don't have to battle one of those fits. But he's stayin'."

Jason's grandmother turned away from her husband after his hard words and began to leave the kitchen. She turned back; and, as usual, she had to get in the last word.

"You'll be battlin' alone, Bob Merritt. A full moon always aids the evil. You can't win. You'll get no help from me. You better stay clear of that evil." As she walked from the kitchen, she began saying the Lord's Prayer.

"Pray for yourself, woman!" yelled Daddy Bob. "Pray for yourself!"

Bob Merritt shook his head and walked toward the back porch.

Jason followed his grandfather out of the kitchen, and they walked out onto the back porch. Daddy Bob looked toward Ray Klim's house. Then he looked up at that full moon his wife had been sure to mention.

"You causin' all Ray's trouble, moon?" He stared upward in silence. "Why you wanna cause trouble down here? Leave us alone."

He sat down on the porch steps and stared out into the woods. Jason was afraid of the way his grandfather talked out loud to the moon. He moved closer to the one he loved. Jason's heart jumped as his grandfather spoke again.

"Sit with me, boy. We'll both talk to the moon. Anything you wanna say?"

Jason looked up at the moon. "No, suh."

"It's easy to talk to the moon. It don't talk back at ya."

Jason was still looking up.

"You scared of that moon, boy?"

"I don't know, suh. I don't think so."

"Ya gramma's wrong, boy. That ol' ball of light don't cause nothin' but the tides. And I ain't even sure it does that. So there ain't nothin' to be scared of. Nothin' at all. Your gramma's livin' in a fairy tale all the time. I guess she just can't handle gettin' so old. She just ain't got nothin' else to think about. Don't pay no mind to her carryin' on."

"Daddy Bob, when's Mama comin? It's gettin' late, ain't it?"

"I don't know, boy. When she gets all fancied up and all, no tellin' when she'll be back. But it ain't late yet. She'll be here in the mornin' when you wake up. All right now, boy, remember what I said about bein' quiet about Ray."

At first Jason didn't understand his grandfather's quick thought change, but he soon understood when he saw Miss Eve and Mr. Charlie walking toward them. Miss Eve was the first to speak.

"Bob Merritt," she said, rather sternly, "we lookin' for Ray."

"Evenin', Eve, Charlie. Ya say you're lookin' for Ray?"

"We thought maybe ya seen 'im," continued Eve.

Jason watched Charlie, and he noticed that he never took his eyes off Daddy Bob.

"Well, I ain't seen him; but if I do, I'll be sure and tell him y'all are lookin' for him."

"He's layin' drunk somewhere. He's good at that," said Eve.

"Did y'all ever think that he's sick, and he needs help?"

"If liquor's a sickness, then he's plenty sick."

Daddy Bob looked at Charlie.

"Did you bring his lovin' brother along for support? Or if he does find him facedown somewhere, is Charlie here gonna kick a few more of his teeth out?"

Charlie smiled.

"Maybe you'll be losin' some of yours one of these days, ol' man. I told you a long time ago that you ain't never scared me, and things ain't changed."

Charlie then looked at Jason.

"You oughta be glad ya got your mama's features, boy, 'cause your daddy weren't too much to look at. So you was lucky."

Jason didn't understand, but he knew he didn't like the way Charlie was talking. Then Daddy Bob spoke.

"Ain't there no good in you at all, Charlie Klim?"

"I do some things good, ol' man. Just ask that big-tittied daughter of yours. She'll tell ya."

Bob Merritt's face was red with anger. Eve interrupted Charlie's crude talk.

"You stop lookin' for trouble, Charlie."

Bob Merritt's insides were raging with anger, but his old age and better judgment told him to stay calm with the likes of Charlie Klim. Bob hated the thought of being afraid of any one man. The fear he had of Charlie Klim was real, and he couldn't ignore it. The air was filled with hate, and Jason could feel the uneasiness around him. He looked at his grandfather and then at Eve and Charlie. Eve tried to act as a mediator, but it was easy to see she enjoyed the heated words.

"If ya do see Ray, send him home." Both Eve and Charlie turned away and walked back toward Ray's house. Daddy Bob looked down at Jason.

"Ya did good, boy. Ray thanks ya."

Jason smiled at the pleasing words. His grandfather got up, and Jason followed him back into the kitchen. As they entered, they were met by Jason's grandmother.

"What did Eve want?"

"Trouble," answered Bob.

"Trouble? Or her husband?"

"Both, I guess."

"You got no right lyin' to her about her own husband. She should know."

"So Charlie can put a few more scars on him? Don't talk to me about rights, woman. You don't know half of what goes on."

"What was Eve doin' with him, anyway? She hates him so," said the old woman.

"She didn't seem to hate him tonight. As a matter of fact, she don't never seem to hate him."

"She's said it before, and I don't blame her one bit. He ain't no good."

"Folks can say things and not mean 'em, ya know. Many times things is said to please others."

"Oh, you ol' goat, you don't know nothin'. And that's a fact. Why you hate Eve so? She ain't never done nothin' against you."

"I don't hate her. I just know what kind she is."

"And what kind is she?"

"She's got them eyes of madness, and I don't like 'em. And I ain't talkin' no more about it. So you go on somewhere and play with yourself and leave me alone. I'm tired of lookin' at ya."

Again, Daddy Bob stopped the argument, and Jason's grandmother left the kitchen. She did, however, get the last word once more.

"Keep that boy away from that evil, or you'll be sorry."

Jason looked at his Daddy Bob after his grandmother's warning.

"Don't you be afraid tonight, boy. You stay with me and you'll see how true friends help each other. Sit down at the table, and I'll see if I can tell ya what might happen so you'll better understand."

Jason sat down at the kitchen table, and his grandfather did the same.

"Now, listen close, boy, and maybe you can help me. But you can't be scared. You gotta be a man."

Jason's eyes locked on Daddy Bob.

"Ray Klim might get bad sick tonight. And that means that we might have to keep him from hurtin' hisself or somebody else. It ain't nothin' to be afraid of. We only got to be careful of it. There's a difference in bein' careful and bein' scared. If you're careful, you think about somethin'. You even study it, so you know all about it. If you try to think about all that happens around, you'll never really be afraid; you'll only be careful. Then you'll find that you can handle most anything. It's how you handle fear that makes you a man, you know."

Daddy Bob's familiar saying rang in Jason's head, but he wasn't sure what his grandfather was talking about; but he nodded his head in agreement with his loved one.

Daddy Bob put his hand on Jason's head as a voice interrupted their moment together.

"Bob."

Both Jason and Daddy Bob turned to see Ray Klim standing behind them in the kitchen.

"Ray...what you doin' down here?"

"I'm feelin' better for some reason. My insides stopped burnin', and I think it's passed."

"Would ya like some coffee?"

"That sounds good, Bob, but I don't think I could hold it down. I better not chance it. But I would like to set a spell."

Jason watched Ray as he talked; and Ray seemed to drift away as he spoke, as if he was there at the table and then his body was there but his words were not. Ray's eyes were bloodshot. Jason became afraid, and his small body shivered as his heart began to race.

"Eve and Charlie come huntin' you a little while ago."

"Did they think I was here?"

"I think they knew you were here, and that's why they stopped their hunt."

"Yeah, they really didn't want to find me, they just wanted to know where I was. There's a difference."

Daddy Bob nodded his head, but Jason didn't understand. Jason watched his grandfather and their visitor as they talked. The conversation was mostly about the past good times that they had known, and Daddy Bob asked a time or two if Ray was still feeling okay. As they talked, Ray seemed to leave his sickness for a while; and he even smiled a few times, showing his few teeth as he grinned. After about a half hour of talk, Ray said he was going home. Daddy Bob walked out onto the back porch with him, followed by Jason. Jason had learned to like Ray Klim as he sat and talked, and he even got used to looking at his eyes.

"Good night, Ray."

"Bless ya, Bob Merritt. Bless ya. You're a good man."

Ray walked toward his own house, and Daddy Bob and Jason watched him until he reached his own front porch. As Ray walked up the steps to his porch, he was met by the loud-talking Eve as she blasted out at him about being gone. Ray walked past her as if he didn't even hear her, and she followed him into the house, yelling a few more hard words.

Daddy Bob looked up at the moon. "If you do so much, why don't you shut that bitch up?"

Then he turned, and he and Jason went back into the house.

Jason's grandmother passed the kitchen door, and Daddy Bob took the opportunity to let his feelings out.

"The devil went home, woman. So you can rest easy now. We ain't none dead yet."

"You ain't funny, Bob Merritt. You ain't funny at all. Shouldn't Jason be in bed?"

"Your grandmother's right for the first time tonight. It's that time. So good night."

Jason started out of the kitchen.

"Boy!" Daddy Bob stopped him. "You done real good tonight. I liked ya being part of it all. I know you would have helped if you was needed."

Jason beamed with pride after his grandfather's words, and he quickly followed his grandfather's orders.

"Good night, Daddy Bob."

"Good night, boy."

"Good night, Gramma."

"Say your prayers, Jason."

Jason remembered how good he had felt that night and how he had had such good thoughts in his head. Sleep came quickly, but his restful night was soon ended with the sound of voices. He woke up to find the voices coming from outside his bedroom window. Miss Eve was yelling for Daddy Bob to come in a hurry. Jason could see his grandfather running toward Ray Klim's house. Eve stayed outside the window and kept yelling, "He's gonna kill somebody. He's crazy."

Jason's grandmother joined Eve in the yard, and they both cried as they hugged each other.

Then Jason's heart began to race at the sight of his Daddy Bob and Charlie Klim coming out of Ray's house, wrestling with Ray as he tried to fight and kick his way free. Ray almost got away one time during the struggle when Charlie fell down in the slippery pine needles. Daddy Bob had to hold on alone until Charlie got to his feet and could help again. They carried Ray around to the back of the house and took him to the old garage. Jason ran to the other side of the house so he could continue to watch the action of the battle. They worked the wild one into the garage, and Jason could hear objects slamming against the wall of the building. He squinted his eyes as some type of object came crashing through one of the windows. Then Charlie came running out of the garage and yelled, asking somebody to get him some rope so they could tie Ray up before he did something to himself. Jason's grandmother gave Charlie the rope. He went back into the garage. After only a short wait, both Daddy Bob and Charlie came walking out of the building. Eve was still crying and

Jason's grandmother ran to Daddy Bob and began to do something to his arm. As they walked back toward the house, Jason could see that Daddy Bob's arm was bleeding. He ran back to his room as the foursome went into the kitchen. It was hard for Jason to hear what was being said in the kitchen, but he could hear Eve crying and he could hear Charlie say he was leaving.

After about ten minutes, he heard the garage door open, and he ran to the other side of the house again. He was careful not to get spotted by the women in the kitchen. The lantern in the garage was lit, and he could see someone moving about. Then the light went out, and his Daddy Bob came out of the garage. As he closed the door, it made that tin-on-tin clanging sound; and Jason noticed that there was a white cloth of some type around Daddy Bob's arm. Bob Merritt left the door ajar, and he sat down on the ground in front of it. Jason watched his grandfather for a few minutes; and after he realized that he was going to sit guard for the rest of the night, Jason went back to his room.

Jason returned from his thoughts of the past, and he found himself standing in his room, looking out the window toward Ray Klim's house. He didn't remember getting out of bed, but his flashback had been so real that it took him a second to realize that he had returned from the past. Jason's sleepless dream had worked up a sweat on his neck and chest; so he opened the window so he could perhaps cool himself. There wasn't much of a breeze, but the night air did seem to do the job. Jason reached down on the floor and picked up his shirt; then he wiped his face and neck, trying to end his sweating. He moved closer to the window, and he felt a cooling breeze. He looked in the direction of Ray Klim's house. He could see something or somebody moving about on one side of the house. He thought at first that he could see more than one, but a second look revealed what appeared to be one person at the dark edge of the house. The moon was rather bright. The large oak and pine trees that surrounded Ray Klim's house made shadows everywhere. The figure moved to the back part of the house. Jason thought it was rather strange that anyone would be going into the woods at that time of night. He knew the danger of the swamp at night. As he turned away from the window, he heard that strange noise that he had heard earlier on the porch. He closed the window quickly and jumped into bed, covering himself with his sheet. He knew that it was too hot for any type of cover, but his fear kept him from removing his shield. He could hear his heart beating. He could feel the sweat again dripping off his chin. He tried to think of pleasant things and what he would do when daylight came. Again the image of Ray Klim as the devil flashed in his head. He jumped up, flinging the sheet onto the floor, and he knelt down again by his bed.

"Dear Jesus," he prayed, "please help me to go to sleep and stop all these things in my head. And please, Lord, no dreams tonight, please."

Jason jumped back into his bed, took a few deep breaths, lay back on his pillow, and began to stare at the ceiling.

"Maybe Gramma's right," he thought. "Maybe there's evil about. Maybe it walks with Ray Klim. Daddy Bob could be wrong. He might be bein' fooled by the devil. I love Daddy Bob. A man's gotta handle his fears." Jason ran his grandfather's favorite saying through his mind.

"I like Tom Green," he thought again. "But I wish he didn't have that hole in his ear. It's ugly. Mama's so pretty and she smells so good. Sheriff Floyd's ugly and fat. He stinks, too. I hate Sheriff Floyd. I hate to sleep. Maybe I can stay awake 'til the sun comes up, and then I won't have to sleep at all."

A shotgun blast roared in Jason's head. Then he heard his mother's voice.

"You get away from that door, Jason."

Jason closed his eyes to end the mixed thoughts. The vision of his mother and Sheriff Floyd in the bed flashed in his head. In the middle of his thoughts he heard that strange sound coming from Ray Klim's house again. He opened his eyes. He listened to hear the sound once more, but there was silence. He thought that perhaps there had been no sound at all, and it had been only his imagination. Jason shrugged it off as another addition to his already jumbled thoughts.

He remained in his bed and stared at the window.

A summer shower began and Jason watched the raindrops splashing against his window. He knew that all the summer showers were good for was to stir up the mosquitoes. "That's what Daddy Bob said about the evening rains," he thought. As usual, the shower didn't last long, but Jason watched the window until the rain stopped. He rolled onto his side and faced away from the window. Thoughts of not sleeping were gone from his mind. His eyes were too heavy for a struggle. He closed his eyes and allowed the needed rest to take over his body and mind.

Suddenly his leg itched. Then his side. Something stuck him in the chest. He grabbed the spot with his hand. A small bug of some type wiggled under his hand as Jason continued to press it to his chest. The insect could not wiggle free. Jason closed his hand around his prisoner. The bug still moved frantically, and Jason recognized the shape and feel of the visitor. It was a roach. He held the roach tightly in his hand. He didn't want to squeeze it, but he didn't want to hold it either. Jason sat up and threw the roach across the dark room, slamming it against the wall. He heard the insect hit the wall and fall to the floor. He listened for any movement from his victim. Jason wanted to get up and be sure he had killed the nasty pest, but the darkness of the room helped him decide to wait until morning to look. He shivered inside at the thought of the roach's returning if it had not been fatally injured. He wanted to cover himself as a protection against any more of the roaches that inhabited the Big House. The cover, however, was too hot. It clung to his skin, reminding him of his sticky-legged visitor. He tossed and turned for a short while. Then finally he lay still. His body was calm, but his mind was racing. There seemed to be no escape from his uncomfortable thoughts. He heard the shotgun blast. A bobcat screamed. The sun passed in the sky. A voice whispered, "You gotta help me, boy." Then he heard it again. A squirrel fell from a tree. Jason sat up once more in his bed. His heart pounded as he sighed with relief. He was safe in his room. He fell back on his pillow. His heavy eyes closed once more. He slept.

Chapter Four

As Jason slept, his brain raced with thoughts and images. He struggled to fight his way out of the evil flashes, but his efforts were useless. His dreaded dream returned.

Jason saw himself standing in the backyard. His boots shone with wetness from the morning dew. He saw his father standing on the back porch. He had a shotgun across his shoulder. Jason's mother then walked from the house out onto the porch and stood next to his father. She spoke.

"Will y'all be home for supper?"

Then Jason's father spoke. "Why you wanna ask a question like that, woman? It don't make no difference to you if we come back or not."

"I do so care, J.P. You just think what you want."

Jason watched his mother turn away and start to walk back into the house. Then she turned back and looked at Jason.

"Come here, son," she said. Jason ran up the steps of the porch.

His mother hugged and kissed him. Jason's heart raced as he enjoyed that affectionate moment. Then it ended with the sound of his father's voice.

"Quit slobberin' all over the boy, Mary C. He ain't goin' off to the war, ya know. You oughta be thankful I'm gettin' him out of your way for a whole day." Jason looked at his mother.

"You stay close to your father, and I'll see you tonight."

Jason smiled and hugged her once more.

"Come on, boy. Them squirrels is waitin'."

Jason left his mother's arms and walked to his father.

"We'll be here when we get here, woman," said J.P.

Jason looked at his mother as she went into the house. She didn't say anything to his father after his last remark. Jason stood by his father while he looked back toward the house. He seemed to be waiting for his mother to come out again. She didn't. After a short wait, his father turned away and began to walk toward the woods.

"That bitch."

Jason looked up at his father after his two angry words. His father was silent.

They passed the dog pen. The dogs, sensing a hunt, began to make a great commotion. Jason, even at the age of six, knew that squirrel hunting could be done without a pack of hounds. He smiled at the dogs and tried to comfort them.

"You fellas can go when we go coon huntin', but ya gotta stay home today."

The dogs continued to bark and whine until Jason and his father were out of their sight. As they walked, Jason watched the early sunlight dodging in and out of the treetops, and he heard the famed early bird holler a good morning.

Jason marched behind his father for a long time. They passed many areas of the woods that Jason had never seen before. Jason had heard of the great swamp that was deep in the woods, but he had never seen it. They walked into a large clearing, and Jason followed his father up onto a small mound of dirt. Jason was surprised when his father spoke for the first time.

"There it is, boy."

Jason looked. He saw a great marsh and swamp area. Jason thought that this must be the great swamp that his grandfather had spoken of so many times.

"It's a killer, boy." Jason was startled by his father's words. "You should give her respect, boy. She can beat a man down overnight

SWAMP

without raisin' her hand. Just bein' near her at night can tear at a man's mind and body. You should know about her ways, boy. And you should always tip your hat if you should pass her by."

Jason didn't understand very much of his father's talk, but he did know that he didn't like to look out into those dark, dirty waters. Jason watched his father continue to stare out into the swamp. As before, he seemed to be looking for something to happen. Jason looked around at every little sound he heard. A small splash in the water would send his heart racing. He could see that in one section of the waters there were cattails that stood at least ten feet high. They were so thick that you couldn't see through them at all.

"Let's move, boy." Jason's thoughts were interrupted, and he again followed his father's lead.

As they walked, Jason's father mumbled a few times to himself but he never talked directly to Jason. Jason's mouth and throat were both dry from the long hike, and he was rather glad when his father stopped to rest. His father sat on the ground, and Jason did the same. Then his father surprised Jason by acknowledging his presence.

"You want some water, boy?"

Jason's heart nearly jumped out of his chest. "Yes, suh."

His father handed Jason a skin pouch filled with water. Jason took it and turned it up to his mouth as he had seen his father do.

"You've done good, boy, this bein' your first all-day hunt. You handled yourself real good while we was doin' all that walkin'. This kinda stuff will make a good man out of ya. That's a fact."

Jason smiled after his father's kind words, and the long walk seemed to shorten in his mind. "It wasn't so bad," he thought to himself.

Jason's dream became mixed and clouded. He saw many squirrels in the trees above him. He heard many shotgun blasts. The sun passed from one side of the sky to the other. He heard his father speak.

"Sometimes a man's just gotta get away. A woman's a funny creature, boy. She can bring ya sorrow like nothin' else on earth. And then she can turn around and give you such pleasure that all the sorrows fade like an ol' pair of overalls. You're sure doin' good, boy. You ain't scared of the dark, are ya?"

The woods filled with darkness, and the sounds of the night began.

"Ain't no reason to be scared, boy. Nothin' out here gonna hurt ya. If we was near that swamp, it would be different; but we're far enough from that awful place."

Jason saw his father lean his shotgun against a tree. Then he turned to light a small fire on the ground.

"Your mama will be gettin' worried about us, boy. But it's my thinkin' that a little worry might do her some good. She never worries 'bout nothin'. Yeah, it'll do her a heap of good."

Jason sat down on the ground. His father worked with the fire until it burned freely. Then he lay down on his stomach with his face near the fire. It was strange to Jason that his father's face glowed on the other side of the fire. Jason realized that they were settling down for the night, and the thought didn't please him at all. Then a bobcat screamed. Jason jumped to his feet. He looked around and then down at his father. His father looked up but didn't stand.

"That was pretty close. Hand me that gun, boy."

Jason reached for the gun. He gripped it and turned toward his father. The gun was heavy, and he lost his hold as he stepped away from the tree. The gun fell toward the ground. It seemed a long time before the gun struck the ground. When it hit, there was a great blast, and the dark area lit up. The small fire was scattered by the blast. Jason heard a loud scream.

"Perhaps the bobcat is even closer than before," he thought.

There was smoke and dust in the air from the blast. Jason awaited his father's roar of disapproval. The roar didn't come. The fire was out, and the darkness surrounded Jason. There was movement on the ground across from him, and he was afraid.

"Daddy," he whispered. "Daddy." A painful moan pierced his ears. A frightening whisper followed.

"Jason."

The sound stopped. Jason looked into the darkness. Then he

heard it again.

"Jason. Help me, boy."

Jason closed his eyes, but the voice continued.

"I'm hurt, boy. I'm hurt bad. You gotta help me."

Jason fought his fears for a brief moment. He moved in the direction of the voice. After only a few steps, he was standing next to his father. He was still on the ground. He gritted his teeth in pain. His left shoulder and neck were covered with blood. His shirt was peppered with the small pellets from the shotgun shell. Jason stared for a few seconds in disbelief. His father's eyes were closed, but Jason could hear a low whimper coming from his throat.

"Maybe," Jason thought, "he's dead and the noises are noises of the dead."

Jason's insides trembled at the thought of being alone. He became sick as he looked around him into the darkness. Thoughts of being alone overshadowed the thoughts of his father.

Suddenly something grabbed his leg. A sharp pain shot through the boy's heart. His small body became cold. He pulled away and fell to the ground. Then he heard the whisper again.

"Help me, boy."

Jason looked back to see his father's hand reach toward him.

"You gotta help, boy. Do you understand? You gotta help."

The boy only stared at his father; he didn't speak.

"Come closer, so I can tell ya what to do."

Still Jason didn't move.

"You gotta get Daddy Bob."

Jason remained still and thought to himself, "I love Daddy Bob."

"Come closer, boy."

Jason refused and stepped away from his father.

The wounds on J.P.'s neck were making it difficult for him to talk. He looked at his son and seemed to give up his efforts.

Jason's dream again became cloudy and confused. He saw the shotgun. He saw many dead squirrels. There was a loud shotgun blast. A bobcat screamed. The sun passed in the sky. The gun fell to

Bob Cat

the ground. Then, again and again.

He scratched the mosquito bites on his face. He itched all over. His stomach growled and he felt pain and emptiness inside. Darkness was again around him. There was no fire. He drank from the pouch again and stared down at his father. There was no movement. The ground was stained with blood. The sun passed, and the water pouch was empty. He thought of his Daddy Bob.

"I gotta get Daddy Bob. Please wake up, Daddy."

Jason walked alone in the thick woods. He scratched his face and arms. He sat at the top of an old Indian mound and cried. He saw the cattails standing tall. The swamp was near.

His father's words rang in his head.

"It's a killer, boy."

Jason began to run. He didn't know where to go, but he felt he must run. He fought through thickets of briars and vines. He fell and tripped over stumps and fallen trees. He cried as he ran. A small animal darted in front of him, but Jason didn't break his stride. He only ran faster. His little heart pounded, his legs ached, and the sun burned his face. He must stop and rest. He leaned against a small tree and closed his eyes. He heard sounds to his right, and his rest was short-lived. He looked in the direction of the sounds. Again he was afraid. He saw movement through a thick section of vines. He moved closer. He peered through the brush and focused his eyes on a figure that he recognized. His run had brought him back to his father's body. The sounds were coming from two bobcats as they sniffed around his father's body. Jason breathed heavily and felt as if his heart were going to rip through his chest. The cats began to scratch and tear at his father's clothes. The bigger of the two tore a piece of blood-soaked material from his father's shirt and ran into the woods. The smaller cat followed, carrying one of the dead squirrels. Jason sat next to the tree and closed his eyes. His face burned, but he had no strength to move. A mosquito bit him under his eye. It was painful to swallow. His lips were cracked. The bushes around him began to move, and he cried out.

"Please, bobcat. Please don't." He hid his face in his hands.

Suddenly he was pulled from the ground. Again his heart was pierced with pain. He screamed and began to fight.

"Jason! Jason! Stop, boy, stop!"

Jason opened his eyes and stopped fighting. He was being held by his Daddy Bob, and there were men standing around.

Jason fought his way back to reality, and his dream ended. He sat up in his bed. His body was covered with sweat, his heart was racing, and he felt sick. He sighed with relief. He thought of Daddy Bob's words: "It's how you handle fear that makes you a man."

CHAPTER FIVE

JASON'S THROAT WAS DRY, AND HE JUMPED FROM HIS BED. A COOL DRINK was his only thought. He passed the window in his room and he looked out. It was still dark and he knew he hadn't been asleep long. A second look revealed that Ray Klim's house was lit up more than usual. Jason stared out the window for a few seconds. He saw no movement. His throat reminded him of his original objective. He walked toward the bedroom door. He reached for the knob. As he pulled the door open, he heard voices. One voice was Daddy Bob's. The others were too soft, and he couldn't hear them very well. He opened the door all the way and stepped out into the hall. He paused and listened. There was a light coming from the living room. He walked toward the light as he made his way slowly down the hall. As he neared the living room entrance, he heard Daddy Bob's voice.

"Now, Eve, when did you find out he was gone?"

Then a woman's voice spoke with a quivering sound. "About ten, I think. I checked his room and he was gone. We gotta find him."

Jason recognized the woman's voice as belonging to Miss Eve. He could always tell when it was Miss Eve, because she had such a rough voice for a lady. She always sounded as if she needed to clear her throat.

Then Daddy Bob spoke again. "Well, he could hardly get around on his own. So how do you think he could have got out the house? He never went out, did he?"

"No, he never went out at all. I just don't understand it. I just don't."

Jason could hear Miss Eve beginning to cry. Then his grandmother tried to comfort her. "Now, Eve, try not to carry on so. You know it ain't gonna help matters none, and you'll only make yourself sick. You know Bob will find your daddy, so don't cry. Bob'll take care of things."

"Maybe Ray took the old man somewhere. Where is Ray, anyway?" asked Daddy Bob.

Jason moved closer to the doorway so he could hear Miss Eve's answer.

"Ray didn't take him nowhere. He's home in bed."

Daddy Bob's voice got louder. "Bed! Why is he in bed? Does he know the ol' man's gone?"

"No," answered Eve, "He got drunk and passed out, so I put him in the bed."

"I don't believe that. He told me he wasn't gonna drink tonight. He said he felt sick and he was gonna stay away from the bottle. Did you see him drink anything?" Daddy Bob's question had an angry tone to it.

"No," she said, "but I had to drag him out of the front room when he fell down. And I'm sick and tired of cleanin' up after his drunkenness. So I fixed him this time. He ain't gonna break or ruin nothin' tonight."

Daddy Bob jumped from his chair.

"He's not drunk, you fool. What do you mean, you fixed him?"

"I mean I tied him to the bed. That's what I mean. Now, leave me alone, Bob. Just leave me alone." After Eve's words, Daddy Bob went into a rage and began to shout.

"You're the evil in that house, Eve, not Ray. You never have fooled me. You never have."

Daddy Bob ran out of the room and down the hall. He was in

such a hurry that he didn't see Jason standing to one side of the hall. As he passed, Jason could hear him talking angrily to himself.

"That crazy bitch. If there's a devil in anybody, it's in her."

Jason watched his grandfather go out the screen door at the back of the house and turn in the direction of Ray Klim's house. Then Jason walked to the edge of the living room entrance and slowly peeked around the edge of the wall. He could see his grandmother standing in front of Miss Eve, but he couldn't see Eve's face.

Then his grandmother spoke. "Just sit here now, Eve, and I'll get you some coffee."

His grandmother moved away from Eve, and Jason could see her face. He watched her for a few seconds as she looked around the room. She didn't seem to be very sad now that she was alone in the room. Then suddenly Jason thought of Daddy Bob's words and a picture of Miss Eve as the devil flashed in his head. He shook his head to get rid of the thought, and then he looked at Miss Eve. She was looking right into Jason's eyes. Her eyes seemed to widen, and a cold chill ran through the boy's body. He couldn't seem to turn away from her stare. He tried, but he couldn't. Then the devil picture flashed in his head again, and the concentration of the stare was lost. Now free from Eve's visual hold, Jason ran down the hall and out the back door in the direction of Ray Klim's house. The lights from the house and the moon made the way to Ray's house easy to see. When he stopped running, Jason found himself at Ray Klim's front door.

He slowly walked up the steps to the front porch. He thought that he would sure feel better if he could see Daddy Bob. He looked back at his own house with thoughts of making a run back. His thought was short-lived when he saw Miss Eve standing on his back porch, looking in his direction. He couldn't see any of her facial features, but an image of her eyes opened wide popped into his head, and he found himself pushing his way through the front door and into Ray Klim's house.

He looked around, and he could see that he had stopped in the front living room. His heart was racing, but the room was fully lighted and he thought that the room seemed normal. He looked at all the walls, thinking that perhaps they would be filled with evil pictures, but all was normal. He then walked slowly down the hall with hopes of finding his grandfather. After only a few careful steps, he heard a man's voice. He didn't recognize the voice yet; so he continued to walk slowly. He could see a light coming from one of the back rooms. That seemed to be where the voice was coming from. He moved close to the wall as he walked, so that when he reached the room he would be able to peek around the edge of the door. As he slid down the hall his head bumped into something hanging on the wall. It didn't hurt; but when he looked up, he found it was a picture of Miss Eve. It took all of his strength to keep from screaming out loud. The eyes in the picture held him as Miss Eve's stare had done at his house. He would probably have stood and stared at the picture all night, but his concentration was again broken—this time by the voices coming from the lighted room. Jason pulled himself away from the picture and moved toward the room. As he looked around the edge of the door, he whispered to himself, "Please, Jesus." After his little prayer, he focused his eyes on the familiar figure of his grandfather.

Daddy Bob was cutting Mr. Ray's feet loose from the bedpost. Jason could see that he had already cut the ropes from his hands. As Daddy Bob cut the last rope, he cursed angrily. Mr. Ray didn't move.

Jason watched Ray Klim as Daddy Bob threw the ropes to the floor. Ray Klim's eyes were closed, and he didn't seem to know or care that he was being cut free. Daddy Bob closed his pocketknife. Then Ray moved his head to one side and coughed loudly. The cough seemed to bring him around, and he tried to talk. He spoke in a whisper, but Jason was near enough to hear him.

"Bob, you gotta help me. I'm sick. My guts is burnin' out. You gotta get me a drink."

Daddy Bob stopped his wild words and helped Ray sit up in the bed. "You mean you ain't had nothin' to drink tonight?"

"No, I told ya I was really gonna try, but I can't. I just can't."

Daddy Bob thought of the things Eve had said, and then he turned his attention back to Ray.

The bed was wet from Ray's sweat. There were spots of blood on the sheet, and the room was filled with the odor of vomit. Ray had rope burns on his wrists and ankles where he had twisted and fought to free himself. Daddy Bob reached onto a small table next to the bed and poured Ray a glass of water. He handed it to the sick one. Ray began to drink and Jason could hear each gulp as he swallowed. When the glass was empty, Ray rolled to one side and put his head over the edge of the bed and began to vomit on the floor. Jason's eyes widened as he watched Ray. Jason thought to himself that that was the strange noise he had heard from his bedroom window. As Ray continued, he made a painful-sounding growl. It was the same noise that had stopped the conversation on the porch. The clock in the front room chimed once. Then Jason turned his attention back to Daddy Bob and Ray. Daddy Bob helped Ray to get back to the center of the bed. Ray spoke in his whisper again.

"Bob, it's blood. I'm spittin' blood, damn it. Help me, Bob. You gotta help me. I ain't gonna die, am I?" Jason's eyes widened again at the word die. Daddy Bob gave Ray a wet towel.

"You ain't gonna die, Ray. Here, wipe your face off and try to get up if you can. We gotta try and get you cleaned up."

Ray rolled off the bed with Daddy Bob's help and knelt on the floor.

"Come on, Ray. If you get cleaned up, you'll feel better. We just gotta get this crap off ya."

As Daddy Bob struggled with Ray, Jason, not knowing how his grandfather would react to his presence, moved away from the door and stood in a dark section of the hall. Knowing that Daddy Bob was within yelling distance seemed to calm Jason's fears.

Daddy Bob pulled Ray up from the floor. Ray tried to walk, but Daddy Bob had to do most of the work as they moved down the hall to the small bathroom at the far end. Jason followed behind at a short distance and again peeked around the edge of the door.

Daddy Bob sat Ray on the toilet and tore his shirt off him. He tried to tear off his pants, but the denim material was too strong. After about a two-minute struggle with Ray's semi-dead weight, Bob finally got Ray's pants off and wrestled him into the bathtub. As Ray sat slumped over in the tub, he talked.

"She's crazy, I tell ya. She's crazy." While thinking about Eve, Ray pulled out of his sickness for a moment. "The ol' man! Bob, where's the ol' man?"

"We don't know, Ray. He's missin'. Did you know he was gone?"

"Oh, God! I could hear her yelling at him. I heard something break. I couldn't get my hands free. The room was goin' 'round. I think she came into the room and looked at me. I think the ol' man was with her. Or somebody. Bob, we gotta find him."

Bob thought again of Eve, who was sitting in his living room. "You don't think Eve would hurt her own father, do ya?"

"I don't know, but she's crazy, I tell ya. But I just don't know. Help me up."

Bob helped Ray out of the tub. He seemed stronger because of his concern for the old man. Daddy Bob turned and saw Jason.

"What the hell? What's wrong, boy? Did your mother send you over here?"

"No, suh," Jason said. "I just come on my own. I'm sorry." Jason hung his head.

"Well, since you're here, go and fix me and Ray some coffee. And you hurry, boy." Jason ran into the kitchen and obeyed his grandfather's order.

"Now, Ray, tell me what happened."

"Bob, I'm really not too sure. I got dizzy and fell in the front room. I was in a kinda half sleep. I could hear talkin' and then some-body—Eve, I guess—was helpin' me up off the floor. I could see the furniture in the living room goin' by as she helped me toward the bedroom. Then I was movin' faster down the hall, like maybe I was bein' carried. I remember hittin' the bed facedown, and then Eve was turnin' me over and tyin' me up. I told her I was sick, but she didn't listen. She left the room and I was in a half sleep again. I don't know how long I was like that, but in a little while I could hear voices in the hall. Mostly Eve's. But somebody else, too. Maybe the ol' man, but he don't talk so loud." Then Ray thought about Charlie.

"Charlie! That's it! It was Charlie. The other voice was Charlie's. He was arguin' with Eve about the ol' man. He told her to stop yellin' at him, and Eve told Charlie to remember whose house this was. Then I didn't hear no more. Where is Charlie, anyway?"

"He's not here, and Eve didn't mention him at all," answered Bob.

Ray thought for a second. "Sometimes Charlie don't stay here. He's got a few lady friends, ya know. Sometimes he stays out all night. Bob, I don't think the ol' man could even walk today. He had something wrong with his leg. It was swelled up. If he's gone, somebody had to help him. He never went out. So why would he go out at this time of night? But as old as he is, he might have just done somethin' crazy. You never know."

"Well, crazy or not, we've gotta find him. So let's get some coffee in ya and get ya dressed. Jason, boy! Where's that coffee?"

"Comin', Daddy Bob! Comin'!"

Jason returned to the small room with two hot cups of coffee.

"Here, Daddy Bob."

Daddy Bob took both cups and gave one to Ray. "Drink it slow this time, Ray."

Ray pushed his hair out of his eyes. "Where's Eve?" he asked.

"She's over at my place. She wanted me to help her find the ol' man, but when she said she tied you up, I came over here first." Ray took a slow sip of his coffee and then looked at Bob.

"She's crazy. But I guess me and the ol' man don't make things too good for her around here. What time it is, anyway?"

"One-twenty. Let's get that coffee down. And if you can try and get up and move around, maybe your head will clear. We gotta find him. Where ya think Charlie is? We could sure use his help."

"Somebody mention my name?" Jason, Daddy Bob, and Ray all turned to see Charlie Klim standing in the doorway.

His shirt was open as usual, showing his muscular chest and stomach. He was wearing a black derby hat, and he tipped it to the threesome.

"Hey, what's goin' on here? It's past y'all's bedtime, ain't it?"

"Where ya been?" asked Ray.

"Now, brother, you know I can't give away such information."

"Charlie, if you could try and be serious for a minute, maybe you could help us. The ol' man is missin', and I know I heard you and Eve fightin' about him."

"Yeah, we had a few words about the ol' fella, and I left. But he was here when I left."

"What did y'all fight about?" asked Bob.

It was easy to see that Charlie didn't want to talk to Bob Merritt, but for some reason he answered the question.

"Oh, she was yellin' at him for knockin' over somethin' in his room, and I got tired of hearin' it. I told her to ease up. When I did, she started yellin' at me too. So I left."

"Well," said Ray, "we gotta find him, and you can help."

Charlie didn't like the idea of helping in the search. "Come on, Ray. I'm beat. Maybe he just took a walk or somethin'."

"Maybe, shit! Now, shut up," Ray yelled, "you know damn good and well he ain't took no midnight stroll. So stop actin' stupid. You're gonna help us, tired or not."

"Okay, okay, brother dear. Don't get pissed. I'll help, but don't call me stupid."

Daddy Bob turned to Jason. "Jason, you go back to the house and tell your grandmother that we're gonna go hunt for the ol' man. And you stay home—you hear me?"

"Yes, suh, but. . ."

"No buts. You stay home."

"Yes, suh." Jason knew by the tone of his grandfather's voice that he had better not argue.

CHAPTER SIX

JASON WENT OUT ONTO THE FRONT PORCH. HE MADE SURE NOT TO LOOK UP at the picture of Miss Eve as he made his way down the long hall. Once on the porch, he looked toward his house. It seemed such a long way from where he stood to his own back porch. Even if he was to run, it might take forever to reach the steps. He thought that perhaps his grandfather would go back with him. He decided to wait. He turned back and looked into the house. The adult threesome was walking toward the front of the house.

"I guess we'll start out back and work our way into the woods a ways," said Daddy Bob.

Jason watched them as they neared the front door.

"I'm gonna get somethin' to drink first," said Charlie in his deep voice.

"Well, don't take too long. We need all the help we can get. And don't disappear, please," growled Ray. Jason couldn't hear Charlie's reply, but he did hear the two mumble something to each other.

Daddy Bob reached the front door and saw Jason waiting on the porch.

"You ain't gone yet, boy? I thought I told you to get home and tell them what we doin'. Now, you git!"

Without a word, Jason jumped off the porch and ran straight for

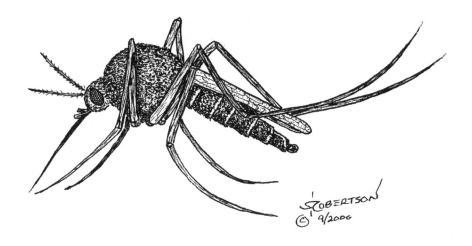

MOSQUITO

the light on his back porch. His feet began to slip on the pine needles, but he didn't break his stride.

"I gotta tell Mama. I gotta tell Mama," he repeated to himself several times.

His little arms pumped like two pistons as he sprinted the entire distance. As he neared the back steps, he could hear his grandfather's dogs barking. He paid little attention and ran up the back steps without slowing down at all. He became startled as he ran into his mother. She had just walked out onto the porch.

"Jason, what's wrong? Slow down."

"Oh, Mama! It's you! I'm sorry," he panted.

"What are you doin' runnin' from over there at this time of night?"

"Daddy Bob told me to come tell ya that they was gonna hunt for the ol' man."

"Who's they, boy?"

"Daddy Bob, Mr. Charlie, and Mr. Ray."

"That still don't tell me what ya was doin' over there."

Jason looked down and didn't answer. The dogs were still barking, and they began to make a great deal of commotion. Both Jason and his mother looked out toward the dog pen.

"What's wrong with those crazy hounds? Jason, did you feed them dogs this evenin'?"

Jason looked down again.

"You didn't, did ya?"

"No, ma'am, I forgot."

She shook her head. "Sometimes, Jason, you..."

"I'm sorry."

"You're always sorry about somethin', ain't ya?"

Again he looked down.

She stared at him for a few seconds. She was disgusted with his forgetfulness. "I don't know 'bout you, Jason. I just don't know what we're gonna do with you." She sighed and added to the boy's shame. "Now, you get out there and feed those dogs before they wake up the entire county. Then you had better get to bed. We'll talk about this again in the morning."

Jason looked out into the darkness at the dog pen. His mother turned away from him and walked into the house. He didn't want to do it, but he knew she was mad and a refusal would only make things worse. He could see a couple of the dogs moving about in the darkness. Then he walked to a small wooden cabinet that was located in the corner of the porch. He opened it and took out a sack of dry dog meal. He poured the food into two large buckets. He put the bag back into the cabinet and picked up the buckets. They were heavy, and he struggled with them down the steps. After having reached the ground, he headed in the direction of the howling dogs.

Jason stopped every few steps and put the buckets on the ground in order to rest his small arms. The weight of the buckets was too great for him to carry without stopping. His struggle with the heavy burden took his mind off the fear he had felt before he began his chore.

The dog pen had a thick wooded area on its left side and a small creek on its right. The moon was reflected in the water, but the trees around the pen still made it difficult to see. He made his way to the gate of the pen, and he set the buckets down. He unhooked the gate latch and worked his way through the opening with the buckets.

"What you fellas so fired up for? Y'all hungry?"

Three of the hounds began to gather around Jason as he tried to carry the buckets to the middle of the pen. They almost knocked him down before he could get to the big tub, where he dumped the dry food. He emptied both buckets into the tub, and the hungry dogs began to eat the dry meal.

"If you pigs will just wait a minute, I'll add some water to it and there'll be plenty for y'all. It sure will go down easier, too." The dogs continued to gobble up the food. Jason then took the two empty buckets and left the pen. He walked toward the creek, where he always got the water for the dogs. As he walked, a cold chill ran through his body. He opened his eyes as wide as he could, swallowed, and tried to whistle, but his mouth was too dry. He heard the high-pitched hum of one of those night pests, and as it neared his ear, he slapped himself, hoping to end the mosquito's flight.

He reached the edge of the creek and bent down to fill the buckets. He knew the water would be heavier than the meal. The struggle began again.

He took only about five steps before he stumbled and fell. He dropped both buckets, and the water splashed all around him. He braced his fall with his hands, and he could feel the muddy ground. When his hand hit the ground, there was a great swarm of mosquitoes. He jumped up quickly and began to swat at the insects. They began to get in his eyes and nose. He became frightened by the loudness of the mosquitoes' hum. He slapped his face again and again to rid himself of the creatures. He began to run, hoping to run out of the swarm. He ran for about ten yards and then realized that he was running away from his house instead of in the direction of safety. He stopped, got his bearings, and headed toward his house. He ran past the buckets he had dropped and lost his footing once more. This time his fall brought him face-to-face with a man lying on the ground. The man's mouth and eyes were wide open, and he was looking at Jason. Jason backed away from the body. His fear held a scream inside him. The man stared at Jason, but he didn't move. Jason was almost hypnotized by the stare.

The man appeared to be naked, but his body was covered with mosquitoes. The moonlight showed the man's face. It was drawn and white. His cheeks and forehead were crawling with mosquitoes. His eyes glared through the darkness. Jason continued to back away, and he threw himself against the wooden fence that surrounded the dogs.

"Oh, Jesus! Please help me. Please let this be another dream." Jason put his hands over his face, hoping that when he removed them the body would be gone. Then in the distance he heard his salvation. His mother's call was like a god-sent song.

"Jason! You hurry and get in here, boy. I ain't gonna wait all night on you."

Jason looked up toward the house, and he could see his mother standing on the porch.

"Jason, did you hear me?"

He looked down at the body and then at the porch. He closed his eyes and ran straight ahead. He didn't look back. After about a ten-yard run, he opened his eyes and found the strength he had lost.

"Mama!" he screamed. "Mama!" He ran up the steps and into his mother's arms.

"What is it, Jason?"

He began to cry, and his words were mixed and shaky.

"Calm down, son. Calm down. You're gonna squeeze the life out of me. Now, stop."

Jason held his mother tighter and tighter, while he kept his head buried against her breast. Then the boy heard a strong and familiar voice behind him.

"What's wrong with you, boy?"

Jason released his death grip on his mother and turned to see his Daddy Bob standing behind him.

Jason threw himself into his grandfather's arms. He continued his death grip. Daddy Bob pushed Jason back and held on to his arms.

"Now, that's enough of this carryin' on, boy. Now stop and tell me what's wrong."

Jason looked up at his grandfather and then closed his eyes. The thought of the old man's face flashed in Jason's head. He took a deep breath.

"There's somebody at the dog pen. He's on the ground and he's covered with mosquitoes."

Realizing what the boy was saying, Bob turned and ran to the dog pen. He didn't see the body at first in the dark; but as he neared it, that great swarm of mosquitoes flew up in his face. Then he saw it. He knew it was Eve's father. The search was over. A closer look told Bob that the old man was dead and that most of his blood had been taken by the hungry little bloodsuckers of the swamp. Bob took off his shirt and put it over the old man's face. He turned and walked back to the house.

Jason and his mother, along with Miss Eve, were all standing on the back porch as Daddy Bob walked back. He walked slowly up the steps.

"What is it, Daddy?" asked Mary C.

He looked at Eve. "It's your daddy, Eve. He's dead."

Eve's eyes widened.

"I'm sorry, Eve. I'm really sorry."

Eve began to walk off the porch in the direction of the dog pen.

"Eve, don't go out there. There just ain't no sense in it."

Eve stopped and stared out at the pen. Then, for some reason, she turned back toward the house. She stared at Jason for a second and then walked up the steps and into the house.

Jason found himself becoming more and more afraid of Miss Eve. Jason's mother was still standing on the porch, and she turned to him.

"You okay, son?"

"Yes, ma'am," he answered with a quiver in his voice.

"You don't look too good. Are you sure you're all right?"

"Yes, ma'am."

"Don't you do no faintin' on us now, ya hear?"

"I ain't, Mama." Jason looked at his Daddy Bob.

"You ain't sick, are ya, boy?"

"No, suh."

"You gotta learn to handle these things, ya know."

"Yes, suh." Jason's stomach churned inside him, but he dared not mention his discomfort. His mother spoke.

"What you gonna do now, Daddy?"

"Well, I guess I should try and find Sheriff Floyd. I hate to fool with that bastard, but I expect it's got to be done. He'll most likely spend his time with Eve instead of doin' his job and findin' out what happened to the ol' man."

"Oh, Daddy."

"Don't 'Oh Daddy' me. I seen it for years, girl. This is a crazy night, and Floyd won't help matters none. But he is the law, and the law should know about this."

"Daddy, you know you don't like him 'cause he chews 'bacco and dips snuff. And you know that's the reason."

"You don't know my reasons, girl. But I will say, like I have before, that it ain't clean or natural for a man to be spittin' on the ground all the time. And there ain't no way for you to say I'm wrong in sayin' it. But there are other reasons that don't concern you. So don't you be tellin' me nothin' 'bout Floyd."

Mary C. knew she shouldn't continue about the lawman.

"Well, you better go find him. Me and Jason are goin' to bed."

Mary C. took Jason's hand and pulled him with her toward the kitchen door. Daddy Bob stopped her.

"I'm takin' the boy with me."

Mary C. looked at her father. "But, Daddy, it's so late."

"That don't matter none. He ain't gonna be able to sleep, and I think he'd be better off away from here for a spell."

Jason's heart nearly jumped out of his chest. He knew his mother would do what Daddy Bob said. He stepped away from her.

"You stay on the porch 'til I get back. Then we'll go."

"What you gonna do now?" asked Mary C.

"I gotta put somethin' over the ol' man so he'll be covered. I just don't feel right 'bout him not bein' covered."

Daddy Bob walked to a dark corner of the porch.

"There was a mess of ol' blankets over here. Here's one."

Daddy Bob came out of the darkness carrying an old patchwork quilt.

"This should do it."

Jason watched his grandfather walk back out to the dog pen. The sight of the old man's face flashed in Jason's head as he watched a large moth beat itself against the lone lantern that lit the porch. His mother was still standing at the door. She, too, watched her father walk into the dark toward the pen. Her thoughts were of Floyd.

"I know Floyd better than anybody," she thought. With that, she began to think about her first experience with the fat lawman.

Chapter Seven

She was only fourteen at the time of the encounter. Floyd was about thirty years old, and he had never married. He was considerably overweight, and his fat gut always made his pants roll down at the waist. His face had been scarred because of a bad complexion. The sun kept his fair skin always peeling. One hardly ever saw Floyd without a fever blister on his lip. The Florida sun was too much for his fair features. He had what folks called "bug eyes," those eyes that looked as if they might pop out of his head at any moment. His teeth were stained from tobacco, and he had a snuff callus below his lip. The smell of his chew didn't add to his beauty. His meanness had kept him as the county sheriff, and the fact that no one ever ran against him also assured him of his job.

Mary C. recalled that day when she was walking down the old path. She had been sent to the store by her mother, and the path was the fastest way to get to Miss Coleman's store. The path was wide in some spots but narrow and overgrown in others. As she walked, she didn't realize she was being watched by a pair of bug eyes.

She was halfway to her destination when she saw Floyd standing in front of her, blocking the path. At that time in her life many changes had already taken place in her body, and she was developing into a rather attractive woman. She stopped when she saw Floyd, and she stared at him, waiting for him to speak. He only stared back.   His stare made Mary C. uneasy, and so she turned away and began to walk back in the direction from which she had come.

"You Bob Merritt's girl, ain't ya?" Floyd asked quickly, hoping to end her retreat.

Mary C. didn't look back at him after his question.

"I didn't mean to scare ya, girl. I just heard somebody, and I wanted to see who it was. But I sure didn't mean to scare ya."

She looked back at him. "You didn't scare me none."

"Where ya headed, girl?"

"To Miss Coleman's."

"You is Bob Merritt's girl, ain't ya?"

"Yes, suh. Do you know my daddy?"

"Sure. I know your daddy real good."

Her fears began to leave her as she talked to the ugly one.

Floyd sat down on the ground and leaned back, supporting himself with his arms. "You gonna buy yourself somethin' good?"

"Heck, no. Mama just gave me enough money for the things she needs. We ain't never got no extra money."

"That's too bad. A pretty thing like you oughta have some extra now and then for some nice things."

Mary C. liked the way Floyd talked even if he wasn't good to look at. She held her head down when he said she was pretty.

"How old are ya now, girl?"

"Fourteen."

"My, my. You ain't no little girl no more. You on the edge of bein' a full-growed woman. And a mighty fine one, too."

She continued to look down.

"I'll bet ya got more boyfriends than ya know what to do with. A girl like you just gotta have lots of fellas."

Mary C. lifted her head. "Mama don't want me to have no fellas yet. She says the devil gets in a man when he's near a woman."

"Well, I don't know 'bout no devil, but it sure makes me feel good to see a pretty lady like you."

She smiled and looked down again.

"What else did your mama tell ya about men?"

Mary C. looked up once more. "She said that men was only after one thing when it comes to a woman."

"And what is that?" Floyd asked with a serious look.

She hesitated, trying to find the right words to answer the question. She looked at Floyd. He was still waiting. "Once a woman gives herself to a man..." she began, then stopped.

"Go on," said Floyd.

"Well, once a woman gives herself to a man. . .she loses her goodness." Mary C. looked down again.

"Is that so?" asked Floyd.

She nodded her head but didn't look up at Floyd. She didn't notice that Floyd had stood up and had begun to walk toward her. She became startled when she looked up and the fat one was standing next to her. She didn't know what to do, and so she only stared. Floyd stared back at her, but for only a few seconds. Then he spoke.

"You'll be able to make up your own mind about men someday, girl. Then we'll see what ya think."

Mary C. smiled, trying to ease her tense feelings. "I gotta get to the store. Mama's gonna be mad if I don't get home."

"I sure hate to see ya go, but if ya have to go I guess there ain't nothin' to make ya stay."

Mary C. began to walk past Floyd.

"I sure enjoyed talkin' to ya. It was real nice."

Mary C. continued to walk as Floyd talked.

"Here, let me give you somethin'." With the words "give ya somethin'" ringing in her ears, Mary C. stopped and looked back at Floyd. He was holding up a big silver dollar. Her eyes lit up at the sight of the shiny coin. The sun reflected off the silver as Floyd turned it in his hand. The reflection seemed to be a signal for Mary to reach out and take the desired item. She walked back to Floyd and reached for the solid circle. He pulled it out of her reach.

"You want it?"

She looked surprised as the coin moved away from her grasp. "I sure do."

"Yeah, you could buy some nice things with all this money

here."

"I sure could," she agreed.

"If I do give it to ya, ya gotta promise not to tell nobody. I don't think your mama would like it."

Mary C.'s eyes widened at the thought of getting the coin. "I ain't gonna tell nobody. I promise."

Floyd moved the coin slowly in her direction. His movement tantalized her, and she reached for the coin again. This time he let her take the coin. She squeezed it in her hand and stepped away from Floyd.

"Now you hold it first," he said. "Then we'll both decide if you should get to keep it or not. Okay?"

Mary C. nodded.

"Sit down and talk for another minute."

The offer seemed fair, and she did want the money. She sat down on the ground, and Floyd did the same. She was surprised when Floyd sat down next to her. He was almost eye-to-eye with her when he spoke.

"Do you think I'm ugly?" he asked.

Mary C. was shocked at his question, but was quick to lie with her answer. "No, suh."

"A lot of people say I'm ugly."

Mary C. looked down.

"Do you want that silver dollar?" he said gruffly.

His change in tone puzzled Mary C.

"Well, do ya?"

She looked at Floyd. His eyes were wide open. He glared at her, and his forehead seemed to bubble with sweat.

"If ya don't want it, give it back."

"I do want it." She held it tight in her hand.

"Well, all right, then." Floyd seemed calm. "Are you willin' to do a little work for it?"

"Sure, anything." The words came out of her mouth before she realized what she was saying.

"Just sit here with me for a spell and the money's yours."

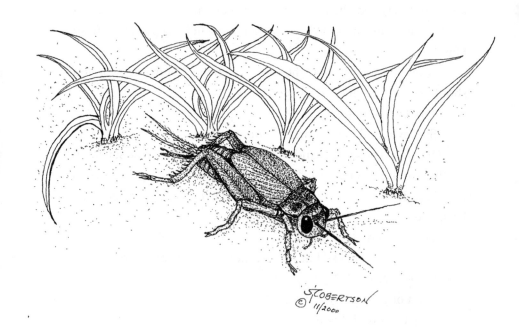

CRICKET

The smell of tobacco filled the air around the two as they sat. Floyd reached out and touched Mary C. on the knee. "I sure like bein' with ya, girl."

She smiled at his kind gesture, but she trembled inside when he left his hand on her leg. He rubbed her thigh gently. Then he reached out and touched her face. He sensed her fear.

"I'm not gonna hurt ya. So don't be afraid. And you don't have to do anything. You just sit there and I'll do all the work. Then the money's yours. You do want the money, don't ya?"

She closed her eyes and nodded. The thought of the dollar overshadowed her fears.

"You are a pretty thing," he said as he reached out again, this time touching her neck. He stroked her neck for a few seconds, then moved his hand down her shirt. He moved his hands slowly, touching her young, developing breasts. Mary C. shivered inside at his movements. Her small nipples stood up, joining her already present goose bumps. He unbuttoned two of her buttons and maneuvered his hand until it was underneath her shirt. She kept her eyes closed as he touched and squeezed her skin. His hands were cold at first, but they soon became warm. She thought that it didn't feel so bad after all. She thought of the silver dollar, and it felt even better. He kissed her on the cheek, and the tobacco smell became stronger.

"Does that feel good?" he asked while he squeezed one of her breasts. She turned her head away and didn't answer. He didn't ask again.

"Just a little longer and you can keep the dollar," he said, tempting her, "just a little longer."

Mary C. thought that, well, he wasn't really hurting her, and she could buy some nice things.

Then Floyd reached down and unsnapped her jeans. She reached down to stop him. He pushed her hand away roughly and continued with his movements. She tried to stop him once more, and he pushed her hand away again.

"I told ya I wasn't gonna hurt ya, and I ain't. Do you want the money or not?"

Again she nodded and closed her eyes.

Floyd unzipped her pants. She felt his hand slide down her flat stomach. He rubbed the lower part of her stomach for a second and then continued his downward movements. His fingers began to move around in her recently grown hair, as if they were frantically searching for something. She tried to move away once, but Floyd held her close to him. The odor of tobacco was stronger than before, and Floyd was beginning to sweat heavily. As his fingers groped around, she began to feel pain. It wasn't a great deal of pain, but it was uncomfortable. She opened her eyes and looked at Floyd. He had his eyes closed as he continued moving his fingers. He pushed her down on the ground. He took his hand from under her shirt as he pushed her. He leaned forward and kissed her on the stomach. He took his now free hand and began to rub himself between the legs. He did, however, keep his other hand in her pants. She began to squirm around as she realized the pain was becoming more intense. It was, however, combined with a good feeling where he touched her. She wanted to pull away, but every movement caused more pleasure. It seemed the pleasure was beginning to outweigh the pain. She found that if she spread her legs wider she was more comfortable. She did so. Her movements were now only for more pleasure; she had no thoughts of escape.

Floyd began to make moaning noises as he rubbed her and stroked himself. Once it was very painful, and she tried to pull her legs together, but Floyd would not let her. She squeezed the silver dollar each time she felt pain.

Suddenly, Floyd pulled his hand from her pants and sat up with his back to her. He continued to stroke himself. She couldn't see what he was doing, but he shook as he sat next to her. Floyd stood up quickly and walked away from her. Mary C. watched him zip up his pants. She had not seen him unzip them during the action. She reached down and rubbed herself between the legs. She didn't know why she touched herself. It just seemed to be the thing to do. She felt around where he had touched her. She wanted to see if she was injured in any way. She felt moisture. She didn't understand and became frightened. She quickly pulled her hand away and zipped and snapped her jeans.

"Keep the dollar, girl."

She looked up at Floyd, who was standing over her.

"See, girl, I like ya. I don't want to hurt ya in any way at all."

Mary C. thought of how good it was beginning to feel. She nodded and smiled at Floyd.

"Remember our secret, girl. Maybe we'll see each other again."

Mary C. nodded as usual. Floyd walked away.

She felt a small amount of pain as she walked on to the store. She thought that it was sure nice to know where to go if she wanted another silver dollar.

Mary C.'s reminiscences were interrupted by her father.

"Hey, girl. You here? You act like you're off somewhere else. This night's filled with enough craziness without you addin' to it. Wake up and pay attention to what's goin' on."

As Daddy Bob talked, Mary C. thought to herself once more. That silver dollar had been the first of many she would receive from Floyd in her lifetime. When times had been bad, Floyd had eased some of her needs. Over the years she had learned to overlook his ugliness.

"Girl, I'm talkin' to you."

"I'm sorry, Daddy. I'm just tired."

"Well, you had better get some rest. I'm takin' the boy with me." Daddy Bob looked at Jason.

"Get in the truck, boy."

Jason ran to the truck and climbed in on the passenger's side. He looked back at the porch. His mother walked into the house, and Daddy Bob walked down the steps of the porch and headed toward the truck. He passed the window where Jason sat. He stopped. Jason looked up.

"You done good, boy. Ya done real good."

Jason felt proud after his grandfather's words. Daddy Bob got into the truck and turned the key. The engine didn't turn over at first, but Jason knew that wasn't unusual for the old vehicle. After a few more tries the old girl cranked up. They headed down the dirt road in front of the Big House.

Mary C. watched from the kitchen window as the two rode away. She turned away from the window and saw Eve sitting at the kitchen table with her head down. She appeared to be asleep.

Mary C. watched her for a few seconds. She couldn't bring herself to feel any sorrow for Eve. Mary C. was sorry that the old man was dead, but she enjoyed seeing Eve in any kind of pain. Eve didn't lift her head as Mary C. continued to stare. Thoughts of the past touched Mary C. again.

She saw Ray Klim standing in front of her. He reached out his hand and touched her face. Then he turned and walked away without a word. She smiled to herself at the pleasant thought. Her smile changed as she continued her flashback.

She saw Eve standing next to Ray. They were at the Fourth of July picnic. They sat together and laughed. They ate watermelon and laughed again. She imagined their naked bodies clinched in passion. She shook the thoughts from her head.

"What you starin' at?"

Mary C. cleared her head and realized that Eve had sat up and was speaking to her.

"I said, what are you starin' at?"

"Oh, Eve. I wasn't starin' at you. I was kinda lookin' past ya. I'm sorry 'bout your daddy."

"You ain't sorry for me and you know it," snapped Eve.

"I can't say I am at that, but I will respect the dead. I ain't gonna do no fightin' with ya." Mary C. walked out of the kitchen, leaving Eve to herself.

CHAPTER EIGHT

THE OLD TRUCK SHIMMIED AND SHOOK AS IT MADE ITS WAY DOWN SEMINOLE Road. Jason looked out the front windshield and recognized the old road leading to the beach. He remembered his grandmother's saying once that she could never live near the ocean as Sheriff Floyd did. "Them waves crashin' all night would drive me plumb crazy," she had said. Jason smiled as he thought of his grandmother's funny words.

The Big House was located only one mile from the ocean, but in order to get to Sheriff Floyd's place, Daddy Bob would have to turn off the main road and drive another mile through the woods and sand dunes. After the turn, Jason rolled his window up because, for about three hundred yards, the crickets were so loud that it seemed to be unnatural. Neither Jason nor his grandfather had spoken before they passed the crickets. Daddy Bob broke the silence inside the truck.

"There's them damn crickets. It's always been crazy how they all gather here. Nobody seems to know why, but they're always here. Yeah, it's crazy. . .but there's a lot crazy in these parts. That's a fact. We 'bout past 'em now." With that, the crickets stopped. "You can put that window back down now, boy. It's too hot to leave it up. We'll hear them bugs again on the way back."

As Jason rolled the window down, he looked out at the woods

that surrounded the truck. The moon was full, but the thick area didn't allow much of the moonlight through. Jason enjoyed hearing his grandfather's voice, so he tried to start another conversation.

"Daddy Bob, we didn't get a chance to tell Mr. Ray or Mr. Charlie."

Daddy Bob ignored the boy's words.

"Daddy Bob?" Jason tried again.

"What is it, boy?"

"We didn't tell the others about the ol' man."

"Ray got sick and had to go back home, and Charlie was supposed to be lookin' on Seminole Road. But I doubt he really went to look. He ain't too dependable when it comes to serious things. Don't worry, they'll find out soon enough. What about you, boy—you okay?"

"Yes, suh." Jason looked out the side window of the truck.

He closed his eyes, and the thoughts of the darkness around him brought back memories again. He saw himself sitting alone in the dark woods. His body shivered and he felt cold from the night air. A shotgun blast roared in the distance. Jason opened his eyes quickly to reassure himself that he was still safe in the truck with his loved one. He looked over at his grandfather. The boy yawned and leaned his back against the back of the seat. Comfort was impossible as the truck bounced its way through the woods. Jason began to fight with his heavy eyelids to stay awake.

"We'll be there in a few minutes now, boy." Daddy Bob's words brought Jason back to his senses, and he continued to struggle to keep his eyes open. Then the truck began to slow down.

"There it is. I knew we was gettin' close."

Jason looked out his window as the truck stopped. He could see a small boxlike house. There were two old wrecked cars in the front yard and a small wooden shed to the right of the house. There was a lamp burning in the front of the house, but Jason didn't see any movement. The truck came to a complete stop, and Daddy Bob opened his door.

"Stay near me, boy. If I know Floyd, he'll have some big dogs somewhere around here."

Jason slid over to his grandfather's side of the truck and stepped down onto the ground behind Daddy Bob. They walked slowly toward the front of the house. They passed one of the old cars. Jason stumbled over a pile of old rusty tools that lay next to the old car.

"Be careful, boy."

Jason picked himself up. He looked down. He saw that he had fallen over a broken shovel and he had almost landed on an old rusty machete. Jason picked up the large knife to take a good look.

"Put that thing down, boy." Daddy Bob's stern voice cut through the night air. "You always gotta fool with stuff that you ain't got no business foolin' with." Jason dropped the machete and continued to follow Daddy Bob.

Then suddenly, as they passed near the shed, it seemed to explode with wild noises and movements. Jason grabbed his grandfather as his eyes fell upon the sight of three large dogs as they ran out from the shelter of the small shed. All three dogs were tied to a post, and they stretched the ropes as far as they could, trying to get at the intruders. The shed shook as the three pulled at the ropes. It looked as if the little building would give way and collapse at any second, freeing the wild hounds to attack the two visitors. Daddy Bob yelled a time or two for the wild ones to get back, but they didn't pay any attention to his stern warning.

The two made their way to the front of the house. They were greeted by a loud voice.

"Who's there? What ya want?"

The dogs were still barking, so Daddy Bob had to yell in order to be heard. "It's Bob Merritt. I know it's late, but I gotta see ya."

Floyd pushed his face against the window of his front door. "Is that you, Bob?" he shouted.

Daddy Bob still had to yell. "Yeah, it's me. I got my grandson with me. These damn dogs is scarin' him to death. Open the door."

Floyd hesitated as he looked out the window, making sure he recognized his visitors. Then he opened the door. Daddy Bob and Jason were greeted by the fat and ugly sheriff and a large black pistol. As they walked into the house, Floyd put the gun down on a small table.

The front room had an awful odor to it. The braided rug on the floor had been stained many times by the dogs. The smell of tobacco and ammonia made Jason's stomach feel even worse than it had before. The walls were covered with pictures of naked women on calendars.

"What brings you out here at this time of night?" asked Floyd.

Daddy Bob answered quickly. "Jason found Eve's daddy dead out near our dog pen. And I don't think it was an accident. So we didn't touch anything. I thought we'd better get you to take a look."

Floyd wrinkled his face and gave a sigh.

"Always somethin', ain't it? There's always somethin' happenin' around here."

"It seems so," Bob agreed.

"Let me go wash my face so I can think better," said Floyd. Then he left the room.

Jason watched the ugly one as he left the room. He looked around at all the pictures. There were hundreds of them. They were all side by side, covering every inch of the walls. All the women in the pictures were beautiful to Jason. He thought of his mother. He could hear Floyd in the next room as he splashed himself with water. Daddy Bob walked to the front door and looked out.

"Them crazy hounds is stopped now. I'd hate to see them bastards untied."

As his grandfather watched out the window, Jason continued to look at the pictures. He moved his head all around, being sure not to miss any of the ladies. As he turned he could see that the hallway was also covered with the beauties. He slowly walked down the short hall, still gazing at the parade of flesh. He stopped at a door leading to another small room. The door was half open, and Jason looked into the room. There wasn't much light in the small room, but Jason could make out the figure of a young girl sitting up in a bed. She had pushed herself up into the corner of the room, and she held a blanket up, covering her body. Her shoulders were bare. Jason could see her eyes through the darkness. As they stared at each other, the thought of Jason's mother ran through his head. He closed his eyes and moved away from the door. He leaned against the wall and opened his eyes. His thoughts were interrupted.

"Jason, get in here, boy. We gotta get home."

Jason walked back into the front room. He came eye-to-eye with Floyd.

"You oughta not be roamin' 'round a strange house, boy. No tellin' what you might find," said Floyd.

Jason was frightened at Floyd's remark, and he was ashamed that he had seen the girl. Again Daddy Bob's voice broke into his thoughts.

"Why you gotta have all these pictures, Floyd? I sure hate the boy seein' all them pictures."

"They bring me pleasure. And I ain't asked ya to bring the boy with ya. You done that. You seen my house before."

"Yeah, I guess you're right. I just didn't think."

Floyd smiled.

"Besides, ain't nothin' better to look at for man or boy than a good-lookin' woman." Floyd grinned once more after his remark, showing his tobacco-stained teeth.

"Ugly men like me don't get much pleasure in life. So we gotta find it wherever we can." Floyd looked at Jason.

Daddy Bob walked out onto the front steps and Jason followed behind. He didn't look up as he passed Floyd. Floyd startled Jason.

"How's your mama doin', boy?" Floyd whispered, with another nasty grin.

Jason's heart raced after Floyd's question, but he didn't answer. Thoughts of how he hated the fat man filled his head. He walked quickly to catch up to his grandfather. Floyd stood at his door as the two headed for the truck.

"I'll be there in a little while," yelled Floyd as the dogs started again.

Reaching the truck was salvation for the boy. As Jason jumped into the cab of the truck, a strange voice cut through the noise from the dogs and the night air.

"Bob Merritt!"

Bob stopped and listened.

"Bob Merritt!" Again the voice called out.

"I'm here," said Bob. "Who is that?"

"It's me, Tom Green."

Daddy Bob squinted, trying to see in the darkness. "I can't see ya, Tom. Come into the light."

"I'm at the edge of the house, suh. I needs help. I is hurt bad."

Daddy Bob ran in the direction of the voice. Jason jumped from the truck and followed. When they reached the side of the house, they found Tom Green tied to a post.

"What the hell you tied here for?" Daddy Bob bent down and reached for the rope.

"Let that nigger be," roared Floyd's voice.

Both Jason and Daddy Bob turned to see Floyd, standing behind them, holding that big black pistol.

"What's wrong with you, Floyd? You can't tie a man up like this."

Jason looked down at his friend Tom Green. The little man's face was cut and bleeding. His hair was covered with white sand from the beach. His shirt was torn half off, and one of his eyes was swollen shut.

"Now, don't you be tellin' me what I can or can't do, Bob Merritt. 'Cause you ain't got nothin' to do with the law around here. You gettin' a mite ol' to be tellin' folks what to do."

"What did he do to deserve bein' beat and tied like this?"

"I caught him diggin' turtle eggs, and that's breakin' the law. I'm takin' his ass to the county jail in the mornin'."

Daddy Bob looked down at Tom. "But you can't just leave him out here all night."

"Well, he sure as hell ain't comin' in my house. So he stays right here. Now, you best be gettin' on home. And don't be obstructin' justice."

Bob's face was red with anger. "This is the last time you gonna do anything like this."

Then Floyd pointed the pistol in Daddy Bob's face.

"I done tol' you once that you gettin' too ol' to be threatenin' folks. Now, you walk on back to that truck of yours and get home. I'll be over to your place in a while."

Bob started backing up toward the truck. Floyd held the pistol in his face. Jason walked too, but he was behind the sheriff.

Jason looked back at his peanut friend, and he could hear Floyd still talking to his grandfather. As Jason walked he stepped on something lying on the ground. He looked down. It was the machete. He looked at the knife. He looked back at Tom Green. Then he looked at the sheriff. Floyd was still watching Daddy Bob. Jason's heart raced once more as he bent down to pick up the big blade. Without another thought, he ran back to Tom Green, carrying the knife. He stopped and stared at his friend for only a second. Then he dropped the machete on the ground. It fell next to Tom's leg. Tom Green looked up at the small boy. Then he looked down at the knife. Then suddenly Jason leaned over and kissed the old man on the forehead. The black man's eyes widened as the young boy stepped away from him. Jason smiled and ran back to the truck. Floyd had been so busy with his many cruel words to Daddy Bob that he had forgotten about Jason.

When Jason reached the truck, Floyd turned quickly and ordered him into the truck. Daddy Bob was already seated in the cab. Daddy Bob started the truck and backed away from Floyd. As they drove away, Jason watched Floyd walk back to the house. He also looked at the side of the house where Tom Green was tied, but it was too dark to see him.

The ride home was fast, and Jason didn't notice the crickets at all. Daddy Bob cursed out loud as they made their way home. Jason smiled. He knew his friend would soon be free.

CHAPTER NINE

WHEN JASON AND HIS GRANDFATHER RETURNED HOME THEY WERE GREETED ON the front porch by Gramma.

"What's the idea of leavin' us here with that body out there? You just don't care 'bout nothin', do you?"

Daddy Bob looked at his wife. "Don't start with me, woman. It's been a bad enough night without all your talk."

"Well, I told ya that devil friend of yours would do somethin' awful one night, didn't I?"

"Yeah, you sure did, but your so-called devil's been tied to a bed all night." Daddy Bob walked past her and went into the house. Jason followed. The two were met next by Jason's mother.

"Daddy, did ya see the sheriff?"

Bob was quick to answer. "I saw the bastard. I wish I hadn't."

"What's wrong?"

"He ain't no good. No damn good at all. But I ain't gonna talk about it. I'll do somethin' 'bout it in my own time."

"Well, is he comin'?"

"I reckon he'll come, but I don't want to see his ugly face."

Mary C. knew not to continue the conversation about Floyd. "Would you like some coffee? You really look beat."

"I sure would, honey. Between all the excitement and your mother's mouth, I need somethin' stronger than coffee, but that'll do for now."

"Sit at the table and rest. It'll be ready in a jiffy."

Daddy Bob sat at the kitchen table, and Jason did the same. Daddy Bob looked down the hall. "Where's Eve?"

"She's in the livin' room on the couch."

He looked back at Mary C. "Did y'all go tell Ray we found the ol' man?

"No, suh. Mama wouldn't let me go over there."

"That's all right. I'll go in a little while."

Mary C. gave her father a cup of coffee and sat down at the table with a cup of her own. She looked at Jason. He sat with his head resting on his arms.

"Daddy, don't you think Jason should be goin' to bed?"

Jason sat up.

"I don't think he's gonna sleep much if he does. And for some reason I want to keep him in my sight. It ain't gonna hurt nothin' for him to stay up. He'll sleep all day. Give him some coffee."

Mary C. fixed the coffee and then walked toward the hall.

Daddy Bob turned to her as she was leaving. "You gonna check on Eve?"

Mary C. kept walking. "No, I ain't checkin' on her." She left the kitchen.

Jason could see that his grandfather was in deep thought as they sat at the table.

As Mary C. walked down the hall, she heard a knock at the front door. She looked up and saw the well-known bug eyes of Sheriff Floyd peering between the white curtains that hung over the window of the door. She walked to the door as Floyd pushed his nose against the glass of the window, making a hideous face. Then he smiled.

She opened the door, and the ugly one stepped in.

"Evenin', Mary C."

"Evenin', Floyd."

"I ain't seen ya in a while, girl."

"I ain't been doin' much lately."

"How's that boy of yours?"

"About the same, I guess. Daddy says he's better, but I can't see it."

"That daddy of yours is really somethin', ain't he?"

"I don't know what you mean, Floyd."

"Oh, it don't make no difference. Where is the mighty Bob Merritt?"

"He's in the kitchen waitin' on you."

"And Eve?"

"She's in the livin' room. Daddy said you'd be more interested in her than what you was here for."

Floyd smiled.

"Well, I guess I'll talk to your daddy first. Since he always seems to know so much more than the rest of us."

As Mary turned to walk away from Floyd, he grabbed her and squeezed one of her buttocks.

"You're a lot of woman."

She slapped his hand away and made her way to the kitchen.

Jason and his grandfather were still sitting quietly at the table.

"Daddy, the sheriff's here."

Jason looked up quickly. Daddy Bob didn't look toward the fat man. He continued to drink his coffee.

"Well, Bob, where's he at?"

Daddy Bob looked up at Floyd. "If you mean Eve's father, he's out by the dog pen."

"Who the hell else would I be talkin' about?"

"Oh, I don't know, Floyd. I'm just tired of the whole thing. I don't like havin' you around here. But since you're here, you might as well see the body. I doubt you're gonna do anything about it, but . . . well, like I said, since you're here . . . "

"Just show me the body, and I'll do the rest. I don't need none of your preachin'. You come and got me, if you remember."

"That was a mistake, but it's done." Daddy Bob stood up and stepped toward the back door.

"Oh, yeah," said Floyd, "we had better find Ray, too."

Daddy Bob stopped. "Find Ray? For what?"

"Well, you have to admit that if it is foul play he's the prime suspect. As crazy as he is and all." Floyd's words angered Daddy Bob.

"Bullshit, Floyd! That's bullshit, and you know it!"

"Well, you call it what you want, but let me do my job." Floyd stared at Daddy Bob for a second. "Now, will you take me to the ol' man?"

"Come on, I'll show ya. But you do what ya have to, and then you get off my place." The two walked out onto the back porch, leaving Jason sitting at the table.

Jason put his head down on his arms, and it wasn't long before the lack of sleep had him in a battle again to keep his eyes open. He realized that he was losing the battle. He closed his eyes.

Just to rest them a second, he thought to himself.

As he rested he could hear the clock in the hall chime three times. He began to drift away from reality. In his mind flashed the sight of the old man's face covered with mosquitoes. Then Ray Klim as the devil. Then Eve's black eyes. Then he saw Tom Green. The rusty knife appeared. The young girl sat in the bed. Jason turned his head back and forth to fight the dream. He fought through the ugly thoughts and returned to the reality of the kitchen. He kept his head buried in his arms. He reassured himself that the ugly thoughts came during sleep. He took a deep breath of relief. He lifted his head and opened his eyes.

Fear ripped through Jason when he found that he was sitting across from Eve. She was at the table with a cup of coffee held up to her face. Jason didn't know if this was part of the dream or not. He could only see her eyes. Her black eyes. He found himself being held once again by her evil stare. The trancelike stare was strong, but Jason's fear was stronger. He pushed away from the table and tried to run. He fell once as he lunged for the door. He had to crawl out onto the back porch. Panic overtook him as he jumped to the ground. He got to his feet and began to run. After only a few steps, he ran into the sheriff.

"Hey, slow down, boy. You're gonna knock somebody down."

"Where's Daddy Bob?" Jason panted as he waited for an

answer.

"He went over to find Ray."

Jason looked toward Ray Klim's house. He could see his grand-father standing on the front porch. As before, Jason's fears were lightened at the sight of his loved one. Jason ran toward Ray Klim's as Daddy Bob walked down the steps.

"What is it, boy?"

"I'm scared."

"I know, boy. I know. I'm scared, too. This is an evil night. I ain't never seen nothin' like it. I don't know why, but there's evil in this night."

"Ah, you ain't scared."

"Sure, boy, everybody gets scared. But it's how you handle bein' scared that makes you a man. Right?"

Jason nodded, agreeing with Daddy Bob's favorite saying.

CHAPTER TEN

DADDY BOB PUT HIS ARM AROUND JASON, AND THEY WALKED BACK TO THE Big House. As they walked up onto the back porch, they were greeted by Eve.

"Did ya tell Ray?"

"He ain't there."

"He ain't there? Where is he?"

"I don't know. Maybe he went with Charlie to look some more."

"He's probably out drunk somewhere. That's where he most likely is. Drunk. He don't care nothin' 'bout the old man."

"I don't think he's drunk, Eve. I'm too tired to talk about it now. You was wrong in tryin' to keep Ray tied up like ya did. You was wrong. He ain't never gonna get no better if you don't help him. I don't think you want him to get better."

Eve stared at Bob as he walked past her and went through the back porch door, followed closely by Jason. Jason was careful not to look up at Eve for fear of meeting her eyes. The two were met by Sheriff Floyd and Mary C. as they walked into the kitchen.

"Another cup of coffee, Daddy?"

"No thank ya, honey. What ya think, Floyd?"

Sheriff Floyd rubbed his red, peeling face with the back of his hand. "Well, Bob, I'll admit it's strange as hell. I ain't at all sure about it bein' foul play. The way he's naked and all, I think maybe he just went a little crazy with ol' age and wandered off. Ol' folks is funny that way when they nearin' the end and all."

"Maybe so, but you know he didn't walk too good. He ain't been able to for some time now."

"Yeah, I know, but he coulda found some last hidden strength. They do it, I tell ya. Ol' folks'll surprise ya, Bob."

"And you think this is one of those crazy times, do ya?"

"I don't see it no other way, Bob. I just don't. I don't know what you're tryin' to see, but that's the way I see it right now. You act mighty funny 'bout all this, Bob. You want me to say that it was a killin', but you don't want there to be no suspects."

"Suspects! You call Tom Green and Ray Klim suspects? Tom Green never hurt nobody in his life. Ray Klim was tied to a bed all night. So there's your two suspects."

"You don't know all that for a fact. You just talkin'. I'm not sure, but it looks like some kinda heart attack to me. We'll see what the doctor says. If he says the old man was killed, I'll look into it. But until then, there ain't much more I can do. I'm gonna get him now. So leave things like they is. I shouldn't be too long."

"Whatever you say, Floyd. I'm just tired of it all. I wanna get this night over with. It's the worst I seen in many a day."

Sheriff Floyd left the kitchen. Jason's mother saw him to the door.

Floyd and Mary C. walked out onto the porch. Floyd turned to face her.

"You need any money, girl?"

"In a few days, Floyd. In a few days."

Floyd smiled. "Just say when." Floyd reached out and gently touched Mary C. on the chin with his fingertips.

"You need to rest, girl. You too pretty to be missin' your rest."

Mary C. smiled at the ugly man and kissed the tip of his hand as it rubbed across her face.

"You're a good man, Floyd. You been good to me. There's a place in my heart for ya."

"You ain't been too bad to me either, girl. It works both ways. If it hadn't been for you, this ol' ugly face of mine would have never been close to a real woman."

"I'll see ya, Floyd."

Floyd nodded and walked off the porch. Mary C. watched him get into his car and drive away. She didn't understand why, but she did have feelings for the fat, ugly lawman. She knew now that what he had done to her as a child had been wrong. She tried not to think about it too much. He had never really hurt her. He had helped her many times. So giving him a little pleasure seemed a small thing. She walked over to the swing and sat down, trying to relax for a second or two. How confused the night had been. She felt afraid for the first time. The fear came mainly because this was the first moment she had had time to think about what had been happening. More thoughts of Floyd entered her head. She was reminded of the time that being with Floyd had been a big mistake.

It all happened because she had seen Floyd earlier that day near the swimming hole. She had told him that her mother and father would be gone for the evening and if he would like to come sit on the porch and keep her company, he could. Floyd agreed and arrived just at dark.

She made coffee, and they sat on the porch and talked about all the people in their little town. Her husband had been dead for about six months, and this was the first time she had been with the ugly one since sometime before her wedding. Floyd had not bothered her during her five years of marriage. All of their encounters had been before J.P. began to court her. But now that times were hard, she knew how free Floyd was with those silver dollars as long as he got his pleasure.

Then there was the problem with Jason. Since his awful ordeal in the woods, he had been acting strange and would at times cling to Mary C. for the length of a day. At other times, he would keep to himself and stay quiet for hours and hours. Jason's love for Daddy Bob was growing during this time, and it seemed that the old man was the only one who could bring him out of his withdrawn patterns of behavior. Mary C. was concerned about Jason; however, she had become discouraged and disappointed in his slow improvement. Her patience had waned regarding the boy. She didn't give him many tender moments. Jason would soon be six. When he did talk, he talked a mile a minute and asked hundreds of silly questions that had no meaning to anyone but to himself.

Mary C. remembered how on that night Jason was extremely quiet for the first part of the evening. He seemed to be fascinated by their visitor. She was afraid the boy would say something about Floyd's appearance, but he never did. Floyd let Jason look at his gun, and he told Jason one or two of his sheriff stories while Mary C. was getting the coffee.

It all started as a nice evening on the porch. It wasn't long, however, before things began to change. Jason began to talk and ask his needless questions. He became restless and sleepy, fighting sleep as it began to overtake him. Mary C. had to tell him three or four times to go to bed. She finally persuaded him with two good pops on his backside. She walked with Jason to his room to make sure that he got into bed, closing the door as she left. She rejoined Floyd on the porch.

"I just don't know about that boy. I have to give him a beatin' almost every day."

Floyd didn't say anything as she sat down next to him.

"What you thinkin' 'bout, Floyd?"

"Nothin'."

"Ah, you thinkin' 'bout somethin' all right. I can tell."

"You ain't been with me for years, girl. How can you know what's in my head?"

"I just know."

"Then you tell me."

"Well," she smiled, "you're thinkin' about touchin' me and you're glad that I asked ya to come here."

"Is that what I'm thinkin'?"

"Ain't it?"

"Maybe, but it's a little different now."

"Why is it different?" Mary C. raised her eyebrows.

"'Cause if it's gonna work, we got to treat it like business."

"What you mean, business?"

"Well, I'll pay ya good for your services, but you gotta come when I want ya. We just ain't gonna meet when you need some money. We gonna meet when I say."

Mary C. thought for a few seconds. She didn't understand the need for his demands; but the words "pay ya good" overshadowed any of her thoughts, and she agreed.

"Whatever you want, Floyd."

Floyd smiled and leaned back in the swing.

"We oughta get things started tonight, girl. I could sure use some good feelin's. It's good to see ya, and I would sure like to be close to ya again." Sweat began to streak down his face.

Mary C. thought about her promise, and she realized that Floyd was going to test her to see if he truly had command.

"If you want to now, then let's go inside. Daddy won't be back 'til late."

Mary could see that Floyd was becoming excited by the mere thought of being with her. She knew that the encounter would be a short one. They both stood up, and Floyd put his arms around her. They went into the house, making their way to her room. As they walked into the room, Floyd began to work frantically to unbutton her blouse. He was so nervous and excited that he only managed to fumble around. He didn't make any headway with the buttons. Mary C., seeing the problem, tried to help.

"Hey, calm down. Let me."

Floyd stepped away from her and wiped the sweat off his forehead. He then rubbed his mouth with the back of his hand. He took out his handkerchief so he could get rid of the snuff around his mouth. He continued to watch Mary C. undress. She first took off her shirt. His eyes watched her hungrily. Floyd stepped to her quickly and grabbed one of her breasts roughly and squeezed it.

"Oh, take it easy! You don't have to hurry or be so rough. I'm not goin' anywhere. You'll bruise me. Be careful."

Floyd stepped back again and licked his lips.

"I want ya, girl. I wanna touch ya all over. I want ya to kiss on me, ya hear?"

"I hear ya, Floyd."

Mary then stepped out of her jeans and stood there with only her panties on.

"Take them off, too," Floyd ordered.

"Sure, Floyd." Mary C. smiled. "But ain't you forgettin' somethin'?"

Floyd looked puzzled. "What?"

"Well, I just don't see how you gonna be able to do anythin' with all your clothes on. That's all."

Floyd stood there fully dressed. Suddenly he began to laugh.

"You're somethin', girl. You're really somethin'. You always say somethin' funny. I was watchin' you so hard I plumb forgot about me."

Floyd began to undress quickly as Mary C. stretched her naked body across her bed.

"You can hurry any time, Mr. Sheriff."

"You're somethin'. You know that? You're somethin'."

Mary C. watched Floyd as he struggled with his pants. He didn't take his shoes off first, and getting his pants over his big shoes became somewhat of a problem. He fell down twice before he finally got himself free of the hold. It was hard for Mary C. to keep from laughing at the fat one as he fought with the garments. His legs were snow-white, and his big gut hung down like a sack of mud. The hair on his chest crawled all the way down his back. It looked unnatural to Mary C. She didn't remember Floyd's body as being as ugly as it was. It was hard for her to see how she could get any pleasure from going to bed with someone like Floyd. She would have to take pleasure in thinking about the money she would be paid.

Floyd was now finished undressing. He had just kicked off his shoes, and he made his way to the bed. He stood over Mary C. for only a moment and then he jumped on her like a wild pig. When his fat body landed, he almost knocked the breath out of her.

"Oh, Floyd, you gotta be careful. You could hurt me somethin' awful. I got little bones and tender spots. So take it easy."

Floyd was now breathing heavily, and the sweat poured off his face and body.

"I'm sorry. I just don't know why I do things like that. You just make me act so crazy. Are you all right?"

"Oh, I'm fine. Just be a little more careful, okay? Be gentle. That's the thing to be—gentle."

Floyd lay alongside her for a few seconds and then began to touch her in all his favorite places.

"You still got that good feelin' to ya, girl."

Mary C. didn't answer, but she did smile, closing her eyes as she did.

"Does that feel good to ya? I sure want it to feel good to ya."

"It feels fine, Floyd."

Floyd smiled and rolled his big body over on top of Mary C. He was rather heavy, but some of the pressure was taken off her as the soft mattress gave way to their weight. Floyd was no longer talking or worried about Mary C.'s comfort. He had no thoughts of foreplay. He only wanted to satisfy his hunger. All thoughts of gentleness left him. He began to grab Mary C. as if he were trying to get all he could in one night just in case there were no other nights. He moved his hands wildly as if he didn't know where to start. He seemed to settle for a moment, and then he reached for another spot. Mary C. was becoming uncomfortable and began to stop his wild hand movements so he would not bruise her.

"What's wrong?" he said.

"What's wrong? You're about to peel all my skin off—that's what's wrong. Now, you gotta take it easy or we ain't doin' nothin'. So you decide what you're gonna do."

Floyd was embarrassed about the way he was acting.

"I'm sorry," he said in a low, husky voice.

"Hey, come on. Let's try again. But this time, take it easy, please."

Floyd nodded and smiled and began again.

"I'll tell you what. Let me get on top. I think it'll be a lot easier on both of us—at least one of us anyway."

Floyd didn't seem to care how they did it as long as they did it, so he positioned himself in the middle of the bed and Mary C. climbed aboard. As Mary C. mounted her business partner, she giggled as the thought of Moby Dick went through her head.

"What's so funny?" he asked.

"Oh, nothin'. I was just thinkin' about you fallin' down on the floor when you was undressin'."

Floyd smiled. After the two began to work toward the same goal, it wasn't long before Floyd entered her body and began to fill his need. As they continued, she sat up straight and arched her back, moving her hips for more sensation. She closed her eyes and forgot about Floyd's ugly body and cared only that he penetrated deep within her. She even overlooked the sweat and body odor that emanated from the fat one. As they both began to move, hoping for more sensation, the bed began to squeak and the headboard began to bang against the wall. It seemed as if the entire Big House were shaking. Being in the height of the encounter, neither Floyd nor Mary C. paid any attention to the noises around them. They continued their wild act until suddenly they heard a new sound.

"Mama?"

The two lovers froze.

"Is that you, Mama?"

They both looked toward the sound. Jason was standing in the doorway.

"Mama, I'm scared."

"You better get back in that bed, boy."

"But I'm scared."

Mary C. pulled a blanket over her.

"Did you hear me?" she shouted.

"Why you fightin' with Sheriff Floyd? Is he fightin' you, Mama?"

"Jason, you get away from that door. Go back to sleep. Now get, ya hear?"

Mary C. remembered hearing Jason cry as he walked back down the hall to his room.

Her thoughts were broken by the sound of Daddy Bob's voice as he stepped out onto the porch.

"What you doin' out here, girl? You should try to get some sleep."

Mary C. shook the unpleasant thoughts of that evening from her head and looked up at her father.

"I'm just sittin'. Did you tell Ray yet?"

"No, I couldn't find him or Charlie. Everything's so strange. I just don't understand any of it. Where's your mother?"

"She went on to bed. She was dead on her feet."

"That's good. She needs to rest. I'm nervous enough without hearing her do all that talkin'. She just adds to all the problems. She seems to be weaker in her old age."

"Oh, Daddy, she's just afraid, that's all. This night's enough to scare anybody."

"Boy, that's the truth all right; but sometimes she . . . "

Before Bob could finish, Eve came through the back door into the kitchen.

"Where's the sheriff?" she asked.

"He went to get the doctor."

"Oh, I guess you have to do that, huh?"

"I guess so."

Eve's face had a sad and tired look, but there were no tears.

Jason didn't look at her as she talked to his grandfather. As she talked, Mary C. left the kitchen.

"Bob, would you walk me back to my house? I'll be fine once I get over there. I'm gonna try and get some sleep. Please let me know what the doctor says."

Jason was surprised at her tone of voice. It was strange and really didn't sound like her at all. He could see that his grandfather didn't notice the strangeness of her request.

"Sure, Eve, maybe you can get some rest. There ain't much you can do here. The sheriff will take care of things now. Maybe Ray's back. We should try and tell him and Charlie. They might still be huntin' for your daddy."

Bob stood and walked to the door, where Eve was standing.

"Boy, I think maybe you can get to bed now. So get."

Jason wasn't too excited about the idea, but as usual, he did as his Daddy Bob said. He wanted to give a warning to his grandfather, but he didn't know how or why. He just felt as if he should say something, but he didn't.

Jason walked slowly down the hall, thinking of Eve's words. He passed his mother's room and then paused to look in. She was lying on the bed with a pillow covering the top part of her head. She must have sensed his presence because she removed the pillow and looked at him.

"What you doin', son?"

"Daddy Bob sent me to bed."

Mary C. extended her arms.

"Come here. Lay by me."

Jason's heart almost leapt out of his chest again. He darted to his mother's arms and pulled himself close to her. Her body was warm, and her good smell again enveloped him. He thought that maybe he was in the middle of another dream. This one was rather pleasant.

"You okay, son?"

"Yes, ma'am."

"You sure been brave tonight. Your daddy would have been real proud of ya."

Jason smiled, but the sight of a dead squirrel flashed in his head.

"Daddy Bob's proud of ya, too."

Jason thought how much he loved his Daddy Bob. His mother hugged him tightly. She soon ended his tender moment.

"Why don't you go on now to bed? I'll see ya in the morning. I'll bet you really sleep late this day."

Jason, always expecting to lose his tender moments, was not surprised at his mother's words. He left her side and walked to the bedroom door.

"Good night, Mama. I love you."

"Good night, son."

Jason walked to his room and took off his shirt. He looked out the window in the direction of Ray Klim's house. He saw his Daddy Bob and Miss Eve walking up the steps of the porch. They both went into the house. He looked at his bed. He yawned. He began to feel how sleepy he really was. He got into bed, still wearing his cutoff jeans. It felt as if his whole body sank deep into the soft mattress. His arms and legs felt weak, and he had a small headache. The clock in the living room chimed four times as he drifted away into his dream world. It wasn't long before his mind began to wander. As he fell asleep, his brain filled with earlier images.

His boots were wet with the morning dew as he walked through the woods. Then there was a shotgun blast. The sun passed and there was darkness. A bobcat screamed, and a squirrel fell from a tree. Then Miss Eve's eyes shone through the darkness, and he saw his Daddy Bob's white crown of hair. He felt so much love for Daddy Bob. A swarm of mosquitoes slapped his face. He saw the old man's naked body crawling with the pests. He tried to fight his way out of his dream world, but he couldn't find the way out.

The sun passed again, and he cried out. The water pouch was empty. His stomach hurt and he cried again. Jason's horror was interrupted by the sound of voices. At first he didn't know if the voices were real or a part of his nightmare. He opened his eyes and looked around his bedroom, reassuring himself that he was awake.

He heard the voices again as the clock chimed five times. He got off the bed and then went to the bedroom window. He couldn't see who they were, but he could see three men's shadows near the edge of the house. Then suddenly another group of men passed the window carrying the old man on a piece of plank board. Jason, startled as the body passed near him, moved back from the window and fell over a small nightstand. He fought his way to his feet and sat on the edge of his bed. He could feel his heart racing wildly in his chest. He felt sick. So he lay down again. He thought about how the old man looked. He didn't know how anyone could touch him. He stared at the ceiling for a few seconds, and then he heard someone walking down the hall. He jumped out of bed and pushed open the door so that he could see down the hallway. His mother was standing at the front door with her back to him. She opened the door. A man entered.

"We got the ol' man, and I'm gonna take a good look at him over at my place. We'll let y'all know somethin' later."

"Doc, we sure thank ya for comin' out."

"That's my job, girl. It's been an awful night, that's for sure."

"It'll be a blessin' when it ends," agreed Mary C.

"Is your daddy here?" asked the doctor.

"No, suh. He took Miss Eve home and he ain't come back yet."

"Well, I guess I can tell you—and you be sure and tell him—that we've had another awful thing happen tonight."

"What kinda thing, Doc?"

"Well, Floyd came by my place after he was here. He woke me up and tol' me about the ol' man. When he left he said he'd meet me back here in about thirty minutes. Well, me and my son was headed this way on the ol' beach road when we seen smoke and fire through the woods. It looked to be comin' from Floyd's place. We hurried as fast as we could but we was too late."

"Too late," Mary C. interrupted. "What do you mean?"

"Well, when we got there, the place was all in flames. We got as close as we could, but it was burnin' bad. My boy said he thought he heard somebody scream. He said it sounded like there was a woman in the house. All I heard was them crazy dogs barkin'. You could hardly think with all them dogs goin' crazy. We listened for the scream again, but we never heard it. It was probably them dogs. Your mind can do funny things when somethin' like that's goin' on around ya."

"What about the sheriff? Did ya see the sheriff?"

"Well, now, that's the awful part."

Mary C.'s eyes widened. Jason's did, too.

"We saw Floyd sittin' on the ground next to one of his old trucks. We hollered at him, but he didn't move. I ran over to him, and then

I seen it." Doc swallowed and hung his head. "Somebody had cut Floyd up somethin' awful."

Mary C. turned away from the doctor quickly. She felt sick.

Jason's heart began to pound. The sight of the rusty machete flashed in his head.

The doctor continued. "You gotta tell your daddy, girl. Floyd had lost a lot of blood from the cuts, and he was in shock. I worked on him best I could, but he just couldn't hold on."

Mary C. turned back toward the doctor. "He's dead?"

"I did all I could, girl. He was cut bad. We was hopin' your daddy could tell us if maybe he seen somebody in that area that might have done this awful thing."

Jason moved back into his room. He saw the machete once more. He smiled to think that Tom Green was free. But then he thought of the young girl that he saw when he was at Floyd's. He thought of his mother and how she had lain naked with the ugly one. His eyes filled with tears.

"I love my mama," he thought, "I love Daddy Bob and Tom Green. I hate Sheriff Floyd."

Jason returned to his bed. He didn't want to sleep, but his body demanded rest. He battled with his heavy eyelids, but he was unable to fight for very long. Once again, sleep came to his tired body and torn mind.

The next time Jason opened his eyes, the morning sun was shining through his bedroom window. He heard a rooster crow. He thought that he had only been asleep for an hour or so. He thought that perhaps all of the past night had been one of his dreams. His little head throbbed from lack of rest. He felt drained, and he closed his eyes once more in hopes of sleeping the day away. His mother's voice kept him from falling back into slumber. His mother and grandmother were talking in the hall.

"I don't know, Mama. Maybe he came in and then left again."

"He never came to bed, I tell ya. I don't think he came back at all."

"Well, I'll go over to Ray's and see if he's there."

"No, you ain't. You ain't doin' no such thing. When the doctor and the other men come back, they can go over there."

"What about Daddy?"

"Your daddy can take care of hisself. If somethin' has happened to him, I don't want you gettin' hurt too. We'll just wait and pray."

Mary C. could see that her mother was worried about Daddy Bob, and she was only trying to cover her fears.

Jason suddenly realized that they were saying that his grandfather had never returned home after he had taken Miss Eve to her house. He thought how strange he had felt when Miss Eve asked Daddy Bob to take her home. Jason jumped out of bed, put on his shirt, and went down the hall and out the kitchen door. He stopped on the back porch and peeked through the latticework siding that surrounded the porch. He looked through one of the openings at Ray Klim's house. He saw no movement at all. He thought that maybe they all went off somewhere, and Daddy Bob went, too. Then he walked down the steps; and for some reason, he ran in the direction of Ray Klim's house. He didn't understand why; but he knew that if he found his Daddy Bob, all would be fine. He loved Daddy Bob. Without stopping for a second thought, he ran up to the front of the house and knocked on the front door. At first he thought that someone was going to answer the door because he could feel the vibrations of a person walking in the house, but the door didn't open.

Jason closed his eyes as a cold chill of fear ran through his body. He wanted to run back to the safety of his own house. He looked back toward his house and moved away from the front door. He walked down the porch steps slowly and was startled by the familiar raspy voice that belonged to Miss Eve.

"What you want, boy?"

Jason turned, and his heart began to race again as he came eye-to-eye with Eve.

"I said, what you want?"

Jason was so afraid that he couldn't manage to get any words out of his mouth.

"You go back home, boy."

Then suddenly Jason found hidden strength.

"Where's Daddy Bob?"

"Well, why didn't you say you wanted him, boy? I can't read your mind, ya know. He's around back with Ray."

Jason felt his heart slow at the sound of Eve's words, and he ran down the side of the house to find his Daddy Bob. He heard sounds as he neared the back of the house, and he called out, "Daddy Bob!"

When he reached the backyard, his eyes were blurred by the color red. He stopped to focus his eyes in the excitement. He first saw Ray Klim, who was standing over someone on the ground. There was an ax covered with blood on the ground. Jason saw it. His stomach filled his mouth with hot liquid. He became dizzy. It was hard for him to focus on Ray Klim's face. Ray Klim looked at Jason and then fell to his knees. He continued to look at Jason. He opened his mouth as if he wanted to say something, but he seemed too weak. He didn't speak.

Jason thought of Daddy Bob's words, "Ray Klim will never hurt ya, boy." Jason cleared his head of his grandfather's words and looked back at Ray. Ray's arms and face were all covered with spots of blood, and Jason felt himself becoming sicker. Ray bent over and began to vomit on the ground. Suddenly Jason saw the most horrible sight of all. The body that Ray was standing over was his grandfather's. Jason wanted to scream. The noise only came out as a whine from deep down in his throat. Jason closed his eyes and nausea overtook him. He felt as if he was in his dream world again.

"Please, Jesus." After his short plea, Jason opened his eyes, and the red was everywhere. His grandfather's chest was covered with blood, the ground was covered, the ax was covered and Ray Klim had blood on his arms and face. No matter where Jason turned, there was blood. He couldn't move in any direction. He could only open and close his eyes. He stared at the blood on Ray Klim's arms, and his head spun in a trance.

He remembered his gramma's words of warning to Daddy Bob: "And you'll be the one that gets hurt, bein' you're the only one that spends any time with him. Have you forgotten he almost stuck that ax in your face?"

The thought of the ax ripped into Jason's head, and he closed his eyes again.

Suddenly Jason's trance was broken by a person coming out of the back of the house. Jason turned to see Eve jump off the back porch. She ran up behind Ray and began to hit him on the back with a garden hose. Ray was still coughing and vomiting. The first two hits didn't seem to bother him much, but the third blow cut him across the forehead. Eve began to yell.

"Murderer! Murderer! I'm gonna kill that devil in you once and for all. You ain't gonna hurt no more people."

With each hit, Jason closed his eyes, hoping that each time he opened them it would all turn out to have been a bad dream. Even with his eyes closed, the sound of the hose hitting Ray tore through his head. Jason prayed again and opened his eyes, but the horror didn't stop. Eve continued to beat Ray until he was flat on his back next to Daddy Bob. Then she ran to the faucet and turned it on. Then she began to spray water in Ray's face.

"I'll wash you clean, you pig," she shouted.

Ray coughed and turned his head from side to side to avoid the spray of water, but she kept it in his face. Ray was too weak to get away or fight back and soon there was no movement from him at all.

Eve held the hose in place long after Ray had stopped moving. The water, mixed with blood, ran over Jason's feet; but he was still unable to move. He was frozen with fear. He could only watch the horror. Eve then dropped the hose and laughed out loud. She looked at Jason, and then she turned and looked into the back of the house.

"It's done," she said. "It's all done."

Then Jason heard another voice.

"Good. The time was right."

Jason turned his head and looked toward the back door of the house. Jason's eyes widened as Mr. Charlie walked out of the house and put his arm around Eve.

"Well, my lady, what about the boy?"

They both looked at Jason.

"Oh, they ain't gonna listen to him. He's loony anyway."

"It looks to me like you did everybody a favor gettin' rid of Ray. And gettin' rid of that ol' nothin' of a man was just a plain pleasure."

Jason's eyes met Eve's. How he hated her. He closed his eyes, hoping for the last time it was only a nightmare. In his head flashed the sight of Eve as the devil and then Ray's bloody arms. Then he saw Charlie's smile.

"I love Daddy Bob. I hate Miss Eve. I hate Sheriff Floyd. I like Tom Green. I wish I had some peanuts."

DUCKIN'

PRELUDE

BOBBY MERRITT STOOD AT THE WHEEL OF HIS SHRIMP BOAT, *MARY C.*, AS SHE made her way through the jetties at the mouth of the St. Johns River. He steered her toward the small Florida fishing town of Mayport. Bobby and his one-man crew were physically drained from the all-night trip, but the amount of shrimp they were bringing to the dock made the night's work more than worth the effort.

His cousin, Tommy, had been Bobby's mate on the *Mary C.* for the last seven years. Bobby looked back toward the deck of the boat and nodded with a big grin. Tommy smiled back as he pulled the hatch over the big hole where the shrimp had been iced down. They both knew this would be their biggest catch of the season. Bobby had called the fish house on the radio and informed Mr. Leek that headers would be needed when the *Mary C.* unloaded. He was happy, but puzzled, because no other boat had delivered such a catch in many months. It would lift the spirits of his fellow shrimpers. He didn't know why the shrimp came, but he was glad it happened to him. Tommy joined Bobby at the wheel. The town of Mayport was in the distance. They would unload soon.

Bobby looked at the great tree as he had done many other times. He loved how it towered above the town. Like many shrimpers, Bobby believed in the power of the tree. He knew it was the biggest oak tree on earth. Bobby thought it was surely one of the earth's great wonders and he knew it watched over Mayport.

Bobby had been raised Catholic and he did believe in God, so he did not worship the tree. He did believe it had great powers over the town. He loved the many tales of the tree and he knew the game had to be played so the shrimp would come. Bobby was excited that his sister's son, Jason, would play in the game soon. Jason and his mother, Mary C., the boat's namesake, had lived with Bobby for almost nine years. They had moved from East Mayport after Jason's grandfather, Daddy Bob, had died a violent death. Jason had also lost his grandmother at the same time. She just disappeared three weeks after her husband's death. People said she just couldn't live without Bob Merritt and that she walked out into the swamp near their old house in East Mayport. She was never found. Jason and Mary C. missed their loved ones, but Uncle Bobby had given them a good home.

Bobby loved the game. His time to play had passed, but he would play in heart as Jason played with his body. Bobby knew there was a God, that Jack Daniels was the nectar of the working man, Elvis was king, the power of the oak was real and you were not a man until you played Duckin'.

Duckin' had been a tradition in the town of Mayport forever. No one knew all the details surrounding such an activity, but many generations had taken part in the action-packed game. There seemed to be a need for the bragging rights as to which game had been the meanest and roughest. Most of the talk was about the number of broken bones and bloody noses that had been inflicted during the game. Duckin' had become the test of manhood in the town of shrimpers. The many stories of the game were greatly exaggerated and each tale changed from year to year. The rougher the game, the more satisfying to the oak. There was no limit to the good fortune from the tree if blood fell on the white sand beneath it.

The sand hill was about sixty feet high at its highest point. Its crowning glory was the huge oak tree. It towered above the hill as if it were a god and was there to protect the town and be worshiped. Most folks spoke reverently when they talked of the tree.

Stories of the oak were as wild as the stories of the game. It had been said that if a man had the courage to take a woman and make love to her, after midnight, in the sand under the oak, he would be assured a son. It would be a son that would grow to be a man of great strength. The strength of the oak would be in him. Willis was considered to be a midnight baby from the oak. Few had been thought of as an oak baby.

It was strange how the great tree had survived in the loose white sand. It was a struggle just to walk to the top of the hill, as the soft sand would give way at your feet. People said that lightning struck the tree many times as the years passed, but the great tree would only absorb the power and become even stronger. Some had heard talk from the tree just before the sun would rise. Folks said it was beckoning the players of the game. Others said it was the cries of the oak babies. It was thought that as a man was planting his seed, the tree planted its seed too. If a man had used the tree for the birth of his son, he could never talk of that night under the oak. If the man or his woman spoke of the breeding, the power from the oak would leave the child. If a boy in Mayport grew strong or with a talent of some kind, he was thought to be a "baby of the oak." Many considered the powers of the oak unlimited. If the shrimping was bad it was because the tree had not been satisfied with the game last played, perhaps no brave soul had attempted to breed beneath the great tree.

The oak reached out in over a hundred different directions with enormous limbs. The limbs alone were bigger than most trees. Each limb was shrouded by the many ropes used as swings during the games of the past. Once a rope was on a limb, it would never be taken down. Only nature and the oak would make the ropes drop as time went on. There were, however, many strong and new ropes put there for the more recent games. The sand hill and the oak were both a great contradiction in nature. The north side of the hill was covered only with white powder-like sand. It seemed impossible that such loose sand would support a tree like the oak. However, on the south side of the hill there was growth. There was a large grape arbor on the left section of the south side of the hill. The rest of that side was covered with palmetto fans, briars and prickly bushes. The true oak believers knew that the tree had the power of both good and evil.

CHAPTER ONE

SATURDAY

HEADING SHRIMP ALL MORNING WAS NOT JASON'S IDEA OF THE WAY HE wanted to spend his Saturday, but he did need the money and he wanted to see *Mary C.* unload her catch. Word of his Uncle Bobby's good fortune had already spread through Mayport and all the young people were running to the dock to try to earn some money. There had been very little heading to be done in the past few months. His uncle's catch was big news.

Jason arrived at the dock as the *Mary C.* was sending up her first basket of shrimp. Two dock workers took the basket into the fish house and dumped it on the heading table. As the shrimp fell onto the table, one of the workers said there were other boats coming in with big catches. It would be a great day in Mayport. If you worked all day at the heading tables, you could earn thirty dollars or even more. It all depended upon your speed and endurance as a header. Standing at the tables all day would take its toll on even the youngest and strongest back.

Jason wanted to see his Uncle Bobby, but he knew he needed to get a place at the table. He had to crowd his way into a section at the far end of the table. Not a great spot, but better than no spot. Jason knew from experience not to try to stand next to Miss Bell and her children. Jason had never felt the sting of her stick and hoped he never would. Miss Bell's stick was great for keeping dogs away and it assured her of plenty of elbowroom at the table. It was always fun to watch a newcomer to the tables try to move in and head next to Miss Bell. People who didn't know of Miss Bell would think the area around her was a safe place to settle to do some heading, but all intruders would be dealt with in the same manner. First, she would hit the table three times with her stick. If the intruder could not read between the lines, the next three swings would be to inflict pain. Most people would be moving when the stick hit the table the first time. Jason didn't know how much Miss Bell weighed, but he did know that her head weighed at least one hundred pounds by itself. Her cheeks looked ready to explode. She always seemed uncomfortable and in pain. The slightest move was difficult for her. Jason knew she hurt when she walked. Miss Bell was even blacker than his old friend, Tom Green. He remembered thinking, when he was a little boy, that Tom Green, the peanut man, was the blackest man on earth. Miss Bell had Tom beaten.

"I like black," Jason thought. "I love Tom Green, I wish I had some peanuts."

Miss Bell's six children headed shrimp along with her. They would not stop throughout the day. As long as the shrimp were dumped on the table, they would be heading. Even if Miss Bell struggled away from the table for personal reasons, the children would not stop. Miss Bell would let them get water once in a while and use the bathroom but only one at a time. Jason thought how he had never seen any of them eat during the heading time, even if the work went into the night.

Miss Bell's children were a strange group. Two of the girls looked just like Miss Bell, only smaller. Jason knew it wouldn't be very long before they had one hundred pound heads, too. The three boys were younger than Jason, but they were much faster at heading shrimp than the older headers. Unlike the other young workers, the three boys didn't play or act silly as the day went on. Maybe Miss Bell's stick gave them the strength and discipline to carry out the workday.

The third girl was different from the others. It was almost as if she didn't fit. Her skin was much lighter. Her eyes were green, and Jason found himself looking at her all the time. Jason liked it when the front of her shirt got wet and he could see her skin sticking to the cotton. He liked those green eyes, but she seldom looked at Jason.

Jason thought how strange it was that he only saw the black children of Mayport when there was heading to be done. He thought of his old friend again and how he loved Tom Green. Jason had not seen the little black man since he had moved from East Mayport to live with his uncle.

"Maybe I'll buy some peanuts down by the ferry slip after I head a few," he thought. It was a pleasant thought, but short-lived, as it was interrupted by a loud voice that Jason hated. It belonged to Willis.

Jason turned to see Willis coming through the door followed by Jason's best friend, Eddie Jones. Jason was always happy to see Eddie, but never liked it when Willis was around. He didn't want to admit his fear, but he knew he was like all the others: afraid of Willis. Jason knew it wouldn't take long for Willis to find a place at the table for him and Eddie to head. Anyone with regard for their own safety would move over for Willis. Anyone, that is, except Miss Bell. Not even Willis was that mean. But he was mean enough.

Willis was seventeen years old, but he looked twenty. He was mature in mind and body far beyond his years. Most of the young folks in Mayport followed Willis and all wanted to be his friend. It wasn't very healthy to be one of his enemies. Or at least that was what was said. If oak babies were true, then Willis was seeded by the great tree.

Jason thought that Willis' friends were "fear friends." He did, however, keep that thought to himself. He did not want to be a "fear friend" but he knew, up until now, he had been. With sixteen approaching, he would change that.

Jason's heart raced as Willis moved near him. "Well," the mean one's voice cracked in Jason's ear, "let's head next to the Jay Bird."

Willis had a name for everybody. Some funny, some not so funny.

Most were mean or cruel and meant to belittle the person. Willis had heard Jason's mother say, "naked as a Jay Bird" one time and so "Jay Bird" became Jason's calling card from Willis. Jason hated it, but he dare not tell Willis.

Willis and Eddie pushed their way to the table and began to work. Jason knew Eddie would not have been so forceful if Willis had not been there. Jason hated that impressing Willis was something one needed to do. Again, Willis' voice started Jason's heart.

"So how come the Jay Bird didn't let us know the boats were in?" Willis was eye-to-eye with Jason. Jason was slow with his reply, so Willis continued, "Less headers, more money for the Jay Bird." Willis grinned.

Jason hated what Willis had said. "It wasn't true and you're a liar, Willis," Jason thought. But it was just a thought. He then found the strength to speak. "I just got here, too."

Willis looked into Jason's bucket to catch him in a lie, but he saw no shrimp.

"You won't make no money that way, Jay Bird," Willis grinned again. Jason knew what Willis would say next. He always said the same thing and why should it change today? Willis didn't disappoint Jason's waiting ears. "Why don't we put our shrimp together and divide up three ways at the end?" Eddie, as usual, agreed quickly, but Jason knew he and Eddie would do all the work while Willis shared the money. Jason didn't know how, but he found the courage to refuse the offer.

"You and Eddie can head together if you want, but I'm gonna head alone." Jason couldn't believe those words came from his lips. Eddie had a shocked look on his face, but it was said and Jason could not take it back.

Willis glared at Jason as if he was even more shocked at the refusal than the others. "What did you say?" The glare had not left the mean one.

Jason swallowed and again the courage came. "I'm gonna head alone, that's all." Jason turned away from Willis, pulled his bucket near him and reached into the mountain of shrimp that had just been dumped onto the table. He was surprised when Willis did not speak again. Willis whispered something to Eddie. They both laughed and began heading shrimp. Jason knew Eddie was only trying to impress Willis and Jason was not angry with his friend. They would have good times without the "mean one" around in the days to come. Jason thought about turning sixteen in three days and maybe that was the reason he had found the new courage. He liked the way he felt. He liked standing alone.

"Sixteen's gonna be great," he thought.

The boats unloaded all morning. After four hours of work Jason took a break and weighed his headed shrimp. Mr. Leek, the owner of the dock, would keep a record of the amounts weighed and then pay the headers when they were finished. Mr. Leek came out of his small office and announced that the boats would, most likely, be unloading until the morning hours. The workers cheered out loud. They knew there was money to be made. Miss Bell and her children continued in a nonstop flurry. Miss Bell had left the table only once. Her children were yet to leave or rest.

Willis and Eddie had left after the second hour. Before Willis had left, he took a handful of his own headed shrimp and put them into Jason's bucket. "Let me help ya there, Jay Bird," he said. "As slow as you are, you ain't never gonna make no money. Don't say I never gave ya nothin'." Jason didn't want Willis' gift. He didn't think it would be very smart to owe Willis anything, even a hand-ful of shrimp. He also knew not to refuse the gesture. Willis then told Eddie, "Let's get out of here. I ain't gonna spend my Saturday headin' shrimp and lookin' at niggers."

Jason hated Willis' crude remarks. Willis always had words like that coming out of his mouth. Miss Bell didn't act like she heard Willis at all. She and the children never looked up and never stopped heading. Jason walked out onto the dock where the workers were unloading the boats. He stood clear as the dock workers lifted basket after basket of shrimp from the ice-packed holds of the boats. His Uncle Bobby's boat had been the first to unload and his uncle had gone home to get some rest. He would go out early in the morning to try the shrimp again. Shrimpers had to go while the shrimp were running. They could take no time off because, as fast as the shrimp appeared, they could disappear. One day the boats would be loaded down; the next day, maybe nothing. It was the nature of the life of a shrimper. One day feast, the next day famine.

Jason liked to watch the dock workers as they brought in the baskets. They were all so muscular, as they lifted and pushed the large steel containers. How he wanted to be strong.

"Maybe sixteen will bring a new strength," he thought. He liked the thought of a new Jason. He looked down and flexed his biceps. Jason remembered how one day Willis had said he had weenie arms. All of the others laughed. Jason laughed, too, but he really didn't think it was funny. Jason sat for about twenty minutes, resting his back and watching the workers. He really didn't want to head anymore, but he knew it might not last and he did need the money. He wrestled with two thoughts.

"Do I go home and eat and most likely not come back; or do I go back to the table and make some money?" It didn't take long for his stomach to make the decision for him. His thought of a huge sandwich was just too strong. He got up and walked back into the heading area and turned toward the exit door. He passed the small bathroom as the door was pushed open in his face. He quickly put his hands up to block the door from hitting him in the nose.

"Hey! Take it easy. You could hurt somebody," blurted Jason. He was surprised when he saw that the black girl with the green eyes had been the one who pushed the door in his direction.

"I'm sorry," she said with her head down. Her voice was soft. Jason liked it. He had never heard her talk before. He stood in her path. She still looked down. Neither spoke for a few seconds. During the silence, Jason thought, "I wish she would look at me. I want to see her eyes." Again, Jason found a hidden strength.

"Your eyes are beautiful," he whispered as the black girl looked up quickly, shocked at his words. Her eyes were opened as wide as possible. He loved them. His heart raced and his mouth went dry. She walked around Jason and hurried back to her place at the table. She pulled more shrimp in front of her and continued to head. She did not look up.

Jason forgot about his hunger and walked back to the table. He would head into the night. He knew his Uncle Bobby would tell his mother about the shrimp and she would not worry, knowing he was working. Jason wanted to stay and see those green eyes again. Her shirt was wet in front and he watched her breasts as they rubbed and pushed against the wet cloth. He imagined her naked, standing on the dock with the sunlight shining on her skin as she headed shrimp. It just seemed nicer to have her standing on the dock with the sunlight shining on her skin. He felt his young manhood push against the zipper of his dungarees. He liked that feeling. Again he thought, "Sixteen's gonna be great."

As night fell, the heading continued. Miss Bell and her children would stay until the last shrimp lost its head. Jason would too.

Mr. Leek brought out sandwiches and tea for those who stayed. It was welcomed by all. No one left the table. They ate as they worked. Most of the white headers had left the tables and gone home for the night. A group of new black workers had arrived just before dark. Jason, Miss Bell and her children were the only ones left who had started the day. The faces at the tables had changed. Jason was the only white to remain. He was proud he had been strong enough to stay. Jason had started to look for things of which to be proud. He liked the feeling. Again, he felt he had stood alone. None of the other boys had stayed. As he enjoyed his sandwich he was surprised, but pleased, when he found himself looking directly into those green eyes. He was even more pleased when he realized they did not turn away from his stare. They looked deep within him. He felt funny, as the two stared at each other as a formal introduction. She looked down to continue her work. Jason knew they were friends. He liked that. The work continued.

It was near midnight when Miss Bell pulled the last few shrimp on the table over next to her and popped their heads off. It was done. The table was empty. Jason and the Bell family were the only workers left at the table. All the others had gone home. One of Miss Bell's boys dumped the last bucket of shrimp onto the scales as Mr. Leek added the poundage to Miss Bell's count for the day.

Jason was paid sixty-three dollars for his efforts. He couldn't believe it. Again, something of which to be proud. Once more he stood alone. He thought that Miss Bell must have made a thousand dollars. Miss Bell went into the office with Mr. Leek. Jason liked him. He was fair and was kind to everyone, black and white. Jason knew he would be fair with Miss Bell. "Besides," Jason laughed to himself, "who wouldn't be fair to a lady that was the size of Miss Bell carrying a stick. . . ."

Jason watched Green Eyes walk past him in the direction of the bathroom. He wanted her to look at him, but she didn't. Jason walked out onto the now quiet dock. The workers were all gone. The dock was dark. Jason knew he needed to go home, but he wanted to see her one more time. He looked back into the fish house in the direction of the office. He saw Miss Bell coming out of the office door. Green Eyes walked out of the bathroom as the children walked toward Miss Bell. Jason couldn't hear what Miss Bell was saying, but they all started walking toward him. Jason stepped back into the dark section of the dock and watched Miss Bell and her children walk through the large doors and out onto the wooden boards of the dock. Jason moved deeper into the darkness. He watched in amazement at what happened next.

First, Miss Bell picked up a running water hose, as the three boys took their clothes off. Each boy held up his own pants and shirt while Miss Bell sprayed the water from the hose on the shrimp-stained garments. First the clothes and then she sprayed the boys as the three girls took the hose and rinsed the boys off, one at a time. The boys danced around as if they were chilled by the cold water and early morning air, but none made any noise. The boys stood there dripping, but clean, as Miss Bell handed each one a clean, dry pair of pants and a shirt. The three boys then walked back into the heading area, putting the dry clothes on as they walked. They sat down together on a small bench. They didn't talk. What had just happened was strange enough to Jason. What was to follow he would never forget as long as he lived.

Jason's eyes widened and his heart pounded in his chest as he watched the two fat girls and Green Eyes all take their clothes off, as the boys had done. Jason couldn't believe his eyes as he pushed even deeper into the darkness. He never took his eyes off Green Eyes. From the moment she unbuttoned her shirt his eyes were glued to her. Her body was the most beautiful thing he had ever seen. She looked so strong. Her stomach muscles seemed to ripple as she moved. Her breasts stood out as if they were rocks. Her thigh muscles bulged forward as she stepped. Jason had never seen such a sight. He felt his manhood once again as he watched her. Like the boys, the girls helped Miss Bell wash their clothes first. Then the three lathered up to clean the stink of the day from their bodies. Jason's eyes were still glued to Green Eyes. He was so excited, it was difficult for him to stand still. He knew he couldn't move. She waited to soap herself last. Her sisters were dressing as she moved the white bar over her skin. Jason felt as if she stood alone on the dock, just for him. His fantasy at the table had come true. He couldn't believe it. He saw no others. She moved in slow motion as she cleaned herself. Her body was covered with white suds.

"You hurry now, girl," Miss Bell's voice broke Jason's trance. "Don't rub ya skin off." Miss Bell and the others walked into the heading area toward the tables. Green Eyes smiled at her mother and continued to rub her body.

The huge black woman helped the other two girls dress near the tables. Mr. Leek walked out of his office and handed Miss Bell another glass of tea. She thanked Mr. Leek and then he began locking the windows of his fish house. Miss Bell sat down to rest and wait for her green-eyed child to finish her shower. She looked out to where the girl was still standing, holding the hose to her naked body. Miss Bell shook her head and smiled as her thoughts carried her back sixteen years, to the night the beautiful green-eyed child was given to her.

She had been waiting on the docks all day for a boat to unload. Just before dark, one boat came in and unloaded a small catch of shrimp. Miss Bell was the only header. She headed the entire catch. It was only about one hundred and fifty pounds of shrimp. Mr. Leek gave Miss Bell twenty dollars for her work. She was thankful.

Now, Miss Bell was a true believer in the power of the oak. Her mother had told her that all the happenings, good and bad, in Mayport, were controlled by the tree. She had given thanks and praise to the oak many times during her life. That night would be no different. She would give thanks for the money she had made. Miss Bell left the dock and walked to the sand hill. She would always stand near the grape arbor. The ground was firm there and the climb to the tree was easier. She made the climb to show her respect and as a penance for any wrong she had done. She figured such a painful chore would clean her of her sins. Miss Bell always felt renewed after visiting the oak.

That night was her greatest visit of all. She had made the climb. It had been painful, but she knew the cleansing had taken place. There was a clear sky and the moonlight brightened the hill more than usual. She could feel the beads of sweat drip off her forehead. It was a dreadful climb for a woman of her size. She never talked out loud to the tree. She only gave silent thanks within her mind. Her mother had told her the tree would know her thoughts.

As her ritual of thanks began, a strange noise cut through the night air. Miss Bell was unsettled at first, but she did listen for the sound again. She fell to her knees as the sound pierced the night once more. She knew it was the cry of a baby. Tears filled her eyes. She felt she was blessed in hearing the cry of an oak baby. She knew all the stories of the cries, but in all her visits to the tree, she had never heard them. The cry continued. Miss Bell was compelled to stand and move closer to the tree. The cry became louder and stronger. She felt a baby near. She looked up, but couldn't see it. Her eyes searched the limbs above her and at eye level. Then she saw what appeared to be a limb move. It was almost more than her heart could stand. Her faith in the oak made her reach out and touch the movement on the limb. Her hand fell gently on soft skin. There was no feeling of limb or bark. She knew her hand had touched the skin of a baby. She moved her face closer to the movement. A baby lay naked in a large gash cut into one of the limbs. It looked as if a chunk of the limb had been torn by lightning. The baby fit perfectly into the nature-made cradle. Miss Bell knew right away the child was female. She believed the stories of the tree giving only male babies, so she knew someone had left the baby as an offering to the tree. And now the tree was giving the child to her. She gently worked her hand under the now quiet infant. She lifted her from the safety of the limb. Miss Bell knew it was a black child, but her skin was extremely light. Miss Bell realized the reason she couldn't see the baby at first was because her skin was almost the color of the limb she had lain in. She would protect and raise the child as her own. It would be her tribute to the tree.

Miss Bell's youngest boy brought her out of her visit to the past, as he laid his head on her lap. She looked down at the boy and placed her hand on his head. She loved all her children.

"Let's go home, Mama," the boy broke the silence.

On the dock, Jason was shocked as Green Eyes continued to wash. She reached back and rubbed the bar of soap over her buttocks. She had her back to him as she reached in front to clean herself even more. She still had her back to Jason as she bent over and picked up the water hose. She turned with the hose. She held it to her hair and face, first. Then down her shoulders, her back, her breasts and stomach, then her butt and legs. Jason watched every splash of water. After the soap had been washed away, she dropped the hose. She looked in the direction where Jason stood in the dark. Jason's heart raced from what he had seen. But his heart nearly jumped into his throat when she spoke.

"I know you're there," she whispered. Jason was frozen by her words. His mouth went dry again. He wanted to run, but his feet would not move. They were frozen, along with the rest of his body. She stepped toward him. He could hear his own heart. She continued to move closer. He closed his eyes.

"It's a dream," he thought. He opened his eyes. Now she was near enough to reach out and touch. She was dripping wet and naked.

"She is beautiful," he thought. In his wildest dream, Jason never expected what happened next. Without any hesitation, she leaned her wet body against Jason, pushing her rock-hard breasts against his chest. They were eye-to-eye and this time she didn't look down. His mouth was still dry, but he didn't want to run anymore. She reached down and touched him. He felt strange. She never changed her expression as he felt her hand against the front of his pants. She held it there. The stare continued for a few seconds. The hand remained. Jason reached down to touch her. He felt her hair. He was afraid and he moved his hand away. Her eyes burned into Jason's soul. He could feel them burning deep inside him. He wanted to touch her again. He reached up and touched her breasts. They looked like rocks, but they didn't feel like rocks. He felt her nipples. He had never felt a nipple. He liked it.

"Will I wake up soon?" he thought. He hoped not.

The real-life dream went on. She still had not moved her hand from the front of his pants. She reached out with her other hand and took Jason's hand. She placed his hand between her own legs even lower than where Jason had touched before. He didn't move his hand or his fingers. Like her, he just held it there. After a few more seconds, she began to move her hips slowly up and down, pushing against Jason's hand. His fingers were wet. He felt funny again. They did not talk. Jason pushed one of his fingers slowly into her body. She didn't stop him. His fingers were wet. He liked it. She opened her legs wider for her comfort and Jason's pleasure. He didn't know what to do next. He knew he should do more, but he wasn't sure what. Suddenly the sight of Miss Bell with her stick flashed in Jason's head. He moved both of his hands. She looked surprised but smiled. She then stepped back to allow Jason a moment to admire her. She liked the way he looked at her.

"Are my eyes really beautiful?" she asked in a low whisper.

"You're beautiful," Jason answered.

With his reply, she stepped toward Jason once more and again he felt her firm breasts against him. Jason was ready to start again when Miss Bell's voice cut through the night air. The contact was broken.

"Get in here, girl. We gotta get home."

She turned quickly, picked up her clothes and ran into the fish

JESSIE'S SHOWER

house. Jason heard Miss Bell's voice again.

"Get them clothes on, girl. You can't run around naked like that. I never seen a child that wanted to be naked all the time. Is you crazy? You gettin' too big to be showin' ya self." She dressed quickly and followed Miss Bell out the door.

As Jason walked home, he knew it all had truly happened, but it did feel like a dream. He wanted to touch her again. He smelled his hand. She was still with him. He liked that. He smelled his hand again.

Jason showered on the back porch and then went into his house. He looked in his Uncle Bobby's room. He was asleep. Jason knew his uncle would be getting up soon to go shrimping again. His mother's bedroom door was closed. He wanted to open the door just to look at her, but he didn't. Jason knew he would sleep late. He thought he would fall asleep as soon as his head hit the pillow, but it was not to be. He lay there for over an hour with thoughts running through his head.

He could see her body as if she were standing in the room. He wrapped his legs around his pillow. He was hard again, as he thought of her breasts. He smelled his hand once more. Sleep took him.

Chapter Two

Sunday

Jason's sleep was deep and long. He had slept most of Sunday away. A person can sleep too long. He would not feel good during the day. His head would ache, but he would suffer within himself. Eddie had stopped by earlier that morning, but Mary C. would not let his friend wake him. She knew her son had worked hard at the tables and he needed his rest. She had seen the money on his dresser. She was proud and she knew Jason was, too. She promised herself she would not let Jason give the money to his Uncle Bobby. But she also knew Jason would offer the money to her. He always did. He wanted to help out and do his part as a working member of the house. She vowed that it would all be Jason's this time. The shrimp were running and the boats were catching. They didn't need to use Jason's hard-earned cash.

Jason woke to the sound of voices and music coming from the front of the house. When he heard Elvis singing, he knew his Uncle Bobby was home. As the music opened his ears, the smell of shrimp frying opened his nose.

"Now," he thought, "if I can just open my eyes."

It was not an easy chore, but he did manage to sit up on the edge of the bed. He figured he could walk to the bathroom with his eyes closed. He stood up and leaned against the wall. He reached down and touched himself. His morning bulge pushed at his underwear. He thought of last night with Green Eyes. His eyes popped open and he smiled. He ran to the bathroom.

Fried shrimp and Elvis filled the house. Jason walked into the kitchen and was treated to the sight of his mother standing at the stove, watching over a pan of shrimp as they fried. He knew it was too late for breakfast, but fried shrimp were good anytime. Mary C. turned toward him as he stood in the doorway.

"Well now, have you decided to join the livin' today?" Jason nodded his head and gave a half smile at his mother's question. Jason's head hurt. He sat at the table behind his mother. She spoke but did not take her eyes off the cooking shrimp.

"You hungry?"

Jason nodded again.

"Are you hungry?" she repeated her question.

"Yes, ma'am," Jason put his head down on the table. It still hurt.

"Too much to drink last night, boy?" Jason lifted his head when he heard his Uncle bobby's voice.

"Mornin'," Jason greeted his uncle.

"You mean good afternoon, don't ya, boy?" Uncle Bobby's question was loud and Jason's head throbbed again.

"Good afternoon," Jason said. He was hoping to quiet his uncle's loudness, but Uncle Bobby had no intentions of allowing the boy any peace at all.

"Was you really headin' last night or was ya doin' some jukin'?" Jason smiled at his Uncle Bobby's inquiry. "Well, was ya?" Jason had to answer. His smile was full now. He had come to life. "Oh, so you was jukin' then," Uncle Bobby continued.

Those green eyes flashed in Jason's head. "Maybe," Jason replied as he thought of the black girl.

"Did you hear that, Mary C.? Your baby boy said 'maybe.'" Uncle Bobby was still working Jason.

Mary C. responded. "I heard him. Now ya'll stop actin' so silly."

Uncle Bobby, as usual, was not ready to stop just yet. "Did you do some breedin'?"

Mary C. was quick to stop her brother's crude comment. "I said stop that foolishness and I mean stop, now."

Uncle Bobby laughed at Mary C.'s interruption of his last question. "He's gonna be sixteen in two days. There's no tellin' what he's been doin'." Uncle Bobby winked at Jason.

"You can tell your ol' uncle later when Mama's not here." Uncle Bobby left the kitchen singing "Don't Be Cruel."

Jason's stomach growled as his mother put a plate in front of him, filled with fried shrimp and grits.

He wondered, "Who popped the heads off these," as he reached for one of the seafood tasties. As usual, they were cooked to perfection. Mary C. stepped to the kitchen door and yelled into the front of the house.

"Come on, Bobby, eat something while it's hot. And turn that record off." Jason was surprised when he heard the music stop. Usually Uncle Bobby ignored Mary C.'s wishes or at least put up an argument about her order, especially when Elvis was singing. But this time the music stopped, as she had requested. Uncle Bobby walked back into the kitchen and sat down. Mary C. gave him a plateful too.

"Thanks. They smell and look great. I hope they taste as good as they smell."

"They do." Jason was quick to add his opinion.

"Oh, you ain't sixteen yet, boy, so you don't know nothin'."

Jason smiled at Uncle Bobby's joke as Mary C. sat down and joined them. The three sat in silence and enjoyed the meal. Jason became lost in his thoughts.

The game, Willis, sixteen, the green-eyed black girl, her breasts, Tom Green, peanuts, his mother—all ran through his head. His thoughts kept him quiet as his mother and uncle talked of the shrimp season and how good things were. Jason loved his Uncle Bobby. He knew the story about how his uncle's wife had just been too wild and Uncle Bobby had to let her go. Folks said she had left him unsettled and searching. Jason heard all the stories about his uncle and all his women, but he never saw his uncle with a woman. He always went out and never brought his lady friends home. Jason knew his uncle worked hard and treated him as if Jason was his own. Jason loved his uncle and he had to play the game for him. Jason's thoughts were broken by his Uncle Bobby's voice.

"Well, boy, Friday's the big day, huh?" Jason's heart raced as his throat went dry.

"Yes, suh."

"You'll love it, boy," Uncle Bobby continued. "It'll be somethin' else. And Friday night we'll sit here and talk about how wild it was."

Jason nodded his head and smiled.

"Yeah, that Duckin' is somethin' else." Uncle Bobby still wanted to talk of the game. The word, Duckin', sent a chill through Jason as if his blood flow had changed directions. The word was disturbing to him. He didn't like it. He didn't like the word "nigger" either.

"What a stupid name," he thought.

"What a stupid name," said Mary C. Another chill ran through Jason as he heard his exact thought come from his mother's mouth.

"She can read my mind," he thought.

"Why do they call it Duckin'?" she continued.

"Well, I don't really know," said Uncle Bobby. "It's just always been called that. But I'll tell you one thing, it's really somethin' when you swing down from that tree. It's really somethin'."

"But, do you have to play?" questioned Mary C. Jason liked his mother's question and was anxious for Uncle Bobby's reply.

"No," Uncle Bobby began, "I don't guess you have to play, but what real Mayport boy wouldn't want to play? Now that just doesn't make any sense at all, does it boy?" Uncle Bobby looked right at Jason. Jason smiled again and shook his head.

"Well, I don't know if I want Jason to play." Mary C. was concerned.

"Oh, girl, you just bein' a mama now." Uncle Bobby smiled. "You just don't want the boy to be grown up. It's time for you to let the boy go. He'll do just fine."

Jason wanted to tell his mother how he had been feeling about the game, but the words would not come.

"Maybe later," he thought. After Uncle Bobby had gone, they would talk.

"Yeah, boy, it's gonna be somethin' else out there on Friday. Really somethin'." Jason thought if his uncle said "It was really somethin'" one more time he would surely throw up. Jason was tired of any talk of the game. Mary C. began a new subject. A subject that would bring sadness and pain to Jason's heart.

"Jason, did your Uncle Bobby tell you what happened to Miss Bell?" Jason looked at his mother, alerted by her serious tone. Mary C. continued, "Was Miss Bell workin' at the tables last night?"

"Yes, ma'am." Jason thought of the fat lady. "She was there all night. Why? What happened?"

"They found her this morning dead at the sand hill. Uncle Bobby helped carry her."

Uncle Bobby joined the sad conversation. "Yeah, it took six of us to put her in the back of that truck. She was heavy enough without bein' dead." Jason didn't know what to say about the awful news. His head ached again. His uncle had more to say. "Somebody had caved the back of her head in with somethin'. It was an awful sight. They don't know what she was hit with, but it did the job. Yeah, that was an awful sight here on Sunday morning. She still had a death grip on that ol' stick of hers. We had to pry it from them fat fingers."

Jason's stomach burned. He could eat no more. He thought of Green Eyes. He still didn't know what to say.

"Why would anyone want to hurt poor ol' Miss Bell," Mary C. questioned.

"Money," answered Uncle Bobby. "Her and them kids of hers had been headin' all day and all night. She probably had made a good amount workin' that long."

Jason looked at his uncle. He knew what he was saying was true. "A thousand dollars," Jason thought.

Uncle Bobby added more. "And after what that one girl of hers said, well, we know it was the money."

"What girl?" Jason found the strength to talk.

"That strange lookin' girl of Miss Bell's. The one with the funny eyes. The one they call Jessie. She said Miss Bell went to give thanks to the oak for the money they had made. She always thanked the tree, the girl said. Miss Bell took that bunch of hers home and went back to the tree by herself. People say ol' Miss Bell talked to that tree almost every night. She was a true believer, they say."

The heading table and the oak flashed in Jason's head.

"What will happen to the children?" Mary C. was concerned again.

"Somebody in Nigger Town will take 'em in," replied Uncle Bobby.

Jason loved his uncle but he hated the word "nigger." He was sad that his loved one said that. He wished he could take it back. It was said. Jason's head still hurt.

Jason left the house later. He hoped to see the girl his Uncle Bobby had called Jessie. He wanted to tell her he was sad about Miss Bell. But he knew he would not walk to the part of town where the blacks lived. He walked down to the ferry slip and watched the fiddler crabs hurry back and forth into their holes in the mud. The tide was low and the small crabs were out in force. Any other time Jason would have been in the mud, trying to catch as many of the little crabs as he could. They were great to sell for bait. But his thoughts were on the events in his life. His mind raced with all manner of thought. His headache throbbed. He sat down on one of the bulkhead pylons. He rubbed his forehead and closed his eyes. He thought of Jessie and how she looked standing in front of him on the dock, how the water dripped off her body. He liked that. The splash of jumping mullet opened Jason's eyes and broke his thoughts. He didn't see the fish, but he recognized the sound. He looked up, as if someone had called his name. His heart raced once more, as he could see the huge oak at the top of the sand hill in the distance. His eyes were locked on the tree as if he and the mighty oak were staring at each other. A cool breeze touched Jason's face.

"Can the oak do the things people say?" he thought. "It's not so ugly during the day." His mind continued. "But at night, I wouldn't go there at night. Miss Bell went at night. She's dead."

A loud splash startled Jason and he almost fell off the pylon as he turned to see what could make such a noise in the water. His search for the sea creature ended quickly when he saw Willis and Eddie standing near him, laughing. Willis had thrown something into the water to scare him. It did. Jason's skin crawled like one of the fiddler crabs when he heard Willis' evil laugh and then his voice.

"What's the matter, Jay Bird? You look like ya seen a ghost. Ain't his face real white?" Willis directed his question to Eddie.

"It sure is." Jason knew that could be Eddie's only answer. Eddie laughed along with Willis.

"Maybe," Willis' voice dug into Jason again, "he saw the ghost of Miss Bell."

Jason's head throbbed even more. He couldn't believe Willis said that. If he could have, he would have buried Willis in the same grave with Miss Bell right that moment.

Eddie saw that Jason didn't like what Willis had said. He stopped laughing. Willis had not finished yet.

"Was the tree callin' ya when we walked up?" Willis for some reason had changed the subject.

How did he know? Jason thought to himself.

"You was lookin' real hard at the oak, Jay Bird. You thinkin' 'bout a midnight breed?" Willis laughed again and continued, "I'm gonna take a woman up there and breed one night."

Willis always talked about women and sex. Sometimes Jason liked it, because he found out things he didn't know. Willis just seemed to know everything about sex and girls' bodies. Jason didn't believe all the things Willis would say. But even the things Jason didn't believe when he first heard them, he later found out were true. Like the time Willis said a woman had the bleed every month. And if she didn't, the blood made a baby. That was one story Jason hadn't believed was true. He found out later it was. All the young boys in Mayport liked it when Willis would tell them about women and sex.

He knew so much.

"The oak has called me before," Willis bragged. "But when it calls me, I go up there and I swing. Do you swing up there, Jay Bird?"

Jason was slow with his answer, but he did finally shake his head "no."

"You mean you have never been on the swings up there?" Willis taunted. Jason shook his head again. "Then how ya gonna play in the game Friday? If you don't get some practice, you gonna get killed when we play. If you don't know how to swing down, you gonna get killed, I tell ya. You need to swing one time before you play. Come on. Let's go up there while it's still light.

Jason's heart raced as he looked at Eddie, then Willis, then the oak. For the second time that day he didn't know what to say.

Willis' voice cut deep once more. "The tree was callin' you to swing. It knows you ain't never done it. It knows you have to swing once, before you play. Now, come on."

Again, Jason did not speak as he continued his stare with the oak. A cool breeze touched his face. Jason didn't know why, but he felt a need to give Willis and Eddie a glimpse of his new strength. He got up off the pylon. Eddie and Willis were both standing near, but Jason felt he was standing alone. He liked that. He walked alongside of Willis all the way to the bottom of the sand hill. Eddie always walked behind Willis. Jason made sure that during the walk to the tree he stayed even, side by side, with Willis. One time during the walk, Jason felt he was leading the way. He liked that.

Jason and Willis stopped at the same time. Jason could feel the hesitation in Willis. The great oak stood above them. It was even bigger than Jason had thought. He had passed near it before, but it never looked as big as it looked then. Hundreds of ropes moved and dangled in the breeze. Eddie stood behind. The three were silent in respect and fear. Jason's grandfather had told him that respect and fear go hand-in-hand. The sight of Miss Bell with blood and sand on her face flashed in Jason's head. The vision made his heart beat faster. Jason scanned the sand looking for the place where the old black woman went down. The sand all looked the same. There was no evidence of her death. He didn't know what he was looking for, but he saw nothing unusual. The only unusual thing at that moment was the fact that Willis had been so quiet as the three stood beneath the tree.

"Now what?" Jason broke the silence.

Jason's unexpected question revived Willis. He looked at Jason. "Now, Jay Bird, we swing. That is, if I can get you up there. The sand's real soft and it ain't too easy goin' up this side." Jason looked down at the white sand as Willis continued. "Why don't we race to the top? It takes a man to run up this side." Willis made the challenge.

Without hesitation, Jason met it. "O.K." All three were surprised at Jason's reply. Jason most of all. It was said. He felt alone. They formed a starting line of three. Willis looked back toward the river. He saw the ferry as it was leaving the other side.

"Now," he said, "when the ferry horn blows to cross, we go." They were set. Willis had drawn the line for the three to stand behind. Jason looked up the hill, checking for any obstacles that would interfere with his run. He could hear his heart pound in his chest. He hoped the others couldn't hear it.

The blast of the horn scared the three boys. As they took their first step, Jason felt the sand give way under his feet. Willis knew what to expect from the soft white sand and his first steps were short and strong. Willis took an instant lead. Jason was close behind. Jason could see that even with Willis' strength, the oak baby would have no easy time with the sand. Within seconds, they were no longer running. They were using legs and arms, as their feet and hands sunk deep into the soft powder. They were now crawling up the hill. Jason only thought of Willis in front of him. He did not think of Eddie at all. He knew at the starting line Eddie would not challenge Willis. Again, Jason stood alone. Willis' hard-driving legs threw sand up into the air. Jason had to keep his head down, so he would not get blinded by the sandstorm above him.

Jason could hear Eddie making noises behind him. Jason and Willis were giving out their own grunts and groans, as their muscles began to tire. Progress was slow, but they were moving upward.

At the halfway point, Jason could reach out and touch Willis' leg. They were close. Willis still led, but Jason had lost no ground at all. Jason wanted to stay close. Willis could not lead gracefully. He was too evil and filled up with himself. As usual, the evil one taunted his victim.

"Come on, weenie arms. Be a man." Willis gave Jason an invitation. As the words left Willis' lips, he lost his footing and began to slide back down the hill. Jason could hear Willis curse the sand as the mean one went by moving in the wrong direction. Jason dug in with all his strength and some he didn't have. He lifted his head. The ropes and the tree were near. The sand stopped moving. He stood level with solid sand beneath his feet. He wanted to give way to his aching legs. He wanted to fall. Something kept him up. He was breathing heavy and he could hear his heart again. He felt as if his lungs would burst in his chest. His thighs hurt. He turned back to Willis.

All pain and fatigue were shocked from his body at the sight of Willis kneeling at the bottom of the hill. Eddie stood next to Willis, brushing the white sand off Willis' shoulders. Willis had lost his balance completely and he had rolled all the way to the bottom of the hill. He knelt near the starting line. Jason could not contain his victory. The burning inside was too great. With a new strength, Jason clinched his fist and thrust his two weenie arms over his head and shouted. He didn't shout anything in particular. It was a victory scream. Willis glared with hate. Eddie glared in shock. Jason stood alone. He liked that. He turned to face the tree and share his victory.

Jason knew instantly there was nothing on earth like the oak. His heart beat, as it had done when Jessie stood dripping in front of him. He had seen two incredible sights: Jessie and now the oak. He wanted to touch the tree. His hand shook as he reached out. He pulled his hand away, as he had done with Jessie. A cool breeze touched his face. He had felt that breeze before. He liked it. He felt good. He flexed his biceps, took a deep breath and reached for the

SWING DOWN

tree again. A chill ran through his body as his fingers touched the bark of the tree. His heart was still pounding, but there was no fear. He only felt strong. He held his hand on the tree as he slowly walked around, sliding his hand gently as he moved. He circled the tree three times without breaking contact. He looked up at all of the ropes shrouding the mighty limbs. He stepped away, breaking his contact, so he could see more of the ropes. They hung as if moss had turned to rope. Again, his hand trembled as he reached out to touch the nearest rope. He wanted to swing. The rope had a large knot at the end of it. He had been on a swing like that once before. Eddie had one in his backyard. The knot was for sitting. Jason knew you stood on a limb, held the rope out and jumped, sitting on the knot as the rope did the rest. You just had to hold on.

Jason was no longer tired from his climb. His victory had taken away his fatigue. He wanted to be up in the oak. He started to climb. It was effortless. He felt as if he was being pulled upward by powerful arms. Each limb seemed placed perfectly for his feet as he stepped. Jason felt as if the limbs and branches were reaching for him, instead of him reaching for them. He couldn't stop. He didn't want to. As each limb appeared, he went higher and higher. There was no fear, but he could still hear his heart. That cool breeze touched his face. It pushed Jason on. Suddenly, he stopped. There were no limbs left large enough to support him. Jason could see the blue sky through the few small limbs left above him. He was at the top of the great oak. He could see the entire town and beyond. He could see far on the other side of the river. He could see the shrimp boats coming through the large jetty rocks at the entrance of the river. He had fished off those jetties before. To the east he saw the ocean. Jason liked the ocean. He saw Willis and Eddie sitting back down at the ferry slip. Again, Jason could not hold his excitement.

"Willis," he yelled. "Willis!" As if his voice was being carried by that cool breeze, the sound reached the two boys. They both turned and with eyes opened wide, gazed at the oak in the distance.

"Willis!" Again Jason's voice flew through the air. Willis and Eddie could not see Jason as he stood high, surrounded by leaves and branches. Willis and Eddie jumped from the pylons and ran. They were afraid. Jason laughed out loud, as the two took flight. He had no idea the two boys would think it was the oak calling out to Willis. He just wanted them to see him. The joke was even better than he had hoped.

His eyes scanned the town once more. He took another deep breath. Jason knew he was standing where no one had stood before. He was proud. Again, he stood alone.

Jason's descent was as smooth as his climb. It was nonstop and he was not afraid. When he did stop, he found himself on the strongest limb of them all. It was the limb with the most ropes hanging from it. It was the limb most used by the players of the game. The swings on that limb would take you down into the clearing below, where the captives would be held during the game. Many of the swings in the tree were for fun, but the swings on that limb were the "swings of manhood." He knew he had to ready himself for the game. Jason could not leave until he had ridden one of those ropes down into the clearing. He searched the limb. He found the rope he wanted.

"This knot is perfect," he thought. Jason held the rope extended out in front of him. He stepped out onto the limb. He could see the clearing below. He jumped, wrapping his legs around the knot.

Jason dropped, like a pelican diving for a fish in the river. It was much faster than he had expected. It took his breath and tickled his belly. In a brief moment, the knot beneath him was a mere three feet off of the ground. But without hesitation, his momentum threw him upward again. He was surrounded by palmetto fans, as if he were in a green tunnel. Then they were gone, as the swing lifted him high again. The rope seemed to hesitate at its highest point above the clearing and the green fans. The return pelican plunge was as fast as the first time; back down through the green tunnel and upward toward the tree once more. Jason's feet touched the tree and he pushed off, driving the swing downward for another trip. He could feel the power each time the rope dropped and then rose. He pumped his legs to go higher and pushed off stronger each time his feet touched the tree. He didn't want to stop. He sat on that knot and held that rope until the sun began to set. He knew he had to be home before dark. He pumped and pushed no longer. The swing began to slow. Jason and the rope came to a stop in the middle of the clearing. He slid down off the knot and stood on the ground. He looked around at the briars and the pricklies.

"Duckin' is played here," he thought. He looked back up at the great oak. It looked even bigger from that side. That cool breeze touched his face. It was as if the oak blew a cool wind down on his body. He closed his eyes to enjoy the feeling. Jason raised his arms above his head and thought of his victory. He thought he was alone. He didn't know of the pair of green eyes watching him from under the grape arbor.

Jessie had watched him swing. She came to stand where Miss Bell had died. She came to ask the oak why her mother had been taken. Jessie knew of the tree and believed. Jessie also knew her mother had not told all the secrets of the tree. She watched Jason walk from the clearing and in the direction of the grape arbor. He did not see her. Jessie could feel from where she stood that Jason was different. A cool breeze touched her face as Jason passed. She lost her breath for a moment.

The daylight was almost gone. Jessie knew she would not stay near the tree if dark fell. She let Jason pass without calling out to him. Her mission was to seek answers from the tree. Her heart raced during her climb to face the oak. She stood and stared at the huge base of the tree. She thought of Miss Bell. Miss Bell had told her, "If you ever stand alone at the oak, be strong and with no fear." It was difficult for the green-eyed young woman not to tremble as night fell around her. She wanted to run down the hill, but she could not turn her eyes away from the tree. Miss Bell had said, "Show your true self to the oak. It will know you."

Jessie knew she must humble herself before the tree.

"We owe the great tree," Miss Bell had said many times. With her mother gone, Jessie must be the one to give thanks and pay tribute. She felt light-headed and dizzy as her stare with the oak continued. A chill ran through her young body. She began to feel a heat inside.

She reached up and rubbed her neck. The chill was taken by the heat. Blood rushed through her veins. Sweat ran between her firm breasts. She thought she had only touched her top button, but her shirt fell down off her shoulders. It laid in the sand. A cool breeze touched her bare skin. Her nipples hardened. Jessie shook her head to free herself from the spell. She could not. Her knees quivered and a weakness pushed her to the ground. Jessie laid in the sand looking up at the limbs of the oak. The sand beneath her massaged her back. Her thighs burned. She found the strength to unsnap her dungarees and pushed them down over her hips. She kicked them off her ankles. She lay naked. Jessie, like Jason, had met the great oak tree.

CHAPTER THREE

MONDAY

JESSIE WOKE THE NEXT MORNING COVERED WITH SAND. SHE COULD SEE imprints of her body, as if she had rolled over and over many times during the night. Her mouth was dry and her legs and back ached. There was a burning in her stomach. She stood up slowly as her eyes searched for her shirt and pants. They, too, were covered with white sand. She shook the sand out and hurried to cover herself. She was weak and dizzy as she dressed. She snapped her pants and worked her way down the hill. Jessie was dazed and shaken from the ordeal and introduction to the oak. She would rest all day and think of the tree.

Jason's night was filled with dreams of the oak and touching Jessie. He was up early, fresh and new, and looking forward to the day. He wanted this summer Monday to move quickly. He would be sixteen tomorrow. Jason knew his Uncle Bobby was out shrimping and his mother had left early to spend the day with some friends in East Mayport. He dressed quickly, ate no breakfast, and walked out into the morning air.

Jason wanted to walk through the little town he had seen from the top of the tree. He knew he had made claim to uncharted territory. The limb he had stood on at the top of the tree belonged to him and him alone. He flexed his biceps and smiled.

As Jason walked toward the docks and the river, again his head raced with many thoughts. He knew he would stand at the tree again sometime during that day. He wanted to touch Jessie. He wanted to swing. He wished Tom Green was there. Jason knew they would talk about the tree and the game and maybe even Jessie.

"I wish I had some peanuts."

Jason remembered how he used to love to see his friend, Tom Green, coming down the road carrying his baskets of peanuts. Boiled or roasted, you could take your pick. Even though Tom Green's face was badly scarred, Jason still loved the small black man. It was sad to think he would never see Tom Green again. Jason missed the peanut man.

His walk first took him to Mr. Leek's fish house. There were no boats unloading, but he did sit and watch the workers prepare a shrimp boat for three nights at sea. He liked to see the huge blocks of ice slide down the long wooden chute and into the ice machine where it was chopped into a fine snowlike powder. A long thick rubber hose would carry the powdered ice down into the section of the boat called the hold. The ice would be kept in the hold until it was needed to ice down the catch of the day. The workers would hook the huge block of ice with metal tongs and then pull the heavy solid block to the long chute above the ice machine. Jason flexed his chest and arms each time the workers' muscles would bulge. He wished he could pull the ice, too.

"Maybe," he thought, "when I'm sixteen, I can ask Mr. Leek for a job. Then I'll pull the ice." Jason liked the thought of being a working man.

He walked over and stood where Jessie had dripped in front of him. He could feel her green eyes. He wanted to touch her breasts and nipples. He wanted to see the muscles in her back and stomach. His zipper moved. He smelled his hand.

The sound of the ferry's horn interrupted his exciting thoughts, as the big carrier began its crossing from the other side of the river. The blast of the horn reminded Jason of how he had stood next to Willis at the starting line at the bottom of the sand hill. Again, he smiled as a cool breeze touched his face. Jason knew that as long as the ferry ran, he would be reminded of his victory at the oak.

Jason left the dock and walked to greet the ferry as it would soon land on the Mayport side of the river, bringing cars and people from the other side. Jason sat on one of the pylons near the ferry slip. He stared at the oak as the ferry pulled into the huge slip. He turned away from the tree as the floating car carrier bumped into the large black support pylons that made up the ferry slip. The ferry would bounce to a standstill. Two ferry workers jumped from the huge boat to the docking area and attached the ramp that would allow the cars to drive off into Mayport. Jason liked to see men working.

"Maybe I'll work on the ferry," he thought. He hoped soon he would be a working man.

Only four cars drove off the ferry. An old man riding a bicycle and carrying a cane pole also rode off the ramp. As Jason watched the fisherman pedal past him, a welcome and familiar smell touched his nose. At the same time, a loving sound from the past came to his ears.

"Peanuts! Peanuts! Get ya fresh peanuts!"

Jason turned quickly toward the smell and the sound. "Tom Green," he thought. Jason lost himself for a moment. He did, however, return to the present as quickly as he had left when his eyes focused on a young black boy standing with a basket of peanuts. The boy was hoping his "peanut call" would be heard by the people in the cars waiting to board the ferry for its return trip to the Fort George side of the river. Jason walked over and stood near the black boy as he made his call once more.

"Peanuts! Peanuts!"

"Hey, boy," Jason interrupted the call. The young boy turned and faced Jason. Jason recognized the boy right away. He was one of Miss Bell's boys. He looked to be about ten years old. He was dressed in only a pair of cutoff dungarees. One leg of the shorts was split up to his waist, exposing the black skin on his butt and the side of his leg. As he and his grandfather had done many times in the past with Tom Green, Jason made his request. "I'd like to have one each, please." The black boy smiled and pulled two small bags out of his basket. Jason knew at a glance which bag contained the boiled and which contained the roasted. He was truly a peanut expert. Jason had put two of his hard-earned dollars in his pocket that morning. He reached into his pocket and took one out.

"How much do I owe ya?" Jason looked at the boy.

"Twenty cents." the boy stated his price.

Jason handed the boy the dollar and thought of Miss Bell. "Keep it all," Jason said.

The boy's eyes widened as he reached out and took the money.

"I'm sorry 'bout ya mama," Jason said.

The boy looked down as he put the dollar into his pocket.

Jason knew that Miss Bell would have been proud of her ten-year-old "working man."

"What's your name?" Jason asked.

"Benjamin." He still had his head down.

"Do they call you Ben?" Jason continued.

"No. Benjamin." The boy looked up. "Is you Jason?"

"Yes. Pleased to meet ya, Benjamin." Jason stuck his hand out to the boy.

Benjamin had never touched anyone that was white. He liked this white boy. Benjamin shook Jason's hand. They both felt good as they smiled at each other. Benjamin stepped away from Jason.

"I gotta go now. I gotta sell lots more before night."

"Good luck." Jason meant what he had just said. He wished the boy well. Benjamin walked on down the road making his peanut call.

The sight of Miss Bell, bloody and covered with sand, flashed in Jason's head. He shook free of the unpleasant thought. He wanted only good thoughts running through his head. He put one of the small bags up to his nose. He shoved the other bag into his pocket. How he loved that smell. Jason sat on the pylon, ate his peanuts and dropped the peanut shells into the river. He felt good as he looked at the tree.

As Jason finished his first bag of peanuts, he heard someone hollering. He turned to see the fisherman, who had ridden off the ferry on his bicycle. The man was yelling about the size of the fish he had just hooked. Jason ran to the man's side and looked into the water.

"It's just a big cat," Jason thought to himself.

"It ain't no catfish either, boy. I know you think it's a cat."

Jason was shocked to think the old man could read his mind. He tried not to think of anything else as he watched the water. Soon the catch appeared. It was the biggest sheephead Jason had ever seen taken from the river. It took both hands and all of the man's strength to throw the large fish up on the wooden boards of the small dock they stood on.

"Holy Moses," the man yelled with even more excitement. "Boy, now that's a fish, ain't it?"

Jason agreed. "Yes, suh, that's a biggin'."

"The biggest boy. The biggest! I knew today was gonna be a good one. It's my birthday today, boy. I ain't gettin' older, I'm gettin' better," the man laughed.

Jason liked the man. He was funny and so alive. Jason also liked the white buck shoes he wore. They reminded Jason of his Uncle Bobby. Jason thought of Elvis and smiled. The man broke into Jason's thoughts.

"You think there's a brother to this fish down in that water, boy? Or maybe this is the baby of the family and now I'm gonna catch his daddy."

The man laughed again. Jason liked him. They sat together and Jason shared his other bag of peanuts with the fisherman in the white bucks. After a few more small fish were landed, Jason decided to continue his walk through Mayport.

Jason left the small dock and his new friend. His next stop would be the sand hill and the oak. While walking to the hill, Jason never took his eyes off the great tree. He looked up to where he had stood high above. A cool breeze moved the hair from over his eyes. He felt good. Jason stood at the starting line that Willis had drawn the day before. The ferry horn made a blast and Jason relived his victory. He clenched his fists and pushed his "weenie arms" toward the sky as he thought of his victory over Willis. He yelled again.

Jason's victory cry was interrupted by the sound of voices coming from the other side of the sand hill, near the grape arbor. He heard yelling. He knew something was wrong. He walked quickly toward the voices. As he approached the arbor, Jessie ran out from under the hanging grape leaves. Jason knew she was afraid.

"Please," she cried. "Help my brother." Jason reached to stop her run, but she would not stop. Jason watched Jessie for only a second. He stepped under the hanging leaves and came eye-to-eye with Willis.

"Hey, Jay Bird, where ya been, boy?" Willis was not alone. Eddie and three other boys stood beneath the grapes.

"What's goin' on?" Jason looked at his friend, Eddie. Eddie looked at Willis.

Willis answered, "We was gonna do some swingin'. But this little nigger here, asked us if we wanted to buy some peanuts."

Jason turned and saw little Benjamin on the ground next to one of the posts that supported the vines of the grape plant.

"Oh no!" he thought. "Please, no!" Benjamin's black eyes stared through him. The black child's face was covered with sand. His mouth and nose were bleeding. His basket lay empty on the ground at his feet. The small bags were scattered on the sand. Jason didn't know what to do.

He was truly lost. He never expected anything like what was happening. Willis continued. "Why ya think this little nigger thought we would buy peanuts from him?"

The sight of Benjamin shaking his hand flashed in Jason's head. Jason was sorry it had turned so ugly. Willis was not finished yet.

"Then to top it off, when I started to run his little black ass away from here, that big-tittied sister of his come walkin' up here, like she owned the place. The bitch told me to leave the boy alone. Do you believe that shit?"

Jason held back a scream of pain, as Willis' evil words beat against his skull. The verbal assault continued as Willis went on.

"I pushed that green-eyed bitch down and I wanted to kick her teeth out, but then this little bastard jumped on my back and she ran off. Why didn't you hold her for me?"

Jason couldn't believe Willis' question. He didn't answer. He looked at Benjamin. Jason knew he had to do something, but he was afraid. He looked at his friend Eddie and the other boys. He knew they were afraid, too. To deal with Willis in his rage would be more than any of them could handle. Willis was so angry he didn't notice that Jason had not responded to any of his questions or words. Willis still had more to say.

"If this little shit hadn't jumped on me I might have got me some nigger pussy, right here today. But I'll get another chance at that one. I ain't forgettin' this." Willis stepped toward Benjamin. The little boy crawled in the sand and fell near Jason's feet. A cool breeze touched Jason's face as he stepped over the boy. He stood between the injured child and Willis. Jason said nothing. His eyes would speak for him. Willis had eyes that made his stand clear, too. He knew that the other boys were watching the eye-to-eye confrontation. Jason was afraid and he wanted to run. He had no idea why he faced Willis. He was sorry he had. Suddenly, like a bolt of lightning, his stomach was pierced by Willis' fist. Jason felt as if the fist went through his body and out his back. All the air in Jason's lungs exploded from his chest. He fell to the ground and lay across Benjamin, gasping for the air that had been knocked from his body. Jason thought he would surely die at the hands of Willis. His entire body shook as Willis stood over him and the black child. Then, with savage, clenched teeth, Willis bent down close to Jason. He made his threat. "If you ever get up in my face again, nigger lover, I'll kill you." Willis' words of death were the last of the beating. He walked away, leaving the others under the purple grapes.

Jason rolled off Benjamin and lay on his back, trying to fill his empty lungs. He couldn't believe how badly it hurt. He felt something touch his arm. It was Benjamin, brushing the dirt off. The boy didn't look at Jason, but the child's gesture eased Jason's pain. Eddie pushed Benjamin away from Jason.

"Get away from him, nigger." Jason hated that word, but he couldn't speak or stop Eddie. Benjamin stared back at Eddie.

"I said get. Ain't you had your ass beat enough?" prompted Eddie. Benjamin looked at Jason, then back at Eddie. He turned and ran. Eddie and the other boys helped Jason get home.

Jason didn't go out anymore that day. His Uncle Bobby would be shrimping until late and he knew there was no telling what time his mother would be back. Jason was alone. He was ashamed over the fear he had felt at the hands of Willis. He was sad that such a fine day had been ruined. He lay on the couch in the living room. He closed his eyes, as the racing in his head began again. He wanted to touch Jessie. He thought of white buck shoes. He thought of Elvis. He saw the oak. He loved his grandfather, Daddy Bob. He missed Tom Green. His stomach hurt. He wanted to touch Jessie. Sleep took his pain.

Chapter Four

Tuesday

"Happy Birthday to you. Happy Birthday to you." It was another morning that music greeted Jason's ears as he opened his eyes. It was not the voice of Elvis. It was the voices of his mother and uncle as they sang "Happy Birthday" to the sixteen year old, as he still lay on the couch.

"Wake up, Birthday Boy. It's time to greet the world and start another year." Jason woke up to a pleasant thought. The day he had been waiting for had arrived. He knew his life would be different. Uncle Bobby's greeting joined Jason's thoughts.

"Get your ol' ass up, act your age, get out and get a job, take on some responsibility, make somethin' of yourself."

"What are you talkin' 'bout?" interrupted Mary C.

"Well," continued Uncle Bobby. "that's what people said to me when I got grown. I just thought I'd get it all said to Jason at one time, so he don't have to listen to it again. This way, he's already heard it all."

"You are a fool," said Mary C. "A complete fool." She turned to Jason. "Well, now, what does the Birthday Boy want for breakfast?"

"French toast." Jason knew what he wanted right away. His mother's french toast was second to none.

"Me, too," Uncle Bobby joined in. Mary C. smiled and went to work in the kitchen. Jason got up and went down the hall to the bath-room. Uncle Bobby sat at the kitchen table, waiting for the toast.

Jason's stomach hurt when he coughed or breathed deeply. It was bruised and if he turned a certain way, a sharp pain would cut through his body as if Willis was still driving his fist into him. He knew he had to be careful not to show his discomfort in front of his mother. She would question him and he did not want her to know. He was sixteen now. He could take care of his own problems. He hurried to finish his morning business and went to the kitchen.

The french toast was stacked as high as Jason had ever seen it. It was a feast fit for a king.

"Oh! Thanks, Mama." He felt great because of the special break-fast. Jason made sure he matched his Uncle Bobby, piece for piece, as the stack of toast went down. They could be nothing but full, at the end of such a feeding. Jason felt as if he would pop if he moved too fast. He walked slowly into the living room and eased himself back down on the couch, where he had slept all night. His mother and uncle both followed him.

"What are you doin' today?" his mother asked.

"I don't know yet." Jason hadn't thought about what he would do on this special day.

"Well, you gotta get married," suggested Uncle Bobby. Jason laughed. Mary C. shook her head.

"If you decide to go fishin', you can use this." Jason's mother handed him a new rod and reel with a new red tackle box. "And the box has everything in it a fisherman will need," she added.

"Is there a red snapper in that box?" Uncle Bobby laughed at his little joke. Jason did too. Mary C. didn't. Jason thanked his mother and kissed her. She smelled like french toast.

Then Uncle Bobby gave Jason his gift. Jason's eyes almost popped out of his head when his uncle handed him the most beauti-ful hunting knife Jason had ever seen. It had a leather case and a belt for his waist.

They first shook hands as a joke, but then Jason hugged his Uncle Bobby. As they squeezed each other, Uncle Bobby whispered in

Jason's ear. "I've got you somethin' else, but you can't tell ya mama." The hug ended. Jason couldn't wait to see what the other gift was. Uncle Bobby made himself comfortable in his easy chair to let the french toast settle. Jason admired his gifts in silence.

The events of the last few days began to run through Jason's head. He wanted to see if Jessie and Benjamin were alright. He wanted to touch her. The image of Willis with clenched teeth flashed in his head.

"Uncle Bobby?" Jason broke the silence.

"What, boy?" His uncle had his eyes closed, but he did respond.

"Do you believe in the oak?" Uncle Bobby's eyes popped open at his nephew's question. Jason continued. "Do you think Willis is an oak baby?" Jason's question was twofold.

"Well," Uncle Bobby said, "let me see. What were the two questions?"

"Come on." Jason knew his uncle was playing, but he did want a serious answer. "Tell me what you think." Jason would not let it go.

Uncle Bobby took a serious tone. "I don't believe all the stories I hear 'bout the oak," Uncle Bobby began. "I do think there is a strange power about the tree and sand hill." Mary C. walked into the room to hear what her brother had to say. He continued. "The oak can bring good shrimpin' if the game is good." Jason's eyes were wide open as he listened to his uncle talk. Mary C. listened too.

"Duckin' is part of the tree. The games is for the making of men and to show how strong and clever you can be. We play for the tree and we play for ourselves. It will make a man of ya." Jason wanted to hear more.

"Are there oak babies around?" Jason still wanted to know about Willis. Uncle Bobby continued his statement.

"I never tried for no oak baby, myself. I'd be too tired by the time I made it to the top of that hill. I wouldn't be able to do no jukin'." Uncle Bobby couldn't resist the humorous thought.

"And if you want to know if Willis is an oak baby," Jason was all ears, "I only know two true oak babies."

"Who?" Jason couldn't believe what his Uncle Bobby had just

said.

"Who?" Mary C. was curious too.

Uncle Bobby took what his audience thought was a serious breath. "One of the oak babies is Elvis and the other is Jerry Lee Lewis." Uncle Bobby fell out of his chair as he roared with laughter. "I used to think Fats Domino was one too, but I found out he was black." Again he roared with his wild laughter.

Mary C. couldn't pass up the opportunity to add her own humor to the already wild atmosphere. "I've got one more question for ya," Mary C. said.

"And what's that, sister dear?" Uncle Bobby quivered his top lip like Elvis.

"When was it that you was dropped on your head as a baby?" Mary C. and Jason added their roar of laughter at Mary C.'s joke on Uncle Bobby. Uncle Bobby laughed too. Jason wanted to know more. He enjoyed being with the two he loved. His birthday had started out great. Mary C. left the room and went into the kitchen. Uncle Bobby motioned for Jason to follow him.

"Oh! The other present," Jason thought. He had forgotten. He followed his uncle down the hall and into his uncle's bedroom. Uncle Bobby reached under his bed into a box. Jason was shocked when his uncle handed him a thick magazine. It had a naked woman on the front of it. Jason's heart raced. . .

"Wild, huh?" Uncle Bobby smiled. "It's time for you to learn." Jason smiled, nodded his head in agreement and ran to his bedroom, locking the door behind him. Birthday or not, he thought perhaps he would stay in his room for awhile. As Jason looked through the book, his desire for Jessie increased with each turn of the page. After a long inspection of his secret gift that took about an hour, Jason went out to face the world at sixteen.

Jason first walked to the ferry slip, hoping to see Benjamin. He wanted to ask the young boy about Jessie, but Benjamin was not there. Jason thought the boy was afraid of another encounter with Willis.

"It was best for Benjamin to stay away," Jason thought. He walked toward the sand hill. He wanted to swing on his birthday.

When he reached the sand hill, he could see some boys were already swinging from the oak. They were practicing for the game. Jason recognized the boys who were swinging. They were Ted Farley and his brother James. The Farley boys had always been nice to Jason. James was sixteen and, like Jason, would play Duckin' for the first time. Ted had played before. He had been a player during the game last year, the game that Willis' father called "the sissy game." That name was given because there had been no blood shed and no bones broken during the playing of the game. In fact, there were no injuries at all, not even a bloody nose. Willis' father had ridden him for an entire year about "the sissy game." He felt that Willis could have made the game rougher and better, but he didn't. Most of the players from the "sissy game" would not play this time. Only Ted and Willis would repeat, to make up for their failure a year ago. The curse of "the sissy game" had been carried by Willis for twelve months. Anytime something went wrong at Willis' house, his father would say, "It's your fault, boy. The oak hates ya, boy. You gotta make up for that sissy game you played in." Those words haunted and drove Willis.

Willis' father had many stories of the time he had played Duckin'. He talked of the injuries inflicted and how brave and strong he had been, when, in reality, he had never set foot on the sand hill. He tried to live through his strong son.

Jason joined the Farley boys. They practiced for the "swing downs." Jason was glad when Eddie came walking up the hill and began to swing with the others. He had not seen Eddie without Willis lately. Jason was pleased to be with his good friend, without the influence of Willis. Willis had gone shrimping with his father. Jason knew the day would be pleasant. It was becoming a great birthday. After a while, Eddie suggested fishing at the jetties. Jason was quick to agree. He hurried home. He would be able to show off his birthday gifts. He met Eddie at the rocks. They sat talking, laughing and fishing. Jason liked Eddie. He always would. Jason told Eddie of the man with the white buck shoes and the big sheephead. The boys did not talk about the confrontation with Willis at the grape arbor. They did not speak of the game to come. It was a great afternoon for two sixteen-year-old friends.

Jason told Eddie about the magazine his Uncle Bobby had given him. Eddie couldn't wait to see it. They both lay back on the rocks. It was a sunny day. Jason thought only pleasant thoughts.

"If I could see Jessie, the day would be complete," he thought. "If I could touch her again, it would be the best birthday, ever."

Eddie broke Jason's thoughts. "Ya got any money?" his freckled friend asked.

"I've got a couple of dollars." Jason always tried to have a dollar or two with him. His Uncle Bobby had always told him, "Don't go nowhere without a little money on ya."

Eddie continued, "I got sixty cents. Let's go buy a big bag of hush puppies from Strickland's." Jason was hungry and the suggestion was most welcome. Jason gathered their fishing gear and walked to the little restaurant. They knew two dollars and sixty cents would buy a load of hush puppies and two cold drinks.

They carried the big bag of hot puppies to Mr. Leek's dock. They sat in the shade on the steps of the fish house. Eddie would reach into the bag, then Jason would do the same. Eddie, then Jason. They reached in the bag and pulled out the tasty spheres, always remembering whose turn it was. True friends remember whose turn it is.

There were still a few puppies left in the bag. It was Jason's turn. Eddie waited. Jason couldn't reach in.

"Well," Eddie was ready for his turn.

"I can't eat no more." Jason leaned back against the side of the fish house. Eddie didn't ask again. He popped the remaining puppies into his mouth. Jason couldn't believe it. Eddie said something with his mouth full of the hush puppies. Jason wasn't sure what it was, but he knew it had something to do with Eddie loving hush puppies. Jason had enjoyed two great meals so far: French toast and now hush puppies. What else could a man ask for on his sixteenth birthday?

The two boys lay back on the ramp next to the steps. They couldn't move. Eddie moaned and said, "Be careful. Don't hit anything sharp or there will be hush puppies all over the dock." Jason was too full to laugh at Eddie's joke. Jason's stomachache made him think of the punch he had taken from Willis. He was quick to shake the unpleasant thought away. Nothing was going to ruin his day.

Eddie forgot his discomfort as he thought of Jason's gift. "Let's go look at that book you got." Jason knew Eddie had another good idea. They managed to get to their feet and headed for Jason's house.

As usual, at that time of day, no one was home. Uncle Bobby was shrimping and Mary C. had left a note:

Jason,
Be back a little after dark.
Love ya,
Mama

The two friends lay across Jason's bed and took in every page. They were amazed at some of the sights. They laughed and joked about others. They both thought all the women were beautiful. They laughed each time Jason would have to remind Eddie to "close his mouth." Eddie had to go home after an hour of turning pages. Jason was alone again.

The sun was gone from the sky, but there was still plenty of light outside. Jason's day had been so great, he didn't want it to end. He decided to walk and see if anything was going on down at the river. Jason's walk took him near the section of Mayport where the blacks lived. He knew he shouldn't be there, but he would do anything, if he thought he could see Jessie. He hated it when people called that area "Nigger Town." He saw two big black men come out of a small tavern called the Blue Moon. They looked at Jason, but said nothing. He could hear music coming from the "Blue Moon." He liked it. He wanted to walk closer to the small tavern. He didn't.

Jason turned to walk away. He saw two figures coming toward him. He was quick to see it was Miss Bell's two fat daughters. They both hurried past him. Neither girl looked his way. He wanted to ask them about Jessie and Benjamin, but he knew they would not respond. He watched them enter the fourth house on the left side of the road. He wanted to follow them, but even being sixteen had not given him that much courage. He did, however, find the courage to sit for a while and watch the house that the two fat girls had entered. He hoped Jessie would come out. It had been a long summer day, but the night was now taking over. Jason knew he would not be caught at the edge of "Nigger Town" when night fell. He began to walk back to where he belonged. He stopped his exit as he heard voices and laughter. He turned back to see four people coming out of the Blue Moon. One was Jessie. There were two young black men laughing and talking to her. There was an older lady with them, too. Jason heard the lady's words.

"It was a fine buryin', girl. Your mama done herself proud. If she had been here she would be laughin' too. She loved that music, ya know." Jessie said something back to the lady, but Jason couldn't hear. Then, as if drawn by his pleading thoughts, Jessie looked directly at Jason. He knew she saw him, but she did not change her expression at all. She walked with the others until she reached the fourth house on the left. She went in. The other three walked on down the road and disappeared into the darkness.

Jason stared at the fourth house. He was disappointed, but he was pleased to have seen her. Jason knew he had stayed too long. He walked away slowly, hoping Jessie would come back out. She did not. He turned the corner and could see the lights of the boats, as they were coming up the river after a day in the ocean. The boats would be unloading. There would be shrimp to head and money to be made.

"I'll head tonight," he thought as he turned toward Mr. Leek's dock. He walked up to the double doors of the main entrance to the fish house. The tables were almost full of headers already. Jason stood at the door, looking to see if he recognized any of the workers. He saw Eddie and the Farley brothers getting their buckets ready to fill. They did not see Jason at the door. They were too busy. He looked at the other workers, as a chill ran through his body at the sound of the evil voice, belonging to Willis. Willis had been shrimping on his father's boat and they were the first to unload. Jason knew Willis would not work at the tables. Usually working on a shrimp boat all day didn't leave a person with the desire to head at the tables. Jason hated to go out on his Uncle Bobby's boat. He always got seasick and spent the day throwing up. Jason had been teased many times about his weakness on the high seas. He heard Willis' voice again.

Jason stepped back outside, away from the doorway. He watched the activity in the fish house from a small window. He saw Willis talking to Eddie. Willis was standing with three other boys Jason did not know. Willis introduced them to Eddie as his cousins from Georgia. The three boys didn't talk or smile. They only nodded at Eddie. One of the boys looked older and he had his hair cut in a Mohawk style haircut. His face was covered with pimples and blackheads. Jason didn't like the way he looked at all. He looked strange, as if something was wrong with him. Jason decided that to approach the tables would only be trouble for him. Willis would, no doubt, show off and try to impress his cousins at Jason's expense. Jason wanted to avoid Willis on his birthday. He left the window and walked past Strickland's Restaurant. He could smell the fish and hush puppies frying. He looked back at the dock and was tempted to go back. He didn't want to miss the opportunity to make some money. He heard someone running. The noise was coming closer in his direction. He didn't recognize who it was until the runner came out of the darkness.

"Benjamin!" Jason said out loud. The little black boy was the night runner. "What are you doin' here?"

Benjamin was out of breath but managed to answer. "Go to the lighthouse."

"Why?" Jason didn't understand.

The boy repeated his message. "Just go to the lighthouse. Jessie sent me here to tell you that." Benjamin ran back into the darkness. Without any hesitation, Jason began to run toward the old lighthouse.

The lighthouse was an old ruin from the Civil War days. At one time it directed ships through the mouth of the St. Johns River. It was built of red brick and there was a small wooden shack attached at the bottom of the old tower. Jason hurried to see Jessie. He saw the lighthouse. His heart raced. Jessie stood in the doorway of the little shack. He walked toward her. She remained in the doorway. She did not step to meet him. They were only a few feet away from each other.

"Why were you near the Blue Moon tonight?" Jessie began their first real conversation.

"I went to find you," Jason replied. "I've been thinking about you since you ran away yesterday."

"That's why I told Benjamin to tell you to come here. He told me what you did. I wanted to thank you. Are you alright?"

"Yes, I'm fine." Jason's heart was pounding to her every word. He wanted to say the right things, but he didn't know what they were.

"Why are you so different?" she continued.

"Why are you so different?" Jason asked her the same question. Both smiled, but neither answered.

"I'm sorry 'bout Miss Bell." Jason had wanted Jessie to know how he felt since he had heard about the tragedy. He had no chance to tell her until then. Jessie did not comment. She stood quiet for a moment. Jason wished he could say more. He had so many nice things he wanted to say to her. Jessie broke the silence.

"Do you still think my eyes are beautiful?" Jason could not speak. He did manage to nod his head. She went on. "Did you like seeing me on the dock that night?" Jason swallowed and only nodded again. She had not finished. "Will you touch me again?"

"Did she really say that?" Jason thought to himself. He wasn't sure. He listened for her to speak again.

"I want you to touch me." Her words echoed in Jason's head.

Jessie reached out and put her hand on Jason as she had done that night on the dock. She touched him and then moved her hand away. She moved back into the small building. Jason, in a nervous trance, followed. Jason was shocked again when he saw that Jessie had placed a thick quilt on the floor of the shack. She stood next to the blanket and began to unbutton her shirt. She didn't stop until the shirt dropped to the floor. She took her pants off. Jason stood frozen, once more, in front of Jessie, as she was again naked. Jason thought of Miss Bell's words, "I never seen a child that wanted to be naked all the time." She wore no underwear. She stood in front of Jason as she had before. She liked the way he looked at her. She liked the way his eyes approved. Jason was still fully dressed. He didn't know what to do. He knew he wanted to touch her, but he was afraid. Jessie, however, had enough fire in her to overcome any nervous jitters that were present in the little room. She stepped to Jason. He tried not to tremble, but he couldn't help it. She pulled Jason's T-shirt out of his pants and over his head. His chest was bare. His arms and neck were tan. His chest was lily white. He always wore a shirt, mainly because Willis had called him "chicken chest" one day at the swimming hole. He was self-conscious and worried about what Jessie thought of the way he looked. It became obvious that she didn't care about his physique or his lack of one. She pushed her bare breasts against Jason's white chest, as she had done that night. This time, Jason felt the heat of her skin. It was like fire and he knew his blood flow was changing directions again. He thought he would faint, as Jessie unbuckled his belt, pulled his zipper down, unsnapped his dungarees and pulled them down to the tops of his feet. He didn't want to lose those white Skivvies. He was afraid of how he might look to her.

"Is sixteen years long enough to be ready to take your drawers off? What if I look funny to her?"

As that thought ran through Jason's head, he felt his white shorts move down his legs. He looked down in shock again, to see them at his feet with his pants. He didn't look at Jessie. He couldn't take his eyes off the pile of clothes at his feet. The ordeal continued, as he felt Jessie's hot hand touch him. She squeezed him twice. He thought it would hurt. It didn't. Then she moved away, making herself comfortable on the quilt. She laid back and stretched her arms above her head. Jason could have sworn her breasts and nipples said his name. He knew she was the most beautiful girl on earth. Her hair was different, too. It was long and straight, as black as a crow's wing. Jason knew of no other black girls with hair like Jessie's. Jessie again made a request.

"Touch me, please."

Jason stepped out of the hold of his pants and moved to her side. He had hoped for this since that night on the dock. "I can't let this chance get away," he thought. "She's so willing and we are alone." Jason reached out and touched her rockhard breasts. His mouth went dry.

"Squeeze," she whispered, as she pushed up toward his hand. "Hard." Jason followed Jessie's lead. He would take many directions from her as the encounter progressed. Her nipples hardened between his fingers. He moved so he could be next to her. Jason rubbed her stomach and thighs. He could see she liked that. He knew if he felt hair this time, he would not move his hand. Jason was next to her, but he was supporting himself with one arm. Jessie broke his support as she reached up and pulled him down to her. She kissed him for the first time. It was a long hard kiss. It took Jason's breath. Jason knew he was not the first Jessie had kissed. He didn't care. He just wanted her to do it again. She did. As they kissed, Jason reached down and felt the hair between her legs. He knew from the dock to move lower. His hand was wet. Jessie kissed him harder. She opened her legs wider. She reached down to assist him. She touched herself. She made noises. Jason thought of his mother. She moved her hand and allowed Jason to continue as she had done. He was learning and he liked it. Jessie touched him. He liked that, too. Jessie worked her hips as Jason worked his fingers. If he was not doing it right, she would adjust him. The instructions went on for only about ten minutes. To Jason, it was like hours. Jessie did have a final technique for their first time and she was ready to take Jason to school.

Jason's eyes widened as Jessie rolled over on top of him. She sat up with her legs on each side of him. She reached down and held his manhood. With one easy push Jason knew he was inside Jessie's body. Jessie leaned forward and pressed her chest against his. Even if Jason wanted to get up, he could not. He was Jessie's captive as she moved her hips and made her noises. She pushed and pumped her hips, taking all Jason could give. Jason felt strange; good, but strange. He had felt that way before. It had happened to him a few times during the night. He would wake up and that feeling was there. Willis had told him that the feeling made babies.

Jessie worked Jason until he had nothing left. He was exhausted and sweating. Jessie rolled off him and stood up. She used her shirt to wipe the sweat from her face and breasts. Jason watched her.

"I've got to go." Jessie put her pants and shirt on. Jason watched. He knew she had to take the quilt, so he got up too. She folded the blanket as Jason put his pants on.

"I'll walk with you," Jason broke the silence this time.

"No!" Jessie was quick with her reply. "It would be bad if we are seen together." Jason didn't like that thought, but he knew she was right. Jessie moved to Jason and kissed him. Not too hard that time.

"You did good," she whispered, as if she knew he was concerned with his performance. She left the shack and walked into the night. Jason watched her. She didn't look back. As Jason stood in the doorway, he had two thoughts: he knew he loved Jessie and he knew she had done that before.

Jason wished himself a "Happy Birthday" with a smile, as he stepped from the shack and into the darkness. He took a different way home than Jessie. His path would take him past the oak. Jason felt that after such a great day, it was only right to see the oak close up. He wasn't sure, but maybe the tree was the beginning of a new life for Jason. If so, he would thank the tree. His head and body were beginning to calm after the wild encounter with Green Eyes. He sang "Don't Be Cruel," in his best Elvis voice, as the oak appeared ahead in the darkness. He felt good as he approached the great tree.

His feeling was short-lived. "Happy Birthday, Jay Bird." Those four words sent a chill through Jason, like he had never felt before. His stomach burned. He knew it was Willis. It came from the darkness. He knew Willis was near. He thought he would throw up. He became sick within, as Willis stepped from the darkness, followed by his three cousins. The Mohawk stood tall above the others.

"Kinda late for you, ain't it, Jay Bird?" Jason could not speak. Like a wild dog, Willis sensed his fear. That made it easy for Willis to continue. "Jay Bird," Willis began again, "these are my cousins,

Sammy, Luther, and the Indian there, that's Roy. He don't talk none." Jason looked at all three as Willis added more. "Fellas, this here is a nigger lover." Jason looked at Willis. His eyes showed his hate, but his quivering showed his fear. Willis lived for that look of fear. Willis would feed on his fear. "Eddie told me you got some real nice stuff for your birthday." Jason thought of his new hunting knife. The sight of the knife cutting Willis' throat flashed in front of Jason's head. His hate stare continued. "You know, Jay Bird, a birthday is never complete 'til you get a birthday spankin'. You know, with one to grow on and all that stuff."

Jason couldn't believe his eyes as Willis unbuckled his Jack Daniels belt buckle and slid the thick black belt from around his waist. Jason's fear gave him new strength. He ran. Within a few steps, Jason was at full stride. He could hear Willis and the others running after him. The sand was soft, but Jason knew his pursuers would also have to fight the sand to catch him. He felt he had a good chance to get away. Jason looked back to see how much of a lead he had. His heart ached as he saw Mohawk only a few steps away. Mohawk's long legs had closed the gap on Jason. Jason's legs were doing all they could. His chance of escape was slipping away. He heard Mohawk only a few steps behind him. He knew he would be caught. He felt a strong hand grab his shoulder. Jason was pulled to the ground. He came nose-to-nose with the pimple-faced Mohawk. Willis and the other Georgia boys were close behind. Willis spoke:

"Oh, Jay Bird! Can't nobody outrun Roy." They all laughed. All but Jason. Then the words Jason hoped would not be said came from the evil mouth of Willis. "Hold him down. I want to make his birthday complete." The Georgia boys grabbed Jason and held him on the ground. Mohawk pushed Jason's face into the sand and sat on his shoulders. The other two cousins held Jason's legs. Jason couldn't see, but he knew Willis stood over him. Jason wanted to cry. He held it. Jason closed his eyes, hoping it was a bad dream. Willis' voice proved it was real.

"You count 'em, Jay Bird, and tell me when I get to sixteen. And don't forget, one to grow on." Jason tightened his body, preparing for the first hit. The first swing by Willis sent a shock through Jason. He had no idea it would hurt like that. He jerked, but there was no way he could free himself from the grip of the Georgia boys. Jason took two, three, and four. Number five brought his first scream of pain and tears.

"Please, Willis, stop," he whispered. Willis heard, but paid the plea no attention. The sixth lick cracked in the night. Jason knew he would surely die before the sixteenth was thrown. He continued to cry, but there was some numbness through seven, eight, and nine. Ten, eleven, and twelve hit him on the backs of his legs. He screamed again on all three that hit his legs. Jason cried openly and begged Willis to stop. The more Jason pleaded, the more Willis bathed in the abuse. Thirteen, fourteen, fifteen, and sixteen put Jason into a semi-conscious state. He heard Willis say, "And one to grow on," but he didn't feel the lick at all. He knew the Georgia boys had released their hold. He didn't move. He couldn't. He heard voices around him, but the words were not clear. They stopped. They were gone.

Jason pushed the ground with his hands to raise himself up. The pain was too great. He spit the sand from his mouth as he lay his cheek back on the ground. He cried. Only thoughts of his hate for Willis filled his head. Every evil deed that he had seen Willis perform flashed, one at a time, in his mind.

Jason was ashamed of the times he had been too afraid to stand up to Willis and his evil ways. He remembered the time Willis made Ted Farley bite the head off a green lizard. Willis had started a club and if Ted wanted to be a part of it, he would have to prove worthy. The lizard was the test. Jason was among the boys who watched as Willis forced the lizard into Ted's mouth. Jason was ashamed.

Jason thought of the time Willis tied Johnny Wade to a tree and then shoved chinaberries up his nose. Jason remembered how swollen Johnny' face was. Johnny told his mother he had done that to himself as a joke, but then he couldn't get them out. The doctor had to remove the berries from his nose. No one ever told on Willis. Fear will always keep secrets. Jason's trip through Willis' past continued.

Jason recalled the day Willis took one of Mr. Shimp's chickens.

Willis had a powerful Black Cat firecracker. He put Vaseline on it and forced it into the chicken's tail hole. As the bird ran across the yard the Black Cat exploded, blowing the backside out of the poor creature. Jason hated seeing that chicken in pain. The blast didn't kill it at first. It suffered. Willis and the others ran. Jason ran too. He watched from the woods as Mr. Shimp came out of the house and killed the chicken so it wouldn't suffer any longer. Jason wanted to tell him he was sorry, but he was afraid of Willis.

Willis would put a dead fish on a board, float it in the river and then wait for a pelican to dive down for a meal. The speed of the dive and the impact when the pelican hit the board usually injured the bird. Sometimes the pelican would drown, as it lay in the water.

There was no telling how many cats were killed by Willis. He was always throwing a dead cat on somebody.

Jason thought of the day Willis let the pigs out of the pen in "Nigger Town." Willis ran the big mama sow up into Mr. Steen's yard and closed the gate. Willis wanted to keep the big pig from getting away. Willis then stood at the fence and watched Mr. Steen's four pit bulls tear the pig to pieces.

Jason's hot wounds were cooling as the evils of Willis still raged inside him. Jason knew that many dogs in Mayport had lost their tails to the swing of Willis' machete. Jason was sitting up now. He looked at the oak towering above him. A cool breeze touched him. He stood up. His walk home was slow and filled with pain. Each step brought back the lash of that Jack Daniels belt.

Willis' evil deeds haunted Jason as he continued his struggle toward home. Jason hated the memory of the time they were all out in the woods and came upon a group of black boys building a fort. Willis had just gotten a BB rifle for Christmas. Willis scared the black boys away. As they ran, he shot two of them in the head with his new gun. Jason could hear the black boys crying as they ran into the woods. On that same day, before they met up with the black boys, Willis had killed a defenseless otter as it sunned itself on the bank of a small creek. Jason's thoughts had carried him home. He had survived.

Like many times before, he stood alone in his house. He filled the bathtub with warm water, but he could only kneel in it. His skin was cut in two places and there was blood. Blood vessels were broken and red blood bruises marked all sixteen licks. He touched his wounds gently with a wet washcloth. After his slow and gentle bath, he lay on his stomach in his bed. He was sick. Willis had taken his wonderfully day away. He had two thoughts as sleep eased his pain.

"I love Jessie."

"I hate Willis."

Chapter Five

Wednesday

Jason woke up Wednesday morning, after a long night of throbbing pain. He opened his eyes. His face was pushed into his soft pillow. He thought of the beating he had endured. He had not died, as he thought he would. He made a promise to himself.

"Nobody will ever beat me again." There had been a hardening in his heart during the pain-filled night. He was sixteen and a day. He had taken sixteen and one to grow on. He wanted to see Willis and the Georgia boys. He wanted to show his enemies he still lived. He would show no pain when he saw them.

Jessie had moved him toward manhood, then Willis had beaten him the rest of the way. In one night of love and hate, Jason had stepped out of childhood. Game or not, Jason was a man. He heard no movement in the house. He thought perhaps it was too early for his mother to be up. He knew his Uncle Bobby would also sleep late. He made his way to the bathroom and was reminded of the beating with each step. He was surprised when he heard his mother's favorite clock chime eleven times. It was much later than he thought. He had slept the entire morning away. Jason walked past his mother's bedroom and pushed the door open to see her. She was not there. Her bed was made. He was even more surprised when he saw that his Uncle Bobby was gone too. He was hungry.

The kitchen was his next stop. There was a note from his mother on the table:

> Jason,
> We let you sleep, but when you wake up, come to the jetties.
> The mullet are running.
> Love ya,
> Mama

Like everyone else in Mayport, Jason had been waiting for the mullet to make their run past the jetties, making their way out to the ocean. The mullet would be fat and many filled with roe. When the mullet made their run each year, a call for the small gill nets would ring through Mayport. All knew the mullet had been spotted. The fish would run past the jetties most of the day. The small boats would bring in thousands of pounds of the roe-filled fish. The men would fish all day and the women would keep the cooking fires on the shore. Mullet fillets would fry all day and the smell of hobo coffee would fill the air. The young people would keep cleaning the fish as they were needed for the frying pans. The small children would spend the day crabbing between the rocks. They would catch many blue crabs and toss them into a large bucket of water that boiled over one of the fires. The women of Mayport would bring many tasty extras to add more to the mullet and crab feast. Sometimes the mullet run would last only a few hours, but other times the fish would run all day. At the end of the run all would gather on the shore and on the rocks for fine eating, music from guitars, banjoes, fiddles, and harmonicas. Singing and dancing in the sand would go on into the late night hours. Many stories would be told, new and old. The laughter and the music would be carried through the air for miles. Jack Daniels whiskey would flow like water. Jack Daniels ran through the veins of most shrimpers in Mayport. It wouldn't be a mullet run unless gallons of Jack Black were consumed. Uncle Bobby called it "the nectar of the working man. If Duckin' didn't make a man of ya, Jack Black could." The love of the strong liquid was represented by the many Jack Daniels belt buckles and caps worn by the men of the shrimp boats.

Jason dressed quickly. He had already missed the morning of the run. He could not miss the rest of the great event. He strapped on his new knife and hurried to the jetties to join his mother and uncle.

As Jason approached the huge rocks, he could hear the voices of the crowd on the shore. He saw the boats out in the river, with the men pulling the nets full of mullet. The young boys were picking the live fish from the nets on the shore. Mounds of mullet lay everywhere. Jason felt as if he were the only person in town who had slept late. He hurried to join in. He liked being a "working man."

The other workers were too busy to notice Jason's late arrival. He passed through the crowd searching for his mother. He knew Uncle Bobby was, most likely, out in one of the small boats. Jason saw Eddie near the rocks cleaning mullet. Eddie was scaling, Ted was cleaning and James was running the fresh fillets to the frying pans. Jason smiled at the mullet disassembly line. The smell of coffee and fish frying reminded Jason of his hunger. In his excitement, he had not eaten. But he had done no work, yet. He knew he had to earn a side of the crispy fried mullet. He pulled his new knife from its leather case and joined the mullet cleaners. Eddie smiled at the sight of Jason and continued his scaling. Jason was cutting on his third fish when his mother walked by and patted him on his backside. He felt pain, but said nothing.

"How long ya been here, sleepyhead?" she asked with a smile, not knowing of his pain.

"Not long." Jason was happy to see her. He loved her so much.

As usual, Mary C. looked better than any of the other women. Even in old faded dungarees and a shirt tied at the waist, Mary C. was a "cut above," as looks went. She was an eye pleaser. She had given pleasure to many men and had much more to give. Jason watched her as she started to talk to one of the other ladies.

Mary C. was only thirty-five. She and Jason had almost grown up together. Jason's father had died in a hunting accident when he was five. Mary C. had been hardened by her many encounters with men. Before she had come to live with her brother, she had learned that her beauty and body were the answer to many of her early money problems. She was not as active as she had been, but now and then she would allow the old habit to take over her thoughts. Once you are good at something, you always go back just to see if you still can. Mary C. could. But, if she was going to use her talents, she would be paid.

Jason continued to watch his mother. He thought of how he hated it when she went out at night. He hated it more and more as he got older. He recalled that when he was much younger, he saw his mother in bed with an ugly man. He had hoped it was a dream, but, as he grew older, he knew it wasn't. Jason wished she would be like Uncle Bobby and stay away from the house with her friends. For some reason, Mary C., from time to time, would bring her men friends home. They would stay late into the night. Jason hated that. He hated the noises that would come from her bedroom. Jason shook his head free of the thoughts of his mother's vice and returned to the mullet.

Mary C. ended her conversation. She picked up the fillets Jason had cut and carried them to one of the fires. Women and men alike all seemed to watch Mary C. as she would walk past. It was just the way she carried herself. Women desired to have a body like her and men desired to have it. Jason watched her too, as his new blade was sliding through the thick fat mullet. He was keeping pace with Ted, cut for cut. Ted was one of the best at the cleaning and Jason was proud that he was keeping up with his friend. Uncle Bobby had taught Jason how to clean most fish. He knew that the mullet had to be cut down the back first, so as not to damage the roe. Jason didn't like to eat the roe. It made his mouth feel funny.

Mary C. passed Jason again. She was carrying a plate piled high with crispy fillets. She walked to a group of men who had come ashore. Jason noticed that the men were happier to see his mother than they were to see the plate of fish. He didn't like the way they looked at her. Men always seemed to say something or laugh as she would pass by or walk away.

"You boys can stop now," someone hollered from the crowd. It was like a voice from heaven to Jason and the other workers. They had cleaned enough fish for the feast and they could now join the eating. Jason washed the blood off his hands and his knife. He pushed the big blade back into the leather case that was hooked to his belt. Even though Uncle Bobby and Mary C. had swallowed their share of Jack Daniels, Jason did not have a Jack Black buckle of his own. "Maybe," he thought, "I'll get one this year."

The young cleaning crew all got in line for a chance at the fried fish and tasty extras. After they filled their plates, they found a group of flat rocks to use as a table and seats. Jason liked sitting with his friends. They ate and talked. They ate and laughed. They ate and ate.

It was fun to watch the men and women as the "nectar of the working man" took control. The mark of Jack Black began to show on some red faces and in some weak legs. Most of the men had settled on shore with food and drink. Only a few still remained in the boats, manning the nets. The mullet had been running since nine that morning. They had filled and emptied the nets for five hours. The catch had been a good one and they were hoping for another run before nightfall. The more nectar they drank, the louder the music and singing became. Jason and his friends roared with laughter, as Uncle Bobby gave his version of "Blue Suede Shoes," complete with the rubber legs and quivering lip. Mary C. only shook her head at her fool brother. Jason thought he was great. So did the rest of the crowd. Uncle Bobby took his bow. Jason knew his uncle could do Elvis even if he wasn't drinking Jack Black, but the nectar did add to his rubbery legs. As all clapped and cheered for Elvis, a roar cut through the air. All turned in the direction of the noise to see Mr. Strickland driving his skeeter, like a race car driver, down the shell road leading to the jetties.

Dust and shells were flying everywhere. His skeeter was an old blue '55 Chevy he had cut down. He used it for running the beach and hauling the catch of the day. As Mr. Strickland approached the large rocks, he turned the skeeter on two wheels. The crowd moaned, anticipating the vehicle to roll over in the sand. The moan turned to a cheer, as Mr. Strickland used his driving skills to avoid the rocks and to stand the skeeter upright safely. The crowd cheered even louder when Mr. Strickland stood up in the seat of the skeeter, tipped his Jack Daniels hat and toasted the crowd with a bottle of Jack Black. It was a great entrance. Mr. Strickland was always famous for his grandstand arrivals. The skeeter was still running as Mr. Strickland hollered above the crowd.

"Couple you boys jump in and we'll go get a load of hush puppies." Eddie didn't have to be asked twice. He grabbed Jason by the arm and they both jumped into the back of the skeeter. Without hesitation, Mr. Strickland floored the gas pedal. The boys held on for their lives as the crowd cheered and laughed. It was a scary ride, but later they would speak of how much fun it had been. The crowd roared even louder, as Jason and Eddie rolled around on the wooden flatbed of the half-truck. Mr. Strickland drove down the road with one hand on the wheel and the other hand wrapped around a Jack Daniels bottle. Once during the ride, he had both hands on the bottle. Jason had to close his eyes at that sight. Jason and Eddie were both relieved when the skeeter came to a sliding halt in front of Mr. Strickland's restaurant. The two jumped from the back quickly, before Mr. Strickland decided to take off again. The rough ride didn't help Jason's bruises. He was reminded of the beating he had taken. He shook the hateful thought from his head.

The smell of hush puppies filled the air around them. Mr. Strickland yelled to his kitchen workers to "get the tub." Jason followed him into the kitchen area, where they were privileged with an incredible sight. On the table in front of them sat a number ten washtub filled with piping hot hush puppies.

"Don't wake me up," Eddie said as he gazed at the mountain of round puppies.

"Now that's a shitload of puppy dogs, ain't it, boys?" Mr. Strickland yelled with pride. The boys both agreed as Mr. Strickland told them, "Grab a side, boys." It took all their strength to get the tub off the table and outside to the back of the skeeter. They struggled, but did manage to get the silver container onto the flatbed.

The skeeter roared once more as Mr. Strickland turned the key.

Jason and Eddie both jumped onto the flatbed again. Their feet hit the wood as Mr. Strickland hit the gas. As the back tires dug in the dirt, the old Chevy headed back toward the jetties. Eddie was thrown head first to the tub of hush puppies. Jason steadied himself by holding onto the slat side of the flatbed, as Eddie pulled his head out of the tub. Jason knew Eddie had taken advantage of the situation, when he saw him chewing on a puppy. They both exploded with laughter as they hung on for life. The tub bounced a little, but it was too heavy to move very much. Both boys grabbed the tub handles and became human anchors. Eddie had made a hole in the middle of the hush puppies with his head. They couldn't stop laughing. They couldn't let go of the handles. The jetties were only a few hundred yards away. The wild hush puppy ride would soon end.

A crowd had gathered in the roadway, in anticipation of the arrival of the famous Strickland hush puppies. They formed a gauntlet to greet the brave boys, who had risked their lives to bring in the supply of round tasties. At the sight of the crowd, Mr. Strickland adjusted his course, hoping to bypass the welcoming committee. About ten yards into his new route, he was forced to jump a small mound of sand.

As the skeeter left the ground, Jason knew they were airborne. The old Chevy went grill first into the soft sand. All forward motion ended in an instant. The sudden stop turned the flatbed into a catapult. Jason and Eddie also found themselves airborne. They were both too scared to yell as they sailed through the air. Both landed, side by side, seat first, in the water. Mr. Strickland landed flat, stomach and face down in a mud bank, killing at least a hundred fiddler crabs as they crawled across the mud. The number ten washtub, along with its cargo, sailed through the air as if it were a shot out of a cannon. Five thousand hush puppies fell like hail from the sky, bouncing off the spectators, as they ran to aide the three heroes. The hush puppy blizzard would be the highlight of the mullet run that year. The seagulls and pelicans would have a hush puppy feast. The drinking and laughter continued into the night.

The fishermen were all on shore as night began to fall around the rocks. The nectar would flow heavy now and the fires would burn high for light. The music and laughter would be nonstop deep into the night. Many of the young people had gone to find their own activities, leaving the adults to get drunk and act foolish. Jason and Eddie were walking home for dry clothes. With all the excitement and their newfound popularity, the two had not given Willis much thought during the day. Eddie was the reminder. "I guess Willis took his cousins back to Georgia today." Eddie's statement unsettled Jason, as the Mohawk flashed in his head.

"I hope he stays in Georgia," Jason thought to himself as Eddie continued.

"Boy, Willis is gonna be mad he missed the mullet run." Jason didn't say anything. He knew if Willis had been there, he and Eddie would not have had such a great time together. He didn't care if Willis ever came back. The two parted company at the path next to Mr. Johnson's grocery store. They planned to get cleaned up and meet back at the jetties. They wanted to sneak up into the rocks and spy on the wild carrying-on from the Mayport white folks.

Jason's house was in darkness as he stepped up onto the back porch. He knew no one was around, so he took his clothes off. He left the light off and showered with a hose outside. Mary C. always had a bar of soap on the window board on the porch. Cleaning up before you entered the house was usually a good idea when someone had the smell of fish on their clothes and body. As Jason picked up the bar of soap, he heard a voice in the darkness. "Can I do that for you?"

Jason turned quickly, covering himself with his hand as he did. "Jessie!" He was shocked. "What are you doing here?" he whispered.

"I wanted to see you." Jessie stepped toward him, becoming more visible. "I've been hoping I would see you sometime today." She wanted to make that clear. She continued her first question. "Can I do that for you? You watched me wash, once. Now, I'll watch you." Jason was embarrassed. He had no response for her request.

"You just stand there. Let me do the work." Jason didn't say anything as Jessie stepped closer. She took the bar of soap from his free hand. She took his other hand and he was covered no more.

"You've gotta be natural with me. Don't be ashamed of nothin', never." Jason took a deep breath and tried to relax as Jessie worked her magic on his chest and shoulders, with a bar of soap. She washed the front of his legs and touched him to make his blood rush. She wanted to see his manhood. She did. In the dark, Jessie didn't notice the bruises from the beating. Her touch gave him no pain. She rubbed his buttock cheeks. He only felt chills and tingles, but no pain.

Jessie liked being a teacher. She now realized she was dominant in their relationship, because of her sexual knowledge. Jason was a most willing and eager student. He was enjoying the bath, but he was nervous about being outside. The backyard was very private, but he was still afraid someone would see them. He picked up the hose and interrupted Jessie's work. Jason dried off quickly and put on a pair of shorts, hanging on a hook by the screen door. Jason knew it was probably a mistake, but he couldn't help it. He asked her to come in the house. Without a second thought, they found themselves standing in the kitchen.

Jason's hair was dripping onto his bare shoulders and chest. Jessie kissed him hard like before. He was ready for that one. Jessie liked the way they hugged each other. It was strong and Jason squeezed her hard. Jessie stepped back and opened her shirt, exposing the "rock hards." Jason liked seeing her naked as much as Jessie liked being naked. She pushed against him. Jason felt the heat as he had the night before. Jessie wasted no time. Jason felt his shorts fall to the floor. He stood naked once more. With Jessie, however, one would not have to stand naked alone. Jason watched in amazement as her clothes hit the floor too. Jason was a little more relaxed inside. He knew his mother and uncle would not be home until late. They would be able to enjoy each other. He couldn't believe it was going to happen again. His thoughts were only of Jessie. He was ready for lesson number two. Jessie was ready to give it. All Jason had learned the night before, he was sure to use as they continued.

He took Jessie to his bedroom, locked the door and went to school again. He would take any directions she gave. Jessie liked the control she had. She had never been in the position to be the one with the knowledge. She had never felt needed and now she felt Jason needed her for his advance into manhood. She liked her new responsibility. Jessie was creating a new man; she enjoyed that thought. Once the physical activity began, there was no gentleness from Jessie. She worked hard and gave her all. She, too, had learned her lessons well. She didn't have to guide Jason as much as she had done the first time. He remembered what she liked. They pleased each other until Jason had to, again, give in. He was still in his novice stage. Jessie didn't mind the early ending to the encounter. She understood.

Jessie made the ending official. "I've got to go. I shouldn't stay any longer."

Jason hated to see her go, but he knew, once again, she was right. Jessie dressed, kissed Jason and went out the back door. He watched her disappear into the darkness. Again, Jason thought, "I love Jessie. I think she's done this before." He walked into his bedroom and remembered.

"Eddie's waiting for me!" He had forgotten his meeting at the jetties with his friend. He hurried to dress and ran toward the rocks. He knew where Eddie would be waiting. They didn't want to be seen by the adults. They wanted to watch how the flow of nectar had taken over the crowd. Jason walked up to Eddie. Eddie had chosen a good hiding place.

"Where ya been?"

"Sorry," was the only thing Jason said as Jessie's naked body appeared in his mind.

"Well, ya been missin' it. Jack Black is kickin' butt out there." The two looked out at the fires. They could see the mullet run aftermath. Empty bottles of Jack Daniels lay all over the sand. Three couples danced to a slow soft guitar. Jason couldn't see their faces. Except for an occasional outburst of laughter, it was rather quiet. The flow of the "working man's nectar" had taken its toll on all. The two watched for a few minutes, hoping to see some wild carrying on. They watched as a green truck drove up and stopped near the fires. They knew the truck belonged to Willis' father. Their view of another man was blocked by the truck. The man wore a Derby hat. Jason was uneasy when he saw the hat. He thought of a man he once knew in East Mayport. He hated that man. His name was Charlie Klim. Jason's heart raced as he thought of that name. Jason knew that Charlie Klim had something to do with his grandfather's death. He also knew Charlie Klim liked his mother. That made Jason hate him even more. Charlie Klim wore such a Derby hat. Jason didn't like his memory from the past. He watched the man walk past the fires. He thought of how he missed Daddy Bob.

Jason's heart pounded harder as he saw his mother walk out of the darkness. She greeted the man with the Derby. She hugged him as Jason's eyes glared. The man took off his hat and put it on Mary C.'s head. They stood near the fire together. Jason's fear became a reality. It was Charlie Klim. Jason couldn't stop the rage of the past as it ran through his head. He saw his Daddy Bob on the ground. There was blood. He saw Charlie Klim standing in a doorway. The thoughts of the past filled Jason's throat with hot liquid. He wanted to throw up to ease the discomfort. He turned away and stared into the darkness behind him. Eddie broke the silence.

"Let's go. There ain't nothin' happenin' here."

Jason agreed. He couldn't stay and watch his mother wear the Derby he hated so much. He wanted to cry, but he was with Eddie and he was sixteen now. They left the rocks and went back down the road toward home.

As the two passed Strickland's they were greeted by a group of their young friends. Ted Farley was the first to speak.

"We been lookin' for y'all."

"What for?" Eddie joined in.

"We're all goin' to Mr. King's house. He told us to come tonight. He's gonna tell some stories."

Eddie and Jason knew what that meant. They were excited. Like many other towns, Mayport had its haunted house. It just so happened that Mr. King lived in it. Mr. King had thrilled and frightened the children of Mayport for many years. Like Duckin', Mr. King was a Mayport tradition. Mr. King was getting older now and he didn't invite the children as often as he had in the past. The young people knew it was a treat and an honor to sit, candles burning, with Mr. King.

Jason didn't know two of the young people with Ted. He knew James, Ted's brother. He knew Wade Collins, Judy and Jane, the Sallis sisters, but there was a new boy and girl he had not seen before. The boy had freckles, like Eddie, but looked older. The girl was small, yet mature in build. Jason liked the way her half shirt exposed her stomach. Ted continued.

"This is our new neighbor, Billy Bell. He moved in next door, Monday." The new boy stuck his hand out to Jason and Eddie. Jason shook it first. He liked Billy Bell's manly handshake.

"And this is my sister," Billy added after he shook Eddie's hand. 'Her name is Terry, but we call her Tinker." Jason and Eddie both couldn't believe what Billy had said.

"Tinker Bell," they both hollered. The young girl smiled as her brother continued. "Yeah, people always say that, but she's used to it. It's fun when folks think what her name is. Our dad thinks it's a riot." Jason nodded a hello to Tinker Bell as he and Eddie joined the group. Ted led the way to Mr. King's house.

Seeing Mr. King standing on his front porch, ready to greet the young group, was enough to make you change your mind about going. Knowing what was to come made even a sixteen-year-old's heart beat faster than normal. Mr. King was a master at telling the many ghost stories about the house. Even if you had heard them before, they were still as thrilling each time. Mr. King would have a pleasant greeting and ease the minds of any newcomers. Jason had heard Mr. King's greeting many times and he knew that once you entered the house, Mr. King's voice would change and become more frightening. It was all in fun, but it was unnerving.

Mr. King's house was supposedly built over an old Spanish graveyard. The original house was a boardinghouse for pirates and sailors of long ago. Many violent deaths had taken place during the time the boardinghouse was operating. The house had eventually burned down and the present replica was built in its place.

Mr. King escorted all the wide-eyes into the living room. The room was lit up by candles, making shadows on the walls. Mr. King was truly the master. He knew they needed atmosphere. Jason watched Tinker as she looked around the room. Eddie watched her too. Eddie nudged Jason with his elbow to get his attention. Eddie then licked his lips toward Tinker.

"I guess that means you like her, huh?" Jason asked.

"I'd like to get her in the cemetery," Eddie said.

"Well, don't tell her brother that, or you might stay in the cemetery."

Eddie swallowed and agreed. They both smiled and watched Tinker. She returned Jason's stare every now and then. Jason thought he would like to show Tinker the things he had learned from Jessie. He liked her stomach. Mr. King was in rare form that night. Jason could see the fear, interest, and amazement in Tinker's face, as she took in every word. He saw that Tinker's brother was interested in Judy Sallis and he never saw the looks Tinker was getting. Judy seemed interested in Billy too. It was a matter of time before they were partners for the evening. Jane had always liked Ted, so they sat together. Jason knew Eddie would act too silly and Tinker would not be impressed by his actions. Eddie had no chance to be her partner in the cemetery. Jason had a new confidence when it came to the opposite sex. Jason knew Willis wasn't going to like Billy being with Judy, but he figured that was Judy's business, not his. Eddie would most likely tell Willis.

Now, anytime Mr. King had told his tales, he would have the group of listeners, two at a time, walk upstairs in the house alone. This was to see if any of the spirits might appear to the already scared couple. Jason knew the tradition and he made sure he stood near Tinker. As if Mr. King had read Jason's mind, he began the pairing.

"Jason, you take that pretty little new lady and see if they will appear to her, upstairs."

"Yes, sir!" Jason agreed and took Tinker by the arm, as Eddie's mouth fell open. Eddie was not at all happy with Mr. King's selection. Tinker wasn't sure she wanted to go, but Jason assured her that there was no problem.

"I've done it before. It's really O.K." Tinker looked at her brother after Jason's comment. He gave her encouragement.

"Go ahead, Judy says it's alright." Reluctantly and wide-eyed, Tinker walked up the stairs. Jason liked the hold she had of his arm. Again, he tried to ease her mind.

"I've done this a hundred times. I've never seen anything." Tinker said nothing. She squeezed Jason's arm tighter. She pushed against him as they walked slowly from room to room. He could feel her breast against him. He liked that. The tour of the room ended without the appearance by the ghosts of the past. They stood back at the top of the stairs. Tinker had kept her eyes closed throughout the entire walk. Jason looked down at the others awaiting their turn at the spirits.

"If there was a ghost up there, Tinker would have missed it anyway." Mr. King and the others all burst into laughter at Jason's comment. Tinker hurried Jason down the stairs. The others all took their turn hunting for spirits.

Eddie asked Tinker if she wanted to go again, but she said, "No, thanks. Once is enough." Eddie passed up his turn as his partner would have been James. They all thanked Mr. King as they stepped out of the house onto his front porch. Mr. King ended the visit with his usual warning; "Please be careful as you walk home tonight. You may have a spirit follow you. If they like you, they do that sometimes. But don't worry, they always find their way back here to see me. You see, I understand them."

Tinker was glad as the group moved away from the house and walked down the road. Ted Farley knew the usual procedure after a visit to Mr. King's.

"Now, who has the guts to visit the cemetery?" His eyes were wide open when he asked his question. Judy and Jane gave an excited approval, Billy smiled a yes, hoping to get closer to Judy, Eddie didn't seem to care, Tinker was in shock at the thought, and James said, "No, I'm goin' home." The night of self-made horror continued as they all walked to the Mayport graveyard.

The visits to the cemetery always had the same outcome. Couples would end up pairing off, in hopes of getting to know each other better. The matchups seemed to be set for Billy and Judy, for Ted and Jane. The problem was the threesome of Eddie, Jason, and Tinker. Tinker didn't show much interest in either of them as they walked down the dark road leading to the graves. She was quiet. She was afraid. She didn't want to go. She couldn't hold back her true feelings.

"Billy," she got her brother's attention away from Judy, "I don't want to go."

Billy smiled. "You don't have to go, Tink. You know that." Billy understood and respected his sister's feelings. Jason liked that. "Why don't you go back if you want to?"

Tinker smiled and nodded her head. "I'll walk her home," Jason was quick to offer. Eddie was beaten to the punch again.

"Great," Billy said. He was glad he didn't have to take her back. Judy was driving him crazy and he did want to get to know her better. Jason and Tinker turned to walk away. Billy looked at Judy.

"I'd like to see that graveyard now." Judy smiled as a voice cut into the night.

"Not with that one."

They all turned to see Willis standing near. Every boy in Mayport knew that Judy was Willis' girl. All except the new boy. Willis' voice had its usual threatening tone.

"You need to go on home now, boy. That's too much woman for you." Willis stepped closer to Judy. Jason was surprised when he saw no fear on Billy's face. Judy joined the heated atmosphere.

"Leave him alone, Willis. He hasn't done anything wrong."

Willis went on. "Not yet, anyway. If he had of gotten you in the woods over there, now that would have been a different story."

Judy looked away. She was red with anger. She knew Willis was not going to leave the situation alone. Billy remained silent, but he watched Willis.

"You don't own me, Willis," Judy began again. "I can do what I want."

"I know ya, girl. You need a man. So after I kick the shit out of this pretty boy here, you'll come to your senses. Just like before." Willis and Billy stared at each other.

There wasn't much difference in the sizes of the two enemies. Jason thought that Billy might be a little bigger than Willis. It was close. Jason liked the way Billy looked as he stood facing the evil one. He had not seen many do so. He thought either Billy was brave, or he really didn't understand just how mean Willis was. Jason knew Billy couldn't withstand what was to come if Willis decided to carry out his threat. Billy would not be prepared for the evil.

"I'm only gonna tell you one more time to get gone." Willis directed his threat and eyes to Billy. Billy had taken enough.

"Why don't you kiss my ass?" Billy asked with a smile.

Eddie's mouth dropped open. Jason couldn't believe his ears. All the others stood in shock. Not in Jason's life did he think anyone would say something like that to Willis. Willis stood for a few seconds, also in disbelief. Billy added to this insult.

"Maybe you don't hear too good. I said, kiss my ass."

Two times was too much. Willis yelled and charged at Billy. Willis had his head down, as if he were a bull getting ready to spear a matador with his horns. Willis was wild and careless in his anger. He intended to drive his shoulders deep into Billy's stomach, hoping to knock him to the ground. As Willis got closer, Billy lifted his knee. It landed square on Willis' nose. The power of the lifted knee and the force of Willis' charge made the contact echo in the night. Willis' head was thrown back by the force of the impact. Blood flew into the air as Willis' nose seemed to explode. He slammed to the ground, holding his nose and rolling in intense pain. Billy did nothing else and said nothing. It was obvious that Willis would not be able to continue his assault. Billy turned to Tinker.

"I'll go home with you, Tink." He looked at Judy. "Judy, it was fun. I hope I can see you again." Billy and Tinker said good night and walked away from the stunned group. Willis still lay on the ground. Blood covered the front of his shirt. His hands were full too. Judy,

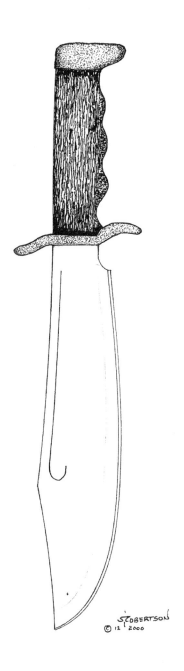

BOWIE KNIFE

Jane, and Ted followed Billy and Tinker. Eddie ran to assist Willis. Jason stood and looked at Willis on the ground. He liked that. He had never seen a nosebleed like that. He was glad it belonged to Willis. Jason wanted to leave with the others, but he also wanted to bathe in Billy's triumph. Eddie helped Willis to get to his knees. Willis looked dazed and sick. Jason turned to see the others getting farther down the road. He looked back at Willis just to assure himself it was true. He smiled openly and hurried to catch the others. Jason knew Eddie would get Willis home. He really liked the new boy. He liked Tinker, too. He wanted to touch her stomach. They didn't talk much on the way back. There was a funny feeling in the air. They were all still in shock. Jason could tell that Judy was taken with Billy. Billy was quiet and Jason liked the way he handled the situation. Jason said good night to the group as his road home came first.

Jason was home quickly and he stepped up on his back porch. He saw the bar of soap. He thought of Jessie. Her body flashed in his head. He saw Willis with his hands covered in blood. He thought of Tinker's stomach. He wanted to see her naked. Jason's late night visions were interrupted by sounds coming from inside the house. He listened. He heard his mother's voice. She was angry. He opened the door and walked into the kitchen. Her voice was louder now, and a man's voice joined hers. He knew the voices were coming from his mother's bedroom. He eased down the hall and stood next to her door. The voices were even louder.

"I want you out of here," his mother yelled.

"You don't mean that." The man's voice cut into Jason's head. He had to help her. He ran to his room for his new hunting knife. The loud voices continued to hurt his head. He looked on the dresser. Then he remembered. "It's on the porch." He had taken it off along with his muddy clothes earlier that night. He hurried outside. He pulled the knife from the case and ran to help his mother. He gripped the handle as tight as he could. As he came to the door of her room, he heard her scream and then he heard a sound as if she was being hit. Jason's heart pounded against his chest as he opened the door. He could not see his mother. His vision was blocked by the intruder.

The man was looking down on the floor at the side of the bed.

"Get up," he yelled. "Get your ass up!"

Jason's rage was too much for him as he stepped forward. He pushed the big hunting knife deep into the unwelcome intruder. The steel blade sunk deep into the man's lower right side. Jason knew from the feel of the knife that it came out of his body in the front. The man screamed in pain as Jason's death grip on the handle pulled the blade back out. Jason pushed again. The blade didn't move easily this time. Jason knew he had hit bone inside the body. The man turned slowly to eye his attacker. Jason stepped back, shaking with fear.

Jason knew he would die when he realized he was standing face-to-face with Charlie Klim. With a face filled with pain, Charlie Klim reached out to grab Jason. Fear gave Jason a hidden strength. He pushed the knife a third time. The bowie blade was driven deep up under Charlie Klim's armpit. Jason pulled the knife away again. His grip prepared for another plunge of the steel. Charlie Klim stood still. Jason shoved it in again. The blade sunk a fourth time, gashing the thigh of Charlie Klim's right leg. The big man Jason had hated since he was a child fell to his knees. The pain was too much for any man to remain standing.

Mary C. ran past the two warriors and out of the room. Jason and Charlie Klim both shook as they stared into each other's souls. Charlie Klim trembled in pain. Jason trembled in fear. They were only a few feet apart. Jason's legs were frozen. He could not move. Jason watched in horror as Charlie Klim reached out with his bloody arm and grabbed his shoulder. The grip forced Jason down to his knees. Jason felt the bloody arm quiver as they both knelt on the hardwood floor. He felt both of Charlie Klim's big hands touch his throat. Jason closed his eyes as the powerful fingers sunk into his skin. Jason thought of Daddy Bob. He saw Tom Green. He saw Jessie. He saw the oak. He thought a breeze touched his face. He opened his eyes. It was the breath of his enemy Charlie Klim. He saw his Daddy Bob again.

Jason screamed and with all his power pushed the knife for the fifth time. He knew it was the deepest cut of all. Jason had driven the blade into Charlie Klim's pelvic and groin area. Jason released his grip and left the knife deep inside. Charlie Klim leaned forward and grabbed the handle of the knife. He only held it. It was over. Jason was still kneeling as Mary C., Uncle Bobby and two other men ran into the bloody bedroom. Jason could feel them, but he couldn't see them. He was in the bed. His Uncle Bobby's face came near.

"You alright, boy?" Jason had no answer. He felt his mother touch his hair. He thought of the people he loved. His state of shock brought sleep.

Chapter Six

Thursday

Jason opened his eyes to the sight of his mother sitting on his bed still stroking his hair. He knew it had happened. Uncle Bobby stood at the end of the bed.

"Mornin'," Uncle Bobby smiled. Jason tried to smile back.

"You did good, boy. You did real good. Too bad you didn't kill that son of a bitch." Jason looked up at Mary C. Her mouth was cut and her eye was almost swollen completely closed. He hated her beautiful face looking like that. The thought of his last push of the knife sparked his mind. He was glad he did it, but he couldn't believe Charlie Klim was still alive.

Uncle Bobby continued. "He's a bad one, that Charlie Klim. You were brave, boy. I'm proud of ya." Jason closed his eyes as Mary C. picked up the conversation.

"He's hurt bad, but he ain't gonna die. And he ain't gonna bother us no more."

"He ain't gonna do much of nothin' because of where you left that knife in 'im," Uncle Bobby interrupted Mary C. "His jukin' days are over." Jason felt sick. He didn't want to throw up. He couldn't help it. He ran to the bathroom.

Most of Jason's morning was taken by a visit from the sheriff. Jason and Mary C. had to tell what had happened. Jason did not like reliving the encounter with the hated Charlie Klim. After the sheriff had gone over the story a number of times, he left Jason with a thought.

"He probably needed killin'. But, it's a good thing he didn't die at your hands, boy. You're too young to have such a thing to live with." The sheriff then looked at Mary C.

"You keep bringing them crazies home with ya, woman, and you gonna get hurt bad one day. You was lucky this time." Mary C. didn't say anything after the sheriff's warning.

The story of Jason's battle ran like a wildfire throughout Mayport. Many folks knew about Charlie Klim and they stopped by the house to say "well done." Some were just curious and wanted to be in on the excitement and gossip. Some blamed Mary C. and her lifestyle for the awful attack. They said it was a shame the boy had to get caught up in her carrying-on.

Jason's recovery would be much faster than Charlie's. He stayed in the house most of the day, until Mary C. suggested: "Why don't you get some fresh air and get away from here for a little while? Go walk down to the docks or something."

Jason liked the idea and went out. He felt good about his bravery. Everyone was calling it brave. He walked to the dock. Mr. Leek greeted Jason as he walked into the heading area.

"Hey, Jason. Good to see ya, boy. You doin' O.K.?" That seemed to be the question everybody was asking Jason.

"Yes, suh. I'm fine."

"Your mama alright?" Mr. Leek was truly concerned.

"Yes, suh. She's fine too." Jason saw his mother's injured face. He hated it.

"That was terrible, what ya'll went through last night," Mr. Leek continued. Jason nodded his head.

"I'm surprised you're out and about like this."

"Mama told me to get away from the house and get some fresh air."

"She's probably right. It'll do ya good. No sense sittin' at home lettin' it eat at ya. Why don't ya go sit out on the dock and just relax?"

Mr. Leek left Jason and walked into his office. Jason looked around the fish house and out toward the loading dock. There was no activity. The ferry horn blew and Jason's visit to Mr. Leek's ended. He walked to the ferry slip to sit on his favorite pylon. He saw the oak in the distance.

He had mixed feelings about the oak and the sand hill. He had good feelings at times, but so much pain and suffering seemed to surround the tree and the hill. He would play the game tomorrow. He wanted to play. It was to be his final step to manhood. The week had seen Jason change. He was becoming a man without the game. Jason wanted to climb the limbs again. Thoughts of the past few days began to overwhelm him; Charlie Klim was in his head. Then Jessie, Willis, Tom Green, Elvis, the oak and Jessie again. He saw her wet dripping body. Her breasts, his birthday beating raged within him. He saw the Mohawk. Jason struggled with his thoughts. A voice helped him fight out of the brain flashes.

"Boy, are you lost in deep thought?" A voice saved Jason. He had been almost hypnotized by his mental flashbacks. He focused his eyes on Tinker. He was pleased to see her and have company.

"Can I sit with you?" she asked.

"Yeah. . .sure." Jason was excited, but nervous. Tinker sat on the bulkhead next to the pylons. Jason watched her.

"I heard how you saved your mother last night. I'm glad you're O.K." She looked at Jason with concern.

"Thanks." Jason really didn't know what to say.

Tinker could sense Jason didn't want to talk about it so she changed the subject. "Billy and Ted went to that ol' sand hill to swing on a tree, or something. Ted asked Billy to play in some game tomorrow. They said they needed to practice."

Jason nodded and looked toward the oak. "I'd like to have Billy on the team I'm on," Jason thought to himself as the sight of Willis' bloody nose came to his mind. Tinker broke his thought.

"You gonna play in that game?"

Jason nodded again.

"I've never been to the sand hill," she admitted. "Judy said it's strange up there." Jason smiled and joined the one-sided conversation.

"The oak is great. It's special. It has a power." He was excited as he talked of the tree.

Tinker could feel Jason meant his words. It made her uneasy. Again, she changed the subject. "Why is Willis so mean?"

Her question ignited Jason within. He paused before his answer. "Willis has always been that way. People say Willis is an oak baby. He is stronger than most."

"Oak baby! What's that?" She couldn't understand.

Jason gave a short explanation.

"People think Willis gets strength from the tree. They say his daddy and mama made love under the tree on the sand hill."

"Oh, God!" she interrupted Jason. "That's awful."

"Everybody wants to be an oak baby. I wish I was. A lot of folks believe in the oak."

"Why do you wish you were like Willis?"

Jason still wanted to make her understand. "I don't want to be mean. I want to be strong." Jason looked at the tree.

"Well, Billy is as strong as Willis, and he ain't no oak baby. And you're strong too." She liked Jason. "You even saved your mother. Willis couldn't do that."

Jason liked her words. He felt good.

"I don't think the tree can make a baby." Her statement was firm.

"Well, folks say it can. But, there's other folks say it can't. My Uncle Bobby don't believe it."

"Do you believe in the tree?"

Her question made him uneasy. He didn't know what to say. He didn't know how he really felt about it. He was confused about his feelings for the tree. He liked the power he had felt because of the tree. All his encounters near the sand hill ran through his head.

Tinker asked again. "Do ya?"

Jason looked at the tree. A cool breeze touched his face. "Yes, I do. It has a power over the people here. I believe it."

Tinker was shocked at Jason's answer. Again, she used her talent for changing the subject. "Thanks for being with me at Mr. King's last night." She smiled.

Jason was glad to end the talk about the oak. "Oh, that's O.K. It was fun. You were funny."

"Funny?" Tinker smiled. "I was scared."

Jason smiled. Tinker's pretty face had helped him forget about Charlie Klim for the time being. She lay across the bulkhead and looked up at the sky. Jason liked her legs. He couldn't see her stomach, like before. Her shirt was tucked into her shorts. Her shorts were cut high and he could see the cheeks of her butt as she moved. He liked that. The desire to see her naked ran through his head. He wondered if he would be able to do that. They both remained quiet. Her thoughts were not as strong as Jason's but she did like him. The two were silent for only a short time, as the moment was interrupted by Billy and Ted. Billy broke the silence.

"Hey, you two. Wake up." Jason and Tinker both turned to see Ted and her brother, Billy. Billy continued, "Come on, Tink. We gotta get home. I told Mom we'd be there in time for dinner."

"Did ya swing?" Tinker asked as she stood up.

Billy smiled. "No problem. Duckin's gonna be fun."

Jason's heart beat at the word, Duckin'.

Ted Farley joined in. "Willis and his wild lookin' cousin came up to the swings. We saw 'em comin', so Billy thought it would be best to just leave."

Billy smiled and nodded at Ted's comment. "No sense having trouble if you can avoid it," Billy said.

Jason liked Billy's way of saying things. Jason hoped he would be a friend of the new boy and his sister. The new friends said good-bye and left for home and dinner.

Jason and Ted talked as they walked away from the ferry slip. "Billy's O.K., ain't he?" Ted asked for Jason's agreement.

"Yeah. I like him."

"Maybe we'll all be on the same team tomorrow," Ted was hoping.

Jason had his thoughts about the game. He shared them with Ted. "You should be a captain tomorrow. You and Willis have both played before. You should."

Ted was concerned with that thought. "It will be tough to be a captain against Willis. I don't know if I want to. What would you do?" Ted asked Jason.

Jason took a deep breath and found his new strength. "I want too play against Willis. I think we can win." Jason felt good after making his statement. Ted was surprised at Jason's attitude toward the game.

"Maybe if you and me and Billy were on the same team, we could do it." Ted had a fire stirring within him as he continued. "You know Willis will pick his cousin to play on his team. You know that's why he has him here. The other two stayed in Georgia, but the ugly one came back. Just to play, I'll bet." Ted didn't like that thought. Jason hated it even more as the pimplefaced Mohawk appeared in his mind. He fought the thought as he relived being run down and beaten in the sand. Ted continued and helped Jason fight his unwanted flashback. "That guy's so goony-lookin'. I think there's something wrong with him." Jason nodded in agreement.

The road to Jason's house was only a few steps away. "See ya tomorrow mornin'. Good luck." Ted had good wishes. Jason liked Ted. As Ted walked away, Jason wished he had had the courage to help him when Willis made him eat the lizard head. He was ashamed. Jason hoped he would never stand by and allow his friend to be treated that way again.

Mary C. greeted Jason as he stepped up onto the back porch of the house. "I was gettin' worried 'bout ya, Jason. Where ya been?"

"Down at the ferry slip with my friends, talkin'. There's a new boy and girl in town. They moved in next to Ted Farley. They're nice."

"I've seen 'em." Mary C. said. "The girl's pretty, ain't she?" Jason rolled his eyes at his mother's question. He didn't answer as he walked into the kitchen. Mary C. smiled, but didn't ask again.

"What's for dinner?" was Jason's question.

"Just sandwich makin's tonight. I ain't felt much like cookin' today. There's some leftover shrimp in the icebox. Cold shrimp is better than hot."

"A sandwich will be fine." Jason made his choice. He sat at the table. He heard Uncle Bobby down the hall. He was preparing himself for a night out. Jason liked watching and learning as his Uncle Bobby put on, as he called it, his "jukin clothes." Jason had learned that jukin' had something to do with goin' out with women. Jason knew he would go jukin' as soon as he could. He wondered how old you had to be to do such a thing?

Jason thought that his Uncle Bobby should have been a singer. He was always singing and dancing. Jason didn't mind at all; he liked it. He knew all the songs by Chuck Berry, Little Richard, and Jerry Lee Lewis, but Uncle Bobby's favorite was anything by Elvis Presley. Sometimes Jason felt his uncle looked like Elvis Presley. He thought it was great when Uncle Bobby would sing "Don't Be Cruel" and he would sound just like Elvis. Jason would try it, too, but he would be sure nobody was around to hear. Jason would stand next to the bathroom door and sing along with Uncle Bobby, as he sang in the shower. Uncle Bobby always smelled so good when he went out. It was the "jukin' smell."

Within an hour, Uncle Bobby had finished the jukin' preparation and he was ready to go. He walked into the kitchen to get the approval of Jason and Mary C.

"Well, folks, am I dangerous or am I just against the law?" Uncle Bobby stood there with his upper lip quivering like Elvis.

Mary C. laughed. "You are one crazy man. We gotta get you some medical attention."

Uncle Bobby couldn't pass up that lead. "I hope I need a doctor after tonight." He quivered his lip again. Mary C. then pushed Uncle Bobby out of the back screen door as they both laughed. Jason liked it when everybody laughed and had such a good time. Mary C. turned from the door, still smiling and shook her head. She looked at

Jason.

"Don't you go and be woman-crazy like that fool brother of mine. And don't ever wear them ugly white shoes."

Jason smiled at his mother's warning, but he couldn't wait to get some white buck jukin' shoes.

Then Jason heard his Uncle Bobby's voice in the backyard. "If I don't see ya, boy, good luck in the morning. Ya'll playin' early, ain't ya?"

"First light," Jason yelled back as his blood chilled once more.

Jason's chill was interrupted by the sound of his Uncle Bobby as he continued his vocal trademark. "Goodness gracious, great balls of fire."

Jason liked that song too. He repeated his uncle's lyrics. He walked down the hall and the most pleasant thought took his mind. He was alone with his mother. What a great evening it was going to be.

Jason walked into his bedroom and fell across his bed. He could hear his mother in the bathroom. She was humming one of Uncle Bobby's tunes. He hoped she was not going out tonight. He wanted to talk about the game. He stared at the ceiling. He wondered why his mind raced so. He just couldn't seem to hold one thought. Tom Green, peanuts, his mother, Uncle Bobby, the green-eyed black girl all raced through his mind. He tried to keep the good thoughts so he wouldn't think about the game.

His thoughts were cut short as his mother's voice interrupted. "Jason, I'll be back in a little while." Jason's fears came true with her words. She was going out. He wanted to ask her to stay but, as usual, he didn't. She left and Jason was alone once more.

His mind raced again. He was restless and uneasy, alone in the house. He thought of his grandfather's words. "It's how a man handles his fears that makes him a man." Jason wanted to be a man. He thought of the past few days. He had fought for his mother. He had taken a savage beating. He had lain with Jessie. He had victory over Willis. He had stood against Willis for another. He had claimed the highest limb of the oak. He had turned sixteen. He would play tomorrow.

Jason carried his many thoughts outside into the night air and sat on the steps of the porch. He looked in the direction of the sand hill. He saw only darkness. The sound of the summer crickets made him think of East Mayport and Seminole Beach. He liked the beach and the swimming hole near the big jetties. He recalled the time he went to the swimming hole with his mother and uncle. It had been a great day. They had a big lunch on the beach, picnic style with all the extras. His mother looked so beautiful in the sun. All the men that day watched her every move. Jason remembered that there were always men talking to her on the beach. He remembered how she looked in the water. She laughed. She was pretty even when she was wet.

His thoughts were ended by movement in the darkness. He was frightened at first; he could feel his heart. His fear eased as he saw little Benjamin run from the darkness and into the light of the back porch. Like before, the little black boy was breathing hard from his run. Again he carried a message. "Jessie says come to the lighthouse." Benjamin's words ignited Jason. Without a second thought, he agreed as Benjamin disappeared as quick as he had appeared.

Jason left the safety of his porch and walked into the darkness toward the old lighthouse. Jessie burned inside him. He felt her deep in his soul.

He passed the sand hill. He didn't want to, but he thought of the beating he took. It was after his first visit to the lighthouse. His drive to see Jessie overpowered the memory of the pain.

Jason stepped through the door of the small building as he had done before. He was eye-to-eye with Jessie. The quilt was laid on the floor. They said nothing. Jessie began her exciting ritual. The encounter began. Her rough manner was present at the first kiss. Jason returned her untamed foreplay. The rougher he was, the wilder Jessie moved. She showed him things he had only heard from Willis. Jason knew Willis had told the truth again. Jason lay on his back. He looked at the ceiling of the old building. Jessie worked her magic on his body. He was so glad to be with her. He was in a different world when he lay with Jessie. Jessie's dominance drove him to exhaustion once again. Her wildness ended. Jason felt sweat dripping under his arms. The two had not spoken yet. Jessie had made her noises, but no words. Jessie dressed, as she had done before. To Jason's surprise she was first to speak.

"When you play tomorrow, think of me. I will be with you." Jason looked at Jessie as she continued. "You will be strong. You can win. You are already a man. The game will make you stronger. You must please the oak." Jason was speechless at her words. His blood ran cold at the feeling he had. He didn't expect such strong words from Jessie. He knew she was a believer. She prepared to leave. She folded the quilt as Jason dressed. As usual, Jason had not found the words he wanted. Her talk of the game had confused him. He didn't know she was interested in the game. Jessie slammed Jason with another unexpected thought.

"After you play, we must breed for the oak." Jason looked up. She had left him with an incredible thought.

Jason didn't think of his fatigue after the wild sexual experience he had endured. He passed the sand hill. He didn't look at the oak. Jessie's words of breeding pounded his head.

He ran nonstop to the safety of the porch he had so willingly left only an hour before. He felt even safer as he sat on his bed. He heard the front door open and his mother's sweet voice.

"It's me. Jason, you here?"

"Yes, ma'am, I just got back. I went down to the docks." Jason couldn't tell her about Jessie. Mary C.'s next question made Jason's blood change directions again.

"You still gonna play that silly game tomorrow? You've been through so much, I don't think you should play." Jason's throat went dry as once again he had no words.

His Uncle Bobby's voice cut into Jason's hesitation. "He has to play!" Uncle Bobby stood at the bedroom door, red-faced from the Jack Black nectar. He continued. "It's time for the boy to play. He was man enough to protect his mother. The game will take his mind off things. The game is for fun. The boy needs to play. Elvis has spoken." Uncle Bobby shook his leg and quivered his upper lip.

"You're drunk. Go to bed." Mary C. joined in with her opinion and order.

"You're right, my sister dear. Bed it is. I'm just sorry I will be alone." Uncle Bobby swayed in the doorway.

"Why don't you get Elvis to sleep with you?" Mary C. was disgusted with her brother. Uncle Bobby was headed down the hall, rubber legs and all. He did not hear Mary C.'s suggestion for his bedmate.

"Don't be a fool like that uncle of yours," she warned. Jason smiled and thought of how he loved Uncle Bobby. Mary C. continued, "Just you be careful tomorrow. And if you don't feel like playin', don't." Jason wished it was all that easy. He knew he had to play. Mary C. kissed him. "Good night, son." Jason bathed in the attention. He was glad they were all home together.

She left his room. His raging thoughts returned. He stared at his ceiling. Jessie and her words of breeding rang in his head. "She was so sure when she said it," he thought. "I don't know if I want to do that." He closed his eyes. He hoped sleep would take him. It did not. He thought of Willis and the game, of Charlie Klim and Daddy Bob, of hush puppies and the mullet run, of Jessie and her love quilt. Sleep freed him from his rage. His dreams were of Jessie. He would wake up during the night in nervous anticipation of the game. He could not oversleep.

Chapter Seven

Friday

Jason's dream of Jessie would wake him early. It would stay with him for years to come. It was so real.

In his dream, Jessie stood under the oak. She was above Jason as he looked up. He struggled through the white sand to stand with her. Her hair and the ropes moved as one in the breeze. She was naked. He could never resist her body. Jason made his climb. He stood gazing into her green eyes. Jessie undressed him as she had done before. The two lay in the sand. Jason wanted to breed for the oak.

As they moved, the sand moved beneath them. It covered them as it sucked the breeders down into the roots of the great tree. Jason felt they would suffocate as the sand moved them deeper. He was afraid. Jessie never changed her expression, as if she understood what was happening. The movement stopped. Jason was deafened by the sound of babies crying.

He wiped the sand from his eyes. He saw the roots of the oak, deep into the ground. Cradled within each root was a baby. The babies moved and cried. Jessie smiled. Jason woke up. He was glad it was a dream, but he would remember.

Jason was awake when Uncle Bobby opened his bedroom door. "Get up, boy. Today's the day."

Jason's heart raced at those early morning words. "I'm awake."

"It's five now. Ya'll meet at six, don't ya? You need to get up and eat somethin'."

Jason didn't answer, but he did sit up on the edge of the bed.

"While I'm headed out through the jetties, you'll be gettin' started. Boy, I wish I was sixteen again." Uncle Bobby envied Jason.

Jason wished he could trade places with his uncle for that day. "You go play and I'll go shrimpin'," Jason thought to himself.

"Go wash ya face and get good and awake, boy. You gotta be ready to go. And, if you play against that crazy Willis, you watch him close. He's a mean one, that boy." Uncle Bobby's warning didn't set with Jason. He didn't need to hear such advice, that early. He did take the advice about washing his face. He got up and walked down the hall to the bathroom.

His mother's bedroom door was closed. Jason knew she would not get up to wish him well. He joined his Uncle Bobby for toast and coffee. Daylight had just begun. It was easy to see it would be a clear day.

"It's gonna be a good day for Duckin'. What you gonna wear?" Uncle Bobby was interested.

"I don't know." Jason hadn't given it much thought.

"Well, don't wear all that heavy stuff everybody else wears. Just wear your dungarees and a long-sleeved shirt of some kind. The idea is to avoid the briars. Be light and quick. Don't let your clothes be your downfall."

Jason was unsure about the advice he was receiving. "I thought," Jason began, "the heavier and thicker, the better."

"No, boy! That just slows you down. You can't move. You gotta be ready to move out there."

"Did you ever get hurt?" Jason asked.

"I was too quick and smart for that." Uncle Bobby looked proud. "They couldn't get me if they chased me. And my swing down was unstoppable." Jason smiled as his uncle continued bragging. "Boy, the first time I played, I was real nervous, like you. But, I really played hard and didn't get hurt at all. It's when you let up or sissy out, that's when you get hurt. Players get hurt because they get careless. Always be on your guard. You'll be just fine. . . ." Uncle Bobby hesitated a moment. "Oh! And one more thing. Always be ready to take a hit. But also be ready to give one."

Jason's head throbbed with the words of wisdom he had taken while trying to eat his toast. He had another question. "Did you ever play with Willis' daddy?"

"No, I never played with ol' Bucky. In fact, if you want to know what I think. . . ." Jason was all ears. "I don't think that Bucky ever played Duckin'. I think he's chickenshit." Jason was shocked by his uncle's statement. As usual, Jason didn't know what to say. "Surely," he thought, "Uncle Bobby's mistaken."

Uncle Bobby continued. "I don't know nobody that played a game when Bucky was in it. He talks like he played, but I don't believe it. He's been a liar since he was a baby. He's chickenshit, I tell ya. He only messed around with Charlie Klim, so folks would think he was bad."

Jason thought of how Eddie acted around Willis. It was the same thing. Eddie was the biggest "fear friend" of all. Jason wished his friend could just be his fun, normal self. But Willis altered Eddie's behavior. Jason hated that. But he knew Willis had done the same thing to him before. Jason felt guilty and ashamed.

Uncle Bobby left the table as another evil deed from the past flashed in Jason's head. He remembered the night they were going to the swimming hole to dive off the rocks in the dark. Willis had dared everybody. He said he had done it before. The tide would be high and the hole behind the big rocks would be deep with water. It was too dangerous to dive when it was low tide, but the tide would be at its highest that night. Willis told some of the girls to come and watch the daredevils. The spectators and divers numbered ten when they reached the swimming hole. Jason thought of who was there that night. "Me, Willis, Eddie, Wade, Ted and James." He thought of the girls: Robin, Judy, Harriet, and Sarah, Wade's sister. Jason thought of how he never really believed the stories about Sarah, until that night. Willis had told different stories about Sarah, but Jason always thought they were lies. That night he found out again that Willis didn't lie about such things.

The ten laughed and talked as they walked to the big hole near the rocks. Willis made most of the jokes as he teased Wade and James. He kept the girls moving by his crude remarks and pinching them on the butt now and then. Jason never liked the way Willis talked around girls, but he dared not mention his feelings. He was ashamed that he had not stood up for his feelings.

Jason laid his head on the kitchen table as his mind continued in the past. He remembered standing with the others and looking across the water to the rocks in the dark. The moonlight helped, but it was still dark enough. Willis was ready to make a new challenge.

Playing and teasing with the girls had whet his appetite for something more than diving off the rocks. Willis took over. "Let's find out who the real men and women are here tonight." All eyes were opened wide by Willis' challenge.

Sarah was the first to respond. "And what does that mean?"

All eyes and ears, again, were on Willis.

"That means if you girls are women enough to handle it, we could have some show-and-touch right here." Willis smiled. He was serious. He had more to say. "Don't you girls think that seein' six men naked is worth seein' four women naked?"

Sarah was still the only one to speak after the question. She was never shocked by the things Willis said or did; Jason knew that Sarah liked Willis. She was a good match for the wild one. She responded again. This time she had her own challenge.

"Well, bad ass," Sarah looked right at Willis, "I don't know about the girls here, but if you will swim out to the biggest rock and jump off buck naked, this woman will skinny-dip with you as long as you want." Jason couldn't believe his ears. All eyes were on Willis. They waited for his reaction.

Willis smiled again and without a word he took off his shirt and his shorts. They both hit the ground. He stood there naked. He smiled again as he stepped toward Sarah. She didn't move or blink an eye. She was a match for the wild one.

"You better start gettin' them drawers of yours off." Willis turned and ran into the water. All eyes were now on Sarah. Jason hoped she would live up to her part of the bargain. Sarah watched Willis as he swam to the big rock she had pointed out. In a matter of seconds, Willis was making his way up onto the big stone. He stood naked at the top. He dove into the dark water and yelled, "Sarah, get 'em off," as he hit the water. Again, Jason couldn't believe it. Sarah's clothes hit the ground. She smiled at the others watching her. She stood for a second or two, as if to let the boys get a good look at her. She looked at the other three girls.

"C'mon. It ain't gonna hurt ya." Sarah ran into the water. Jason could see as Willis and Sarah met. There was laughing and splashing. It was easy to see Willis and Sarah would not be coming out of the water for a while. The group on shore didn't seem to know what to do next. Willis, from the water, made a suggestion.

"Hey, you pussies. The water's great. Sarah's great too." Judy didn't like what was happening in the water. She liked Willis too. She wasn't going to be outdone by Sarah. Everybody wanted to impress Willis. Judy was next to hit the water naked. She didn't linger and give everyone a look, but Jason saw enough. He liked seeing the two girls naked. Willis' voice came from the water again.

"Get your ass out here, Eddie." Like a puppy dog, Eddie followed his master's command. He was naked and in the water. Harriet and Robin were next. They looked at each other, shrugged their shoulders with a grin and off came their clothes. Jason and the boys still on the shore all watched the last two girls. Robin fell in the sand as she struggled with her tight pants. She was heavier than the other girls, but all male eyes turned to her when her shirt came off. Jason's mouth went dry when he saw her breasts. They were big and round.

"Where did she hide 'em?" Jason thought. He had no idea they were that big. Harriet and Robin both screamed as they ran into the water. Ted and Wade didn't waste another second as Robin bounced past them on her way to the water.

Ted looked at Wade, as they, too, stood naked. He couldn't hold his excitement inside. "I just gotta see 'em up close."

Wade had his own thoughts to share. "I just wanna touch one of 'em." They both yelled like Tarzan as they jumped into the water.

Jason stood on the shore with James, Ted's younger brother.

"I'm goin' home. I'm gonna tell Mama," James said as he walked away from the edge of the water.

Jason looked out into the water. He saw four different pairs. He couldn't see if Willis was with Judy or Sarah. He did find out later that Sarah had left Willis to Judy and she had given Eddie a thrill.

Jason turned and followed James toward home.

His hate for Willis grew stronger as he walked away. Willis had to add to Jason's shame. He yelled from the water, "No pussy for the pussy!" Willis' laugh followed Jason his entire walk home.

"Hey, boy. . .you better get dressed. Ya ain't fallen back to sleep, are ya?" Uncle Bobby returned Jason from the past. He was back at the kitchen table. "Y'all meet in twenty minutes." Jason shook the thoughts of Willis from his head. He dressed and prepared for the game. He took Uncle Bobby's advice and dressed for high speed instead of protection. He trusted his uncle's knowledge from past experiences. Jason heard one of Mr. Shimp's roosters crow "a good morning." He stepped out onto the back porch, into the morning air. He took a deep breath. Uncle Bobby walked up behind him.

"I gotta go, boy. Have a good game. Be careful. And remember these two important things." Jason was always ready for his uncle's wisdom. Uncle Bobby smiled.

"Protect yourself at all times," he paused, "and don't forget Elvis swings with ya." He ruffled Jason's hair after his joke. "Good luck, boy." Jason nodded.

Uncle Bobby left for the dock and his boat.

Jason stepped off the porch and into his backyard. The grass was wet and a swarm of gnats flew up into his face. Jason knew the path through the woods that would take him to the meeting place. They would meet in the Baptist churchyard. Jason didn't know who would play, but he would know soon enough. His heart began to remind him of his true feelings about the game. As he walked, his mind was a reminder once more. He thought of Jessie and her words of breeding.

He knew he had to be careful of Willis. He had not talked to Willis since his birthday beating. He had seen Willis once at the dock and then again in the graveyard. They had not spoken. Jason knew he would have to face the evil one.

He saw the little church. Ted Farley, his brother James and Billy Bell sat on the church steps. Jason felt good about seeing his friends first. He knew he wouldn't have to face Willis alone. Eddie and Wade were the next to arrive. Eddie was dressed in a heavy hunting coat and gloves. He smiled at Jason. Jason nodded. The other boys were dressed as if they had taken Uncle Bobby's "dress for speed" advice. Eddie noticed and had to comment.

"You guys are gonna get tore up if y'all hit those pricklies today," Jason smiled and added his thought.

"Speed, my boy. We gonna be quick as cats." Eddie couldn't resist. "Yeah, you gonna look like a wildcat scratched ya if ya fall or have to run through them briars."

After Eddie's warning, they all turned toward the sound of talking coming through the path next to the church.

Jason could hear his heart pounding as he saw Willis walk from the woods. Willis was leading his three cousins to the churchyard. A chill hit Jason when his second sight was the pimple-faced Mohawk. He had forgotten about the tall, ugly one being there. Willis' other two cousins had also returned from Georgia for the game. Willis and his following were dressed in army fatigues. They looked like the National Guard on weekend maneuvers. All four boys wore army jump boots with their pants tucked into the boots. It was an intimidating sight for the others, as the Duckin' soldiers walked up to the church. It was obvious that Willis had already picked his team. Willis wasted no time getting the game underway. He walked up to Ted.

"You a captain, ain't ya?"

Ted looked at the others. "I guess so." His friends seemed to agree.

Willis went on. "I'll take my cousins and Eddie. That makes the numbers even."

Jason could see the joy on Eddie's face. All his catering to Willis had paid off. Eddie wanted to play on Willis' team in the worst way. Jason was sorry he could not be with his friend, but he knew he didn't want to be with Willis.

"That's five to five," Willis added. He continued to take over all the decisions.

He gave Ted no choice with his next statement. "We'll be the chasers. You go hide." Usually, a flip of the coin would decide which team did what. Willis had his idea of what he wanted and Ted knew it would be that way. Ted nodded in a forced approval. No one else spoke. Willis had to add more intimidation to his enemies. The evil one looked at Billy.

"Be real careful today, pretty boy. You might not be so pretty after you play." Billy did not respond to Willis. He could handle the threat. Willis had more.

"Jay Bird," Willis turned to Jason. Jason could see the effect of Billy's knee on his nose. Willis' nose was swollen and he had black bruises under both eyes. He looked to Jason like his Uncle Bobby looked one time when he had a broken nose. Jason liked seeing Willis in pain.

Willis continued, "I want you to wear something to protect you during the game. I know you don't have one and true warriors exchange gifts before they go into battle."

Jason didn't understand, but he knew he wasn't going to like whatever was to come.

Willis went on. "Your gift to me will be that you wear it today." Jason's stomach burned as Willis handed him the Jack Daniels belt Willis had used to beat him. Jason did not reach for the evil gift. Willis would not tolerate Jason's hesitation. The evil one made up a new rule.

"You can't refuse a battle gift." Jason's heart raced as he stared at the belt. Willis still pounded Jason mentally.

"Put it on. Now!" Willis' eyes were serious and blazing. Jason felt his knees quiver. He couldn't move or speak. He had felt like that before. Jason hated that helpless feeling, but he knew it well. His shame was multiplied ten times as Willis gave an order to Mohawk.

"Put it on him. If he moves, beat hell out of him." Jason's mouth and throat went dry as the pimpled Mohawk took the belt from Willis and stepped toward him. Jason was too scared to do anything as the belt was buckled around him. His humiliation and shame almost brought tears to his eyes. He felt as if he had taken sixteen and "one to grow on" again. The pain inside was as great.

"Now, if you take it off during the game," Willis warned, "we're gonna relive your birthday ass-burnin'."

Jason could do nothing. His new strength had been drained away from him. He was ashamed. He hated Willis and the Mohawk. They had beaten him again. Jason looked at Eddie. His friend could not keep eye contact; he turned away. Jason felt so alone. He wished he had stayed at home with his mother. The game had not started, but Jason hated it more than he ever had before. He wanted to reach for the belt with his trembling hands, but it was only a thought. He dared not.

The two teams stood in silence. Willis looked at each of his opponents. He wanted to intimidate them one at a time. Ted was first.

"This won't be a 'sissy game' today, will it, Teddy Bear?" Willis had to humiliate. "We gotta make up for what happened last year; don't we, Teddy Bear?" Jason could see Ted was afraid too. He didn't say anything to Willis. Willis turned to James. Jason thought little James was going to cry. He turned white with fear and his eyes welled with tears as Willis continued.

"I hope you got more guts than big brother here. But, I can see y'all both are a little shaky." Wade was next, as Willis would leave no one out. "And your sister's got more balls than you do. She should be playin'. You should be home cookin'." Wade, like the others, could say nothing. Willis went back to Billy. "Let's you and me make a bet on the game, pretty boy. If you win, you can have Judy with no problem from me." Billy didn't respond to the offer. Willis still completed the second part of his deal.

"But, if I win, me and my team get to fuck your sister." With Willis' awful words, Billy came up off the steps with a killing rage in his eyes. No one used that word. Jason's hate for Willis was eating at his insides. Billy grabbed at Willis in his rage, but Willis pulled away. Mohawk and the other two stepped forward to protect their leader. Billy backed away from the sure beating. Willis stood behind his soldiers. Jason could feel the fire and hate in the air.

Jason knew the day would be hateful, but he had no idea what was to come. He knew that to be on guard was the order of the day. Willis was satisfied now. He seemed to bathe in the fear and hate around him. Jason thought as he looked in Willis' evil eyes, "If Willis was an oak baby, he must be from the bad side of the tree."

Jason knew there was a good side of the oak. "Why," he thought, "would the tree let an oak baby be so evil?" Willis' last words cut into Jason's thoughts.

"Y'all have fifteen minutes. Then the hunt begins." His words sent chills through his victims. All but Billy. He only stared as the hate burned in him. Ted Farley found the strength to speak.

"Let's get goin'." His team walked away from Willis and his army.

"Fifteen minutes ain't long." Willis had to give one last warning.

Ted was quiet. He gave no directions as they walked away. He seemed stunned. Billy took over the leadership role.

"We need to all go somewhere fast and decide on what we're gonna do. I don't want to lose this stupid game to that asshole. We can't just let him treat people like he does. Somebody's gotta put a stop to his meanness."

Jason liked Billy's thought, but he knew it would not be easy. Billy's strong words ignited a small flame in his gut. Willis had taken most of this fire. Billy had given him back a spark. For the first time since Jason had endured Willis that morning, he found words.

"Let's run to my house and we can talk about what to do. They won't come there first." They all agreed and ran to Jason's.

The five stood on Jason's porch. They were out of breath from the run. Billy had the first question. "How do you win this game, anyway?"

They all looked at Ted. Ted wasn't a great player, but he did know all the rules.

"The best way to win, in our place, is not to get captured at all. If we could stay free until the sun is gone, we would win without swinging at all. But, that's never been done. It ain't likely all five of us can hide all day and not get caught. It just ain't easy. People will tell if they see ya. It just ain't easy. Somebody always tells. Folks want ya to have to swing. It's the making of men."

Billy was beginning to dislike the game. "Then, why don't ya just go up there and get the swingin' done?"

"Cause that ain't the game. You must try to stay out of the clearing. The longer the members of your team stay free, the more clever your team is considered. Outsmarting your chaser is as important as swinging. If there were no injuries or bloodshed because we were too smart to get caught, the game would be thought a good one. Last year we had captures and swing downs, but no pain or blood. No game had ever had swingers come away with not even scratches from the briars. So, it was called the 'sissy game.' That's why Willis is going to see to it that we have a rough time today. He just can't take being part of that 'sissy game.' It ain't too likely we'll all keep from gettin' caught. They'll get one of us. So, sooner or later, we'll have to swing."

Billy wanted to be strong. "Let's make it later. Let's give 'em a run for their money. Let's stay free as long as we can. Maybe we'll be the first team to last the day with no one being taken to the clearing."

Billy's words again created a fire in Jason. Jason questioned his new friend. "Do we stay together or do we separate?"

Ted had an answer. "Five of us can't hide that good. It just won't work. But one or two can hide much easier."

"O.K.," Billy interrupted, "Ted, you and your brother stay together. Jason, you and Wade be partners. And I'll be hiding alone. I think I will do better alone." Billy was a good leader. James was glad he would be with his brother. James was scared and Ted was his only protection. Jason knew the fifteen minutes were up and the chasers were now searching for them.

"We need to hide. They'll be comin' quick." Jason's statement sent everyone running in different directions. Ted and James went in the direction of the docks. Jason and Wade went into the woods behind Jason's house. Billy ran toward his house.

He had promised Tinker he would tell her what was happening when the chase started. He would keep his promise. He knew Willis would not go to his house that soon.

Tinker was in the kitchen. She had gotten up early. She was excited about the strange game called Duckin'. Billy told her how awful Willis had been. He didn't tell her about the win or lose deal Willis wanted to make. Billy took his sister into his confidence.

"Tink, I want you to help me today."

She was excited by her brother's words and she would do anything to help. "How?" She was more than eager.

"I'm gonna hide in the top of that ol' lighthouse so I can see everything from up there."

She wrinkled her face. "Can you get up there?"

"I think so. What I want you to do is bring me a sandwich or something later. I'm gonna stay all day if I can. It's better if you don't get caught."

Tinker nodded. She was happy to be a part of her brother's excitement. Billy continued. "Just leave the stuff in that little shack next to the lighthouse and leave a note if you need to tell me something. Don't try to find me or talk to me. That could be trouble. Just leave the stuff." Tinker agreed as Billy ran out the door.

"Be careful." She gave a thoughtful warning.

Billy saw no chasers as he made his way to the lighthouse. He entered the door to the tower slowly. He was ready to run if he had to. He was alone. He climbed the shaky stairs to the top. He sat quietly at first beneath the rusty guard railing. He did not look down at the town yet. He hoped he was settled for the day. He relaxed and thought of Judy.

Ted and James were near their house. James broke the silence that had surrounded the two since they had left the others. "Ted, I'm scared. I don't want to play."

Ted looked at his brother's face. He loved his little brother. He understood his weakness. He wanted to help ease his brother's fear.

"I think I have an idea, but it's gonna be hard for you to do. It will keep you safe and you may not get captured."

James' eyes lit up at Ted's encouragement. "What is it?" he asked, with a spark of salvation in his voice.

"Come on." Ted took James home. He knew their father was shrimping and their mother had gone to her sister's for two days. Ted knew he, himself, would not hide in such a way, but he wanted James to be safe. He took James to their parents' bedroom.

"Here, you get in the closet. Lay down and don't move 'til I come get ya. Just sleep if you want to." James was happy to step into the safety of the closet. "Don't come out. If you have to pee, crawl on the floor to the bathroom and don't flush the toilet. And if you want to take a chance to eat, that's up to you, but don't make no noise. If they think you're in here, they'll come and get ya."

"What about you?" James was hoping Ted would stay in the house with him.

"I'm gonna be alone. Or maybe I'll find Jason and them. I can't hide like this."

James smiled and touched Ted's hand as he moved away. James was sensitive and he loved his brother. James heard the door lock as he laid down on the floor of the closet. James would be safe the entire day. He would not move from the closet. He would not be captured. He would not swing. His day of Duckin' ended as he fell asleep under a pile of sheets. Ted went to find the others. He felt good that James was safe.

Jason and Wade hid in the old closed down icehouse located on the edge of Nigger Town. They knew Willis would search there sometime during the day, but it would be easy to see them coming from the loft window. They would be able to escape through the back and change hiding places.

With his team settled in hiding, Ted was not able to find anyone to hide with. He was alone. He was nervous and unsure of himself. He had thought of going to the closet with James. He just had to play as a man would. He reached in his pocket and felt two dimes. He knew he could ride the ferry twice for twenty cents. He could get his thoughts together during the ride. He liked the idea. He took his ride.

Willis, Eddie and the National Guard were all hunting in a rage. Willis wanted to capture and start the swinging. They would stay together and hunt like a pack of wild dogs. It was their style.

Two hours passed and no captives were taken. The wild dogs had run through the docks and had searched all the boats remaining. They had been to Jason's house and to Wade's house. They would get to the others soon. Ted's house was next. James covered his face when he heard the chasers at the windows. He wanted to cry. He was shocked, but happy, when he heard the searchers moving away from the house. They were gone.

The sun was near the middle of the sky. Four hours had gone by. Still, Willis and his dogs were empty-handed. Ted had gotten off the ferry on the Fort George side of the river. He knew that was not part of the game, but a weakness had made him stay on that side. He sat on the bulkhead, looking back across the river at Mayport.

On the Mayport side, Willis was at his house. The pack of hounds waited outside. Willis walked out of the house with a pair of binoculars hanging around his neck and a police type nightstick hanging on his side.

He was frustrated with the hunt. He had an idea.

"I'm gonna look with these from on top of the lighthouse. I'll tell you where they are if I see 'em." The dogs agreed and followed the evil one to the lighthouse.

Billy heard them talking as they made their way toward his hiding place. He looked over the railing and saw the five chasers step into the small shack. He ducked down and listened to see if the door to the lighthouse opened. He didn't want to move and be heard, so he stayed low. He didn't see Tinker as she approached the little shack. She was keeping her promise to bring him food. Willis saw Tinker walking toward the small building. He made the dogs be quiet. Tinker stepped through the doorway.

She knew, as soon as she stepped into the shack, something was wrong. It was too late. A big hand covered her mouth and a strong arm around her waist squeezed the air from her body. She couldn't scream. Her mouth hurt. She was afraid.

The Mohawk had her under his control. Willis stepped to her and put his nose on hers. He whispered. "Where's big brother?" Tinker couldn't answer even if she wanted. Mohawk's hand would not allow her. Willis stuck his tongue out and touched her on the end of the nose. He smiled as he looked at her legs. She quivered. Willis liked that. Mohawk held her tighter. Willis whispered again.

"If big brother is up in the tower, he ain't goin' nowhere now. And if he was gonna meet you here, we'll just wait. Either way, he's mine." Willis gave her another smile and licked her nose again. "But first, girl, you're mine."

Tinker's heart had a pain shoot through it as she struggled to free herself. She only caused herself more pain as Mohawk squeezed her harder. Willis motioned for Mohawk to take her down. With one movement, Tinker was on the dirty floor. Mohawk's hand never took the pressure off her mouth. Tears came to her eyes. Willis liked it when a girl cried because of him. He loved to see the fear in her eyes.

Willis added to the fear he had created. "Now, ol' Roy here is gonna let your mouth go in just a second. But I'm gonna make a deal with ya. If you say one word or make any noise, we're gonna go up into that tower and throw big brother off the top of it. Do you understand me, girl?" Her tear-filled eyes said, "yes."

Billy still listened for the intruders. He heard nothing.

"Remember," Willis reminded her, "not one word." He put his finger to his lips. He nodded to the Mohawk. He released her. Willis stood over her. He reached down and pulled her shorts up at the waist. They unsnapped. She gave a small whimper, but Willis reminded her with his finger on his lips again. She looked up to see the pimpled one smiling down at her. She closed her eyes as she felt her shorts and panties move down her legs. She squeezed her eyes closed tight as Willis pulled her shirt up exposing her bare breasts to the dogs. She kept her eyes closed as she listened to Willis.

"If she makes one sound louder than a mouse, hit her in the head and go up there and see if big brother can fly."

Tinker's stomach burned and she thought she would die. She felt Willis touch her. His finger was in her. She moved her legs and opened her eyes. "Hold still, girl. This ain't gonna hurt. You'll probably thank me. You'll be wantin' to meet me out here all the time." She closed her eyes as she felt other hands hold her legs. She felt Willis again. He worked harder this time, adding to her discomfort.

"Oh, nice and tight. I like that." Tears ran down her cheeks. Willis licked them off. He reached up and squeezed one of her breasts. She could do nothing as she felt his wet mouth on her nipple. It didn't hurt, but she hated whose mouth was on her.

"You've played doctor before, haven't ya?" She opened her eyes as Willis fingered her again. Other hands held her legs open wider as Willis took his pants off above her. He had to talk to her.

"I don't know if I'll fit in this little thing you got, but you know what they say." Willis dropped to his knees. She tightened her legs when Willis worked his way into her body. It hurt. She made a noise but stopped when Mohawk reached for her mouth. She was quiet again. Willis was deep in her. She could not look at him as he moved over her. He pumped and pushed and made his own noises. There was pain inside her. There was pleasure too. She relaxed her legs. She didn't know why. She just did. She found that if she was not tense the pain was not so bad. Willis felt her muscles ease.

"That's it. I knew you'd like it." He pushed harder.

Eddie was in the corner of the shack. He wanted nothing to do with the evil deed. He did not have the courage or strength to stop it.

Tinker tightened her legs again, but relaxed when the pain shot through her. Willis reached up and squeezed her breast hard. It was painful. She reached for his hand. She couldn't move it. Willis gave one last hard push as his excitement ended. She wanted to close her legs but other hands still held them open. She knew her ordeal was not over. Willis made that clear.

"Batter up!" Willis motioned for the Mohawk to take his turn with their captive. The ugly one hurried to take his pants off. Willis moved from between her legs. The Mohawk took his place. She only looked at her second attacker once. She could not look again. Willis held her arms as Mohawk added to her pain. She tried to relax, but she couldn't. She wanted to throw up. Willis motioned for his other cousins to join in.

Tinker felt a wet mouth on both her breasts. She opened her eyes. She could only see the tops of the two boys' heads as they sucked her. There was less pain as the other two boys took their turn with her. Hands were grabbing and squeezing her as her rape continued. She was helpless and alone. The hands were gone. No one held her.

She rolled to her side and cried quietly. She held her legs together. She heard voices, but paid no attention to the words.

Willis had not offered Eddie a turn. Willis stood over Tinker. Her red and naked body shivered.

"Now, woman: You are a woman now, you know. I want you to tell big brother that we could have gone up there and kicked his ass, but we would rather meet him at the oak." Willis slowly dressed her as if she were a child. He whispered as he brushed the dirt off her legs.

"If you think about it, you ain't really hurt. In fact, you started to like it." He looked deep into her eyes and went on. "Like I said, you ain't hurt and if you want to stay that way, you better keep this little secret of ours. We ain't gonna tell on you, so you don't tell on us. Maybe we'll do it again sometime."

She looked away from Willis as he stepped to the door. He looked up at the tower.

"Hey, pretty boy!" Willis shouted. "Your sister's got nice tits."

Billy stood up and looked down from the railing of the lighthouse. He saw Willis.

"She's in here with the team." Willis pointed toward the shack.

Billy knew it could be a trick. He loved Tinker. He had to take the chance. If he was captured, he would have to deal with that when it occurred. He hurried down the steps of the tower. When he pushed through the door to the outside, he was prepared for battle. Willis was gone. Billy looked around. He saw no one. He looked toward the small shack. He stepped to the door slowly. He saw his sister. His heart fell. He knew she had endured something awful at the hands of Willis. Her attackers were gone. She ran to her brother's arms. She cried out loud for the first time. She hugged him as if she would never let go.

"Did Willis. . . ." He couldn't say it.

She buried her head against his strong chest. She found a strength.

"They all did it to me." Billy's heart fell deeper in pain. He wished she hadn't said that. He didn't want to hear anymore, but she had to tell him.

"They held me down," she said slowly. "I couldn't move. They told me if I yelled, they would throw you from the tower." She started to cry again.

Billy would hold his rage and revenge until he and his sister were home. They walked away from the shack. Willis and his dogs watched from the sand hill. He used his binoculars to scan for the other runners. He moved his head slowly through the town. He saw the back of the old icehouse and he could see Nigger Town.

"We need to check the icehouse." He continued to search. Then he saw a welcome sight. The glasses magnified the image of Ted Farley walking off the ferry.

"Well, that son of a bitch." Willis said out loud. "He's been on the other side all morning. What a chickenshit." Willis knew their captive would be in the clearing within the hour. He prepared his troops. He wanted to be sure when Ted made his run, there would be no escape.

Ted had been on the other side of the river for most of the playing time, so far. He began to feel guilty about hiding that way. He had already been a player in the game where no men were made and he was acting the same way again. He knew he needed to face his fears. He knew he would have to teach his brother James to do the same, but how would he be able to teach James to be a man if he was not one himself? He stepped off the ferry hoping to find Jason and the others. He walked down the main street past Mr. Leek's dock and Strickland's. He saw Billy walking with Tinker. He knew something was wrong. They did not know that Willis and his pack of dogs watched them from across the street. Ted walked up to Billy and Tinker.

"What happened?" He knew there was a problem. Billy didn't want to say much about it.

"Willis scared her and I'm takin' her home. Then I'm gonna go after him. I don't give a shit who is supposed to chase who."

Ted said nothing after Billy's strong words. Billy and Tinker walked away.

Now, the old icehouse was giving Jason and Wade problems. It seemed that many stray cats had taken up residence in the abandoned building. The fleas were driving the two hiders crazy. They had taken all they could. They decided to take the chance and find another place of safety. They left the fleas and headed back towards Jason's house.

James crawled out of his safe closet only once during the day. He lay asleep on the floor again. The others had forgotten he was playing. He would take no pain; he was safe.

Ted would not go home for fear they would catch him there and get James, too. Ted decided to walk to Mr. Johnson's store for a cold drink. He needed to face the fear he knew was in him. Willis watched Ted as he made his way down the narrow path to the store. Ted walked into the front of the store, ordered his drink and thought he would sit out on the front steps and enjoy his newfound courage. He pushed the screen door open and stepped outside. His heart stopped. All five chasers sat on the steps. Willis stood to greet the captive. "Well, Teddy Bear. Have you lost your mind, boy?" Willis took his drink.

"First, we're gonna kick your ass because you are such a chickenshit. And then, we're gonna kick your ass because you were stupid enough to walk in here like it don't matter about us." Ted didn't think he would be that scared if they caught him. He was. He wished he hadn't been so foolish. Willis continued.

"Now, I know you ain't got the guts to try to run. So, why don't we all just walk back to the clearing? Then we'll see if any of those other chickenshits will try to free ya." Ted walked with his enemies as they passed his cold drink around to quench their thirst.

Jason and Wade watched them from the sand hill. Jason whispered to Wade. "Ted's not trying to get away. Willis must have really said something to scare him." Jason's heart pounded when he thought about swinging down into the den of wild dogs.

Willis and his group were about one hundred yards from the opening to the clearing. Willis stopped the parade. "Ted, my boy. This year ol' Willis here is gonna make a man out of you." Ted looked at Willis. They were eye-to-eye. Jason watched and remembered how he had felt when he stood that close to Willis. Jason couldn't hear what Willis was saying, but he knew it wasn't going to be good for his friend, Ted.

Then, like lightning, Willis struck. He hit Ted in the mouth, knocking his unsuspecting victim to the ground. Jason and Wade couldn't believe the sight below them. Willis continued his verbal assault, as well.

"We're gonna beat the chickenshit out of you and you can walk with your head up." The Mohawk stood Ted back up. His lip was cut; there was blood. The Mohawk was next. He knocked Ted down with a lick under his eye. Ted lay on the ground for only a few seconds, as the Mohawk made him stand again. Willis was close to his face again.

"Anybody we catch will take the same punishment. You have to get through all five. You'll either be a man or you'll be dead." Ted took a third hit from Sammy, one of the cousins. His nose bled after that one. He lay face down. Mohawk jerked him up again. Willis called off the beating.

"Let's stop for now and get him to the clearing." Willis and his cousin Sammy, tied Ted's legs together. They carried Ted down the narrow path into the clearing and dropped him to the ground. Ted lay there like a dead fish. He didn't move. He was too scared and he wanted no more pain.

Jason watched Willis as he gathered his troops around him. Again, Jason couldn't hear what was being said. He knew Willis was giving orders.

"Don't look up, but two of our little chickenshits are on the sand hill. Roy, you and Luther go under the grape arbor and be sure they don't get away on the other side. If they are too scared to swing down, we'll draw blood when we bring 'em back to the clearing." Roy and Luther hurried to position themselves. Fear struck Wade and Jason when they heard Willis yell.

"Can we get one of you chickens to swing down and save ol' Ted here from his ass-whippin'?" Wade couldn't stand it. He left Jason and ran down the sand-filled side of the hill. He fell twice in the soft sand, but finally made it to the bottom. He was going home. He would not play.

Jason stood and made himself visible to Willis. He didn't know why, he just did. Ted still was not moving. A cool breeze moved Jason's hair.

"Untie Ted," Jason yelled down to Willis. "How can he run after I tag him free?"

Willis smiled and reached down to take the rope from Ted's legs. He held the rope up so Jason could see it.

"There ya go, Jay Bird. But, you and I both know you ain't man enough to swing down here." Willis heard a noise behind him. He turned to see Roy and Luther dragging Wade into the clearing. Both his eyes were swollen shut from the beating they had given him. Willis was pleased.

"Boys, boys. Y'all just went crazy here. Why have you done this thing to this shithead?"

Luther answered the question. "He tried to outrun us."

Willis smiled again. "Can't nobody outrun Roy." They all laughed. Wade lay about five feet away from Ted. Jason still stood above the clearing watching the horror below. Willis continued.

"If you don't swing down here and take your medicine like a

man, we're gonna kick the shit out of these two assholes down here and then we're gonna come up there and get you." Jason knew there was no game to play. It was a fight and Willis was going to make sure people got hurt. He would then blame the game.

Willis turned to Eddie. "Go up there and bring his ass back down here. He ain't swingin'." Eddie looked up at his friend Jason. Willis spoke again. "Can ya do it alone or do ya wanna take Roy with ya?" Eddie shook his head and began his climb toward the oak. Jason watched Eddie make his way closer. Jason would not run. He was there to stay until he made his decision on what to do about Willis. Jason talked first as his friend stepped near.

"Hey there, buddy." Jason smiled. Eddie nodded.

"This ain't funny no more, is it?" Eddie looked at his friend. He was sad and ashamed.

"Willis has gone crazy. He's gonna hurt 'em if you don't go down." Jason took a deep breath. "Willis has always been crazy and he's gonna hurt 'em if I go down or not. But, I'm goin' and I'm gonna fight him until I can't fight no more." Eddie was shocked and wide-eyed at Jason's statement. He was even more surprised at his own.

"I'll go with ya. Maybe we can stop him together. We gotta get Ted and Wade out of there." Eddie looked down at Willis. "He did Tinker bad." Jason looked at Eddie. He could see it hurt Eddie to say that. He knew Willis had done something awful. He hated him more. Eddie was ashamed of what he had stood and watched. He wanted to pay for his sin. He stepped past Jason and climbed up into the oak. He stood on the big limb with the ropes for the clearing. He looked down. Willis stood between his two captives. The others stood half hidden in the palmetto fans. Eddie knew they were there. Willis was puzzled by Eddie's action above him.

"What ya doin' up there, Freckles?" Willis knew Eddie had changed his loyalty. "You ain't taken Jay Bird's turn to swing down, are ya?"

Eddie's hands shook as he held the rope out in front of him. He didn't know why he was facing Willis. He thought about climbing back down and running. He didn't know what was keeping him on the limb. He knew he would soon swing. Willis felt it, too. "I can't believe it, but I think ol' Freckles is gonna swing." Willis turned toward the palmetto fans.

"Luther, you take him off the swing as he goes through the tunnel." Willis planned to let Eddie swing past him and as he was carried into the green palmetto fan tunnel, Luther would knock him off his swing. Luther made himself ready as he stepped deeper into the fans. Willis would scare Eddie and Jason again.

"Roy," Willis called to Mohawk. Roy stepped from the fans and stood next to Willis. Willis whispered something to the ugly one. Jason's hate grew as he watched the Mohawk turn and kick Wade in the top of the head. Jason looked away as the pimple-faced Indian did the same to Ted. Ted yelled in pain. Wade had made no noise. Willis made another evil deal.

"If I have to ask you to swing down, and you don't, ol' Roy here's gonna keep kickin'." Jason looked at his friend standing above him. Eddie looked at Willis, then at Jason. Eddie smiled and reached in his pocket.

"I'm gonna surprise Willis," he said in a low voice. He pulled a small pocketknife from his pocket. It had a three-inch blade. Jason didn't know how to react to the small weapon. Eddie had one last comment as he put the knife in his mouth, holding the blade with his teeth.

"I've always wanted to do this." His teeth were tight around the small steel blade. He looked to Jason like a pirate preparing to swing to an enemy ship. Eddie jumped on the knot of the rope and the swing down began. Eddie dropped quickly as he took the knife from his mouth. Willis stepped to the side as he had planned. He saw the knife as Eddie tried to stick him as he moved past. Willis pulled his nightstick from his side and prepared for Eddie on his return swing. Eddie's momentum took him into the fan tunnel where Luther jumped from the fans to knock Eddie from his swing, as Willis had ordered. As the two collided, the knife in Eddie's hand sunk deep into Luther's shoulder. Luther screamed in pain as they both fell to the ground. The power of the impact had driven the blade and half the handle deep into Luther's body. He rolled in a fit of pain out of the tunnel of fans. Willis was stunned for a few seconds, watching his cousin on the ground. Luther rolled until the briars stopped his movement. He lay quietly in shock. Eddie was shaken from his fall, but was not injured. He was hidden by the fans. He had to do something quick.

Eddie knew his swing down was a mistake. He was afraid of the punishment Willis had in store for his moment of stupidity. He just wanted to go home. Jason watched in shock as Eddie came running from behind the fans. He was trying to make it to the path out of the clearing. Willis was quicker with his stick. The sound of the heavy nightstick meeting with Eddie's forehead echoed from the clearing. Eddie dropped to his knees. Jason could see the gash the stick had opened on Eddie's head. The second swing of the stick drove Eddie's face down in the sand. He made no noise. There was no movement. Jason's stomach burned as a hot liquid filled his throat. He found himself climbing into the oak. He didn't want to. He felt as if the branches had reached down and picked him up. He stood on the rope-filled limb. Willis, Roy and Sammy stood below among the four fallen bodies. Jason could see the rage in Willis' eyes as they stared at each other.

In a hopeful moment of fear, Wade crawled away from his jailers and tried to make his way out of the clearing. In his frightened and hurt condition, he ran wildly into the briars and pricklies. He fell as the briars scratched and wrapped around him. Willis sent no chaser. He could see his victim would not be able to break free of the thorns. Jason could hear Wade cry as he stopped struggling to free himself. It was a cry of despair. Jason didn't want to swing down, but, like Eddie, he knew he would soon. Jason's thoughts were interrupted by Willis' evil voice.

"Hey, Jay Bird, this sure ain't no 'pussy game,' is it?" Willis' torment was deep. He turned to talk to his remaining jackal cousins.

As they talked, Jason saw movement to his left. His eyes fell on a sight that brought a chill over his body. His heart pounded like a wild drum. Billy stood on another large limb, holding a swing rope in one hand and an object of some kind in his other hand. A cool breeze touched Jason's face as Billy jumped on the knot of the rope he held. Willis turned to talk to Jason. Billy's swing had carried him like a quiet hawk through the air. Willis dropped to the ground. Billy swung the object in his hand as the rope lifted him upward again. Jason's eyes widened as the back of the Mohawk's head cracked open like a dropped watermelon. The sound was horrible. Billy's swing sunk the object deep into Roy's skull. Blood went everywhere. Jason could see a look of shock, pain and horror on the Mohawk's face as he crumbled to the ground. He did not move or make any noise. He was down to stay. Willis stood with the nightstick held high, as he waited for the rope to carry Billy back to him. Billy prepared his weapon as the rope returned him. Jason could see it now. Billy held a metal pipe in his hand. Sammy jumped from the palmetto fans as Billy swung the pipe again. The weapon hit Sammy across the nose. As Sammy fell, Willis swung his nightstick like a baseball bat. It struck Billy on the ear. He fell from the swing. Jason scanned the battleground as the war raged below him. Billy crawled on the ground, trying to avoid another blow. Willis drove the wooden stick across Billy's back. Willis began to swing his stick wildly. He hit Ted again, then Eddie, then back to Ted. Billy took another blow. He swung the weapon into the air, then back down at his victims.

Jason had no idea why, but he left the safety of the tree. He didn't remember reaching for it, but a rope was in his hand. He jumped onto the knot and started down. Willis and the clearing looked miles away. Willis turned to see him coming. Jason could see the evil and the rage in Willis' eyes as he drew near. Jason tucked his head down into his shoulder as Willis swung once more. Jason felt pain when the stick glanced off his arm and the top of his head. Fear kept Jason on the swing. He held onto the rope as it returned to the evil one. Willis jumped on Jason and grabbed him around the neck, pulling him to the ground. The stick was gone. Willis had lost it when he had hit Jason. It lay in the sand. Willis had the advantage position on top. Jason felt buried alive in the sand. Willis began swinging his arms, hitting Jason. Jason returned no punishment. He was only concerned with his escape. He was afraid. He knew he could outrun the wild one; if he could only free himself for a moment, his fear would do the rest. As they struggled, Jason's hand felt Billy's pipe in the sand. It was firm in his hand. He hit Willis twice up around his arms and shoulders. Willis continued his rage. He grabbed the pipe. They both held the steel club. Willis was too strong; the pipe was his. He swung. The pipe hit Jason on the side of his neck. With one push and a cry of pain and fear, Jason was on his feet, standing eye-to-eye with Willis. Willis lunged toward Jason. Again, there was no weapon. Willis had lost the pipe when Jason pushed him away. Jason moved to avoid his attacker. He fell into the prickly bushes, scratching his face and arms. Willis punched at Jason's head and face, using his fist for the first time since the battle began. Jason's mouth was cut on the inside. He bit his tongue. He felt great pain. He thought he would die. Willis cried as he continued to strike Jason.

"This ain't no sissy game," Willis yelled. His father's words haunted them both.

Jason rolled away from Willis and crawled over Eddie's body. He got to his feet. He wanted to run. He heard Willis.

"Come on, Jay Bird. Be a man." Willis reached for Jason. He hesitated and stumbled. Jason looked down and saw Eddie holding onto Willis' leg. Willis kicked Eddie, but he held tight. Jason saw the pipe in the sand. Willis kicked Eddie again. Eddie could endure no more. He released his grip.

Jason grabbed the weapon he had held once before. Willis turned from Eddie to engage Jason. Jason didn't look at Willis as he swung the pipe. He could feel the steel sink deep into Willis' skin. The pipe hit Willis under one eye, high on the cheekbone. Willis fell toward Jason. Jason was surprised and afraid as Willis' face came close to him. Jason swung once more. Again the pipe sunk deep. This time the damage was to Willis' ear and the side of his head. Willis fell to his knees in the sand. Shock and pain covered his face.

Jason had seen that look before. He thought of Charlie Klim, as Willis fell forward, face down in the sand. Like the other victims, Willis didn't move. Jason looked at the bodies in the clearing. It was a battlefield.

Jason sat in the sand. He thought it was one of his dreams. He had a quivering sensation around the outside of his eyes. His head hurt and his shoulder was sore. He could feel sand in his mouth, gritting against his teeth. There was a scratch on his arm and there was blood. He was sick to his stomach and a hot liquid filled his throat. He opened and closed his hand, feeling the white sand beneath him. He looked down. The white sand brought him back to the reality of the game. Jason knew it was not a dream at all. It had happened and he had been part of it. That thought made him even sicker. He had been so happy to be sixteen. Again, he wished it all to be a dream. The sights around him told the truth: it was real.

Jason covered his eyes with his sand-coated hands, trying to clear his confused thoughts. He had heard many stories about the game, but now he knew that all the stories of the past would have no meaning. He had truly played in the meanest and most evil game of all. When folks in Mayport talked of the game in the future, they would only speak of that day, the day Jason played.

"They will never play the game again," he thought. "Not after what happened today." His thoughts were interrupted by the presence of others moving near him. He could hear voices, but could not focus his eyes on faces. He didn't want to see faces. Once again, he closed his eyes, hoping it all to be a dream.

"What will happen now?" he thought. "What punishment will there be? I wish my mama was here. She didn't want me to play. Uncle Bobby played twice."

"It'll make a man of ya," his uncle had said.

Jason knew there would be no funny stories about the day he played. People would remember that day, but tears would flow in place of laughter.

Jason's thoughts were again interrupted by movement around him. He could see two men carry his friend Eddie down the other side of the hill. Eddie wasn't moving. Blood and white sand covered his arm and face. He was missing one shoe. His foot was dirty. Jason's stomach and throat burned; his mouth was cut on the inside.

He saw blood in the sand. Again, his stomach burned. Jason's eyes found Eddie's shoe. It was almost covered with the white powder.

Jason hated Willis. He wondered if Willis' father would be satisfied with the game this time.

Jason thought of how everything had gotten out of hand. He knew he would be punished. His thoughts were again shaken by passing voices. He looked up and saw the men returning without Eddie. He lay back in the sand. "Why do they call it Duckin'? I wish my mama was here." Willis' face flashed in Jason's head. Then he thought of Charlie Klim. He could see the pain on Charlie's face. Jason's body quivered. He shook Charlie Klim from his head.

"Jason! Jason! You alright, boy?" Jason looked up. Uncle Bobby stood over him. He closed his eyes with one more desperate hope that he was waking from a dream. He tried to feel his bed under him. The sand was still there.

"Are ya hurt, boy?" Uncle Bobby's voice cut into Jason's confusion. He had no answer. His stomach burned and he could feel the sand grit against his teeth. He was moving. Arms held him. He was being carried from the hill like the others. He wanted to speak, but no words came. The ferry horn blew. He thought of his victory. He heard voices, and arms still held him, but he felt he stood alone. He liked that. He was cold. Water touched his face. A cool breeze moved his hair. He had felt that breeze before. He heard the cries of the oak babies from his dream. Jason opened his eyes. The tree towered above. The ropes moved. Arms held him, but he was still cold. An engine started and Jason could see he was in the back of a truck. Arms held him tight. Billy lay next to him. There was blood again.

"I like Billy." Jason looked up at the oak as the truck moved away. He saw Jessie near the great tree. A breeze moved her hair with the ropes. He smelled his hand and thought of Jessie and the game.

He remembered Jessie's words of "The Breeding." He knew the tree would be satisfied with the game.

"I wish I was an oak baby," he thought.

"I hate Willis. I love Tom Green. I'm gonna keep this belt. I wish I had some peanuts. Why do they call it Duckin'?"

THE LUNCH ROCK

PRELUDE

JASON SAT ON A PYLON NEAR THE FERRY SLIP AS HE HAD DONE HUNDREDS of times before. He liked being alone with his thoughts while he watched the big claw fiddler crabs run in and out of their small holes, near the bulkhead. His mind was filled with visions of his new job. How he loved the thought of being a working man. He would start in two days and he was filled with anticipation, waiting for his first day on the job. Jason loved to work; he always had. His desire to be a working man was part of him.

The horn on the ferry blasted, as the Buccaneer left the Fort George side of the St. Johns River and headed toward Mayport. The sound of the horn ignited thoughts from his past in Jason's head. He was quick to shake free of the unwanted memories. Jason had become an expert at changing the direction of his memories and moving them deeper into the darkness of his subconscious. He didn't want to look in the direction of the great oak tree, but he knew he would. He always did. He couldn't help it.

A cool breeze touched his face and moved his hair. He knew the feeling well. He tried not to like it, but again he did. Jason had not stood near the tree in almost five years. Not since the final game, Jason's game. He could have gone there, but he had just chosen not to go. There was no reason to go there for the ones who knew and fear kept the others away.

Jason was a true mental wonder. No one knew it or cared, but he was a survivor, created from his battles with evil, ignorance and superstitions. His struggles and ability to survive made him more than different; he was special. To be simple, yet unique, is rare. Jason was both. He had lost loved ones and friends as a child and even more as a teenager. What manhood would bring to his broken world was yet to be seen.

Jason had faced death and he knew evil before it was his time to do so. In spite of his eye-to-eye moments with the darker side of man, a heart full of goodness, beating in his chest, set him apart and sustained him. His experience made him strong, but there are limits to one's humanity and sanity.

He loved to see that floating carrier make its way across that hard-running, north-flowing, St. Johns River. Jason knew he would be working on that river in two days. Jason felt flashes from the past enter his head. He slapped them away and focused on the big boat as it entered the wooden slip and bounced from side to side until it came to a stop and the workers secured it to the Mayport side of the river.

Jason turned toward the road and watched the cars as they moved off the boat and onto solid ground. In a brief moment the ferry was empty of its moving cargo and a new cargo of cars was moving onto the metal grated deck for a ride in the other direction, back to the Fort George side of the river. Jason loved that river.

As Jason admired the workers on the boat, he thought again of his new job and how happy he was to have the opportunity to be a working man. His pleasant thoughts were interrupted by the familiar sound of the peanut call near the ferry slip.

"Peanuts! Peanuts, boiled and roasted!" Jason loved many things, but nothing more than the sound touching his ears at that moment. He turned to add a vision to the sound and recognized the young black boy, selling his peanuts to the people in the cars as they waited their turn to drive onto the ferry. Jason didn't know his name, but he had seen the young boy heading shrimp on the docks. Even though he was only selling peanuts, Jason still admired the boy for working. He knew the boy would work all day.

No matter how hard Jason fought back the memory flashes, the sight of the peanut boy opened the floodgates of the past and Jason gave in and took a moment to remember his friend, Tom Green, the real "peanut man." As long as peanuts were sold at the ferry slip, Jason would remember Tom Green. He really loved that old black man.

The sight of Tom Green's face, covered with blood and white beach sand, appeared in Jason's head. He had to end his memory flash, so he turned away from the cars, ferry and tree. The only memories Jason allowed to linger in his torn mind were thoughts of Jessie, the green-eyed black girl. He would always welcome thoughts of her. He missed her and her "life lessons." He had not seen her since that day of the final game. He often thought Jessie and her lessons were all just one of his dreams. His thoughts were often broken and incomplete. There was never an even flow in his head. Jason's walk home was fast and memory free. It was his choice.

CHAPTER ONE

JASON STOOD AT THE STEPS TO THE PORCH OF HIS HOUSE. HE KNEW HIS Uncle Bobby was home because he could hear Elvis singing from the speaker of the record player. Uncle Bobby did love his rock 'n roll, especially Elvis. Most folks in Mayport thought Bobby looked like Elvis. Jason just thought his uncle was funny when he moved his upper lip and sang along with the records. His likeness to Elvis had become Bobby's trademark. He worked at looking like the "King." Everybody needs a trademark, something that sets them apart from others.

Jason loved his Uncle Bobby. He was second only to Jason's mother, Mary C. He struggled with his mother's trademark and was sad and angry with her poor relationships with men. She was good to Jason, but he just wanted her to be good. He was still standing at the steps, lost in his thoughts, when he was interrupted by a voice he loved.

"You gonna stand there all day, boy?"

Jason looked up to see his mother standing on the porch above him. To Jason, there was no more beautiful sight on earth than his mother. She was forty-one years old but her tanned muscular body gave her the look of a much younger woman. Her hair was still raven black, with no gray at all. It was true, she was beautiful and the aging process had not hurt her yet. Some people are lucky that way.

"Sorry, Mama." Jason had a dazed look as he came back to the reality of the porch.

Mary C. had seen that look in Jason's eyes many times before. "You gotta stop driftin' off like that, boy. People gonna think you still ain't right." His mother was concerned, but Jason didn't like what she said.

"I'm fine. I was just thinkin' 'bout stuff."

"You'll be workin' soon and maybe you won't have so much time for thinkin'. Sometimes thinkin' ain't that good for ya." Mary C. had no wisdom in her "gems of wisdom." She walked back into the house. Jason followed her.

As Jason entered the house, the sound of another voice he loved touched his ears.

"Now that's what I call motherly advice. Just don't think too much, it ain't good for ya."

Mary C. didn't hear Bobby's sarcasm.

"Where you been, boy? You been havin' breakfast with one of those young girls around town?"

Jason smiled at his uncle's questions and shook his head "no."

Mary C. joined the conversation. "It ain't that early, Bobby. You just slept late. It's almost lunchtime." Jason made his way to the kitchen table as the others talked. He didn't pay any attention to their words. He was a master at not paying attention. It was a needed skill from time to time. They continued, but Jason didn't hear them.

"Bobby, do you really think this job is a good idea for Jason? He still ain't right to me."

"Yes, I do. He needs something like this. It's time for him to grow and move on. It's been long enough. He really seems better to me. This could be the answer."

Mary C. stared at her brother. She had taken his advice before and awful things had happened. She wanted to remind him of the past, but she didn't.

Mary C. knew Bobby loved Jason and wanted his mental wounds to heal. They both wanted him to be normal. She still had concerns. "He drifts away so much. What if he gets hurt, or gets somebody else hurt because of one of his confused moments?"

Bobby was concerned too, but he felt the responsibility of the job would be just what Jason needed to proceed into manhood. "He's twenty-one now and he needs to move on. He needs to make new memories, if there is such a thing."

Mary C. had made her share of mistakes with her life and Jason's. She wanted to do the right thing, but she just never seemed to. "He seems so strong and normal at times and then so fragile and strange other times." Mary C. looked toward the kitchen, where Jason sat. It was easy for her to see Jason was in his world of deep thoughts. She knew "the look." Bobby knew it too.

It took almost a full year before Jason talked to anyone after that day of the final game. He just woke up one morning and asked for french toast, as if he had been talking all along. The doctor said it was a type of self-inflicted amnesia and his mind found its way back that morning when he smelled the french toast cooking. The year of silence had taken its toll on Jason and his two caretakers. He was not the same as he was before the game. Nobody was the same.

Jason's appearance had also changed. He really had matured physically and the look of a handsome man had replaced the child-like features of a boy. He had the strong facial features of his mother and was naturally muscular. His look was totally the opposite of what folks had expected from the weak skinny boy he had been. If you had not lived with him from day to day, you would not rec-ognize him as being the same little boy he was five years ago. The change in his appearance was nothing short of remarkable. If any of the believers or the old-timers saw Jason they would mark him as a true oak baby. He had the look. Few folks talked about the oak babies anymore.

Jason sat at the table with Jessie's green-eyes burning a hole in his heart. He remembered touching her and the noises she made. He watched the water from the hose run down her naked body. He saw her rippled stomach muscles and her rock-hard breasts. She was naked as she straddled a limb of the tree. It was hard for Jason to see where Jessie began and the limb of the tree ended. She was like one with the tree, yet separate. He had mixed feelings about being rescued from his moment with Jessie.

Mary C. and Uncle Bobby stood next to him at the table. Uncle Bobby brought him back to the reality of the kitchen table.

"I saw one of those big barges go by yesterday, on its way to the end of the jetties." Uncle Bobby gave Jason a pleasant thought as he entered the reality of the kitchen. "It was huge and had all kinds of equipment on it."

Jason visualized the barge moving on the river. He liked what he saw. "I was hopin' to see one this mornin', but I didn't. Just the ferry."

Uncle Bobby was glad Jason joined the conversation. "Well, you'll be able to see all you want soon enough. Hell, you'll probably be on that barge, come Monday mornin'."

Jason smiled at Uncle Bobby's comment. He knew he was going to like working on that barge. Mary C. wanted to be part of the conversation. "What are they gonna do out there, anyway?"

Bobby knew the answer. "They're gonna make the channel at the mouth of the river longer by extending the jetty rocks another hundred yards on the south side. Somethin' to do with making the big ships go farther out before they turn south. It will also help control the amount of trash that washes up onto the beach near the rocks. It will take about a year to finish the job because it's so deep. They'll need alot of those big rocks."

Mary C. had all the information she wanted. She had no more questions. She started lunch. Uncle Bobby walked out onto the front porch and Jason drifted away, looking for Jessie. Jason didn't eat any lunch, or he didn't think he did.

The day was gone; he didn't know where it went. That happened to him quite often. He heard the ferry horn blast in the distance. It was one of his favorite sounds. Jason knew Uncle Bobby's "jukin'" ritual had begun when the sound of Elvis and the smell of Old Spice filled the house. Saturday night was Bobby's big night out and only a death in the family could possibly change that fact. And maybe not even that.

Mary C. used Saturday night too, but any night could be special for her. They both loved Jason, but he was not always a priority, especially now that he was older. Jason liked to hear Uncle Bobby's stories about his wild Saturday nights. He knew he would be left alone. He liked it sometimes.

Jason lay back on his pillow and stared at the ceiling over his bed. The Old Spice had faded and Elvis was silent. He heard his mother say, good-bye, as she left, but he didn't see her. Jason didn't like the way she dressed when she went out at night. Mary C. had not learned from the bad experiences she had from time to time. Jason wanted her to be more careful. Actually, he wanted her to stay home, but he never told her.

Jason knew that if he closed his eyes, he would sleep. If he slept, he would dream. If he could choose his dream, he would close his eyes willingly. He knew it didn't work that way. It would be a serious gamble and he was afraid. He wanted thoughts of Jessie to create the dream state he desired. The need to be with her would be worth the chance. He closed his eyes and invited sleep.

Mary C. walked into the Fish Bowl and stood in the doorway. She looked great, as usual, and even though she was a regular on Saturday nights, all eyes greeted her. She wore a black silk blouse tucked into a leopard print short skirt. The blouse hugged her upper body, making the position of her nipples easy to find. The hem of the skirt touched her upper thigh muscles and a pair of leopard print three-inch high heel shoes made her calf muscles bulge, with each step as she made her way across the room. She was easy to look at. The men loved her, the woman hated her, but they all looked.

Mary C. liked the locals who came there. And she really liked the sailors from the Mayport Naval Base who would buy her drinks at the bar. She enjoyed the atmosphere at the Fish Bowl. Bobby said it was dull and too tame. Mary C. thought it had class. She was tired of the honky tonk atmosphere, with the noise and the fights. She wanted to have class.

The Fish Bowl was a restaurant with a bar area and small dance floor. There were no pinball machines and no quarter-eating jukebox.

If you wanted to dance, it would be to the mellow sounds of the orchestra music coming from the ceiling speakers. The building was located in East Mayport, only about a hundred yards from the gate of the Naval Base. The sailors could walk over for drinks and good food. The bar was full of young sailors. Mary C. knew she would be able to drink her fill of Jack Daniels and not spend a dime of her money. She moved directly to the bar.

It became a treat for James, the bartender, to watch Mary C. make her entrance and walk to the bar. It was always one of the highlights of the night. James was only a few years older than Jason. He had been crazy about Mary C. since he was twelve years old and played with Jason in their yard. He remembered when he cut his bare foot and Mary C. tended to his wound. He always remembered the way she smelled when she was near him.

It was on a hot summer day and Mary C. was wearing a two-piece bathing suit as she doctored his cut. There wasn't much of her body he hadn't seen and now, at twenty-four, James wanted to see the rest of her. She reached the bar.

"Hey, James, how are ya?"

"I'm good, Miss Mary C. I'm always good when you come in."

She was used to James's comments and how he flirted with her. She didn't mind. The key for Mary C. was the attention, and it really didn't matter where it came from.

"Ya wanna drink now, or you gonna eat something first?"

"Just a little easy one for now."

"One easy Jack Black, comin' up." James began mixing her request.

"Bar boy, put that easy Jack on my tab."

James had heard that request before and turned toward a huge young sailor sitting a few bar stools away from where Mary C. stood. James didn't care much for the "bar boy" comment, but he would definitely charge him for Mary C.'s first drink. She nodded to the big man in appreciation, as another young one, not quite as big as the other, gave up his stool so she could sit down. James had seen this reaction to Mary C. many times. It was a given. She was something else and James was glad she was there.

Bobby walked up the steps to Bill's Hideaway, the honky tonk of honky tonks. It was his favorite place. It was located on the beach about one hundred yards off the Atlantic Ocean. The building was supported by huge stilt pylons in case the tide rose that far during a hard northeaster. The jetties, at the mouth of the St. Johns River, protected the building on the north side. You could stand on the huge red rocks and see the Atlantic Ocean on your right, then turn to your left and watch the ships and boats leave and enter the St. Johns River. It was a unique place to have a real honky tonk bar.

As usual, Bobby was greeted by the wild group of regulars when he walked in through the western-type swinging doors. He needed the attention, too. Even if you didn't know Bobby, you would have to give him a second look. He really did look like Elvis. His hair, sideburns, upper lip and clothes could have all belonged to Elvis. It was a common thing for his friends, and only a stranger would consider it odd. He was too good of a man not to like. In fact, he was easy to like. He was funny, manly and talented. He had to be handsome; he looked like Elvis.

Bobby returned all the greetings with smiles, waves and his usual "How y'all doin'?", as he made his way to the jukebox. If he was looking for a woman, the song would be slow for the dirty dancing he needed. If he was ready to drink, dance and be loud, the first song of the night would be a rock 'n roll fast song. As he scanned the musical selections he noticed two familiar female friends staring at him from a dimly-lit corner of the room.

Peggy and Betty were both crazy about Bobby and had been that way since grade school. They had always been best friends and the few arguments they had during their many years together were about Bobby. He had dated, bedded and left them both. He really tried to stay clear of them because he caused such a strain on their relationship. From time to time they had fulfilled his needs. Some folks thought they were queer for each other, but Bobby only knew they both screwed his brains out when he would give one or the other the opportunity. Elvis's "Teddy Bear" blasted from the speakers of the jukebox. Everybody in the room moved to the music and sang along with Bobby. Peggy and Betty loved him.

Jason's dreams had taken him back to the oak tree, the place he didn't want to be. He walked around the huge trunk, as he had done before. He felt strong and afraid at the same time. He looked up to see if the swing ropes were still hanging from the limbs. He heard the muffled cry of a baby coming from under the white sand beneath his feet. He sat up in the bed to break the hold of the dream. He didn't want to see Jessie if it was at the tree.

Mary C. had finished her one easy Jack Black, plus three hard ones. She felt great as she bathed in the Jack and the attention from the big sailor. He was feeling good, too, because when the Jack Black took her, Mary C. became a "toucher" and it drove men crazy. She touched whoever she was talking to and usually didn't mean it as an invitation, but any man would have taken it as the "green light." It was seldom that her interest was on the same level as the individual she was talking to. It was just her way, but it did cause her problems now and then, especially with strangers.

The old Mary C. "MoJo" had "big boy" by the throat, and he was in love for the moment. James watched her work her magic and wished she was casting her spell on him. He knew he had no chance with her, but his fantasies had sustained him since he was twelve. James knew the type of men Mary C. was attracted to and he knew "big boy" was spending his money and spinning his wheels at the same time. He just hoped "big boy" would be understanding at the end of the night. James didn't think he looked like a very understanding person.

Mary C. talked and touched, talked and touched. She was driving "big boy" crazy. His confidence level was rising each time she squeezed his arm, rubbed his back or touched his leg. When the fourth hard Jack Black was placed in front of her, it was worth a small kiss, dead on "big boy's" lips. The confidence builder of all times. He wanted to eat her alive.

Bobby was a dancing fool by any standards. Bebop, Jitter Bug,

Shag, Dirty Boogie, you name it, he could do it. And do it good too. Once he took the floor, his dance card would be as full as he wanted it to be. Unlike his sister, both men and women liked Bobby. He had the qualities men wanted and women admired. The men wanted to be like him and the women just wanted him. Looking like Elvis added to his charisma. While Mary C. was tearing up the Jack Black with "big boy" and "bar boy," Bobby was tearing up the dance floor with Peggy and Betty.

Jason was awake and would not sleep again until his eyes slammed shut from fatigue. He left his bed and walked out onto the front porch. It was a clear Saturday night in Mayport, with a beautiful full moon to the east. It was as if the moon jumped out of the ocean. Jason remembered how his grandfather, Daddy Bob, said, "That ol' moon causes things to happen on this earth. That ol' boy has alot of say-so." Jason missed Daddy Bob, but he didn't miss living in East Mayport in the Big House. He missed his grandmother and Tom Green. Memories of dead loved ones surrounded him. He saw their faces and heard their voices. He wanted to walk with the three of them. He stepped off the porch.

A single blast of the ferry's horn ended his walk and he returned to the reality of the porch. The Buccaneer was making its last run from Fort George to Mayport, where it would rest and spend the night. Jason was sad the sound of the horn ended his time in the past. He was very good at making journeys into times gone by. Sometimes he wasn't sure what was real, because his visions and dreams were as clear as reality. He had the ability to exist in the real world or a dream world. It tore at him, day and night, slowly stripping him to his bones. A cool breeze touched his face and his hair moved. He turned quickly and looked in the direction of the oak tree. It was too dark and far away, but he knew it was there and it was calling to him. Jason also knew he would not go to the tree, not with that moon so full.

He ran back into the house as the clock began to announce the arrival of eleven o'clock. Each chime became louder than the one before it. By the time Jason had counted eight chimes, the entire house was shaking. On the ninth and tenth, Jason watched two pictures fall off the walls of his room from the vibration. He held his hands over his ears, but he could still hear the thunder of the last chime. The tree's effort to run him from the house did not work; he had said "no" and survived again. He reached for the fallen pictures. They had not left the walls.

The crowd at Bill's Hideaway had standing room only. It was packed and the music was loud. Bobby sat between Peggy and Betty. They were working him on the dance floor and rubbed him, top to bottom, at the table. He would enter uncharted territory and have his manhood tested before the night was over. He wanted them both and he had put the idea in their heads. They had discussed the possibility on a trip to the bathroom and had decided to take him to Peggy's house; she had the biggest bed.

Mary C. knew if she tried to stand up and leave the bar stool, she would fall on her face. She was much drunker than she wanted to be. "Big boy" knew his money had been well spent and he knew he would fulfill his intentions.

"I really have to go to the bathroom, but I think I'll need a little help gettin' there." Mary C. was vulnerable and "big boy" knew it. James knew it too, as he watched the huge sailor put his hands and arms around Mary C.'s body. She leaned into him as she stood up and pressed her breast deep into him. He was like a raging bull; it was in his eyes. Mary C. had no chance at all as he walked her to the bathroom door and waited outside, like a jackal, for his prey to show herself again.

Bobby was feeling little pain, as he sat in the back seat of Peggy's blue Volkswagen Beetle. It sounded like a big lawnmower as it rolled down the beach, away from Bill's Hideaway and toward the ramp at Seminole Road. Peggy drove and Betty sat up front with her. The two had decided neither of them would be with Bobby until they got to the house. It wouldn't be fair to the driver. Bobby tried to lie down in the backseat.

"Why the hell you like this little car? It's like ridin' in a tin can."

Peggy was ready. "Don't you talk bad 'bout my Blue Lady Bug. She don't burn no gas, she gets me where I want to go, the radio works, she's paid for, and need I say more?"

"No, ma'am, you've said it all. I'm sorry I mentioned it. If that radio works, turn it on now and turn me on later."

The ladies smiled at each other; they did love Bobby Merritt.

As the Lady Bug turned onto the ramp, leaving the white sand of the beach, "Great Balls of Fire" by Jerry Lee Lewis blasted from the radio. They all sang along.

They were on Seminole Road and only a few miles from Peggy's house. That particular section of the beach road was surrounded by sand dunes, cabbage palms and cattails. As usual, the sound of a million crickets drowned out the music coming from the radio. No one knew why the small black insects gathered so heavily there each night. It was a Seminole Road mystery. Betty didn't like it at all.

"I hate riding through here. It gives me the creeps."

"Big boy" scooped up Mary C. as soon as she walked out of the bathroom. She could hardly stand on her own. He moved her, non-stop, past the bar, through the restaurant and out into the parking lot, in a matter of seconds. She had no idea what was happening; she only smiled through her drunkenness and held onto his arm. He walked her to the back and darkest section of the parking lot, opened the door of a big, late model, white Cadillac, and threw her into the backseat. She had no control over what was happening to her. She came out of both her shoes when he pushed her into the backseat. The sight of her panties and her butt, when her skirt flew up, added to his rage. He leaned down to follow his victim into the car.

A strange noise filled the night air, as a blinding pain ripped through "big boy's" body. The unusual sound was that of human bones shattering. His bones. He fell to his knees and only saw darkness. His thoughts of Mary C. were gone; he had no thoughts at all. He didn't know at the time, but his collarbone and shoulder blade had been crushed by the swing of a baseball bat. After the bat hit him in the back of his head on the second swing, he would remember nothing for days. He dropped like a ton of bricks to the ground. He would not move again until somebody moved him. James stepped over his victim and pulled Mary C. from the white car. She had no idea what was happening as he moved her away from the fallen sailor and into his truck. Mary C. didn't know much, but she knew she was moving somewhere fast. James had changed her fate and saved her for that night, or perhaps that moment.

Peggy's bed was more like a boat than a bed. There was plenty of room for the three of them. When the mini-orgy began, Bobby thought of the rodeo. He was going to have a wild ride; he just had to hang on. The girls went crazy, trying to top each other. He was kissing Peggy, then Betty, then back to Peggy. While one kissed him, the other sucked him. Then they would switch places. He only saw one at a time, but he always knew where the other one was. At one time the kissing stopped and he saw the tops of both their heads as they took turns. He liked to see the top of a woman's head. The double-suck was too much for him. He thought, "Not even Elvis could withstand such pressure." He exploded. He didn't know which one, but he did know the warm lips around him did not leave during the explosion. He guessed they stopped sharing.

The release fatigued him and he closed his eyes. The room was silent, or at least it was silent to him. He knew he would work to please the girls until he was ready again. He opened his eyes to the vision of both women kneeling on the bed, one on each side of him, with big smiles on their faces. They both laid down next to him. It was his turn to do the work.

James drove his truck off the main road into the woods, stopped and turned off the lights. He sat a passed-out Mary C. up in the seat and kissed her as if they had been on a date and were parking in the woods. She slept while he unbuttoned her blouse, exposing her still firm and round forty-one-year-old breasts. She seldom wore a bra, because she was very proud of the way they stood firm.

James squeezed them hard, one then the other. He sucked them both as if he could suck them off and take them with him. His bites were even harder than his squeezes. She would be sore and bruised if she made it through the night of abuse. His rough and painful actions forced a moment of consciousness in Mary C.'s Jack Black soaked brain. She saw the top of his head as he pulled one of her nipples with his teeth. She moaned deep in her throat, but could not speak. The moan made him suck and bite harder; he took it as a pleasure sound.

He reached down between her legs and with one pull ripped the crotch out of her panties. In his same abusive manner, he began to work his fingers deep inside her. She was wet and he considered that as another sign of her pleasure as he worked four fingers as deep as he could go, and even deeper. She made another noise as he took his hand from inside her. She saw the top of his head once more, as he began to bite and tongue her between her legs. He sucked, bit and pulled on her skin the same way he had done her breast. Mary C. was no stranger to sexual pain, but it was usually on her terms.

She was too weak to stop him, but she was awake. She widened her legs and touched the back of his head, hoping for some relief from the attack.

"Easy," she whispered. "Please don't hurt me."

In one move his lips covered hers. She tasted herself on his lips, as he continued his painful, savage kiss. He held her face and she couldn't breathe. It was so dark, even eye-to-eye, she could not identify her attacker. She thought of the big sailor, but she didn't think it was him.

In another sudden move, he turned her toward the passenger door with her back to him. She grabbed the side of the door with both hands as her head was pushed out the open window. It was pitch-dark and she had no idea where they were. She was scared.

"Don't hurt me," was her plea again.

He knelt down of the seat behind her and slammed his growth deep inside her. She felt a moment of pleasure, but only a moment as he began pumping her, like a wild animal. His strokes were hard, deep and many. She held on to the door and tried not to scream. The pounding stopped, and he pulled away from her. She could not relax because even in her foggy state of mind, her instincts told her he was not finished with her.

When she felt an electric-type shock of pain run through her body, she knew he had changed holes in her body. The inhuman humiliation and rape was complete as he again drove his growth deep inside her. She wasn't sober, but she was fully awake. The Jack Daniels had numbed her, somewhat, but not nearly enough to curb the pressure and pain of his anal attack.

The sexual beating she was enduring had taken what little strength she had. She made more noises as he completed his evil act. He began making his own noises and she knew he was leaving his mark inside her. The pressure left her body. She was scared to move; she was scared to see his face.

Mary C.'s fear and ordeal continued when something was wrapped around her head and face. She thought at first that he was going to choke and suffocate her, but he only draped it over her head. She sat back in the seat and left the cloth object on her head. She didn't know, at the time, that her own black silk blouse was her shroud. Her short skirt was rolled up at her waist, she knew her panties were gone and she was naked from the waist up. Mary C. sat quietly, hoping the covering on her face was there so she would not be able to see him and he would set her free. Her safety and even her life might depend on that cover staying on her face.

James started the truck and, as it started to move, he grabbed Mary C. around her neck and pushed her head down in the seat. The truck moved back out onto the main road. During the fifteen minute ride she could hear when other cars were passing them on the road. She kept her head buried in the seat next to him. The truck stopped and he sat her up in the seat. She heard the driver's side door open, then his hands pulled her past the steering wheel. Her bare feet touched the ground. The cover remained on her face and she felt the cool night air touch her naked body. He pushed her in the back and she walked a few steps away. The door of the truck closed and she knew the truck was moving away. Keeping the cover on her head had saved her life up to that point, so she left it on until she knew the truck was gone.

She uncovered her face and realized the shroud had been her black blouse. She hurried and pulled her skirt into place and put the shirt on. When she looked around and focused in on her surroundings, she couldn't believe it. She was behind the old Mayport light-house, a five-minute walk from her house. Her attacker had brought her home. She was alone and hurt, but she was alive.

Bobby opened his eyes and he knew he was face down on the edge of Peggy's big bed. His arm dangled toward the green shag carpet on the bedroom floor. No one was touching, sucking or kissing him. He was glad the rodeo was over. The two women at one time were too much for him. He just hoped they didn't know it, but he thought they probably did. He heard a noise as he pressed his nose against the sheet of the boat bed. He knew he heard someone, but he couldn't see the girls. The noise was coming from the other side of the bed on the floor. His curiosity gave him the strength to slide his worn body in the direction of the noise. When he reached the opposite side of the bed he saw a most interesting sight. There, on the green shag carpet, lay Peggy and Betty, lip to lip, titty to titty and bush to bush, making out like crazy. He dropped his nose back into the sheet. He hoped he hadn't turned them into queers, but he did enjoy watching them for a little while.

The unwanted sleep had taken Jason, and his dream world was his reality for the rest of the night. He did not hear his mother when she entered the house and slowly made her way to the bathroom next to her bedroom. He heard nothing as she turned on the hot water in her deep bathtub. She took off the two pieces of clothing she had left, and dropped them on the floor. Then, she stepped into the tub.

The hot water attacked every tender spot it touched on her body. A few bruises and blood marks were visible already and she knew the red areas would be bruises in time. She was full of fingerprints, bite marks and scratches. She burned in the areas he had abused and her breasts hurt when she splashed them with the hot water. To clean herself completely was impossible. She did the best she could do.

Jason would dream about his new job and Jessie. Mary C. would sleep from fatigue and Jack Black. Uncle Bobby would not make it home that Saturday night.

CHAPTER TWO

JASON WAS UP EARLY SUNDAY MORNING, WITH ONE DAY LEFT BEFORE HE started his new job. He stood and listened at his mother's bedroom door. There was no indication whether or not she had come home at all the night before. He wanted to open her bedroom door to see if she was in her bed, but he didn't. Uncle Bobby's bedroom door was open and Jason could see he had not slept in his bed.

Jason always did his share of the housework. He didn't mind because all three of them worked at keeping Uncle Bobby's modest house in order. He would do whatever was needed, as he waited for the others to return. He didn't want to leave the house until he was sure his mother was alright. He never worried much about Uncle Bobby. He made his bed, picked up around the house and cleaned the kitchen. He liked being busy and he knew his efforts would please his mother. He loved pleasing her.

The clock began to chime on its way to nine. He had been up over an hour. The chiming was not as loud as it had been before and no pictures fell off the walls. As the eighth chime was fading away, Jason heard the toilet flush in the bathroom next to his mother's bedroom. It was like music to his ears. She did come home; he was excited and happy. He didn't have to see her; just knowing she was there was enough. Noises continued to touch Jason's ears, as the lawn mower sound of Peggy's blue Lady Bug filled their front yard.

Jason ran to the front door to see Uncle Bobby jump out of the blue beetle. It looked funny to Jason, but before he could comment, Uncle Bobby beat him to the punch.

"Don't you say one word 'bout it, it grows on ya."

Jason had to laugh.

Uncle Bobby pointed his finger in Jason's face. "Not one word."

Jason smiled and looked back at the little car as Uncle Bobby walked into the house. He loved Uncle Bobby.

Jason followed his uncle into house, hoping to continue the fun conversation about the car. His anticipation was short lived when Uncle Bobby walked toward his bedroom and looked back at Jason.

"I've gotta get some rest. Don't let me sleep past three o'clock. I want to be offshore by six." Jason knew it was the time of year for shrimping at night.

Jason walked past his mother's bedroom door. She had left it open on her return from the bathroom. He stopped and looked in, hoping to see her. She was back in the bed, under the covers. He could only see her black hair. He knew she was awake, because she had been up only a few minutes before. He couldn't help himself.

"Mama, you awake?"

"Go on, son. Leave me alone. I'm sick. Let me be."

Jason backed out of the doorway and closed the door. It didn't matter what she said, he still loved hearing her voice. He would not bother her again. He stood in the house, with the two people he loved, yet he stood alone.

With no conversation in his immediate future and the house-work done, Jason left the two remains of Saturday night to rest and recover. He would seek conversation elsewhere.

Jason walked to Mr. Leek's dock and stood where he would stand Monday morning and wait for the small shuttle boat to take him and the other new workers to their new job. He wondered how many others would be going with him. Uncle Bobby had said, "They were sure hiring a bunch of the local boys." Jason was excited about being a working man. Mr. Leek's office door was closed and Jason knew he was at church. Uncle Bobby always said he talked to the

Lord no matter where he was, he didn't need to go to a big building. Mary C. considered herself a "lost soul," so Jason's only experience with church was when he was younger and living with his grandparents in East Mayport. His grandmother had taken him with her to the Catholic Mass service, now and then. He also remembered praying with his mother before he went to bed, but that was when he was real little.

Jason's next stop was Miss Margaret's store. One member of the family kept the store open all the time. It was nice for the citizens of Mayport to be able to buy what they needed, whenever they needed it. It was hard work, but she had made a good living with the store. It was a true general store and had everything.

Miss Margaret's youngest daughter, Sofia, was minding the store while the rest of the family attended church. It was her turn. She was sixteen and the prettiest of Miss Margaret's four daughters. Jason thought she was beautiful. She had long blonde hair that touched her waist in the back, deep blue eyes that didn't look real, and perfect skin. Jason noticed skin; he had seen pretty skin before. Sofia had two other traits Jason liked. She was taller than the other girls and her eyelashes, surrounding those blue eyes, were extra long. He liked everything about her.

"Good morning, Jason, may I help you?"

Jason found himself eye-to-eye with Sofia. He should have said, "I'm looking for someone to talk to me," but he didn't. He lied.

"No, I'm just lookin'."

She smiled at him. Jason noticed her perfect teeth. He had learned from Uncle Bobby, that pretty teeth were very important to a person's appearance.

"Well, just take your time and if you need me, let me know."

Jason liked that thought as he walked around the store. He couldn't believe his ears, when Sofia started the conversation he had so desperately needed. She was perfect in every way.

"I heard you got hired to help put the new rocks down at the jetties. Doesn't that scare you?"

Jason quivered inside as he searched for the proper answer. "I'd be too scared to work out there." Her second comment gave him the time to respond.

"Heck no, it'll be safe. You just have to be careful when you're working on the water." Jason took a deep breath in case he had to talk some more. Sofia made sure he did.

"I saw one of those big barges go by Friday. Did you see all those machines and cranes? They looked dangerous and scary to me." She was beautiful and Jason liked her even more because she was talking to him. "Will you work on those machines?"

It was his turn to talk again. She gave him no choice. "I'd like to learn." It wasn't much, but his statement made the conversation less one-sided.

"Not me."

Jason thought, "Of course, not you," but he didn't say it.

"You could probably learn, if somebody showed ya."

Her smile was too much for Jason. He was excited and he liked the way she made him feel. He picked up a honey bun and walked to the cash register where Sofia was standing. It would be his breakfast.

"Thirty cents, please."

Jason always had a few dollars in his pocket. Uncle Bobby taught him that. He gave Sofia a dollar and she gave him his change. As he put the seventy cents into his pocket, he couldn't believe his ears.

"Do you have to go? It's kinda boring here this early in the morning. You're my first and only customer. If I made you a cup of coffee to go with that honey bun, could you stay and talk awhile?"

Jason's mouth went dry. He had experienced that feeling too. She was full of surprises and he wanted his fill of her. He knew what he wanted to say and found the courage again.

"Yes, I can stay. I'd like that."

Sofia's smile was bigger than before as she poured Jason his coffee. They sat down at a small table next to the front counter. She had a cup too. He couldn't believe he was having coffee with Sofia.

Jason unwrapped the honey bun and almost dunked the end of it into the coffee. He caught himself before he revealed his childhood habit of dunking toast, donuts and other pastries into his coffee. He didn't usually drink a full cup of coffee. He just used it for dunking and poured the rest out. For some reason, this particular cup of coffee would be consumed in adult fashion and he would accept the second cup Sofia offered. His day got better with each sip.

The sound of the bell on the door made Jason's heart jump when the second customer of the morning walked into the store. Sofia and Jason turned to see a tall, skinny, black man walk in. They both knew it was Jake. He was a strange man, who walked the streets of Mayport. He was quiet and never bothered anyone, yet he was still considered strange. Different means strange to so many people. He wore the same long black trench coat, no matter what the temperature. His other clothes were old and dirty and his body odor was most evident. Jason could see Sofia's discomfort as she watched Jake walk to the meat counter. She walked behind the counter and greeted him, as she did all her other customers.

"Good morning. May I help you?"

Jake pointed a long skinny finger from one hand at a roll of bologna and then held up two other skinny fingers on his other hand. Sofia cut him two slices of the red round meat. He made the same gestures to a block of cheese. Sofia cut him two slices of the square yellow cheese.

"Anything else?"

Jake walked over to the cold drink box, pulled out a bottle of Pepsi Cola from the ice and met Sofia at the cash register. The meat and cheese were wrapped and bagged. He paid his bill and was gone. Jason watched Sofia move as she walked back to sit with him at the table. He understood how women move. Jessie taught him that. He missed Jessie's lessons. He liked being her student.

"Jake gives me the creeps. I hate it when he comes in here, especially when I'm by myself. I'm sure glad you were here with me. Can he talk?"

Jason didn't know the answer to her quick question. He had never thought about it before, but he couldn't remember ever hear-

JAKE

ing Jake talk to anyone.

"He always points at stuff. He scares me. I wasn't that scared with you here."

Jason loved to hear her talk; she said all the right things.

Sofia had a quality about her that Jason couldn't understand. He knew there was something different and special about her, but he had no concept of innocence. She faced him again at the table. He waited for her, as the ferry horn blasted in the distance. She didn't disappoint him.

"Don't you just love to hear the ferry horn?" She was, no doubt, a woman after his heart.

"I've always loved that sound, ever since I was a baby. Don't you just love it?" She had no idea what the sound of that horn meant to Jason. It began his journey into manhood when it said "go" and started Jason's race against Willis up the sand hill to the oak tree. It was his first victory and he would never forget that day. He had stood next to the tree and lifted his arms above his head.

"Jason, did you hear me?" Sofia's voice broke through Jason's ferry horn memory. He knew he had left her for a moment. He was embarrassed and worried she would think he was strange, like the others.

"I daydream too, sometimes. I just go away. Then, when I open my eyes, I haven't gone anywhere. Isn't that crazy?"

Jason didn't like the word "crazy," but he still thought she was wonderful. He was afraid he would drift off again.

"Well, I need to get goin'. Thanks for the coffee."

Sofia didn't want him to leave, but she didn't say it.

"Good luck tomorrow on your new job. You be careful."

He wanted to stay with her, but his embarrassment had him already out the door. He didn't realize it at the time, but Sofia was a true light in his dark world.

Jason was walking on air. He hadn't felt that way in a long time. His time with Sofia and thoughts of his new job would carry him through the day. He waved to Mr. King who was sitting on the porch of his haunted house. Jason thought he would like to take Sofia there one night to hear Mr. King tell his ghost stories. Mr. King waved back. He knew all about Jason.

Jason would try Mr. Leek's dock again, hoping to find more company and conversation. He turned the corner at Strickland's Restaurant and the aroma of hush puppies, frying for the Sunday lunch crowd, took his breath away. He loved those little round balls. He could eat a bagful. In fact he had eaten a bagful before. Jason sat down on the steps leading to Mr. Leek's fish house. He had sat there before with his best friend, Eddie, as they shared a big bag of the tasty circles. Eddie was one of the boys who died during the last game of Duckin'. Eddie's family moved away from Mayport after the funeral. Jason missed his good friend. He was sorry he played the game.

Jason was startled back to the present when his eyes focused on Jake sitting directly across from him in the shade under the fish house. Jake didn't see Jason, as he gave all his attention to the bag Sofia had fixed for him. Jason watched the old man take the food from the bag. He put the bag on a rock and unwrapped the white butcher paper from around the meat and the cheese. He then took one slice of the meat and one slice of the cheese and laid them on top of each other in his hand. He rolled the meat around the cheese, like you would roll a cigar into a round tube. He repeated the same process with the second slices of meat and cheese. He ate both bologna-cheese tubes and washed them down with the Pepsi. Jason didn't know it, but that was Jake's lunch every day.

Jake put the white paper back into the bag and walked away, drinking his last swallow of Pepsi. He put the paper bag into a trash can behind the restaurant and the empty bottle into the pocket of the trench coat. Jason was surprised when he saw Jake throw his trash into the can. He didn't think he would that. Jason had the urge to follow Jake and see where he went during his walks, but it was a passing urge. He walked into the fish house.

Mary C. slowly stepped into her bathtub full of hot water for the second time that day. She was hoping the heat would ease her pain. She had no marks or serious bruises on her face. A beard burn, that makeup would cover, was no worry to her. She would be sure her clothes would cover the other evidence of her ordeal. She looked at the small round fingerprint bruises on her tender-to-the-touch breasts. She decided to burn the secret of that night deep into her belly. What else could she do?

Jason walked passed the empty heading tables in the fish house. He had stood at those tables many times when they were piled high with shrimp, waiting to lose their heads. He had seen Jessie for the first time at those tables. He made his way out onto the main dock.

Jason's heart raced when he saw the two shuttle boats tied to the dock. Mr. Leek had agreed to use his dock as the staging area for the workers to board the shuttles and be transported to the jetties. Jason stood next to one of the boats and put his foot on the side wooden railing. The boat moved up and down in the water and pressed against his foot. He knew one of those boats would take him to his new job in the morning. The sound of a familiar voice ended the moment.

"Mornin', Jason." Mr. Leek was standing behind him.

"Mornin', Mr. Leek. I didn't hear you come up."

"Well, you were thinking pretty hard there, son. You have always done some hard thinkin'. Those boats will be filled with workers tomorrow." Jason nodded in agreement.

Mr. Leek continued. "You'll be right there with 'em too. It sure is a good thing, all these jobs for you young people to get some real good experience and for the old-timers to use some of their skills again. It's a good thing, I tell ya."

Jason liked listening to Mr. Leek.

Mr. Leek liked Jason too. He knew about all the turmoil and adversity the young man had faced in his short, twenty-one years. He also knew Jason was different because of his past and had strange moments of confusion. The folks who knew Jason hoped time and maturity would heal his mental scars. There was no doubt that Jason was not normal, but he was as normal as he could be, considering his past. Mr. Leek prayed for Jason many times, asking God to give the young man the strength to heal. He wanted Jason to make it. He thought Jason deserved a chance to be a good man. The sound of a horn blowing alerted Mr. Leek that someone was at the front of the fish house.

"It's probably Brownie with his gill net catch. He usually shows up about this time." Mr. Leek left Jason on the dock.

Jason stood alone. He had stood there before. The ferry horn blew and it was all Jason needed to drift into the past. He stood on the dock in the dark and watched Jessie wash her naked body with the water hose and a bar of soap. It was the most wonderful sight he had ever seen before. He could feel her wet, rock-hard breasts against his chest. He missed her.

"Jason, you want to make twenty dollars?"

Jason shook the vision of Jessie out of his head.

"Jason, come help me weigh and box Brownie's fish."

Jason realized Mr. Leek was talking to him. "Yes, sir. I'll help." Jason knew how to weigh and box the fish. He had helped Mr. Leek before. The job was completed in about two hours.

"It is always a pleasure to work with you, Jason." As Mr. Leek handed Jason his money he looked up at the clock on the wall of Mr. Leek's office. It was two-fifteen. Uncle Bobby's words rang in Jason's head, "Don't let me sleep past three o'clock."

Jason thanked Mr. Leek and headed home. He had plenty of time, but he wanted to be sure he didn't disappoint his Uncle Bobby. He would run all the way home. He saw Sofia standing in front of the store, talking to another girl. He saw Jake, walking on the other side of the road. He saw a police car parked in front of his house. His run ended, as he walked slowly past the police car. He heard voices in the front room. He was afraid to walk through the front door, so he went to the back door and walked into the back hallway of the house.

Jason heard a man's voice. He looked around the corner of the hallway and recognized who was talking. Sheriff McIntosh was talking to Mary C. and Uncle Bobby. The sheriff had visited them before when Jason cut Charlie Klim with his hunting knife. Jason avoided the thoughts of that night and listened to the sheriff.

"Now, Mary C., we know you were there. We found your pretty shoes on the ground next to him. These are your shoes, ain't they?" He held a pair of leopard print, three-inch high heel shoes.

"I've already said they look like the shoes I lost. Yes, they are probably mine. I told you I don't remember what happened. And that's the truth."

The sheriff had dealt with Mary C. before. "Were you really that drunk? Can a person be that drunk?"

She didn't answer.

"Seems like every few years, somebody gets hurt 'cause they want you. What do you do to these poor devils?"

Mary C. didn't like the way the sheriff was talking to her. "I was drunk, that's all. I didn't hurt nobody." She sat across from the sheriff, wearing a big white terry cloth bathrobe. Mary C. had to keep her bruised body hidden. She knew the sheriff would not be able to examine her without a female assistant and a court order. She gave him no reason to think she was injured. She showed no discomfort, even though it was painful each time she took a deep breath. The sheriff continued.

"I don't think you hurt the man, but I do think you need to try and remember what you did see. Hell, he was probably gonna hurt you, or at least have his way with you. Somebody either stopped him before he could get to you, or they hurt him after. You tell me which one. Did you pleasure the man before a jealous ol' boyfriend cracked his head open?"

"I didn't do anything with him and I ain't got no ol' boy-friends."

"If you don't remember nothin', how you know y'all didn't do nothin'?"

"I just know, that's all."

"Yeah. If you say so." The sheriff realized Mary C. was not going to answer his questions or help him in any way. "There's no doubt in my mind, you know somethin'."

Uncle Bobby sat quietly. He was there to support Mary C., if she needed him. The sheriff wasn't finished with her yet.

"Ain't you just a little bit curious about how bad the man was hurt? Since he didn't do nothin' to you, I thought you might be just a little interested."

Mary C. stared at the lawman.

"You are an amazing woman, Mary C. I don't think I've seen many as hard as you."

She continued her silent stare.

The sheriff shook his head. "Well, just so you'll know, he ain't dead. He has five broken bones in his neck and right shoulder, a cracked skull and he don't know who he is. Other than that . . . he's just fine." The sheriff stood up.

"Don't leave town, Mary C. We gonna talk again. Bobby, keep her home."

Bobby didn't respond as the sheriff walked out of the house.

Jason walked out the back door. He didn't want to talk to his mother and he didn't want her to know he was listening. Jason waited for the police car to leave the yard, then walked to the front of the house and up the steps of the front porch. Mary C. and Uncle Bobby stopped talking when they saw him. His mother greeted him.

"Hey, Jason."

Uncle Bobby did the same. "Hey, boy. Where ya been?"

"On the docks. I made twenty dollars. I didn't want ya to sleep late."

"Hell, I've been up. I need to get ready and get gone." Uncle Bobby walked out onto the front porch and spotted the blue Lady Bug. "Oh man! I gotta get that tin can back to Peggy."

Jason joined his uncle on the porch.

"Take this poor excuse for a car back to Peggy for me. She'll bring ya back home."

Jason couldn't believe Uncle Bobby's request. "I never drove one before."

"It's easy. You drive my truck, don't ya? The gearshift is the same. Nothin' to it." Uncle Bobby walked back into the house, then turned to Jason.

"Wait a minute. You gotta take the can back to Peggy and then have her take ya to get my truck. I forgot about my truck at Bill's. Them damn women fried my brain. I ain't doin' that no more."

Jason wasn't sure what Uncle Bobby was talking about, but he was sure he had no choice in the matter. He would have to drive the tin can back to Peggy and get the truck. Jason looked at the little blue car as Uncle Bobby returned.

"Come on. You can drop me off at the dock and go get this stuff done." Uncle Bobby picked up a duffel bag from the floor and headed out the door.

"Mary C., we're goin'. I'll see ya in the mornin'. Jason's gonna go get my truck. He'll be back in a little while."

Jason watched his mother move slowly off the couch and walk toward her bedroom.

"I'm still not feelin' too good. I'm gonna lay down. Get me up, when ya get back. I don't wanna sleep too much. I'll be up all night. I just need to rest some."

Jason was worried and sad about his mother and he hated the way the sheriff had talked to her. Jason was disappointed when she closed the bedroom door. The horn of the Lady Bug squealed.

"Come on, boy! I'm late enough as it is now." Uncle Bobby sat in the driver's seat of the bug. Jason jumped into the passenger's side and off they went.

As the noise from the engine of the little car faded, Mary C. stood naked, in front of her oval shaped full-length mirror. She was much blacker and bluer than she had been before. She would hide her injuries until there was no trace of abuse.

Uncle Bobby drove up to the dock, left the bug running and jumped out.

"Be careful, boy. Don't hurt my truck." With that request, Uncle Bobby was gone. The car engine was still running, the driver's side door was open and Jason still sat in the passenger's seat. He moved his body over to the driver's side, clearing the stick shift as he moved. He was glad he didn't have to back up. He could go forward and still be going in the right direction. Jason pushed the stick shift into first gear. The car jumped for a second, closing the driver's side door, and rolled onto the main street in Mayport. Second gear was smooth, third was even smoother. By the time Jason passed the little jetties, he was enjoying his first ride in a Beetle Bug. It was fun to drive.

When something is fun, time usually goes by quickly. Before Jason knew it, he was driving into Peggy's front yard near Seminole Beach. He was sorry the fun ride was over. He turned off the engine and walked to Peggy's front door. On the first knock, Peggy hollered from somewhere in the house.

"Come on in, Jason. I'll be out in a second." Jason walked into the house as Peggy continued to yell from another room.

"I thought that crazy uncle of yours forgot me. I need my car to get me to Mama's for dinner, later today. Have a seat. I'll take you back home as soon as I get dressed. I slept in this morning. I hate it when I sleep too late. I was gettin' out of the tub when I heard you drive up. I thought it was Bobby at first. You almost got a real surprise and good look at me." Jason liked the way Peggy talked. She was a true girl of the South.

"If you're thirsty, there's beer and an RC Cola in the icebox. Don't drink the grape Nehi, that's Betty's."

The offer of a cold drink set just right with Jason. He walked to the kitchen and took the bottle of RC Cola from the icebox. He didn't like the taste of beer. When he turned to walk back to the living room he saw Peggy's reflection in a mirror on the wall in the hall, next to her bedroom. She was completely naked, as she powdered her upper body. He watched her until she moved away from his sight. He stood in the same place, waiting for another look. Jason liked seeing her and wanted to see her again.

Jason was surprised when Peggy walked down the hall, wearing her bra and panties. She had her back to him and didn't know he was standing where he could see her. Peggy did see him, when she walked back to her room. She liked his young eyes looking at her. Then she really shocked Jason when she walked into the kitchen, still in just her bra and panties. He couldn't believe it. He thought it might be a dream or one of his fantasies. No matter, he loved it. Peggy took the bottle from his hand and took a drink. Her bra and panties were made of a see-through material. Jason could see everything. Hair, nipples, whatever he wanted. Peggy was a full-figured woman and her big breasts excited Jason.

"You have really turned into a handsome man. How old are you now?" She acted like there was nothing unusual about her standing there.

Jason answered her, but didn't take his eyes off her nipples. "Twenty-one." He couldn't break the trance of her sexual vision.

"You are a man, ain't ya? I didn't realize you had grown up so."

Jason felt the front of his pants move in her direction as his manhood became even more apparent. Peggy saw it too and his excitement excited her. Her nipples got hard and she reached down, touching Jason on the outside of his dungarees. He didn't hesitate. Jessie had taught him what to do. He reached down and touched her in the same way. His hand was on the outside of her panties, but they were so thin, it felt like he was touching her skin. Her panties were wet instantly. Peggy was surprised that her aggressiveness did not intimidate him. She was even more excited at his response.

"You ain't bashful at all, are ya? Come with me." Peggy took Jason's wet hand and led him to her boat bed where his Uncle Bobby had attended the rodeo the night before.

Once again, Bobby Merritt stood at the wheel of his shrimp boat, the Mary C. He had spent a great amount of his life and time in that position. He could see the oak tree on the sand hill, as the boat cleared the jetties and headed out to deep water. He knew the nets would be lowered within the next hour. Bobby and his one-man crew would shrimp all night. He loved the life and freedom of being a shrimper.

For the third time that day, Mary C. sat in a bathtub full of hot water. The heat eased her pain, but it also made the blood run, making the bruises darker. Her body hurt inside and out.

Peggy lay facedown on the edge of her big bed. She was in sexual shock, as she focused her eyes on the green shag carpet on her bedroom floor. She had just experienced the ultimate physical satisfaction of her life. She could not believe it came at the hands of the young man she knew as a boy.

Jason's ability and knowledge as a lover shocked her. He was gentle and caring at the right times and knew when to be wild and rough. He was the perfect size for her and he had touched places inside her that had never been touched. The pleasure she experienced was more than she ever thought possible. She had never been with anyone who was more concerned with her pleasure than their own. Peggy was drained of all her body fluids and strength. Her stomach muscles were sore from contracting each time she exploded inside. It was a good pain. She had never exploded so many times, or for so long. They were continuous and at one time she thought she was going to pass out from the actual pleasure. Jason stood naked at the icebox, drinking another RC Cola. He wanted the grape Nehi, but he knew it was Betty's. He didn't know Peggy would have given anything, including Betty's Nehi. He just had to ask. He liked being naked. He liked pleasing Peggy. Jessie taught him that.

Mary C. stood at her mirror again and patted her body with a soft towel. It was too painful to rub the water away. She covered herself with the white terry cloth robe and walked toward the kitchen. She had felt too sick to eat all day, but she knew she needed to eat something.

As she entered the kitchen she heard a noise on the front porch. She recognized the noise right away. It was the squeaking of the wooden bench swing hanging on the front porch. She stopped and listened, to be sure. She could tell someone was sitting in the swing. She walked toward the window.

"Jason, is that you?" She moved closer to the window for a better look.

"Guess again, girl."

A man's voice scared her and she quickly moved away from the window. "Who's out there? You're scarin' me."

"Not likely, Mary C. Hell, I'm the one oughta be scared."

She recognized Sheriff McIntosh's voice. She was mad. "Oh that's great! The law goin' round scarin' folks in their own homes.

I'm glad I didn't shoot ya. I would have been in big trouble then." She stepped to the front door.

The sheriff greeted her. "Well, you gonna stay inside or join me out here in the nice cool air?"

Mary C. stepped out onto the porch.

The sheriff shook his head at her again. "Damn, woman, you sure stay wet all day. Don't you ever put on no clothes?"

Mary C.'s wet hair dripped on her shoulders. She was disgusted with her visitor, but knew he would not leave until they talked.

"You stay there and I'll get some clothes on. We'll talk out here, but I've already told ya all I know."

"Well, tell me again. And you don't have to get dressed on my account. I'm gettin' used to seeing you with wet hair and in that robe. Don't change your style for me." He kept swinging.

Peggy's legs were shaking as she pushed the clutch pedal down and fired up the Lady Bug. Her perfect sexual match sat next to her. She still felt him between her legs. She actually quivered inside when she looked at him.

"What did you do to me in there?"

Jason didn't know what to say. He had no answer, but she really didn't want one. They were rolling to Bill's Hideaway to retrieve Uncle Bobby's truck. Jason didn't tell Peggy, but he wanted to drive the bug.

Mary C. endured a great deal of pain trying to dress herself. Each time she felt a sharp pain, the sound of the swing on the porch added to her discomfort. The sheriff was waiting.

The Lady Bug stopped in front of Bill's Hideaway. Jason could see Uncle Bobby's truck parked in the sand. The honky tonk was closed on Sunday. Peggy had an idea.

"Jason, how 'bout me followin' you home and you ride with me to my mama's. She'll be surprised how you've grown up. I promise to get you home early. I know you have to start your new job in the morning. I don't want to drive by myself. Come on, please."

Jason really didn't want to go, but she talked so fast and he always had a hard time saying "no." The Lady Bug followed Uncle

Bobby's truck as they left the beach.

Mary C. had to surrender to her pain and put the robe back on. It was the only way she would be able to sit and talk, without the sheriff seeing some evidence of her ordeal and her discomfort. She looked out the window at the lawman still swinging, back and forth.

He reminded her of Sheriff Floyd, from her past. Floyd died years ago, but he had left his mark on Mary C. He had sexually abused her when she was a young girl and then later paid her for sex when she became a woman. Sheriff McIntosh wasn't ugly like Floyd, but she still hated the uniform. She walked out onto the porch.

"Did you think I'd get tired of waiting for you and leave?"

"No, not you, Sheriff. I knew ya wouldn't leave." She slowly sat down in an old wicker chair across from the swing. She was miserable.

"First of all, call me Mac. My friends call me Mac."

He sounded different to Mary C. She would be cautious with him.

Mary C. thought Mac was in his early fifties. He wasn't the best looking man she had seen in her life, but he wasn't the ugliest either. He had a rough but manly look to him and she did like the gray in his hair. His teeth were straight and whiter than most men she knew. She still hated the uniform.

"I know you don't believe this, but I ain't here to bother you. I just want to talk to you and I want us to start with a fresh hand."

Mary C. was not very trusting and she was confused at his words. She would continue to be cautious.

"Maybe you don't know who hurt the sailor. I wish you did, so I could find him. I also hope you really don't know because I want you to be telling me the truth. I want you to trust me."

Mary C. liked the way he was talking, but it was strange.

"I ain't gonna ask you no more questions about the other night and that sailor. If and when you remember and you want to tell it, you let me know. Maybe you can't tell what you know. Maybe you don't know nothin'. Either way, I won't ask you again."

Mary C. had settled in the wicker chair and made sure she didn't move. She felt her sore ribs with each breath. The one-sided conversation continued.

"If you don't mind, I'd like to sit here with you for a little while. If you do mind, I'll understand and leave. I know this all seems strange to you."

Mary C. thought, "Strange pretty well covers it." She kept her thought to herself and continued being a good listener.

"I want it to be alright with you."

Mary C. didn't understand or care. "It's fine, but I don't know what to say to you. You make me nervous." She looked down at the floor of the porch.

"Well, we're both nervous then. I just talk too much, when I'm nervous."

Mary C. smiled at his comment. "I have a feelin' there ain't much makes you nervous, but if ya say so."

He smiled at her comment. "Mary C., I'm gonna tell you somethin' that I've wanted to tell you for a long time, ever since I came here the night your boy cut Charlie Klim up so bad. Now, when I tell you this, I'll have to leave 'cause I won't be able to sit here and face you no longer." He stopped a second as if he needed a moment to collect his thoughts.

"When I saw you today, I decided to tell you. I can't keep it inside me no more."

Mary C. was confused, nervous and cautious, but nothing on earth could make her leave that wicker chair at that moment. She had to hear his dark secret.

"Please don't say nothin'. This is the hardest thing I've ever done."

Mary C. sat up and looked deep into his eyes. She was mesmerized with anticipation. He took another deep breath.

"I think you are so much more than you think you are. You are very special, you just don't know it. No one has ever told you that. I knew it the first time I saw you. I was in love with you the first time I looked into your eyes."

Mary C.'s heart raced as he continued his "true confession."

"I also know that a woman like you would never look in my direction. If a man like me could find a way to your heart, he would probably get himself killed tryin' to keep you or protect you from the others who wanted you. I do know one thing and that is, you need someone to take care of you. You need a man to want you for all of you and not just one thing. You gotta stop drinkin' and livin' so hard. There ain't no reason for it. You're gonna die way before your time, and that will be such a terrible waste." He licked his dry lips and took one more deep breath.

Mary C. could not absorb all he was saying. She was in listener's shock.

"I really appreciate you listening to me and not laughing at me. I'm almost finished."

Mary C. was too hard for tears, but she wanted him to keep talking.

"I haven't told you this before because I know a woman like you needs the attention of more than one man. It's a hard habit to break. I would have to be the only one. It's only right that way. So, the last thing I want to say is that, if you ever decide to stop the way you're livin' and you want someone to take care of you, and you alone, it would be to your advantage to call me. You have no idea how you should be treated. I would like to be the one who shows you, but like I said, it's hard to break old habits." He had spilled his guts and heart all over the floor of the porch. He stood up in front of the swing.

"Mary C., you take care of yourself. I'm gonna find out who hurt you last night." He walked past her and down the steps into the yard. Mary C. could only sit there, as he climbed into his police car. He was gone.

Mary C. was still sitting in the wicker chair when Bobby's truck and the Lady Bug wheeled into the front yard. Jason jumped from the truck.

"Mama, we just passed a police car. You alright?"

"I'm fine, son. Everything's fine."

Peggy stepped out of the bug. "Hey, Mary C. If it's alright, I'd like to take Jason to Mama's for dinner. You need to come too."

"Jason can go, but I'm in for the night. I'm really tired. Jason, you go put on a clean shirt."

Jason ran into the house and the ladies talked.

"I know Jason has to work in the mornin'. I promise we won't be late. It'll give me a good excuse to leave early. I can just take so much of Mama and the other old-timers."

Mary C. smiled. She knew Peggy understood how important the job was to Jason and she knew Peggy would keep her promise. "You oughta be ashamed of yourself, talkin' 'bout your mama and her friends. Everybody loves your mama."

Peggy smiled too. "Ain't that the truth. Everywhere I go folks ask me about Mama. They do love my mama."

Mary C. agreed. "Well, she helps everybody. She never says nothin' bad about nobody. She goes to church and reads the Bible. She's like a saint or somethin'."

"Well, I don't know about Mama bein' a saint or not. I do know she cooks a hell-of-a Sunday roast."

Mary C. shook her head as they both laughed. Peggy noticed how slowly Mary C. was moving, but she didn't say anything about it. Peggy was good at minding her own business.

"Your Jason has sure turned into a fine handsome young man. I know you must be proud of him."

"Yes, I am. He has always been so good. He's been through a lot, but he's doin' better now."

Peggy nodded her head in agreement as Jason walked out of the house, ready to go. The scent of Old Spice touched Mary C.'s nose as Jason came closer.

"I won't be late, Mama."

Mary C. wrinkled her nose and could not let him leave without a comment. "Did ya fall in the bottle? Go easy on that stuff. The gnats will be swarmin' round ya, if you go outside."

"Oh, Mama." Jason wanted to hug her, but he walked by her.

"Don't be late, you promised."

"Bye, Mama."

Peggy had it all worked out. "We'll say hey, eat and say good-bye."

As they reached the bug Jason found a new strength. "Peggy, can I drive?"

She could refuse him nothing. They were off.

Mary C. walked back into the house to ponder on Mac's words of care and love. No one had ever talked to her that way before. A sharp pain clouded her thoughts and she was still hungry. She would think about him later.

The ride to Miss Margie's house was quiet at first. Jason seldom started a conversation. He really only liked it when people talked to him. Peggy usually didn't mind doing the talking, but she sat quietly, thinking about her unbelievable sexual encounter with her lover's nephew. She was truly amazed.

Jason didn't mind the quiet ride. He was more interested in driving the little car. He was having a great time. Peggy finally broke the silence.

"You'll love Mama's cookin'. That's her specialty. She loves to see people enjoy eatin'. I sure didn't take after her when it comes to cookin' for anyone. I'd much rather be eatin' it, not cookin' it. Mama will love seein' you."

Jason had a flash in his head. "I remember your mama. She came to the house and visited with me when I was sick. I like your mama."

"That's Mama, alright."

Jason was enjoying his thoughts of Miss Margie when Peggy gave him something else to think about.

"You know my Aunt Margaret, from the store, don't ya?"

Jason nodded his head.

"She'll be there tonight with her four girls. Do you know the girls?"

Jason had to be sure of what she said. "Miss Margaret from the store is your aunt?"

"That's right. She's Mama's sister. She's a good woman too. Her and Mama are like two peas in a pod. You would think they were born twins, but actually Mama's a year older. My cousins will be there too. Did you say you knew the girls?"

"I've seen 'em goin' to church and in the store, but I don't know their names." Sofia's face flashed in his head.

"Well, you know Aunt Margaret has worked them girls pretty hard and they go to a private school. She ain't let 'em do much regular stuff. Uncle Joe wanted more for his girls, so they've been more sheltered and isolated as they grew up. They're all gettin' to be women now and I just wonder how long before they all four break loose. You can just keep somebody wrapped up so long, before they come unwrapped. And you know they never played with the other Mayport kids. I think that was a mistake on Aunt Margaret's part of raisin' 'em."

Jason thought it was true; he had never seen the four girls out and about in Mayport.

Peggy continued. "Hell, them girls ain't never been to Mr. King's house to hear ghost stories. Do you believe that? Now, that's ridiculous, don't ya think?"

Jason's earlier thought of taking Sofia to the haunted house had possibilities. Peggy was on a roll.

"There's Margie, the oldest, named after Mama. Peggy's my namesake. Then there's Susan and Sofia, Sofia spelled with an f. She's the baby. We all take care of Sofia. She's like a little princess to the family."

Jason wanted to hear more. He was excited at the thought of seeing his new friend. He stepped on the gas.

CHAPTER THREE

SHERIFF MCINTOSH, WALKED INTO THE HOSPITAL ROOM OF "BIG BOY," THE sailor who had been beaten with the baseball bat. He was hoping he would be able to talk to him about that night and why Mary C.'s shoes were on the ground next to him. Morphine had taken away his pain and sleep was the answer, if he was to heal. A nurse entered the room.

"Sir, he won't wake up tonight. He's out for quite a while. The more sleep he gets, the less he'll suffer. He's really hurt bad. It's a wonder he isn't dead." She checked his blood pressure.

"When do you think he'll be awake?"

"Not until the morning, or even later."

"Is there any way that I could be called, if and when he comes around?"

"Give me a number to call and if he wakes up on my shift, I'll try to call you. I'll be gone by the morning, so it isn't very likely he'll wake up with me here. I'll tell the others, but I can't promise they'll call you. I can't speak for them."

"That'll be fine. Whatever you can do. Thank you." He gave her his number at home and at the station. He left the room.

The thirty-minute drive ended as the Lady Bug rolled to a stop in front of Miss Margie's two-story house. Jason recognized the station wagon parked in front of them. He had seen Sofia and her sisters riding in that car. He was nervous, but his desire to see Sofia again overshadowed any thoughts of not going into the house. Peggy was out of the car and didn't know it, but she was leading her new lover to his new love.

Jason could hear talking and laughing, coming from the front room, as he and Peggy walked through the front door. It became even louder when Peggy joined the festivities. It was as if everyone screamed when they walked in. Peggy hugged and kissed everybody in the room and others coming from other rooms because they heard the commotion. Jason recognized Miss Margie when she hugged her daughter. She stepped to Jason.

"And who is this handsome young man?" Miss Margie truly didn't know him.

"Mama, you'll never guess who this is. I tell ya, you'll never guess."

Miss Margie didn't want to give Peggy the satisfaction of her giving up. "Now, don't tell me. I know those eyes." Miss Margie felt herself quiver inside. The others couldn't see the effect Jason had on her. She knew him.

"Oh, dear Jesus! Jason, you darling young man. How are you?" Her heart went out to the little boy she knew before. She liked Jason and had been one who prayed for him.

"I'm fine, Miss Margie. How are you?"

She hugged him and held him close to her. "I'm fine too, Jason. Just gettin' older."

Jason experienced an instant calming and comfort as she held him. He thought of his mother. Miss Margie lifted his heart and he bathed in the moment. Peggy broke the spell.

"Oh, Mama! You know everybody. Nobody changes too much to get past you. I don't believe you guessed it."

"As soon as I saw those eyes. I'd know those beautiful strong eyes anywhere, at any time. We go way back, don't we, son?"

"Yes, ma'am. We do." Jason remembered her sitting on the edge of his bed reading to him, during his silent year. He had not had that memory before. It was one he would save and have again. He was happy to be at Miss Margie's house and he hadn't even seen Sofia yet. Once they realized who Jason was, all the older women hugged and greeted him, just like they had done to Peggy.

Peggy's best friend and sometimes roommate, Betty, hugged Jason too, then turned and whispered to Peggy.

"Where you been, girl? I've been waiting on you for over an hour. You shouldn't have left me here with all these people. I have experienced serious generation gap problems. There ain't nobody here in the middle. Either they're young or old, nothin' in between."

Peggy laughed and hugged her friend. "Poor baby. Stop all that whinin'. It will all be worth it when the table is set. You know you're here to eat."

"Oh, ha-ha! Ain't we funny."

Peggy couldn't wait to tell Betty about Jason. She buried her nose in Betty's ear. "God almighty, girl, do I have something to tell you. You're gonna die, I tell ya. Just flat die." Peggy took Betty's arm and they disappeared toward the back of the house.

Miss Margie added to Jason's pleasant thoughts. "I'm so happy Peggy invited you to eat with us. This is a great surprise. All of the young people are out in the backyard. I guess these old grannies ain't cool enough." She smiled and touched his arm again.

"You're cool enough, Miss Margie."

She smiled at Jason's attempt to compliment her. "Now the real cool one is that uncle of yours. How is Bobby?"

Everybody liked his Uncle Bobby. "He's fine too. He's night shrimpin' tonight."

"Oh, he would love a piece of this roast. He does love to eat my roast. Now, you go on out back and say hey to the girls. You don't need to stay in here with this old crowd."

Jason didn't need any extra encouragement. He was ready to see Sofia. The backyard was his destination.

Peggy and Betty sat together, on a small couch, in Miss Margie's sewing room. Betty couldn't believe what she had just been told.

"Have you lost your mind? Jason?... Jason? You must have had some type of dream or somethin'. You been drinkin'?"

"No, dammit! It happened, I tell ya. And I ain't felt nothin' like it in my entire life. I didn't know I could feel like that. I been missin' out."

"You're serious, ain't ya?"

"As a heart attack. Hell, I thought I was gonna have a heart attack one time durin' it. I almost passed out."

"What? You are just playin' with me. This is a joke, ain't it?"

Peggy shook her head. "Not hardly. This is as real as it gets. I thought I had felt it all and you know just what I mean. But, the boy took me to the mountain and threw me off. I almost passed out, I tell ya. Out cold. And I'm ready to make that climb any time he wants."

Betty's eyes looked like they would fall out of her head. She had never heard Peggy talk that way before. "You have lost your mind. We need to skip dinner and get you to the doctor."

"The cure for me is out there talkin' to my mama. I'm tellin' ya, he is the answer for women. I'm glad I discovered him before I died. Even if it don't happen again, at least I know it was possible. But, it ain't the last time, not if I can help it."

Betty was still sitting in amazement, waiting for the punch line that wasn't coming.

"I'm considerin' sharin' him with you, but I ain't sure yet. I don't know if you're ready to appreciate his talents."

"You are crazy. Somethin' bad has happened to you. We gotta talk to your mama."

Peggy started laughing. "Alright, I'll share him. I can't wait for you to get thrown off that mountain. Then, we'll see who's crazy." Peggy grabbed Betty and kissed her on the lips. "I'm gettin' excited, just talkin' 'bout it. Come on, let's get back up front before Mama catches us back here, butt naked."

"You're scarin' me, girl. You ain't kiddin', are ya?"

"Not one bit. It's all true. How 'bout stayin' close to me while we visit? Keep me from attackin' the boy in front of the family."

Betty laughed with her, but she still found it all hard to believe. They left the little room.

Miss Margaret's four daughters were playing badminton in the middle of the backyard. They were running, swinging their rackets, missing the birdie, and laughing. Jason had never seen such a game, but it was easy to see the girls were not very good at it. It didn't seem to matter; they still seemed to be having a good time. Everything about Miss Margie's house was a good time. At one time all four girls were on the grass, flat on their backs, laughing. Sofia was even more beautiful when she laughed. He liked watching them as they played. He couldn't believe he was there with her. Sofia was the first of the sisters to notice Jason.

"Hey, what are you doing here?"

The game and laughing stopped and Jason knew all eight eyes were looking at him. "I came with Peggy." Peggy's big breasts flashed in his head, but the vision didn't linger.

"That's great. Do you know my sisters?" Margie, the oldest, joined in. She was Jason's age. "We've all seen him, but never been introduced. How do you know him?"

"We talked in the store. He stayed with me when Jake was in there."

Margie reacted. "Oh! I hate it when he comes in. He's creepy. Can he talk?"

Jason felt as if he'd had that same conversation before. "I don't think so. I've never heard him talk. I don't think he's ever hurt nobody either."

"Well, he's still creepy. He scares me. He scares us all when he's in the store."

The girls agreed with "big sister," and they all three nodded their heads.

Sofia was so proper with the introductions. "This is Jason."

He could feel the eight eyes looking him up and down and over again.

"This is my sister, Margie, she's the oldest."

Margie smiled and Jason could see she was proud to be the oldest and the boss.

"This is my older sister, Peggy. And this is my other older sister, Susan."

Margie had to join in again. "Sofia, you are so silly, sometimes."

Jason loved being with them all. Sofia was, no doubt, the most beautiful and she really stood out when they stood together. The others, however, had their own beauty and qualities. Each one had her own look. A different look. They did not look like sisters at all.

Margie was twenty-one, like Jason. She had dark features, totally the opposite of Sofia. Her hair was short and her body was hard. She had a muscular look and she reminded Jason of Jessie. He liked the way Margie looked.

Peggy had long hair, like Sofia, but it was raven black, like Mary C.'s. Her ice blue eyes gave her an exotic look. Jason had only seen such a look once before, when he looked into Jessie's green eyes.

Susan had auburn red hair, tied in a long ponytail that touched the cheeks of her butt when she walked. Jason had never seen hair that long before. Jason stared at the small amount of freckles that crossed her nose. He was impressed with all four sisters. He could look at them all night. He appreciated each one of them.

"Supper time!" Miss Margie's announcement ended the backyard introductions.

The table was like a dream to Jason. He had never seen such plates, glasses and table settings. Everyone was so happy and polite. He could not remember ever experiencing such an atmosphere. As he gazed at the surroundings, he lost track of Sofia, while Miss Margie was directing her guests to their seats. Jason experienced another great moment when Miss Margie asked him to sit between Sofia and her older sister, Margie.

"Jason, you sit here." She didn't have to repeat her request. He sat down in the chair he would have chosen if given the chance. Jason hadn't noticed something very interesting, until he sat at the table. He was the only male at the dinner. He was surrounded by women of all ages. It could have easily been one of his better dreams. Miss Margie continued her hostess duties.

"Sofia, would you like to ask the Lord to bless our gathering?"

Jason didn't turn his head toward Sofia, but he wanted to.

Everyone bowed their heads.

"Dear Lord, thank you for this day and making all this possible. Please bless this food, those who prepared it and those of us who can't wait to eat it. In Your Holy Name. Amen."

They all said, "Amen," as they laughed at Sofia's prayer. Margie had to say something to her little sister.

"You are so silly, Sofia . . . but that was funny."

Jason liked the way they treated each other. He was in a different world. The roast beef feast began.

Jason watched at first, as the others passed the containers of food around the table. He wanted to do the right thing. He watched everything. Peggy was even different when she sat at her mother's table. The room was filled with respect.

Miss Margie generated that respect and gave it back to all in the room. He wanted his mother to be respected like that. While Jason was watching the activities around him, Sofia filled his plate with food. She gave him the same choices she made. No one had ever done such a thing for him.

"I hope you don't mind. You were daydreaming, and I didn't want you to miss out on the best stuff."

"No, that's fine. Thank you. It looks great. I'm really hungry too." Jason hadn't talked that long in weeks.

Margie couldn't help herself. "Sofia, maybe he doesn't like what you like and now he can't hurt your feelings by telling you he's allergic to all that stuff."

Sofia looked at Jason. "Are you?" She had a concerned look on her beautiful face. They all laughed. Jason was in heaven.

Jason ate and listened to the many pleasant conversations around him. He and Sofia were quiet as the others talked. Jason liked being with everyone, but he knew if he and Sofia were alone, they would talk more to each other. She would make sure of that. He'd had breakfast with her in the store that morning and now dinner that night. It was a great day.

Margie talked the most. The other girls had learned to be good listeners, like Jason. Sofia talked the least. The other two added their comments, but never began or ended a subject. That seemed to be Margie's job. The older ladies had little separate conversations, as the dinner moved on.

Jason looked up one time and found that Betty was staring a hole through him. She had an amazed look on her face. It made him uncomfortable, so he looked away and tried not to look at her again. Throughout the rest of the dinner, he knew she was still looking at him. Peggy smiled at him once, and he could see her eyes glaze over. His head was on a swivel. He had Sofia and Margie on each side, Peggy and Betty directly across from him and he tried to pay attention to Susan and sister Peggy, whenever they joined the conversation. He had never had so much fun. Miss Margie got Jason's attention away from the others.

"Jason, how is your mother?"

He was surprised that the subject was directed at him and he would have to respond. The table was quiet after Miss Margie's question.

"We talked about your Uncle Bobby, but we didn't talk about your mother." Her second comment gave Jason the time he needed.

"She's doin' fine." He was afraid his answer was not enough, but Miss Margie made sure it was.

"Your mother has always been so pretty. She never seems to age. What a wonderful thing. Please tell her I said, 'hello,' and tell Bobby too. That Bobby is a mess."

"Yes, ma'am. I will." Even with a few words spoken, Jason felt he had been a strong part of the conversation.

Peggy wanted to add to the conversation. "Betty and me saw Bobby last night at Bill's. He ain't changed a bit."

Miss Margie was interested. "Does he still dance and sing like Elvis?"

"Yes, Mama, he can still dance. And, Mama, he is Elvis." Peggy had a serious look on her face, as the whole table errupted into laughter.

"Y'all laugh if ya want to. I think he's really Elvis." The laughter continued. Betty had to speak up.

"You have really gone crazy, this time. You gotta stop ridin' in
that little car. All that bouncin' up and down is doin' somethin' to
you."

They all laughed again. Peggy did too. Jason loved it. He wished
his two loved ones were there with him. The roast beef was the best
he had ever eaten. Everything at Miss Margie's was the best ever.
He emptied the first plate Sofia had fixed for him and a second one
that he filled. The apple pie covered with vanilla ice cream was the
crowning touch. It was a great day.

Everyone helped with the clean up. Jason followed Sofia's lead
as the young people cleared the table. It took no time, with everyone
helping. He loved being part of the family activity. Jason ran into
Susan while he carried a stack of dishes to the kitchen sink. It was a
chest-to-chest, face-to-face collision. There were no injuries, but they
knew each other much better than they had before. Even though it
was an accident and a brief moment, Jason still liked being close to
her. She liked it too. He liked the freckles on her nose. Jason had no
idea of the number of eyes watching him as he helped with the cleaning. All four sisters were attracted to him. He had a rare look and
way about him. Women were drawn to him.

Sofia saw his kindness and his childlike vulnerability. She
wanted to ease his confusion. Her sister Susan, who had been part
of the body-to-body collision, liked him from the day she saw him
talking to Mr. King across from the store. Sister Peggy paid the least
amount of attention to him, but she did think he was handsome.
Margie, the oldest, didn't like the attention Sofia was giving to Jason.
She had more mature ideas for him and Sofia was just a silly child.
The other Peggy watched Jason from time to time as the evening progressed. He excited her so. Betty watched him in amazement. And
Miss Margie looked at him and recalled his young life of adversity.
If he had known he was being watched by so many eyes, at once,
he would have crawled into his world of dreams. He was too busy
watching the ladies, who were watching him. He did have a way of
touching the hearts around him. Jason lost sight of Sofia again and
took a solo mini-tour of the house, hoping to find her.

Miss Margie's house was a big one. It reminded Jason of the house he lived in when he and his mother had lived with his grandparents in East Mayport, near the naval base. That house was actually known as the Big House. Miss Margie's house was much cleaner and had pretty things in it, but it was similar in size and structure.

Jason turned the corner of the main hallway and found himself facing a set of stairs, leading to the upper floor. He could hear voices in the rooms near him, but the upstairs area was quiet. The walls on both sides of the stairs were lined with pictures. He looked at each one as he slowly climbed the steps one by one. Miss Margie's family history was captured in the squares and ovals hanging on the walls. He recognized some of the faces in the pictures. An instant chill ran through Jason's body when his eyes fell on a picture of a group of young boys standing at the bottom of the sand hill in Mayport, below the oak tree. It was faded and looked old and Jason's blood flow changed directions in his veins. His heart raced in his chest, at the tree above the young boys. Jason knew the boys were going to play the game. One of the boys in the picture waved at Jason and motioned for him to follow them. He watched the boys in the picture run up the sand hill toward the tree. Jason was quick to shake free of the impossible vision. He was standing at the top of the stairs looking down, as if he had made the climb to the tree with the boys. He was confused and scared. A sweet voice called him back from his fantasy.

"Daydreaming, again?"

He turned quickly and found himself face-to-face with Sofia. She had saved him. He hoped she didn't hear his heart as it beat against his chest.

"I was lookin' at all the pictures."

"Aunt Margie has pictures all over the house and albums full too." She added to his racing heart. Sofia knew he was stressed and she sensed his discomfort. She knew something had ignited a dark moment in his head. Sofia touched his cheek with the palm of her soft hand. "Are you alright?"

Jason's head cleared, instantly. Only Sofia filled it now. She moved her hand from his face and took his hand.

"You don't have to be afraid." She led him down a hallway to a small room. As they entered the room, she turned quickly and kissed him on his lips.

"I've been wanting to do that all day. I hope you don't mind. I just wanted to so bad. Don't be mad. I know I'm just a baby to you and my sisters, but please don't be mad. Don't tell Margie. I know you like her."

Jason was surprised and speechless. He knew she was talking to him, but he only heard a few words. She still stood close to him. He wanted to kiss her again, a real kiss. He couldn't help himself either.

Jason reached out and put both of his hands around Sofia's tiny waist and gently pulled her to him. Their bodies touched and they were as close as two people could be. Sofia was not afraid at all. It felt natural to her, as if she was part of him and belonged there. She had no experience at all with such a moment, yet she felt she had touched him before. No one had to move first. They kissed as if they had been practicing for years. It was long and breathtaking for them both. Their lips were a perfect match. Jason felt it too. They melted together, like they had entered each other's body. Laughter and footsteps, coming up the stairs, broke the passion.

Sofia moved across the room and took a box off of the shelf. She began taking items from the box and placing them in some type of order, on a table. Jason didn't move as the three sisters and cousin Peggy entered the room. As usual Margie was the first to talk.

"I knew she'd be up here, gettin' ready for the big game. She never wins, but she keeps tryin'."

Sofia smiled at her sister. "Today's the day. I can't lose."

The three sisters moved to the table and helped Sofia. Peggy stood with Jason.

"I hate Monopoly. I never win, either.

She patted Jason on his butt, as she passed him and moved toward the girls at the table. Peggy couldn't help herself.

The sisters were talking and laughing. Jason could see that they were excited, as they prepared to play the game. He had never played Monopoly before. He knew nothing about it. Sofia's voice caressed his ears.

"Peggy, are you going to stay and play?" She wanted Jason to stay.

"I told y'all, I hate that game. Besides, that game takes too long and I've got to get Jason home early. He starts his new job in the morning and I promised Mary C. I'd have him home early."

Jason wanted to yell, "No! No! Let's stay! I want to stay," but he didn't.

Peggy had more reasons. "I can't take much more of the old talk downstairs and I ain't playin' Monopoly. It is time for me to fire up the Lady Bug and head out. We've stayed longer then I planned already. It was fun seein' y'all." Peggy passed Jason.

"I'll meet ya at the car. I need to say bye to everybody." She left the room.

Jason knew he had to say good-bye to the others too, and thank Miss Margie for the dinner. He looked in the direction of the four sisters across the room, but he saw only one pair of eyes. Sofia returned his stare. She gave him courage.

"It was very nice finally meeting y'all. Thank you. I had a good time." He could feel all four sets of eyes on him again. Each one of them liked something about Jason. He was easy to like. He probably got that from Uncle Bobby. The girls were settling down to play their board game, so he knew Sofia would not leave and follow him downstairs. Their good-bye was done and he would have to see her another time. He knew then he would buy more honey buns.

Jason didn't look at any of the pictures on the walls as he hurried down the stairs. Miss Margie met him with a good-bye hug. He had never been physically touched, so many times, by so many different people. It was a great day.

"You take care of yourself, son. And don't be a stranger. It was so nice seeing you. You made this a very special Sunday for me."

"I had a good time. Thank you for dinner. I'll tell Uncle Bobby he really missed a good time." The praise and the comfort gave Jason courage.

Peggy kissed her mother and yelled toward the living room. "Betty, I'm leavin'. I'm gonna take Jason home now. I'll see you back at the house." Peggy took Jason's arm and led him to the blue bug.

"You want to drive?" It was a great day. They were off again.

Mary C. sat in her porch swing, enjoying the night air and waiting for Jason. It was only about nine o'clock, so she wasn't too concerned. She knew Jason would be up early no matter how much sleep he had. He would probably be too excited to sleep. She wanted him to be at his best for his new job. Mary C. was glad Peggy had taken him to the dinner. It would keep him busy and he needed to get out and be with other people. She was just a little worried about his moments when he drifted off into deep thought. People might not understand about that. Mary C. didn't know she was being watched by a pair of eyes, as Sheriff McIntosh sat in his car near her house, in the dark.

Peggy was singing along with Little Richard's "Tutti Frutti" as the Lady Bug rounded the curve at the little jetties.

"I sure wish I didn't have to get you home tonight. You are somethin' special, Jason. Somethin' special." She looked at him with want in her glazed-over eyes. The road to his house was at the next turn. Jason kept his eyes on the road and hands on the wheel. Peggy reached over and rubbed him between his legs.

"I hope I get to see you again, soon."

Jason's foot pushed the gas pedal. Peggy laughed and started singing again.

Miss Margie walked into the room, as Sofia was celebrating her first win at Monopoly.

"I told y'all I couldn't lose tonight." Her sister Margie had a disgusted look on her face, but didn't respond, while the four of them put the pieces of the game back in the box. Sofia didn't care who knew it, she wanted to know more about Jason.

"Aunt Margie, what happened to Jason? Everybody seems to know something about him that they don't talk about. I can see you like him, but you feel sorry for him too. I feel sorry for him and I don't even know why. Will you tell us?"

Her sisters were quiet. They were surprised by her question, but they wanted to hear what their Aunt Margie had to say. Miss Margie seemed to be ready to share the stories about Jason.

"There is so much to tell about Jason. He was a very special boy. He had this look about him and he had a sensitive side, very rare for the boys in Mayport. He has lived through so much more hardship in his short life than most would see in ten lifetimes." Miss Margie continued for her captive audience. She began a story that would cause all four sisters to fall in love with a young man they had met that day.

"When Jason was five years old, his daddy, J.P., took him hunting one day. Somehow his father accidentally shot himself with a shotgun. Jason tried to get help and was lost in the woods for a day or so before someone found him. When they did find his daddy, he was dead. Some animal had torn his body up, but folks said he was probably dead way before the animals got to him." All four girls had the same look on their faces. Miss Margie had much more.

"When he was seven, his grandfather, Bob Merritt, they called him Daddy Bob, was killed along with a man named Ray Klim. Folks said Ray's brother Charlie killed Ray to steal his wife and he killed Bob for pure meanness. The wife's name was Eve, and she was pure evil. I always thought she had something to do with the killings. The story was that Jason saw the killings being done, but his young mind couldn't hold such evil deeds and God won't let him remember now. They never could prove it was Charlie or Eve, so nothing was done. About a month after Bob was killed, his wife, Jason's grandmother, just disappeared. I think she killed herself out in the swamp."

The four girl's were spellbound by the story they were hearing.

"Two or three other people got killed during that time and all of them had something to do with Jason and his family. There was death all around that poor boy." Miss Margie shook her head and took a breath before she added to the unbelievable tale.

"That's when Jason and Mary C. came to live in Mayport with Bobby. Bobby's named after his daddy, Bob Merritt. Jason and his mother had put all those awful things behind them and they were happy, living with Bobby. When Jason was going to turn sixteen, Bobby wanted him to play in this crazy game the boys played in Mayport. It was to prove you were turning into a man. It was strange and some people in Mayport actually felt the game was needed so the shrimp would come."

The girls looked more amazed.

"I know it sounds crazy, but there are still people in Mayport who believe that big oak tree on the sand hill has a power and it can give it to a baby. They used to call them oak babies. I'm not going to tell y'all how they said you became an oak baby. Your mama can tell y'all about that."

The information from Miss Margie was almost too much for the four girls to take in. They all took a deep breath along with their aunt.

"Well, Jason was going to play this crazy game. Mary C. told me later that he didn't want to play because of a group of evil boys, who were going to play too. She thought Jason was scared, but he wouldn't tell Bobby. A few days before the game it was Jason's birthday and Bobby had given him a big hunting knife. Jason came home one night and the same man who people said killed his Daddy Bob was tryin' to hurt his mother. Jason took the big knife and stabbed the man a bunch of times. He cut Charlie Klim up bad. It was self-defense and he saved his mother, but it was still another awful moment of violence in his life."

The sisters were exhausted and they all felt as if they had taken a beating. The story was mentally pounding them. They couldn't believe Miss Margie had more.

"A day or so after the stabbing, Jason played the game. it was crazy, what they did. The game was called Duckin'. It was a rough game and you had to try and capture members of each team. When you were captured you would be put in a place under the oak tree. You could not run free until a teammate would swing down on rope swings from up in the tree and tag you. Then you could run free. The rough part came in when people would try to knock you off the swings. They say the collisions and injuries were real bad. In the games before that day, the young men who played only broke a few bones or got a bloody nose, stuff like that. The day Jason played, for some reason the boys had weapons and used the weapons when the players would swing from the tree. No one has been able to find out what really happened that day. Folks don't even know how many boys died. Four or five, they say. Maybe more. A lot of others were hurt bad. Jason is the only one people talk about. He survived that awful game. He's special, I tell ya. God's with that boy."

The sisters were silent, as Miss Margie had one more addition to her story.

"Jason didn't talk at all for almost a year after that day. That's when I went to visit him and read to him. It was a wonderful day when he started talking again. He has had so much darkness around him. It was nice seeing him today. He really seems to have put all that behind him."

Mary C. saw the lights of the Lady Bug as Jason made the turn, about one hundred yards from the house. She knew it was them because she knew of no other car with its headlights so close to the ground and so close together. She smiled and was certain it was Jason when she heard the lawn mower engine sound.

Neither Peggy nor Jason saw the police car, parked off the road in the dark woods. Mary C. remained in the swing as Jason drove the little car right up next to the porch steps.

"Well, just drive right on in the house, why don't ya?"

Jason jumped out of the car and Peggy opened her door, so she could move to the driver's side.

"Well, here he is. Just like I said."

"You did good, Peggy. Thank you."

"We had a good time and I'm still stuffed. Mama said, 'hey,' and she wished you hadda come. Maybe next time."

"I'd like that. Your mama's always been so nice to us."

"That's Mama. She loved seein' Jason. She guessed who he was. She's a mess. Thanks for lettin' Jason go. He was great company. I think he enjoyed it."

Jason looked at Peggy, after such an understatement. "I had fun, thank you." Sofia's face flashed in his head.

"Say 'hey' to Bobby for me." Peggy's big breasts flashed in Jason's head when she mentioned his Uncle Bobby. Jason wondered if she would tell his uncle about what they did. Peggy fired up the Lady Bug and was gone.

"That Peggy's been in love with Bobby for as long as I can remember. I've always liked Peggy. I thought Bobby would have settled down with her. But, who knows what he's gonna do. I think it has something to do with that friend of hers, Betty. I don't think they're queer or nothin'. I just think Betty loves Bobby too and it would be bad if he settled with Peggy. I don't know, it's too crazy for me."

Jason followed his mother into the house. She didn't ask him any questions about his wonderful day. He didn't mind; he was just glad she was home and they could be together. She disappeared into her bedroom. It was Mary C.'s unknowing, unfeeling way. Jason was alone.

Jason would be like a five-year-old child on Christmas Eve, waiting for Santa, during the night. He was too excited to sleep. He set two alarm clocks so there was no danger of oversleeping. Mary C. would not wake up and assist him in the morning. The police car drove away.

Chapter Four

Jason turned both alarm clocks off, before they made any noise. He had fallen asleep a few times during the night, but no longer than thirty minutes at a time. His excitement would sustain him for the workday. He knew he was scheduled for the six-thirty shuttle run to the big rocks. He allowed for the time it would take him to walk to Mr. Leek's and he knew he had to leave the house right at six, so he would be sure to be on time. He checked all three clocks in the house, just in case. He would walk out the door when he counted six chimes of the living room clock.

Jason knew his uncle was not home and he hoped his night shrimping trip was full of the brown-colored night shrimp, called "hoppers." He had his lunch, his new required steel-toed boots and his gloves. The first of six chimes sent him out the door.

The dock was alive with people and movement. Mr. Leek was greeting all the workers as they entered the fish house.

"Mornin', Jason. There's coffee and donuts over there on the table, if you're hungry." Mr. Leek was the greatest. He always thought of things like that. Jason was too excited to eat, but when Mr. Leek saw him pass the table he put two donuts into Jason's lunch bag.

"You might need these later." Jason liked Mr. Leek. There were at least one hundred men in the fish house or standing on the dock.

SHUTTLE BOAT

Jason joined the group on the dock. He was ready to take his seat on the shuttle. Most of the workers were older than Jason, but about twenty-five or so looked to be near his age. Jason knew there had never been so many people on Mr. Leek's dock. It was strange to Jason that he didn't know any of the workers. He thought he would know some of them.

Jason's heart jumped when one of the shuttle's diesel engines fired and popped the bouncing air lid on the exhaust pipe. Then, the second shuttle did the same and Jason's heart jumped again. He didn't need anything else to make his heart beat, it was pounding enough without any help. Mr. Leek stepped out onto the dock, carrying a clipboard.

"Listen up, gentlemen. This will be your boarding area each morning. If you are not going to work after today, or you decide to quit at any time, please let me know, so we can replace you. It's fine if you quit, just let me know. The way I understand this shuttle run is that each of you have a group you have been assigned to. If you don't remember your group I have a list and I can find out for you. Group A and B will operate the big equipment. Group C will assist them and handle the tools and Group D, the less experienced workers, will be given jobs they can handle until they learn what is needed and the foreman learns what you can do. If you are in Group C you need to board the shuttle to my left. Group D will board the shuttle to my right. Good luck, gentlemen, have a great day."

Jason was the first one from Group D on the shuttle. He took a seat right next to the outside railing. About twenty-five men boarded with him. The shuttle was full and lines were untied from the dock. The exhaust pipe flipped its lid and they moved out onto the river. The shuttle captain blew his horn to let the other boats know he was coming. The ferry horn blew at the same time, making its first run of the day. The shuttle slowed to allow the Buccaneer to pass. It was fifty yards away as it moved to the Fort George side of the river. Jason watched it with respect.

The second shuttle's horn sounded and Jason looked back to see the full boat pull away from the dock. A few of the workers talked to each other, but most of the men sat quietly. It was too early for very much conversation. The shuttle was making the turn to enter the mouth of the river. Jason could see the channel lined by the huge rocks that lead you out to the open ocean. To the right you could see the great navy ships resting in the water of the man-made basin. Jason's blood ran cold when he made the mistake of looking back toward Mayport. He had forgotten about the oak tree. He saw it on the sand hill, towering above the little town. His mouth went dry and a cool breeze touched his face. He turned away quickly. The shuttle was pulling up next to one of the big barges that Jason had heard about, but not seen.

The shuttle boat was far below the huge barge in the water. Four rope ladders with wooden slat steps were dropped from the deck of the barge. Each man had to make the climb from the shuttle to the barge. Jason was the first to grab the ladder, but he didn't climb up. He held the rope steady so the others could make the climb with the least amount of movement in the ropes. He helped each man as they went up. He even helped one man after his foot slipped off one of the wooden slats. Jason had done a full day's work before he made the climb to the barge. He stood with the other workers. The shuttle captain liked Jason already. As Jason steadied his feet, a man began giving instructions to the first arrivals.

"The reason Group D is here first is because we want you out of everybody else's way before they get here. So follow me to the far side of the deck, before the others get here." Group D followed the man. They stopped in an open area, where there was no equipment of any kind. It was as if they had hidden everything from Group D. The man's voice filled the air again.

"My name is Mr. Hawkins. My friends call me Hawk. There is a possibility that some of you will become my friend. However, until that happens, my name is Mr. Hawkins. I will let you know when you can call me Hawk. The last job I was on, nobody called me Hawk. I am one of the foreman for this great company and I am in charge of the new workers; the men who are young and willing to work, but don't know nothin'; the workers who get the experienced worker killed tryin' to do something they got no business doin'. Don't do nothing unless you are told to do it. Even if you have to wait for somebody to be with you, you wait. I will let you know when you can do things on your own. Don't get that mixed up with calling me Hawk. If I tell to do something on your own, that doesn't mean we're friends. It will probably mean you can move a bucket, if it's in your way."

Jason used his listening skills and took in every word. One time during the speech, Mr. Hawkins was looking at Jason and Jason looked directly into the man's eyes. Uncle Bobby had taught him that. Three other men stepped from the crowd and stood next to Mr. Hawkins.

"These men will divide you into three working groups. When one of these men tell you to do something, do it. Only me and the man in charge of your group will direct you. Once you are with a group, you stay there unless I change you. I am the only one who can change you. Please follow these rules. If someone tells you to do something and you don't think he has the authority to do so, talk to me before you do anything. All this may seem uncalled for or elementary to some of you stud boys, but I assure you it is for your safety and well-being. This is a very dangerous job. Men have died on rigs like this. Men far better and smarter than you. One mistake and it could very well be your last. The way to avoid that fatal moment is to follow the rules and do only what you are told. We will tell you when you eat and we hope you are all smart enough to relieve yourself before you get here, at lunch and maybe one other time. We understand emergencies, but don't have more than one a year. If you think you are sick or having stomach problems, stay home. We don't want you here. We will be much better without you. Now, do you have any questions before you start to work?"

Jason knew he had no questions and it seemed no one else did either.

"Good." Mr. Hawkins walked away as the other three men divided the twenty-five men into smaller groups. The man with Jason looked to be Uncle Bobby's age. He was quite a bit overweight and his stomach made his khaki pants roll down at the waist. He had fair skin and his face was red and peeling from days in the sun. He took his group away from the others and put them to work.

Mary C. was up and moving around the house. She was in pain. In fact, the pain was the worst it had been. She found a bottle a Jack Daniels in Bobby's room and used it to ease her pain. She lay on her bed, as the Jack warmed her tender areas. She looked at the clock on her dresser. It was eight o'clock. She hoped Jason made it to the job. She would sleep most of the day.

Bobby's all-night shrimping trip had lasted into the morning. The catch was substantial and it was worth the extra time dragging. His nets were coming out of the water, ending the last drag. If he had shrimp in this load, he would be starting the week on a positive note. The huge net bag full of sea creatures hung dripping over the deck of the *Mary C.* The bag swung back and forth until Bobby and his mate steadied it. It was easy for Bobby to see the net held another large amount of shrimp, mixed in with the other creatures of the deep. He pulled the rope that secured the bag at the end of the net. When it opened the live shrimp and others fell to the deck of the boat, slapping the wooden deck. The shrimp were in the majority, always a good sign. The pile of shrimp were surrounded by and mixed with flounder, whiting, small Spanish mackerel and crabs. The shrimp moved the least, the fish flopped around, but didn't go anywhere. The crabs were a different story. They went everywhere and they were ready to fight. Bobby didn't care much about the aggressive crabs; he was more interested in picking the shrimp out of the pile and getting them on ice for the trip home. It would take a while to clear the deck of the creatures and clean it. He turned the *Mary C.* toward home and put her on automatic pilot. He returned to the stern to help pick out the shrimp and the fish they would save to sell to Mr. Leek.

Sheriff McIntosh stood at the door of the big sailor's hospital room again. He thanked the nurse on duty for calling him when "big boy" opened his eyes. A doctor motioned for him to step to the bed.

"We don't mind if you talk to him. In fact, we hope he responds to you. He has no family here yet and if he'll talk to you, that would be a good sign for him. There is so much swelling in his head, it is a wonder he is not in a coma. He is in bad shape. I hope he talks to you."

Sheriff McIntosh nodded his head and moved closer to the injured sailor. The nurse walked in to take some medical readings.

"He was awake just before you came. He opened his eyes and looked around. I told him where he was."

"I thought he talked to someone yesterday, and he didn't know who he was."

"I don't know about that. No one told me that."

The sheriff sat down in a chair next to the bed. He touched the sailor's hand. "If you can hear me, try to open your eyes. I would like to talk to you. The doctor said it would be good for you to talk to me." The sailor didn't move. He was asleep.

The work on the barge was nonstop for Jason and the rest of Group D. Their red-faced, overweight leader, named Big Jim, had something for them to do every minute. They worked together, carrying pipes, tools and cleaning up after other groups of men after they made messes. Jason worked hard and fast. He was pure energy, as he moved around the deck of the barge, from job to job. He wasn't trying to impress anyone; he was just being Jason. He would finish one job and ask Big Jim, "What's next?" He did love being a working-man. He was in high gear and took pride in each job, no matter how small. One time during the day, Jason was on his way back to Big Jim for his next assignment and he stopped to help another worker, who had dropped a boxful of small bolts and the little silver washers were all over the deck. Jason helped the man pick up the bolts until the box was full again and then Jason helped him carry the heavy box to its original destination. Big Jim was watching Jason, as he helped the other worker. Jason finally made it back to his regular area, where Big Jim waited.

"That box was too heavy for that boy. He ain't got butt enough to handle that weight."

"No, sir. I guess not. Sorry I took so long."

Big Jim liked the way Jason took each job so seriously and he also liked the way he was willing to help where he was needed. It seemed so natural for him to do that. Helping others doesn't come easy for some people.

While carrying a box of metal clamps, Jason turned and found himself in the same path as Mr. Hawkins. He had to dodge to one side to keep from running into the foreman. Mr. Hawkins had to do some dodging too, as he stepped quickly to one side and allowed Jason to pass by him, without a collision. Jason never broke his stride and kept moving.

"Sorry, Mr. Hawkins."

"That's alright, boy. I don't mind steppin' aside for a man doin' his job."

Jason was moving too fast, and was too far away, to hear the foreman's comment. He would have liked what Mr. Hawkins had said.

Jason put the box where he was told and headed back for another. Mr. Hawkins's voice stopped all the action.

"It's lunchtime, gentlemen. You have forty-five minutes. If you don't want to sit up here in the sun, 'cause you burn like Big Jim, you can go down and sit on the rocks in the shade. If you do leave topside, be careful on the ladders and don't fall in the water. Don't make me wait for you. At the end of forty-five minutes, I will blow this whistle. I expect you to be standing on this deck when I stick it in my mouth. You will return to the same job you are doing now, unless I tell you different. If you are not planning to return after lunch, don't just leave. You can ride the shuttle back to the dock, with our blessing. There will be no hard feelings and you will be paid for the half day you have worked. We know this kinda work ain't for everybody. Have a nice lunch."

Jason wanted to sit on the big red rocks. He picked up his lunch from where he had been told to leave it that morning, and walked to the edge of the barge. The ladders on that side were attached and it was much easier to climb down than it was to climb on the rope ladders earlier that morning. He moved down to the rocks and sat on the biggest one he saw. It had a flattop surface and it was big enough to have ten men lie down, stretch out and relax, if they wanted. It was bigger than Peggy's bed.

Jason could see the ocean on one side and the mouth of the river on the other. Only a few other workers had made the climb to the rocks. Jason would call it his "lunch rock." He was surprised when he saw Big Jim working his way over the rocks. He hadn't seen him climb down while he was hunting the best rock. Big Jim was working extra hard to keep from falling, as he looked for the right rock.

"Mr. Big Jim. Come over here and sit with me. This rock's easy to sit on and there's plenty of room for both of us."

Big Jim looked at Jason and realized it would be an easy climb over to Jason's rock. Jason helped him step onto the flattop of the huge red rock.

"There ya go, Mr. Big Jim. It sets good, don't it?"

"Thank ya, boy. I didn't think it would be so hard to get down here. I just had to get in the shade. The sun is cookin' me alive." Big Jim's forehead was beaded up with sweat. His blue company shirt was soaking wet.

"I'm sweatin' like a damn pig here, boy. I've got sun blisters on my lips and my face is peelin' slap off. I just had to get out of the sun before I busted into flames. I gotta lose some damn weight before I drop dead out here."

Jason thought, "Then you wouldn't be Big Jim."

One area of the rock's flattop was shaded by a pile of other rocks. You could sit on the big rock and lean your back against other rocks that surrounded it. Jason motioned to Big Jim.

"You need to sit over there. That's a good shady spot."

Big Jim moved into the shade and sat down, resting his back against another rock. The shaded rock was cool on his back and he felt better. He closed his eyes and took deep breaths, trying to calm his overheated heart. Jason interrupted his cool quiet moment.

"This is a great rock, ain't it?"

Big Jim opened his eyes. "What?" Big Jim wanted to be sure he heard what he thought he heard.

"This rock. It's a great rock. I wonder where it come from." Jason was serious with his praise for the rock and his question.

"They cut 'em out of some mountain and float 'em here on barges. We gonna see some in a few days, maybe sooner. Then the work's gonna start. You think you gotta be careful now, just wait 'til them damn big rocks get pushed off the barges and dropped in the water. Or a smaller one is hangin' from a crane overhead and you're on the drag line, keepin' it from swingin'. Then tell me about being careful."

Jason was all ears. His specialty was listening. Big Jim had forgotten about Jason saying it was a great rock. He originally wanted to know why he said that, but talking about the dangerous rocks had taken that thought from him.

Jason opened his lunch bag and took a container of water out first. He used the lid of the container as a cup and poured some water into it. He handed it to Big Jim. He didn't ask him if he would like a drink; he had it ready for him so he couldn't refuse. He knew Big Jim needed it more than he did at the moment. He had plenty and he would drink as he ate. Big Jim took the lid and enjoyed the water.

"Thank you, son. That sure went down easy. I didn't realize how thirsty I was. I've been sweatin' so much I've probably dehydrated myself. I've been tryin' not to eat so much and with this heat, this diet and this job, I'm on the edge. I tell ya I'm on the edge."

Jason wasn't quite sure what Big Jim meant, but he knew Big Jim was miserable. "I know you're tryin' not to eat too much. But I always get sick or a headache whenever I don't eat somethin'. It ain't too good for ya to starve yourself. It might make you sick. That's why you feel so weak. You need to eat somethin'." Jason reached into his bag and pulled out a big jelly-filled donut, compliments of Mr. Leek. Big Jim's eyes looked like double flares going off.

"I got two of these and I think you should eat one. You have to make that climb back up that ladder, and you will need your energy."

Big Jim could not argue with Jason's logic. The jelly-filled was history. Jason gave one of his two sandwiches to Big Jim and shared the water until it was gone. Jason knew he could get more water when he was back on the barge. They had plenty of water cans and they did allow you to drink whenever you wanted. Jason jumped up and his eyes almost popped out of his head when he saw the *Mary C.* entering the river after her night at sea. Big Jim saw Jason's excitement.

"What is it, boy?"

"It's my Uncle Bobby's boat, the *Mary C.* He's been night shrimpin' and he's headed home. He's too far on the other side; he couldn't hear me from here if I hollered."

"What's your name, son?"

"Jason, sir."

"Well, Jason, we gotta get back, before that whistle blows."

"Yes, sir. Thank ya for talking to me."

"Thank you for lunch."

Jason stayed close to Big Jim as he made his difficult climb to the deck of the barge. Jason assisted him when he needed it and made sure he was safe. They were back in plenty of time. Before the whistle sounded, Big Jim stepped to Jason.

"I'll bring us lunch tomorrow. That is a great rock."

Mary C. watched through her front window, as Sheriff McIntosh got out of his car and walked toward the front porch for another one of his visits. She wondered if it was for business or pleasure. Either way she was in too much pain and too miserable to be interested. She knew he would notice her discomfort if he saw her; she would not be able to hide it this time. She had no idea it would hurt so much more on the second day. At first, she wasn't going to answer the door and act like she wasn't there. That plan went out the window when he sat his butt down in the swing, like the night before. He was going to swing until someone came home or someone opened the front door.

Mary C. decided she would talk to him, but it would be through the window and that was it. If he didn't like that arrangement, he could leave. She stepped to the window and before she could speak up, she saw her salvation. Bobby was walking up to the front porch.

"Hey, Bobby." The sheriff greeted him first. Bobby didn't like him being there. "Ya like swingin', don't ya?"

"I like it alright. I was hopin' to talk to Mary C. again, but there ain't nobody movin' in that house."

"She was gonna be gone all day. I don't know when she'll be back. I do know she didn't leave town, 'cause you told her not to."

"Bobby, why don't you help your sister and get her to talk about that night? That sailor's hurt bad. He don't even know his own name. He could still die from this thing. He was probably doin' somethin' wrong and maybe he deserved it, but there ain't no person or evidence that says that. All I've got is a vicious attack on an innocent person, as he walked to his car. I think Mary C. was walkin' to that car with him. I know her shoes did."

"Mac, if I knew somethin', I'd tell ya. If she told me somethin' and didn't want me to tell ya, I wouldn't tell ya. That's the way it is. But, I can tell you one thing that's true, and that is, she ain't said one word about anything that happened that night. I don't think she knows nothin' 'bout it. Now, I'm really tired and after I take a bath, I'm goin' to bed and dream about the eight boxes of hoppers I just unloaded. I hope you have a nice evening, Sheriff, but it won't be on my front porch." Bobby walked into his house and closed the door. Sheriff McIntosh left.

Jason stepped off the shuttle boat and onto Mr. Leek's dock. Group D may have been the first group to leave for the barge that morning, but they were the last group to leave the barge at the end of the day. They were, no doubt, the lowest working species and only the crabs, running in and out of the jetty rocks, were respected less. Not once did Jason think he was less important than any worker he saw that day. He had respect for the more experienced equipment workers and the knowledge of the foremen and bosses, but they were all the same to Jason. They were all workingmen. He waved to a busy Mr. Leek and walked toward the front door, leaving the fish house. Mr. Leek wasn't too busy to share good news he knew Jason would like.

"Jason, Bobby had eight boxes of "Hoppers." Jason smiled at the information.

"You look tired, Jason. Get on home. We'll talk about your first day some other time."

Jason nodded his head, but he was more excited than tired as he made his walk home. Perhaps his pace was slower than usual, but he didn't feel any difference. He looked into the window of the store, as he passed by, to see if Sofia was working. Her mother was at the counter waiting on a customer. He remembered about Uncle Bobby's eight boxes of hoppers. He wanted to talk to Uncle Bobby and his mother about the shrimp and his first day at the jetties.

Sheriff McIntosh stood in the hospital hallway, talking on the phone to the owner of the Fish Bowl. They were discussing the beating the big sailor had taken Saturday night. Mr. Daugherty was not there that night, so he didn't have much information about the incident.

"Well, if you hear anything, please let me know. I'm gonna try to get over there and talk to some more of the workers later tonight and take another look around the parking lot. Thank you for your cooperation. I really appreciate it. Good-bye." As he hung up the phone, one of the nurses walked to him.

"Are you the policeman waiting for the young man to wake up?"

"Yes! That's me. Yes!"

"Well, he's wide awake for some reason. I don't know how long he'll be that way."

"Thank you!" Mac moved past her and into the room. The young sailor was looking up at the ceiling and, like the nurse said, his eyes were wide open. The sheriff stepped up next to the bed, where he had stood before.

"Mr. Clark." The sailor had been identified by the navy, earlier that day. "My name is Mac. I'm the sheriff and I'm investigatin' the crime committed against you. I've been waiting for you to wake up for two days. Welcome back."

Mr. Clark's eyes remained open, as he looked around the room.

"Take your time, gettin' your thoughts together. It must be hard to wake up and not know where you are, or what has happened." Mac didn't know what to say. He was nervous because of the young man's serious condition. As bad as he wanted the information, he still didn't want to do anything to make things worse for the young sailor.

"Can you hear me?" Mr. Clark looked at the lawman and nodded his head one time.

"Can you talk to me?"

"Yes," he whispered.

"That's great! That's great!" Mac had to hold back his excitement. "If you could try and answer a few questions for me."

"I'll try," he whispered again.

"Do you remember anything about last Saturday night? Someone attacked you and that's why you're here."

Mr. Clark searched his dulled brain for information.

"Take your time. I really want to find the person who did this to you."

Mr. Clark whispered again. "How long have I been here?"

"Two days. They brought you here early Sunday mornin'."

"What's wrong with me?"

Mac didn't want to answer any questions. "I'm not sure. You have a head injury and some broken bones, but you need to ask the doctor about that." Mac was excited until he heard Mr. Clark's next question.

"What did you say my name was?"

Mary C. and Uncle Bobby were sitting at the kitchen table when Jason walked into the house.

"Well, well. If it ain't the workin' man. You look beat, boy."

Jason didn't understand why the others thought he looked tired; he felt great. "I'm fine. I don't feel that tired."

"Well, you look it. They really worked y'all huh?"

"I saw you go by at lunch, but you were way on the other side of the river. I couldn't holler that loud."

"I couldn't hear ya, if ya had hollered, 'cause Elvis was bringin' us and eight boxes home." Uncle Bobby used his best Elvis voice. He was excited too. Eight hundred pounds of shrimp was an exceptional night's work. He knew he would go out again that night. You had to be there when they were running, because they could be gone as fast as they came. It was a crazy business.

Mary C. joined the conversation. "How was it out there today, son? Did ya do good?"

"It was fine. I liked it and I think I did good."

"Of course, he did good. He just had to do whatever they told him. He's new and with no experience, he's just gotta do whatever they tell him and he'll be doin' good. Right, boy?"

"I was in Group D. We stayed together and did most of the cleanup work. It was steady 'til lunch and there was even more work after lunch. But, I liked it." Jason wanted to talk and for some reason the others let him.

"I had lunch with the boss of my group. We sat on a great rock. He ate one of my jelly donuts. I had to keep him from fallin' off the ladder. He's gonna bring me lunch tomorrow."

"Hold on a minute!" Uncle Bobby stopped Jason. "You're tellin' us that your boss sat on a rock with you and ate a jelly donut?" Bobby looked at Mary C. and then back at Jason.

"Yes, he did. His name is Big Jim."

Bobby still had his doubts. "And this Big Jim is gonna bring your lunch tomorrow?"

"Yes, sir. He said he would."

Bobby looked at Mary C. again. "This son of yours is somethin' else. He does live in a dream world, but it's a funny one." Uncle Bobby couldn't resist. "Anything else unusual happen today?"

"No, sir. I met Mr. Hawkins, the foreman."

Bobby was interested for real this time. "Hawk Hawkins is the foreman out there?"

Jason could tell Uncle Bobby knew something about the Hawk. "Yes, sir. But none of us can call him Hawk. Only his real friends can do that."

"I'll tell ya one thing. He is a bad man. There ain't many tougher than the Hawk. If there is, I ain't seen 'em 'round here. I ain't seen him in years. He's a good one to have on your side. If things get goin' bad, don't be against him."

As usual, Jason listened to every word. Uncle Bobby had

more.

"He's a man, that one. He use to live in Palm Valley and he came out to Mayport all the time to see a girl named Cricket. He was crazy about Cricket. He used to take her to Bill's when he was here. Cricket moved away and he didn't come 'round no more. I'd like to see the ol' boy."

Uncle Bobby always amazed Jason. He knew something about everybody. Jason couldn't resist.

"Do you call him Hawk?"

"Do I what? Hell, boy, I gave him the name Hawk. His real name is Lester. One night he jumped off the railin' at Bill's and landed on a man who had pushed a lady down in the sand. I said he looked like a nighthawk swoopin' down on a rat. He was the Hawk to me from then on. It just caught on. It was perfect, him havin' a last name like Hawkins, anyway. Hawk Hawkins, it just had a good ring to it. I guess he's gotten particular about who calls him Hawk. In the work world Mr. Hawkins fits better. Tell the other workers that if he don't want to be called Hawk, to heed his request, 'cause they don't need him mad at 'em."

Mary C. added to the information. "I remember him and that girl Cricket. She was a pretty girl, but I don't remember him bein' so mean. I remember him dancin' circles around you one night and takin' the trophy home."

Bobby's eyes lit up. "He caught me on a bad night. And he had Peggy, my usual partner. I don't know how he ended up with her out on the floor. I had to dance with Miss Perkins. She was about a hundred years old and didn't know any of the dances. I thought I could carry her, but Gene Kelly couldn't have won with her."

Mary C. and Bobby both laughed. Jason liked the moment with his family. He wanted to tell them about the dinner at Miss Margie's, but he didn't.

"Tell Mr. Hawkins I said, 'welcome back.' Now, I'd like to talk all day 'bout all this stuff, but I've got to get some sleep. I'm goin' after more hoppers at nightfall and I do need my rest." Uncle Bobby walked to the bathroom for his shower.

Mary C. wanted to hear more about Jason's day at work, but his story about having a jelly donut with the boss on a rock made her think he had spent the day in his dreamworld and perhaps his fellow workers thought he was crazy.

"So you liked it today?"

"Yes, ma'am. I did."

"Was it very hard work?"

"Yes, ma'am, but I liked it. Everything was fast and the day went by fast too. I liked sittin' on the rocks in the shade. It really was a great rock. Big Jim thought so too."

Mary C. didn't respond.

"Ya know, Mama, important people always have different kinda names. Like Hawk and Big Jim. You think I'll ever be important enough to have another name?"

"Those names ain't nothin'. It don't make you important. Just 'cause Bobby said he looked like a hawk, it makes him important? And bein' called Big Jim probably means he's been fat all his life. Them names don't mean nothin'."

With her stand, Mary C. ended the brief, but enjoyable for Jason, conversation. Jason listened to his mother, but he still wanted a "name."

Uncle Bobby's shower was quick and he was in his bed. Jason was next in the shower and Mary C. sat on the front porch swing. Jason liked them all being home.

Sheriff McIntosh walked around the back parking lot of the Fish Bowl. He would get no answers or help from Mr. Clark or Mary C. He had talked to all of the workers from that night, except one, James the bartender. The owner of the Fish Bowl walked out into the parking lot to meet the lawman.

"You must be Sheriff McIntosh. I'm Jim Daugherty. We talked earlier." They shook hands.

"I really hate all this happening here. We don't usually have this sort of thing happen. This isn't very good for us. People won't come, if they don't feel safe. How is the young man?"

"He's in pretty bad shape. At least he's awake now. He's got some broken bones, but the big problem is he don't know who he is. I feel bad for the man. We know it wasn't robbery, because he still had his wallet and money. Somebody was mad about somethin' and they beat the hell out of him over it."

"Don't get me wrong, Sheriff. I really do feel bad about anybody getting hurt like this. I didn't mean to sound unfeeling when I mentioned the people not coming to eat. I just hate it happening for all kinds of reasons." The two men both turned toward the noise of a rusty blue truck, pulling up behind the restaurant and parking.

"There's James now. He's the only one you haven't seen yet who was working Saturday night. Let me get him."

James stepped out of the truck and Mr. Daugherty motioned for him to come over to them. James hurried to talk to his boss.

"Yes sir, Mr. Daugherty."

"James, this is Sheriff McIntosh. He's looking into the attack that happened here Saturday night. He's talked to everybody but you."

James shook the sheriff's hand. Mac noticed the strong hand the young man presented.

"How ya doin', sir?"

"I'm doin' fine, but I'd be much better if you could tell me something that would shed a little light on this beatin'."

"Well, I'll try, but I heard about it Sunday mornin', at church."

"Do you remember the big sailor?"

"Yeah, I remember him."

"Was he with anyone? Did he leave with anyone? Did he argue with anyone?"

"Yes, yes and no. Yes, he was with somebody. Yes, he left with somebody. And, no, he didn't argue with anybody."

The sheriff knew he was referring to Mary C., because he already knew Mary C. left with Mr. Clark. "You're talkin' 'bout Mary C.?"

"Right. He bought her drinks for a couple of hours, and then when she got too drunk to sit on the bar stool, she left with him. I'm pretty sure he was tryin' to get her drunk, but she didn't need no help."

"How long after they left did you get off?"

"Not long at all. If I had been parked out back, I probably would have seen 'em."

"You weren't parked here Saturday night?"

"This is my usual spot, right here. The carpenters were fixing the wall over here, next to the outside cooler and they asked me to move, so I parked on the other side. If I had been parked out here, maybe I could have stopped it, or seen somethin'. I feel bad about that."

"Did you like him? I mean, was he a good customer? Was he drunk too?" Sheriff McIntosh was a three question at a time man. James was a three answer at a time man.

"I didn't like him or dislike him. I really didn't think about it much. He paid his bill, tipped me and didn't spill anything, so I consider that a good customer. He wasn't drunk at all. His only intention was to get her drunk. He was stayin' sober."

"Why do you think that?"

"Now, Sheriff, during all your investigatin', you ain't seen Mary C. yet?"

"I've seen her."

"Then you already know why he wanted her drunk and he wanted to be sober."

Mac understood what James meant, but he didn't think he needed to say it. "Well, thanks for talkin' to me. I know you have to get to work. If you think of anything you think might help me, please let me know."

"If I think of somethin', you'll be the first one I call."

Mac didn't like James very much and he knew James had the same feeling about him. He also knew bartenders always know more than they tell. He thanked Mr. Daugherty again and left the parking lot.

Chapter Five

Jason felt like a new man, after his shower. He was too keyed up to stay around the house while Uncle Bobby slept and his mother lay on the couch, nodding off now and then. Each time she drifted into temporary sleep, she would make a painful moaning sound and wake herself up. As bad as Jason wanted to be with her, he couldn't stand the sounds she made when she did fall asleep. He dressed and went for a walk. His path would take him to Miss Margaret's store.

As Jason walked, his thoughts were about going to work in the morning and seeing Sofia that night. His second look into the store for that day did not bring the sight he wanted. Sofia was not working. Miss Margaret was still behind the cash register. Jason walked around to the back of the store so he could look into a small window of the storeroom that was part of the store. He thought maybe Sofia was working, but she wasn't up front. There was a light on and he could see that no one was in the room. He turned away from the window and walked to the corner of the building, headed back to the main road. He turned quickly, when he heard a noise. There he saw Sofia's sister Susan, sitting on the ground with her back against the wall of the building. It was dark and very strange to see her there. The noise he heard was her crying. He watched her for a few seconds. He knew if he said anything, it would scare her and he didn't want her to scream. She picked up something and threw it in anger. Then she put her head down against her knees to cry some more. He had to say something. He thought, maybe, if he whispered:

"Susan."

She didn't scream, but she jumped up to run.

"It's me, Jason. I didn't mean to scare ya."

Her eyes were wide open as she looked back. Her deep, heavy breathing made her chest go in and out. It was very noticeable and Jason watched her body tremble, until she realized she was safe and she calmed herself.

"I tried not to scare you, but it didn't work. What are you doin' out here in the dark like this?"

"What am I doing here? I live here. What are you doing here in the dark? That's the question." She had a point, but Jason had no answer. He lied.

"I was gonna cut through the back here, for a shortcut home, but I didn't know the woods were so thick back here. They used to not be so thick." He knew he needed to change the subject.

"What would someone like you be crying about? You must be one of the happiest people in the world."

"Oh, really? What are you talking about?"

"I'm sorry, I thought you were crying and I just wondered why someone like you would cry out here alone in the dark. It don't seem to fit you." Jason liked those freckles that crossed her nose.

"Some people have lots of reasons to cry and some people cry for nothing. I just felt like crying, that's all."

"Can I sit here with you?"

"Why would you want to?"

"I don't have to. If you'd rather be alone. I didn't mean to bother you. People always bother me when I want to be alone. And I know how it feels. I'm really sorry you're sad. You are way too pretty to be sad about anything. Good night." Jason turned to walk away from Susan.

"Stay with me, please. I'd like you to stay."

Jason sat down and leaned against the wall. She returned to her spot and did the same. Jason found himself out of character, when he started the conversation.

"I had my first day workin' on the jetties today."

"Oh, that's right. How'd you like it?"

"It was fine. I really liked it."

Susan changed the subject and shocked Jason. "Have you had sex with my cousin, Peggy?"

Jason's mouth went dry and he thought he was dreaming. He needed to clarify what he thought he heard. "What?" Jason wanted to be sure he heard the question correctly.

"If you haven't, she wants you to." Jason was speechless and his new role as the conversationalist ended, as he became the listener, once again.

"She really acts like she wants you, but I think what it is, is that she wants you again. The way she looked at you and I saw her pat your butt, upstairs. It was so obvious, she couldn't help herself. Well, have you?"

Jason found a small amount of courage. "The first thing you should know is that you shouldn't ask such questions and the second thing you should know is that a man does not discuss such things with anybody who wants to know."

"Jason! Jason! Good answer." Her voice was coy and playful. "I've always thought Peggy was a real woman and she's my favorite relative. She told me things that Mama would never tell me. If it was up to Mama, us four girls would stay in the house and work in this store until we were all old and gray. Peggy tells us of real-life things and what pleasures are out there, if you have the courage to look for them. She calls it 'havin' the balls' to do it."

Jason's eyes popped open at Peggy's favorite saying, when she talked to her four cousins.

"If a woman like Peggy wants you, I do too."

Jason's heart went crazy in his chest. Susan was dropping bombs on him from all directions. He had no idea what to do or say. She did it for him.

Susan leaned over and kissed Jason, with a "good one." It was an open mouth, swallow your face, deep tongue action, hard kiss. She pushed her body through his as the pleasure attack continued. With no thought at all, Jason had a handful of one of her breasts. He squeezed her and she pushed harder against his hand. He reached down and touched her on the outside of her shorts. The wild kiss continued and she allowed his hands to go wherever he wanted. She became tense when he moved his hand under the elastic waistband of her shorts and found his way under her cotton panties. He had wasted no time and she found herself flat on the ground, still kissing Jason, while his fingers touched her, inside and out. She was scared, but it felt great. She reached and touched him, hoping she was doing the right thing. She touched him and wanted to feel his bare skin.

Susan unsnapped his pants and pulled the zipper down. Her reach found more than she thought. It was hard and full of heat. She had never felt such a thing. It scared her and excited her all at the same time. The heat between her legs, as he touched her, matched the heat she held in her hand. Her hand was empty; his fingers had stopped. Her shorts and panties were moving down her legs. Her legs were pushed open and she knew the second he was inside her. Her foreplay had ignited Jason, and he was in his aggressive state. She felt pain, but would never show it. She wrapped her arms and legs around him and worked as hard as he did. It was young animal sex and great for both of them. Jason continued his strokes long after he had exploded. Jessie had taught him that. It was all a new feeling for her. Susan would always want him. She would have to wait in line with her mentor and cousin, Peggy.

Jason walked to Mr. Leek's dock, while trying to recover from his flash encounter with Susan. Susan went back into the storeroom and would not recover for some time, if ever. Jason went into the public bathroom Mr. Leek had built next to the fish house. He relieved himself and washed his face and hands. He wasn't ready to go home and he wanted to clean up. He really liked her freckles. He walked out onto the dock and looked at the two shuttle boats again. The ferry horn sounded and added to his day. It was always a welcome sound and it would always make his heart beat a little faster. He thought he was alone, but he wasn't.

Jake was about ten giant steps away and he was moving fast. Jason stepped back, as Jake went by him, with his black trench coat following behind him, like a vampire's cape. Jason was frozen, with fear and surprise. Jason knew that feeling well. He knew Jake had to see him; they were too close for Jake to miss him. Jason was afraid, but he wanted to find out where Jake would be going, in such a hurry. He walked out of the same door Jake had gone through. Jason turned his head from side to side, looking for that black trench coat. Like a storybook phantom, Jake was gone. Jason felt strange, as he stood there alone. He decided to go home.

As he walked away from the fish house, Jason heard a noise behind him. In his state of nervous fear he turned quickly to face the noise. The door of the public bathroom swung open. Jake stepped out into the fresh night air. Jake looked at Jason, nodded to him, and walked away. Jake's disappearing act was into the bathroom. Jason felt foolish, as he made his walk home.

Mary C. met Jason at the door. She was in her "concerned mother" state.

"Where have you been? I was worried 'bout you. You're here with me one minute, I doze off for a second and when I open my eyes, you're gone. Why do you have to go roamin' the streets?"

Jason was never surprised at his mother's attitude and personality changes. He always listened and responded with respect. He thought she might have been drinking, but he tried not to think about the possibility. He knew she had been sick.

"I'm sorry, Mama. You've been feeling so bad, I didn't want to bother you. I just went for a walk. I know I always stay too long. I was sittin' at Mr. Leek's."

"Well, what's goin' on in our little town that keeps you gone?"

Jason smiled. "Nothin', Mama. Nothin' at all." Jason wanted to shower again before he went to bed. He walked toward the bathroom.

Mary C. had another motherly moment. "I'll make your lunch for tomorrow and leave it in the icebox. Don't forget it."

Jason looked back at his mother. "Oh, you don't have to do that. Remember, Big Jim is gonna fix my lunch tomorrow."

Mary C. shook her head, as Jason closed the bathroom door.

Jason's hard work and sexual encounter with Susan had drained his body and he slept deep and hard. He would dream, but not remember it. He was able to jump out of bed with plenty of time to leave the house when those six chimes started again. He walked faster that morning, so he could stop at the store. He knew the store would be open and he had a craving for a "honey bun" breakfast and perhaps a look at Sofia. He entered the store. Sofia's oldest sister Margie was minding the store. She looked at Jason as he walked through the door.

"Good morning, Jason. May I help you with something?"

Jason knew she had to say that to all the customers, but he still liked hearing it. It was so proper and made him feel important. It was a nice way to talk. This time he had an answer.

"I'm gonna get a honey bun and a small carton of milk. It's for my breakfast."

Margie smiled as Jason walked to the shelf, where he knew the honey buns were placed.

"I'll get you a real cold milk, out of the back. Don't you just love real cold milk with a honey bun?"

Jason knew she was right. "Yes, I do. Thank you. That would be nice." She left for a few seconds and returned with the icy cold milk. Jason met her at the cash register and paid her for his breakfast.

"What are you doing out so early? I hate being up this early."

"I'm goin' to work. It's my second day on the jetty rig."

"Oh, that's right. You're working out there. I forgot. You like it? Or you probably can't really tell in just one day."

"I like it alright. I'm gonna try another day, anyway." Jason knew he had to go. There was no way he would be late for the shuttle boat. "I really have to go. I'll miss the shuttle."

Margie gave Jason something to think about during the day. "Don't tell anyone, but me and some friends are going out tonight. We're going to Bill's Hideaway. Mama would kill me if she knew.

I'm spending the night out at my friend's house. Her mother's out of town and she asked me to stay with her for three days. They live off Seminole Road near the beach. It's only a mile or so to the Hideaway. She's been before. She says it's wild. I can't wait. You can meet us there, if you want to."

Jason liked the idea of meeting her at Bill's, but the only thing he knew at that moment was that he wasn't going to be late for the shuttle. He was out the door.

Jason heard Mr. Leek's voice and the two shuttles fire up at the same time.

"Gentlemen, may I have your attention? You will ride the shuttles in the same groups and at the same times you did yesterday and each day you work. If you are new today, you ride the last shuttle. If you were here yesterday, you ride the same shuttle. God bless you." Mr. Leek touched Jason on the back, as he walked by.

"You sure impressed some people yesterday, son. Keep it up."

Jason got on the shuttle and sat in the same seat as the first day. The boat pulled out and right on schedule the ferry blew to cross over. A light mist of river water covered Jason's face. He began eating his breakfast and drinking his milk. It wasn't still icy cold, but it was cold enough. The barge and the big red rocks were just around the corner. He was mentally and physically stronger that morning; he would not look at the oak tree.

Jason took his place holding the rope ladders and assisting the other workers as they left the shuttle. Again, he was the last to leave and make the climb to the barge. Group D moved to the open area and stood there, waiting for their morning instructions. Mr. Hawkins didn't keep them waiting.

"Well, gentlemen. We thank you for coming back. You are part of a big project and we need good men to be here and work. Remember the rules and we will be just fine. You are to go to your group leader and he will give you your first job for the day. I'll greet the new boys and let them know the rules. After today, there will be no new boys."

Jason saw Big Jim standing to his left and he walked with the

other members of his group to get his morning jobs. Big Jim surprised Jason when he spoke directly to him first.

"Jason, if I don't see ya today, meet me on the rock for lunch. I
got some good stuff."

Jason understood about lunch, but he didn't understand what
Big Jim meant about not seeing him. Big Jim turned and directed the
other members of Group D to their first jobs of the day. Jason was the
only one left standing there, after the others went to work. Big Jim
turned Jason's way.

"Jason, come with me. Mr. Hawkins wants to see ya." Jason's
heart began to race and his mouth went dry. He knew that feeling
too well. He stood in front of the Hawk.

"Mr. Hawkins, this is the young man I told you about. This is
Jason."

Jason looked into Mr. Hawkins's eyes again, but this time it was
at close range. Uncle Bobby taught him that.

"Big Jim here tells me you were his best worker yesterday. Is that
true?"

The right words came to Jason with no interference in his head.
"I'm sure Mr. Big Jim would not lie to you, sir. And yes, sir, I was
your best worker yesterday. I plan to be your best worker every day,
sir."

Mr. Hawkins kept his stern look, but it was hard. "Do you really?"

"Yes, sir, really."

Mr. Hawkins didn't take to people very well, but Jason was easy
to like. "Your job for the day will be to keep the deck of this barge
picked up and clean of any obstacles and any debris that may be left
in the way. You have the freedom to go anywhere you see anything
that could cause an accident. You can use your judgement and you
don't have to ask for permission to do the job you think needs to be
done. Your work today could save a fellow worker from injury. Do
you think you can handle such an important job?"

Jason couldn't believe what Mr. Hawkins had just said. He was
being trusted to use his own judgment and he had the freedom to

CRANE BARGE

move about the barge, without anyone directing him. He was his own boss. What a great morning.

"Yes, sir, I can."

The deck of the *Mary C.* was full of shrimp, again. Bobby and his one-man crew picked out the shrimp and the fish they could sell. They worked on the stern, as the boat headed back toward the mouth of the river. They were about three hours away from Mr. Leek's and unloading another five boxes of hoppers.

Mary C. was awake, but couldn't open her eyes. The Jack Daniels headache took all her strength. She had been miserable enough with all the painful areas on her body and now her head was added to the list. Her full bladder made it impossible to stay in the bed, so after she made her way slowly to the bathroom, she stood in the kitchen with her eyes closed. She stood there for a few seconds, debating whether or not to get back into bed. She thought coffee was the answer. She forced her eyes open. Mary C. had no idea her new friend, the sheriff, was on his way to her, for an early visit.

Jason was on the move. He was a workingman of nonstop action. The barge was clean of any dangerous debris or, for that matter, any debris at all. A nail, a screw, a piece of paper: nothing stayed on the deck of the barge for more than a few seconds. He had even established the best route to take in order to clean the problem areas more often. He never stopped moving and cleaning. He would drink water, as he continued his search for any unwanted object. He picked up tools and put them in order, back in the toolboxes. If a worker dropped something from above, Jason was there to be sure he didn't have to leave his spot. Jason either threw it back or carried it up a ladder, if it was too dangerous to throw. At some time during the morning he had done something to help everybody on the barge. He had even helped the members of Group D carry boxes to a designated area.

Mr. Hawkins watched Jason, as he worked his magic; he couldn't help it. He was easy to like. Big Jim could see Mr. Hawkins was admiring Jason's enthusiasm for his job.

"He's a good boy, don't ya think?"

Mr. Hawkins nodded. "Yeah, I do. He has a spirit that ya don't see too much anymore. Folks used to have it, but it's gone. It's like he's out of place in time. Somebody did a good job raisin' this boy."

Jason went by the two men, carrying some scrap wood to a large trash can. As he dumped the wood someone yelled, "Man overboard!"

Mr. Hawkins and Big Jim, along with a crowd, ran to the edge of the barge. A worker was floating facedown in the water, on the open river side, away from the jetty rocks. He had hit his head on the side of the barge during the fall. Everyone was frozen for a second when they spotted the floater. Jason passed Mr. Hawkins and handed him the end of a rope, as he dove off the barge and into the water, holding the other end of the rope.

Everyone was frozen again, as Jason popped up in the water next to the floater, lifted his head up out of the water, and started tying the rope around him. It took Mr. Hawkins a second look to realize he was holding the other end of the rope that Jason was tying to the injured worker. They all watched in amazement, as Jason pushed the man toward the side of the barge, keeping his head out of the water and holding the rope. Two other men grabbed the rope with Mr. Hawkins and began pulling the man up, out of the water and back toward the deck of the barge. He was still unconscious and he was dead weight. They could see blood on the side of his head and it looked like his arm was broken. Big Jim dropped one of the rope ladders down to Jason, waiting in the water. Jason was up the ladder and standing on the deck, dripping wet, before the injured worker was untied.

Jason didn't notice that everyone on the barge was standing and looking at him. The silent amazement was more respectful than any other form of praise. They had just witnessed an unselfish act of bravery and kindness, by a young man they had never seen before yesterday. Two first-aid workers attended to the man's injuries and called for a shuttle boat. Jason was still standing near the injured man and he was still dripping on the deck. For some strange reason no one said anything until Mr. Hawkins looked at Jason and broke the silence.

"What the hell did you have for breakfast?"

"A honey bun, sir."

The entire barge exploded into laughter. Even Hawk couldn't hold it back. They all gathered around Jason, as two big workers lifted him on their shoulders in a gesture of respect and praise. It was really a great day.

Uncle Bobby made sure he brought the *Mary C.* into the mouth of the river, near the south jetties, taking his load of hoppers to Mayport. He wanted Jason to see the boat from the barge and he thought he could see Jason through his binoculars. He held the big glasses to his eyes and focused in on the big red rocks at first. His movement to his right brought to his eyes an unbelievable image. It looked like a riot of some kind was taking place among the workers on the barge. They were all concentrated in one area and some of them seemed to be jumping around the deck. As he scanned the commotion, the high-powered lenses of the glasses found an image that was not only unbelievable, but dreamlike. He thought he saw Jason being carried around on someone's shoulders, above the others. Bobby moved the glasses away from his face and wiped his eyes. When he focused the binoculars again, it was true. He didn't know what was happening, but he knew they sure looked happy. He couldn't wait to dock the boat at Mr. Leek's.

The coffee helped Mary C. wake up. She still had the headache, but she could keep her eyes open. Another hot bath was on her mind and she carried her second cup of coffee into the bathroom with her. She turned on the faucets, full blast, took off her robe and sat down in the tub, waiting for the water to fill around her. She couldn't hear Sheriff McIntosh knocking on the front door. He waited for about thirty seconds. He knew she had to be there and he wasn't leaving until he saw her, even if he had to get her out of the bed. He walked around to the back of the house and knocked on that door too. Mary C. only heard the water rushing in around her. Mac decided to walk back to the front of the house and sit in the swing again. As he passed the bathroom window he heard the water running and he knew she was home, or someone was home. He would sit in the swing like he had the night before. Mary C. lay back in the hot water, hoping to relax, heal some more and steam away her headache. The sheriff waited.

The injured worker was being taken off the shuttle boat at Mr. Leek's dock. Lunchtime had calmed the celebration on the barge. Jason sat on his big red rock with Big Jim and six other workers, who had joined them in the shade. Big Jim had a great lunch for him and Jason. Mr. Hawkins looked down from the deck of the barge and watched the eight men talk, laugh and eat together on Jason's rock. It was a great rock.

Uncle Bobby threw a rope to one of Mr. Leek's dockworkers, tying the *Mary C.* secure to the dock. He could see the fish house was alive with excitement. A man was being carried on a stretcher toward the front of the building. Mr. Leek saw Bobby and hurried to him.

"That Jason is somethin', ain't he?"

Bobby had no idea what he was talking about.

Mr. Leek was excited. "I always said he was special and had a purpose in this life."

Bobby couldn't take any more mystery. "What are you talking about? What is goin' on out at that barge and who are they putting in the ambulance?

Bobby was a three question man.

"Oh Lord! You don't know yet, do ya?"

Bobby shook his head. "No, I don't know yet. So tell me."

"The man in the ambulance is Mr. Steve Robertson, the famous crane operator."

Bobby stopped Mr. Leek. "You mean to tell me, that the man on the stretcher is Steve 'the Crane' Robertson? The Steve Robertson from down in South Florida?"

"That's him, in the flesh."

"What the hell happened to him?"

"He fell out of his crane and into the river. He hit his head on the side of the barge when he fell."

Bobby thought he understood. "No wonder there's so much excitement around here. He's a famous man."

Mr. Leek had to bring Bobby into the "know." "Well, him bein' famous ain't the half of it. We're all happy the man ain't dead and all, but the real news is what happened when he fell. Your nephew, Jason, jumped into the water with a rope and saved Mr. Robertson's life. He was out and floatin' facedown when Jason jumped in and held his head up out of the water, until he tied him off and the other men pulled him back to the barge. Everybody watched it happen. The two men who came on the shuttle with Mr. Robertson said it was the bravest thing anyone had ever seen on that barge. The boy's a hero. That Jason's a hero."

The vision of Jason being carried above the crowd flashed in Uncle Bobby's head.

Mary C. stepped out of the bathtub and began drying her body off. She had no idea the sheriff sat in the swing. He heard a door close in the house and looked into the window next to the swing. Mary C. was walking through the front room, still drying her naked body with the towel. She thought she was alone and a quick walk to the clothes hamper would be private enough. Mac stared at her through the window. Her beautiful body was covered with black bruises and red scratches. He loved seeing her for the first time, but he hated it too. His heart hurt inside his chest, as she moved out of his sight. Mary C. heard a car door slam, as she pulled a sweatshirt over her sore upper body. She thought she had a visitor, so she looked out the window to see a police car driving away. She was glad she didn't have to talk to the lawman.

Jason, Big Jim and the other six from the rock, were all on the barge before Mr. Hawkins blew his whistle, ending lunch. Jason was prepared to continue his safety cleanup efforts for the rest of the day. As the workers returned to their previous jobs, Big Jim and Mr. Hawkins stopped Jason before he got started.

"Jason."

Mr. Hawkins had Jason's full attention. "Yes sir, Mr. Hawkins."

"I've got the other shuttle waiting and I think you should take the rest off the day off. You deserve it and you won't lose any pay."

All the workers who could hear Mr. Hawkins clapped and cheered at what they heard. Big Jim escorted Jason to the edge of the barge and helped him onto the rope ladder that took him down to the deck of the shuttle boat. The diesel engine fired and the exhaust lid flew up and down once more. Jason had the rest of the day off with pay.

The old black box Helacrafter in Mr. Leek's office cracked with the voice of the shuttle captain. He was proud to be delivering Jason to Mr. Leek's dock. Uncle Bobby heard it too and he would wait for his nephew.

Sheriff McIntosh had his patrol car at high speed, when he passed the little jetties, leaving Mayport. He was frustrated, angry and sad about what he saw through Mary C.'s window.

"If Clark did that to her, he deserved to be hurt," were his thoughts. He wanted to walk the parking lot at the Fish Bowl one more time.

Jason tried not to look at the oak tree, as the shuttle boat headed back to Mayport. He didn't think about being a hero at all. He didn't really want to take the rest of the day off, but it all happened so fast, he didn't know what to say. If Mr. Hawkins said take the rest of the day off, he did. A soft cool breeze touched his face and moved his hair. He knew the tree wanted him to look. A squirrel fell to the ground. Eddie fell to the ground. Willis fell to his knees. The limbs of the tree clawed at his brain. The bowie knife sunk deep into skin and bone. The bounce of the shuttle boat and a light splash of river water released Jason from the tree. Reality was Mr. Leek and Uncle Bobby standing on the dock, waiting to meet the shuttle and its passenger.

Mr. Leek was more proud of Jason than anyone. He shook Jason's hand over and over again and even hugged him a number of times. He was really beside himself with pride. You would have thought Jason had pulled him out of the river. Uncle Bobby was proud, but didn't show it as openly as Mr. Leek. He thought to be more manly with Jason about it, as if it was expected of him.

"Hell, he swims like a fish. Are you sure you weren't just divin' in to take a swim and landed on that man? I'm sure glad we finally found somethin' you can do."

Jason smiled. He did love Uncle Bobby. They walked home together.

Mary C. saw her two men walking toward the house, so she met them on the porch. "What are you two doin' together at this time of day?"

Jason didn't even think about telling his story. To him it was over and done. Uncle Bobby was a very different story.

"Well, the smallest thing that happened today was me catchin' another five boxes of shrimp."

She didn't understand. "Bobby, that's great. Thirteen boxes in two days. That ain't happened to you in years, and that's small to you?"

"I want you to sit down in this swing and listen to the big news of the day. If you could get out of bed, you might hear what's happenin' around here."

She zeroed in on his bed comment. "We don't have to be a smart aleck, now, do we?"

"You're right, I'm sorry. That was uncalled for and out of place. We should be sharing this good news as a family."

Mary C. was growing impatient with her brother's foolishness. "Are you gonna tell me what the hell you're talkin' bout, or am I goin' in the house?"

"You need to sit down before I tell you."

Mary C. reluctantly sat in the swing. Bobby got serious and told her the story.

Sheriff McIntosh walked slowly in the back parking lot of the Fish Bowl. He didn't think he would find anything more than he had before, but for some reason he wanted to walk there and think about what had happened. He saw the place on the ground where the big sailor fell. Mary C.'s shoes made it look as if she was defending herself. Did she take them off on purpose? Did she run out of them as she ran away? Did somebody take them off her? Once again, he was a three question man.

The sound of James's rusty blue truck filled the air of the quiet parking lot. Mac turned to see it stop, hear the engine cut off, and see James step out and go into the back of the Fish Bowl. He didn't like James for some reason. He didn't exactly know why, he just didn't. That happens sometimes.

Mary C. sat there amazed at the incredible story Bobby was telling her. Jason smiled a few times while Bobby was telling what he heard. He had more.

"And guess who he saved."

Mary C. was too spellbound to guess anything.

"None other than, Steve 'the Crane' Robertson. The most famous big rig operator in, probably, the world. He does all the big hard jobs and makes a fortune. He's like the Elvis of the big rigs."

Mary C. shook her. "You are a fool."

Bobby looked at Jason and gave him the Elvis lip. Jason did love Uncle Bobby.

"Whatever possessed you to be the one to jump in that water? You could of drowned yourself."

"I was fine, Mama. It just came to me, what to do, and I did it. It was fine."

"Sometimes I don't know what to do with you." She opened her arms for Jason to hug her. He moved to her and bathed in the moment of affection he was always looking for from her. He would rather be there than up on someone's shoulders. It was a great day.

Sheriff McIntosh looked through the window of James's blue truck. He saw papers and dirty rags on the floorboard, some tools in the front seat and an empty gun rack over the back window. He moved to the back bed of the truck and lifted a piece of green canvas, exposing a case of beer, some more tools and several two-by-fours. He saw nothing unusual and actually didn't really know what he was looking for. The vision and thought of Mary C.'s abused body haunted him and he wasn't sure what he would do with his feelings. He wanted to protect her and punish the culprit, who caused her such pain. He entered the Fish Bowl to sit and relax. Or perhaps talk to James, once more.

Uncle Bobby had showered and was going to bed. The night shrimping was successful, but tiring. Jason had also showered and changed clothes. Mary C. and Jason were both surprised when Uncle Bobby made his suggestion.

"I'm gonna try to sleep for a few hours. Wake me up about six-thirty and we'll all three go eat at Bill's and celebrate all our good fortune. I need a night off and we need to do something together, for a change. We'll make a night of it."

Jason and Mary C. both stood there shocked at Uncle Bobby's proposal.

"Are you foolin' with us? You better not be foolin' with us, Bobby Merritt."

"No, I ain't foolin', I'm serious. I think it will do us all good to get out. Hell, Jason's twenty-one years old and you need to get out of that bathrobe and get out of the house. But, we need to go early to beat the crowd. With all these new workers in town, I'll bet they're stayin' busy. We'll have dinner before the drinkin' crowd gets there. It'll be fun."

Jason listened as the others talked. He wondered if he'd see Sofia's sister Margie at Bill's Hideaway.

Uncle Bobby went to bed. Jason cleaned his room and Mary C. started washing clothes. It was nice for Jason to be home with the two he loved. He carried a handful of dirty clothes to her in the wash-room.

"Here, Mama."

"Jason, I'm so proud of you. But, I want you to be more careful. You don't think before you do something. You just do it no matter what might happen. I want you to stop takin' chances all the time. I am really proud of you." Jason took a deep breath as she took the clothes from his hands. He wanted to hug her again, but he knew to be satisfied with the one earlier.

"I need some more soap powder. I won't have enough to finish this wash. Who uses all these towels? Go to the store and get some Tide. There's money on my dresser." Jason walked to her bedroom for the money. He was excited about his trip to the store and the possibility of seeing Sofia.

Jason turned from the dresser and saw a strange reflection in his mother's full-length oval mirror. The limbs of the tree surrounded his mother's bruised and scratched, naked body. He closed his eyes. He knew the tree wanted him to come. He would not look into that mirror, ever again. He was out the door.

Jason's walk to the store had a good pace to it. It was as close to being a run as you could get without actually running. He slowed down when he turned the corner and stepped on the short piece of concrete leading to the front door of the store. The bell on the door sounded when he walked in and it actually made his heart jump more than it had done before. He knew the bell would alert whoever was minding the store that they had a customer. Jason was polite, but very disappointed, when Miss Margaret walked out of the back storeroom and greeted him.

"Why, Jason, you dear boy." She sounded just like her sister Miss Margie to Jason. "We all heard what happened on that barge today. Are you alright? Did you get hurt at all? What possessed you to jump in that water?" Miss Margaret was a three question woman.

Jason had a hard enough time answering one question, much less three. He did his best. "I'm not hurt. I was fine."

Miss Margaret had to take it or leave it, as the answers she needed. "I know your mother is so proud of you and wait until I tell Margie about it; she will be so proud. She loves you so much. You're just like family to her."

Jason knew she was talking about Miss Margie, her sister, and not her oldest daughter, Margie.

"What can I help you with?"

"Mama needs some Tide for the wash."

"It's right there, to your left on that second shelf."

Jason took the box of soap powder to the register and took out the money. Miss Margaret put the box in a bag and gave him his change. "We sure enjoyed having you out at Margie's for dinner Sunday."

"I had a good time."

"Oh, and I want to thank you for being so nice to Susan last night. She was in one of her moods and she said how nice you were when you saw her crying and took time to talk to her. She was gone so long I got worried, but all the time she was sitting out back talking to you. She was in a much better mood after y'all talked. I guess there is such a thing as a generation gap. She just needed someone closer to her age to talk to."

Jason's mouth went dry while Miss Margaret reminded him of his encounter with her redheaded, freckled daughter. He was out the door and headed home.

CHAPTER SIX

SHERIFF MCINTOSH SAT AT THE BAR IN THE FISH BOWL. IT WAS EASY TO SEE James wasn't too happy about the lawman being there.

"Bartender James, I'd like a Jack Black with a little ice, if you will, sir."

"I didn't think you could drink. You bein' the law an' everything."

"Well, I'm off today and I'll try not to get drunk and shoot up the place."

James fixed the drink and put it in front of the sheriff. "How you doin' with that beatin' case you're on? How's that big sailor? Does he know who he is yet?" Mayport was full of three question people. But that was fine with Sheriff McIntosh, because he had the three answers.

"I'm not doin' jack shit with the case. The big sailor sleeps all day and night. And I have to introduce myself to him all over again each time he does wake up."

"You know, Sheriff, I just don't think Mary C. could have hurt that big boy like that."

"James, I don't think so either. I just can't see it happenin'. She's a strong woman, but I just can't see it."

"She's a woman, alright. Ol' big boy wanted her bad too. He wasn't her type though. Ol' Mary C.'s pretty particular with her men.

When you look like she looks, you can pick 'n' choose. She would've never gone outside with him, if she hadn't been so drunk."

"She was really that drunk, huh?"

"She couldn't stand up by herself."

"Well, she walked out with big boy, didn't she?"

"I wouldn't exactly call it walkin', more like carried while straight up."

"You're a friend of Mary C.'s, right?"

James didn't like the direction the conversation had taken. He became more cautious with his words. He spoke slowly and deliberately. "I've known her since I was a boy."

"Do you like Mary C.? I mean, knowing her all those years you must be friends.

"I'd say we were friends. She's a lot older than me, but we're friends."

Sheriff McIntosh positioned himself across the bar, as close as he could get to James, without any of the other customers hearing him. They were almost eye-to-eye, when Sheriff McIntosh clenched his teeth and asked his next question.

"Then why in the hell did you let that son-of-a-bitch take your friend out in the parking lot, when you knew his intentions was to have his way with a drunk woman? What the hell kinda friend stands by and let's that happen?"

James backed away from the bar. "You hold on, mister. She's a grown woman. I've seen her walk out of here a bunch of times, with her own intentions. Hell, I've seen her in the backseat of a car in the parkin' lot on my way home some nights. Don't try to put no guilt trip on me. You're talkin' to the wrong man. And since you're off duty and you can drink and shit, don't get up in my face like that again. I ain't no scared little boy."

Mac put money on the bar and finished his drink. "I didn't know you liked her so much, James."

Mary C. woke Uncle Bobby at six-thirty sharp. She was more excited about their night out than the other two. She had already ironed clothes for the night and she had even ironed something for

Bobby and Jason. Uncle Bobby must had been excited too, because he got right up out of bed and began his jukin' ritual. He was surprised, but pleased, at Mary C.'s thoughtfulness.

"You ironed my stuff?"

"No, the tooth fairy ironed it. Of course, I ironed it."

"Thanks, sis. You do want to get out tonight and you made such a good selection." Bobby held up his black sharkskin pants and his powder blue, long-sleeve, silk western shirt. "You did good, girl."

Mary C. added a few more ideas on how he should look for the night. "And don't wear those brown Dingo boots, with those black pants. It looks ridiculous. Wear those black Cuban heels, with the pointed toes. You never wear them."

"Every time I wear them damn pointed toes, I just get the urge to kick the shit out of somebody."

"Well, you ain't kickin' nobody tonight. Here." She handed him black, half cut boots. She wasn't finished. "And don't you dare wear those black and white saddle oxfords."

Bobby smiled. "Don't talk ugly 'bout my bebops. They are called bebops."

"Well, I don't care what you call 'em, just don't wear 'em." Mary C. closed the door of his bedroom, as she walked out. Bobby would dress as she suggested and he would wear the Cuban heels.

Mary C. pulled a pair of extra tight Wrangler dungarees over her bruised legs and hips. She still needed to keep most of her body covered a few more days. Then she pulled a 32-inch bust size, black cotton shirt, over her braless 36-inch breasts, tucking it into the already too tight jeans. It looked like she had been spray painted black from the waist up. She walked to another room looking for the belt she wanted to add to her wardrobe. Bobby saw her when she stepped out of her room, ready to go.

"Well, I know one thing. If there's a scavenger hunt tonight at Bill's and nipples are on the list, they gonna be easy to find. That material in that shirt can't take much more pressure."

Mary C. didn't care. "Ain't you just the funniest thing."

Jason walked out of his room and joined the others. His attire was much more conservative than theirs. He was excited about being with his family. It was going to be a great night. They were out the door and headed to the beach.

Jason hated the sound of the crickets on Seminole Road. He knew the exact location on the road where you would begin to hear the awful sound, and about how long it would last. Mary C. held her ears, along with Jason, but they didn't seem to bother Uncle Bobby at all. He just kept driving and acted like he didn't hear anything. Mary C. couldn't stand it.

"Now, don't tell me you don't hear those stupid crickets."

"I never said I didn't hear 'em. I just ain't gonna let 'em mess with me, that's all."

"What do you mean, mess with ya? What they gonna do?"

"Any time I've been drivin' by here with somebody, they hold their ears, like you and Jason did. It makes you look stupid. I ain't lettin' them little black insects make me do something that makes me look stupid. I'm makin' a stand."

Mary C. shook her head. "You are a fool. Where do you come up with these fool notions?"

"It's a family trait."

Jason hadn't been listening to the foolish conversation. The crickets had filled his head with visions of the past. He knew Sheriff Floyd's house was somewhere near the crickets. That night in the truck with Daddy Bob was the first time he heard their sound. He gave Tom Green the rusty machete. Sheriff Floyd died that night. He saw his mother sitting on top of the fat lawman. The crickets were gone; Jason was back in the car with his family.

It was free mullet dip night at Bill's Hideaway. The aroma of shrimp and hush puppies frying filled the room, as the family trio walked through the swinging doors. Even though it was still early, the room was already filling up with customers. Jason loved the smell of the hush puppies. Bill's used the same recipe as Strickland's in Mayport, so Jason would have a familiar taste in his mouth when he bit into one of the tasty balls.

There were only two dining tables left, so Bobby moved them

toward a four-seater in a corner of the room. Uncle Bobby talked to a few of the regular customers as they made their way to the table. Mary C. had her usual walk and look of confidence and what she considered "class." All eyes, male and female, looked directly at the first item on Bobby's scavenger hunt list. She had a way of getting the attention she needed so badly. Bobby was in his environment, Mary C. had what she craved and Jason wanted a hush puppy.

The waitress came to the table with glasses of water. Bobby knew them all.

"Hey, Kelly. How ya doin' tonight?"

"Good, Bobby. I like it when it's busy like this. Y'all want some mullet dip and crackers?"

"Yeah. We'll decide what we want while you get the dip. Oh, and one thing. Can you go ahead and bring us some hush puppies to munch on?"

It was music to Jason's ears.

"I'll be right back to take your orders."

Mary C. watched Kelly as she walked away. "Now, Bobby, she's a nice lookin' woman. She married?"

"I don't think so, but she's got a big ol' boyfriend that picks her up at closin' time. And I'm gettin' too old to fight for a woman."

"Well, you need to think about findin' the one right woman for you and stop all this foolish jukin'."

"Ya know, there just might not be a right man or woman for people like me and you."

Mary C. realized her foolish brother had said something interesting for a change. "You really think that might be true?" She was serious too.

"It does look that way at times. Maybe, we ain't made to be a companion to nobody. Maybe, we're suppose to be with more than one person. Maybe, it's in the blood."

Mary C. listened to Bobby for perhaps the first time in a long time.

"I know I'm hard to live with. I wouldn't want to live with me. The people who like me, like me because they see me once in awhile.

I don't want someone I care about to get tired of me. I would hate that. I need to stay just like I am."

Mary C. had no response for Bobby's serious moment. She liked talking to him on that level and seeing that side of him. She would not talk to him about settling down anymore. She didn't like thinking it was in her blood to be with many and not be able to stay with one man if she wanted. She hated the possibility that Bobby was right about them both. Kelly was back at the table, carrying what could be considered a small bucket of mullet dip and plenty of hush puppies for all three of them.

"Thanks, Kelly. You always take care of me so nice."

"Any time, Bobby. Waitin' on you has always been a pleasure."

They all ordered the fried shrimp special, with fries and slaw. Kelly left for the kitchen.

"'Waitin' on you is always a pleasure.' That don't sound like no woman worried 'bout a boyfriend. Not to me anyway."

"Well, she did have that 'I want you, Elvis' look in her eyes when she put this damn trove of dip on the table in front of me. I did notice that."

"I think she likes you. She made it pretty clear."

"Mary C., ya gotta remember. She's workin' these tables to make as much money as she can, she probably has a lot of favorite customers."

"Well, it was more than that. A woman knows when another woman is trying to get a message across to a man."

"Quit talkin' 'bout it. Ya don't know nothin'."

"I'll stop talkin', but I don't care what you say, I think you like her."

As Mary C. and Bobby talked, and Jason ate his hush puppies, no one at the table noticed a man standing next to their table.

"Well, if it ain't Bobby 'The Bebop Man'."

All three at the table looked up at the man. It was the Hawk himself. Jason couldn't believe Mr. Hawkins was standing at their table. When Bobby recognized his old friend he stood with excitement, shook hands and even had a manly hug. Jason was surprised at the sight of Uncle Bobby and Hawk, actually hugging each other. Uncle Bobby knew everybody.

"I don't believe it. The Hawk Man. I heard you were here, but I had to see it with my own eyes. Damn, you look good, boy."

"You too. I thought I might run into you here one night." Hawk hadn't noticed Jason yet, but he noticed Mary C. while Bobby was talking. "And, Miss Mary C., how are you?" He stuck his big hand out toward Mary C.

"I'm doin' fine, thank you."

"That's good. It's nice to see my friends from Mayport. I've missed this place. I always liked it here. I like the ocean, bein' close by."

"Here, sit with us. Let me buy you dinner."

"I'd like to sit with y'all, Bobby, but you don't have to buy me dinner."

"Hell, I probably owe ya money, anyway. Damn! It's good to see ya, Hawk." He sat down in the chair facing Bobby with Jason and Mary C. on each side. He finally noticed Jason. "Jason! I didn't see ya there, son. Why didn't you say somethin'?"

Bobby jumped in. "Gettin' Jason to speak up and say somethin' ain't the easiest thing to do. He listens more then he talks."

Mr. Hawkins had admiration and respect in his eyes for the young man. "Mary C., this is your boy, Jason?"

"That's my Jason."

Jason loved being hers and the fact she just said it.

Mr. Hawkins continued with a serious tone that filled the table. "I told someone today that I would like to meet the people who raised this young man. And I would like to thank them for restoring my faith in people. You have done a wonderful job with Jason. He is a special breed." Mary C. was teary eyed, Bobby had no foolishness to add, and Jason popped another hush puppy in his mouth. Kelly took Mr. Hawkins's order for another fried shrimp special and the pleasant evening continued.

It was ten o'clock when James walked out the back door of the Fish Bowl. Sheriff McIntosh knew he got off early on Tuesday nights and he waited in the dark for James to leave. James fired up his truck and was out of the parking lot with tires spinning and smoking. The patrol car followed far behind.

The four specials had been delivered to the table and Bill's Hideaway was packed with people eating, drinking, dancing, playing pinball and shooting pool. Mr. Hawkins had given his version of the rescue on the barge, while Mary C. listened to every word, Bobby talked to others around them and passing by, and Jason thought his thoughts. The swinging door up front opened wide and Jason's eyes fell upon an interesting and welcome sight. Sofia's sister, Margie, and two other young women walked in. Bobby noticed Jason's attention was taken away from the hush puppies.

"Well, lookie here now. Mary C., did you see what I saw?"

Mary C. really didn't care at the time. She was giving her attention to Hawk. "No I didn't see anything. What is it?"

"Jason here just lit up like a candle, when those girls walked in."

Mary C. turned to see who they were. "Pretty girls. Who are they, Jason?"

"I don't know all of 'em. I just know Margie. She's Miss Margaret daughter. I don't know the others. Margie and her sisters were at Miss Margie's on Sunday. She's named after Miss Margie.

"So that's one of Margaret's girls. Hell, all four of them girls are lookers. I see 'em in the store. They sure don't look like sisters to me. I see her now. That's the oldest. Yeah, that's Margie. She's about your age, ain't she, Jason?"

"She's twenty-one, too."

"Damn, boy, you learned a lot 'bout this girl at one dinner, didn't ya?"

Jason didn't answer; he was too busy watching Margie. Bobby really didn't want an answer anyway he was just talking to be talking. Mary C. went back to her starry-eyed conversation with Hawk. Hawk was as taken with her and her small cotton shirt squeezing her breasts together didn't hurt his attention span. Margie and her friends were out on the town as a defiant act of rebellion. They were all over twenty-one and lived with parents who had not allowed them to socialize with folks who ate at a honky tonk. It was their night to explode on the scene, as competition for other women and possibilities for the men. Margie was the most aggressive of the three, but the other two were close enough. Margie saw Jason across the room and led her companions directly to his table.

"Hey, Jason. I'm so glad you came."

Uncle Bobby, Mary C. and even Hawk looked at their quiet Jason.

Bobby couldn't help it. "So glad you came? So glad you came? I thought this was my idea."

Jason was speechless, as usual.

Margie wasn't. "I told my friends you might be here. I wanted them to meet you."

Jason couldn't believe Margie's tone. It was as if they had spent hours together and were an item. The rest of the table couldn't believe it either.

Margie continued her forward talk. "This is Jenny, and this is Stephanie. This is Jason, his mother, Mary C., his Uncle Bobby and . . . sir, I'm sorry I don't know you."

Bobby sat back in amazement at Margie, as she introduced everyone.

"I'm Hawkins."

The three young girls were pretty, sexy and they smelled great. Bobby couldn't see any reason why they should sit anywhere else. "I don't think there's any tables left and I know the bar's full. So if you ladies would like to sit with us, we can squeeze three more chairs in here."

Margie continued to be the spokesperson for the trio. "That would be great. Thank you."

Bobby got up and found chairs for the girls. Naturally, Hawk moved next to Mary C., Jenny and Stephanie sat on each side of Uncle Bobby, and Margie sat as close to Jason as she could get. There was no doubt what she had on her mind. She had talked to her cousin Peggy too; she just didn't know about Jason and her sister

Susan.

James pulled his blue truck off the main road and onto a dirt road leading to the beach. He lived in a little cottage about two hundred yards off the beach. The cottages were old and unkempt, but at one time they were full of vacationers from up north, during the winter. There were eight cottages, but only five had tenants. The roofs leaked too bad in the other three.

Sheriff McIntosh kept his distance, as James stopped the truck in front of his cottage. Again the sheriff wasn't sure what he was looking for, but he knew James knew more about that night than he had told. He watched James walk into the cottage and thought, "If he did save Mary C. from Clark, why can't he say it? He'd probably be a hero. And why can't Mary C. say what happened? If he did save her, she would know it." He wanted answers. He needed answers. He parked his car in the woods, got out and walked toward the cottages.

A light came on in the back of James's cottage. The sheriff stayed behind the other buildings as he made his way closer to James's truck. He looked in the dirty window of one of the small buildings. It looked like a department store. It had everything. Boxes stacked up on boxes. Brand new tools, appliances, fishing equipment, fishing nets, and cases of beer and hard liquor. There was enough Jack Daniels to supply the mullet run at the little jetties for years. There was no doubt in Mac's mind that James wasn't just a bartender, he was a big time thief and his stealing days were over, as of that night.

He walked to the truck to see where James was in the cottage. He looked in the side window of the truck, when an object, hanging form the inside mirror, caught his attention. Mac reached inside the truck and took the object off its hanging place. He held it up to his face in the moonlight. It was a pair of women's panties; they were dirty, bloodstained and had the crotch ripped out. Mac knew they belonged to Mary C. He didn't think about how he knew; he just knew. James had them hanging on the mirror of the truck like a trophy or a first place ribbon. He knew he had his man. He put the evidence into his back pocket. There was a noise, and a ringing in his right ear. A blinding pain followed as he fell to the ground. He was in a dream state, with no focus quivering around his eyes. He thought he was facedown on the ground but wasn't sure. He had no idea at the moment that James stood over him, holding the baseball bat, he had swung that night and Saturday night. Mac focused his eyes on two bare feet, as they stood next to his head. Mac knew he was going to die. James reached down and took his cloth trophy out of Mac's back pocket, and then hung it back on the mirror.

Bill's Hideaway was full of jetty workers and locals. Mary C. and Hawk danced every slow dance and sat and talked during the fast ones. Hawk was more interested in her than showing off his dance floor talents. He left that to Bobby for that night. Margie's two friends were taking turns dancing Bobby's butt off. They wouldn't let him rest at all. He complained, but he loved it. The attention of young pretty women was just what he needed. Bobby was attracted to the two young beauties, and every now and then had improper thoughts about their young bodies. He had decided, however, they were too young and inexperienced and they would probably end up being more trouble than fun. Besides, he wasn't ever going to take on two women at one time at anything. He hadn't recovered from the last time. He would dance with them and push up against their firm bodies, but he would keep his sharkskin pants on that night.

Margie and Jason had moved outside and were standing on the upper deck looking at the ocean. Jason looked at the jetties to their left. Margie was a toucher, like Mary C. After she had talked to her cousin Peggy, she wanted Jason. It was the same way Susan had felt. If a woman like cousin Peggy wanted him, they wanted him. She was still the most aggressive.

"Let's go sit in my friend's car."

Uncle Bobby walked out onto the deck. "Jason, you and Margie need to come in here a second."

Margie hated the interruption, as Jason turned and followed his uncle. She reluctantly did the same.

The entire room was quiet. It felt strange to Jason. No music, pool balls hitting and falling, no pinball bells, just a strange, out of place silence. Uncle Bobby took Jason by his arm and moved him to the center area. Jason looked up as he moved and saw Mr. Hawkins standing on the steps above him. He held a glass in his hand. He ended the eerie silence.

"Ladies and gentlemen. Please give me your attention for a moment. Tonight, I would like to take this opportunity to honor and toast a young man, who risked his life so another could live. I know it happened because I was there."

Jason's heart raced in his chest, as Mr. Hawkins lifted his glass, followed by the other customers.

"Ladies and gentlemen, I give you Jason! The 'Jetty Man'!" The room exploded with cheers and applause. Goose bumps covered the women and most of the men. Hawk had moved the crowd to a pitched frenzy of emotion. Mary C. loved him and Jason. Uncle Bobby was almost in tears, because nobody ever clapped for him like that. Margie wanted Jason even more and Jason had a name. He was important. He was the Jetty Man.

James talked to his new victim, as he picked Sheriff McIntosh up off the ground and threw him over his shoulder.

"I told you not to get in my face again. You musta thought I was just playin' with you. I really knocked the shit out of you. You probably don't know your name either." James dropped the sheriff into the back bed of his truck.

Mac could feel the warmth of his blood, as it flowed from the opening on his head, down his back. His couldn't move his arms at all. He was helpless and he knew he was going to die. Mac could feel his life force spilling out onto the bed of the nasty truck. He heard the truck motor, and the vibration and the cool air told him the truck was moving. He could open one eye and he saw cabbage palms and water oaks overhead. The sky was clear and he heard the waves hit the beach. The truck stopped. His body was sliding through the pool of his blood. His body fell from the truck and splashed in water an inch deep. He was moving again as James pulled him by his feet. The deeper water slapped his face. Sheriff McIntosh was right, he was going to die.

Jason had been surrounded by his admirers for about twenty minutes. The barge workers were all paying their respect, because most of them had seen the deed firsthand and understood just how incredible the incident actually was. Margie was in a sexual rage for Jason and all the attention he was getting added to her fire and desire. The crowd around Jason thinned out and he was talking to Big Jim. Margie walked over and whispered in his ear. "Please, meet me outside." She nodded to Big Jim, with a smile.

Big Jim smiled back, shrugged his shoulders and then smiled at Jason too. "I'm sure you'd much rather follow her, than stand here and talk to me. I know I would. I'll see you in the mornin'."

Jason probably would have just as well talked to Big Jim, but he didn't say "no" very often, or maybe not ever. He saw Uncle Bobby dancing with Stephanie and Jenny, at the same time, as he walked toward the door. He didn't see his mother. She and Mr. Hawkins were shooting pool in another room.

Jason walked out onto the upper deck to find Margie. As soon as he stepped into the night air a car horn sounded and he looked down to the beach. Margie drove up to the bottom of the steps in a red Pontiac Star Chief. The passenger side was facing the steps. She reached over from behind the wheel and opened the passenger door, pushing it in Jason's direction.

"Jason, come on, get in. Take a ride with me, please."

Jason walked down the stairs and into the car. They went down the beach.

Margie drove for only about a mile and pulled the car into a secluded section of the sand dunes. She stopped the car, turned off the engine and lights and moved over to Jason with one sliding motion, with a wild kiss at the end. It was wet, long and had all the tongue Jason could handle. She was driving her rock-hard body through his. Jason began squeezing her breasts and rubbing her between her legs, all on the outside of her clothes. He was surprised when she began taking her clothes off. In a few seconds she was naked, completely naked and she had done all the work. Her muscular body excited Jason and reminded him of Jessie. He had the same thoughts when he saw Margie at the roast dinner. Jason was still dressed as she straddled him in the front seat. She buried his head into her young hard breasts and moved her hips against his lap. She stopped suddenly.

"Come on, the backseat is really big." She moved her naked body up and over Jason, touching his face with every inch she could, as she climbed into the backseat. She was flat on her back with plenty of room for Jason. He was excited from seeing her sit there naked. He was ready to work his magic and Margie had driven him to his aggressive state. She would get what she wanted and even more.

James drove the sheriff's police car into the water of the coquina pits, near Wonderwood. He knew there was a strong possibility it would never be found. Nobody worked there anymore and the local children didn't swim there anymore either. Too many had gotten cut by the coquina. It was just too dangerous. Getting away with his hideous crime would be worth the three-mile walk back to his cottage.

Mary C. passed Bobby before the next dance song began.

"Thanks for the night out, big brother. It's been great so far. Have you seen Jason? I haven't seen him in about an hour."

"Yeah, I've seen him. He took a ride down the beach with that Margie. She couldn't stay away from him. She had her plans before she got here. He'll be fine. They'll be back."

"Are you sure?"

"He's a twenty-one-year-old hero of the year. All the young women are going to want to be near him. She was just the first to be here when it all happened. She feels like she's part of the history too. He's fine. Let him be. Let him be a man."

Mary C. remembered the last time Bobby said let him be was the day he played that game. People died that day and Jason's mind died with them for almost a year. She went to find Hawk.

Margie joined the "mountain club" with her cousin Peggy and her sister Susan. Jason had thrown her from the mountain too. She was drained of all her body juices. She didn't want to move. Jason sat up on the edge of the big backseat and looked out of the car win-

LOGGERHEAD

dow. A huge loggerhead sea turtle was slowly making her way back to the ocean after laying a hundred Ping-Pong ball looking eggs in the soft sand of the sand dunes. Jason put his Skivvies back on and surprised Margie when he jumped out of the Star Chief, wearing just his underwear. She hadn't seen the sea turtle, so his quick departure was a bit unsettling. She sat up to see what happened and where he was going.

Margie couldn't believe her eyes. Jason was sitting on top of the big turtle, like it was a horse, and riding it back toward the water. The slow turtle never broke its pitiful stride, even with Jason on its back. It kept moving through the sand. Nothing would keep it from the water.

Jason had his back to the car and Margie, so he didn't see her when she jumped from the car, wearing just her panties, and ran to join him with his ride. Jason got his own surprise when Margie jumped on the back of the turtle with him. She screamed and pushed her bare breasts against his back. If this was Margie's "coming out as a wild woman night" she had more than proven herself worthy. The sea turtle was a little slower, but it kept moving. Margie jumped off first at the edge of the water and ran back to the car. Jason was right behind her. He loved it when she joined him in his ride. It was more than a great night.

Mary C. was as close as she could get to Hawk as they danced. She had touched him all night and he had done his share of touching her. Her body language and sex appeal had its hold on him and he was trying to maintain some sense of control. She knew he wanted more and she did too. But not that night. Not until she was healed. He would not see her yet, but he would see her. She knew she had to tell him. Hawk was in cheek-to-cheek, nipple-to-nipple heaven.

"Hawk, we need to talk about tonight."

"What about it?"

"I've had a great time with you. In fact, I haven't felt this good in a long time."

"That's good. I'm glad I was part of it."

"But, I've got to go home tonight. I would love to stay with you, but I do have my reasons and you'll have to understand and trust me. It ain't you at all. I would love to stay with you tonight, but it just can't happen now. If you can deal with that, it will be worth the wait. If not, then I'm sorry."

"Mary C., I came here tonight to eat, have a beer and go home. I didn't expect to run into you and have such a good time. I would love to stay with you too, but if it ain't to be tonight, it ain't to be. It don't take away from the nice time we had. Maybe we can do it again, when we both don't have go be home early. You know I'm the first one on that barge, every mornin'."

Mary C. liked him even more. An understanding gentleman was something she wasn't used to. She kissed her new friend.

"Thanks, Hawk." Mary C. walked with Hawk to the main dining room, passing Bobby and his two young beauties. He thought she was leaving with Hawk.

"You gone, girl?"

"Whenever you're ready. You're the driver."

Bobby smiled. "Are we leavin' together?"

"We came as a family, we're leavin' as a family. Where's Jason?"

Bobby shrugged his shoulders. "You mean he ain't back yet? You do know that Margie was in deep heat, don't ya?"

"We might not be goin' home as a family, after all. The car they're in belongs to Stephanie here and we may have to give these girls a ride home." Mary C. smiled at both young ladies, but she didn't care if they got home or not. Hawk shook Bobby's hand and told everybody "good night." They all walked with Hawk out onto the upper deck. They all saw the lights of the red Star Chief coming down the beach directly toward them. The red car pulled up to the bottom of the steps, like a taxicab offering everyone a ride. Jason and Margie had returned.

Stephanie and Jenny ran down the steps and created their original threesome. Jason got out of the car and created his original trio, as well. Margie stayed at the wheel, as her two companions jumped into the front seat with her. They all three yelled "good night." Margie blew the horn, white beach sand flew from under spinning tires, and they were off, with two red lights fading, as they moved down the beach.

Hawk pulled away in his company jeep and kicked up a little sand, too. The family trio climbed into Mary C.'s Ford Falcon. Jason looked out the side window of the backseat toward Bill's. It was only eleven o'clock and people were still driving up for a late drink. Most of the barge workers were already gone, but Bill's was open until two A.M.

Jason felt like someone stuck a sharp stick into his heart when a vision of evil touched his mind. His throat filled with hot liquid and he felt sick. He closed his eyes, hoping it was a dream. When he opened them he realized it was real. There, on the other side of the steps stood a man in the dark, wearing a black Derby hat. The man seemed to be watching the three of them, as they got into the car. The Derby stood there for a few more seconds. Uncle Bobby started the Falcon and began driving away, with no sand being thrown. Jason watched the Derby walk up the steps. The man under the hat walked slowly with a bad limp. Jason didn't want to believe it, but he knew Charlie Klim was back. The Derby hat had ruined a great night.

The ride home was quiet for the threesome. Bobby was tired from the dancing and trying to keep his mind off the two young girls he had held all night. Mary C. was thinking about the possibility of a meaningful relationship with Hawk. Jason thought of the Derby hat. All the things that had happened to him that wonderful night took a backseat to Charlie Klim. He hated Charlie Klim. He wanted to tell the others, but he didn't. They all heard the crickets on Seminole Road, but nobody said anything.

Bobby was asleep almost as soon as his head hit his pillow. He was hoping to dream about being double-teamed by his two new friends. Mary C. would take longer, as she would be thinking about what Bobby had said. She hoped he was wrong about them not being able to be with one person. Jason would sleep very little, as visions of the evil in his past would torment him and awaken him each time he would begin to sleep.

CHAPTER SEVEN

JASON WAS UP BEFORE THE CLOCKS WENT OFF AND OUT THE DOOR, HEADED for the store. A honey bun could easily become his permanent breakfast. The bell on the door sounded again, as he walked in the store. Jason's sleepy eyes fell upon the sight he had been looking for each time he was near the store. It was Sofia's turn to open the store and she stood behind the counter. She was even beautiful in the morning. Not everybody can do that. She didn't disappoint him. She was excited and her voice was like soft music to his ears.

"Jason! I was hoping you'd come in. I took Margie's turn, so she could stay with some friends last night."

The mention of Margie sent a slight chill down Jason's back. He had a quick vision of her in her panties, riding the loggerhead.

"I wanted to see you so bad. I really miss you. I never really missed anybody before. It feels funny to me."

Jason loved the way she talked to him. It was always honest and she seemed to know the best words to say. It would flow out of her mouth like she had memorized a poem. Her eyes were still beautiful.

"I was hoping to see you, too. I've been up here, looking for ya."

"I know. Mama said she saw you today, Susan saw you one night and Margie saw you one morning. I knew you were looking for me."

Jason had another quick vision of himself moving his hand under the elastic waistband of Susan's shorts.

"I heard about what you did at the jetties. How you saved that famous man. Jason, you are the talk of the town. Everyone's talking about you and how brave you were. I can't believe you're here. I wanted to talk to you so bad. Come back here." Sofia motioned for him to follow her into the back storeroom. As soon as he entered the room she threw her arms around him and kissed him with more comfort and passion than the first kiss. The perfect kiss sent chills through his body.

"I think you're wonderful. I think I love you."

Jason stared at Sofia.

"I know you think I'm crazy, but I really do. Call it whatever you want. It's love to me and that's all I care about."

As usual Jason had no words. She was amazing to him and he wanted to tell her. He just didn't know how.

"You don't have to say anything. I know I'm just little Sofia. I couldn't feel like this all the time and not tell you. I think you feel something too, but it's hard for you to be with me when I'm so young. I won't be young forever." She didn't want to interfere with Jason's job. "Don't be late for work, because I talk too much."

Jason remembered his honey bun. "Oh! I need a honey bun and a small carton of milk."

Sofia got the milk, while Jason got the honey bun. He didn't want to, but he had to go.

"Be careful. Don't jump in that water today."

He was out the door.

The ride on the shuttle was the same as before. The sound of the diesel engine, the ferry horn, breakfast on board, and the mental battle with the oak tree, all became part of Jason's morning trip to work. They had all made the climb to the deck of the barge, and stood in groups waiting for Mr. Hawkins. They didn't have to wait very long before the foreman walked to the front of the gathering.

"Good morning, men. For those of you who haven't heard, the

"Crane," Mr. Steve Robertson, is recovering in St. Vincent's Hospital in Jacksonville. He is doin' fine, but he will be off this job for the remainder of the time. Before this day is over, some of the big rocks we have been waitin' on will be coming into the river on bigger barges than this one. Then, the real work will begin. We may have some night shift work for those who want it or if you know someone who needs night work let us know. That will depend on whether or not we can get a light system set up. If we do, there will be work around the clock. We realize that you will need all the energy and help you can get to work at your best level and pace today. With that in mind, the management has decided to feed you breakfast this morning. So, you can thank the Jetty Man. Honey buns for everybody." The crowd of men exploded once again into cheers and laughter as Hawk and the other bosses reached into boxes and handed out a sweet honey bun to all the workers. Jason couldn't believe it. He must have been patted on the back a hundred more times in a matter of minutes. After the boxes were empty and the workers were all eating, Mr. Hawkins stood before them again.

"When you've finished your breakfast, we've got a lot of work to do to get ready for those rocks. Be careful today and put those wrappers in the trash cans." The workday began.

Mary C. was up earlier than she had been for about a week. She felt good about herself, the family and her body were healing. She actually had thoughts about ending her bad habits and creating a fresh new start for herself. Mary C. knew it would be difficult for her to make the changes needed. She did like thinking about the possibilities. Her evening with Hawk and her strange talk with Sheriff McIntosh made her realize that maybe she could be a one-man woman, no matter what Bobby said. She needed to make a trip to the store and she decided the walk would do her good. She checked Bobby's room and couldn't believe he was gone. He had gotten up and went out shrimping anyway. He was a worker, she had to give him that.

Mary C. drifted with her thoughts, as she made her slow stroll to Miss Margaret's store. She was in no hurry; she wanted to enjoy being out and being alive. She hadn't celebrated her life very often; it felt good. A wave to Mr. King sitting on his porch was always appropriate. The store was right around the corner.

The bell on the door sounded her arrival, when Mary C. entered the store. Sofia and her sister Peggy were working. Peggy was working the register and helping the customers and Sofia was doing an inventory on the stock. Peggy greeted Mary C. as she had been taught.

"Good morning. May I help you?"

"Good mornin'. I think I know where everything I need is. But thank you."

"Well if you can't find something, let me know."

Sofia stood up from behind a shelf near the back of the store. "Hello. You're Jason's mama, aren't you?"

"Yes, I am. And you're the youngest. You're Sofia."

"Yes, ma'am. That's my sister Peggy."

Mary C. nodded to Peggy. "All of you girls are so pretty. Each one of you looks different, but y'all are all so pretty."

"Thank you. Everybody says we all look so different."

"Y'all really do. And that older sister of yours, that Margie. She's pretty too. Your mama and daddy sure made some pretty babies, didn't they."

Sofia and Peggy looked at each other and smiled at Mary C.'s funny way of complimenting them.

"I never realized you girls were growin' up so. It makes me feel old, 'cause I remember all y'all when you'd be runnin' and tryin' to find Easter eggs in Eloise Leek's front yard. I guess it hit me when I saw your sister Margie last night. She sure ain't no little girl anymore, is she?"

Sofia and Peggy looked at each other again. Sofia was the talker.

"You saw Margie last night?"

"Yeah, over at Bill's."

Sofia wasn't sure what "Bill's" meant. "Bill's?"

"Yeah, Bill's Hideaway, over by the south jetties."

Sofia smiled at Peggy with a shocked look. "Margie was at Bill's Hideaway? Are you sure?"

"Of course, I'm sure. She sat at our table the whole night. She had quite a time, that girl." It was easy to see how shocked and surprised the two sisters were about the information Mary C. had given them. Sofia looked at Peggy one more time.

"Mama's going to kill her, if she finds out."

Peggy agreed. "Dead as a door nail."

They both laughed.

"The girl is twenty-one years old and she wasn't doin' nothin' wrong." Mary C. didn't think the two younger sisters needed to know any more details; she had said too much already. Mary C. had her own code of ethics and putting someone's business out was not part of it. She would volunteer no more information.

"You don't know our parents. I can't believe she had the nerve to go there. She has gone crazy wild."

"Well, good for her. Everybody needs to be crazy wild, now and then. It sure makes life more interesting."

Mary C. was an expert at "crazy wild."

The girls talked together, while Mary C. collected the items she needed. Peggy took her money and bagged the goods. Mary C. left them, still talking about Margie's big night out.

Mary C. walked across the street from the store to Mayport's small post office. She took the mail out of their box and headed back out the door. Mr. Leek held the door open for her as she walked out.

"Well, good morning, Mary C. How's it feel to be the mother of a hero?"

"It feels good, Mr. Leek. Real good."

"We're all so proud of that boy, or I should say, that man. He has really grown into a fine young man. But, I don't have to tell you that, do I?"

"No, but it's still nice to hear it. Comin' from other folks."

"Oh, my goodness! Did you hear about Sheriff McIntosh?"

"No, what?"

"His dead body washed up on the beach under the Atlantic Beach Pier, this mornin'. One of them crazy surfers found him, bangin' against the pylons under the pier."

Mary C. went weak in the knees. Her heart raced like Jason's. She was sick to her stomach, as Mr. Leek continued with the awful news.

"They haven't said how he died yet. He had been in the water all night and no tellin' how many times he hit those pylons, before they found him. They don't even know where he went in the water, or where somebody put him in the water. The way that tide was runnin' last night, he could have fell off the south jetties and popped up at the pier."

Mary had heard enough; she had to go. She had said nothing while Mr. Leek was telling her what he knew.

"Are you alright, Mary C.? I didn't mean to upset you. I shouldn't be tellin' all the ugly details. I'm sorry."

She still couldn't respond, but she nodded and left.

Mary C. walked back across the street, passed the store and passed Mr. King's house. She couldn't believe what she had just heard. She wondered if the big sailor was still in the hospital. She took the bag of items to the house, but she didn't want to be alone there. She took another hot bath and prepared to leave for the day. She would return back home when Bobby and Jason returned from their workday.

Uncle Bobby and his one-man crew were pulling up the nets from their second drag. It would be their last effort of the day. They had two boxes of shrimp and Bobby was too tired to drop the nets again. After they picked that catch, they were headed home.

Mr. Hawkins looked over the edge of the barge, down at the rocks, during lunchtime. There were at least twenty-five workers sitting in the shade, with Jason, on the rocks below him. They looked like a group of pelicans perched on the red rocks. Big Jim walked up next to Mr. Hawkins and looked over the edge too. Mr. Hawkins had a question for him.

"What do you think of that, down there?"

Big Jim smiled. "I wish I was down there with 'em. He makes me think of Jesus."

Mr. Hawkins looked at Big Jim after his strange answer, but didn't pursue it. He wasn't sure how. He looked down again and watched Jason and the others sharing lunches with one another.

Mary C. stopped her Falcon in front of the Atlantic Beach Pier. She didn't remember deciding to go there, but she was there. There were two police cars on the beach near the pylons. The tide was low and there was about a hundred yards of visible beach. Four men were walking under the pier, looking at the pylons and in the sand. Another police car pulled in behind her, and the officer in the car motioned for her to move. She parked her car, got out and walked onto the pier. She wanted to call St. Vincent's Hospital and see if the big sailor was still there. If he killed the sheriff, she could be next.

"Good afternoon. I'm with the sheriff's department and we are still investigating the attack on the young sailor, who was brought to the hospital early Sunday morning. Can you give me any information on his condition?"

"Just a minute, please." Mary C. was nervous, as she waited for the hospital worker to return.

"We sent some information out this morning, but it probably hasn't arrived yet. Mr. Clark expired last night." Mary C. didn't say a word. She hung up the phone. It was all too crazy for her. She had talked to the man three different times in the last three days. He had confessed his heartfelt feelings for her and he said he thought she was special. No one had ever talked to her like he did that night. She headed the Falcon back toward Mayport.

Lunch was over and the human pelicans were back on the barge, hard at work. Jason's safety cleaning continued on the same effective level as before. He kept his torrid pace and took pride in even the smallest job. He was a great example for all who worked with him. As Jason worked, he hadn't noticed that the *Mary C.* had entered the river and was passing close to the barge.

Uncle Bobby held his binoculars to his eyes to find where Jason stood on the barge. He found him and blew the boat's air horn, to get Jason's attention. Jason looked up and saw the *Mary C.* passing nearby. He saw Uncle Bobby looking at him with the glasses.

Bobby put the glasses down and gave out a wild holler. "Jetty Man!!!!! Jetty Man!!!!! Jetty Man!!!!"

Jason had his name. He did love Uncle Bobby. All the workers heard Bobby's cry of respect, as the *Mary C.* moved up the river. Jason would be Jetty Man from that moment on.

Mary C. pulled into her front yard. She didn't want to be there, but she didn't know where else to go. She was confused and her thoughts were fragmented. She waited for the others.

Bobby was shocked when he unloaded his catch and Mr. Leek told him the gruesome story about Sheriff McIntosh.

"I just saw him on Sunday. He was at the house talkin' to Mary C. 'bout that sailor gettin' beat up at the Fish Bowl. She was there that night and he was talkin' to all the customers, just in case they saw somethin'. That's crazy. You talk to a man one day and he's fish food the next day. That's crazy, ain't it?"

Mr. Leek nodded his head in agreement with Bobby's colorful description of life and death.

The workday was over and the crew from the barge filled the two shuttle boats, as they both made their way up the river to Mr. Leek's dock again. The barges full of huge red mountain rocks did not float into the mouth of the river that day. Maybe tomorrow.

Bobby left the dock before the shuttles arrived and stopped by Miss Margaret's. He was dying for an orange Nehi. Sofia and Peggy were still minding the store. The normal polite greeting met him as he entered the bell ring door. It was Sofia's turn.

"Good afternoon. May I help you?"

Bobby couldn't help himself. "You have got some eyes on you, girl."

Sofia knew he meant that her eyes were pretty. She smiled and was embarrassed at Bobby's crude compliment. "Thank you."

Bobby smiled and used his best Elvis voice.

"No, little lady, thank you." His perfect imitation of the King surprised both girls. They smiled at each other, as Bobby walked to the cold drink box and pulled an orange Nehi from the ice. He popped off the cap and turned the bottle up to his mouth and swallowed half the contents in one big gulp. He took a breath and repeated his action. The bottle was empty.

"Girls, I needed that. I do believe I can go on." The two sisters smiled as Bobby walked to the counter and paid for the cold drink. He looked at Peggy for the first time.

"Lord have mercy, where y'all gettin' these eyes from? You two got to keep y'all's eyes closed at all times. The men in this world won't be able to take it. Too many hearts will fall." Both girls smiled again. Bobby was funny to them and he was a pleasant change from most of the customers before him. Sofia knew who he was and she couldn't help herself.

"You're Jason's uncle, aren't you? He talked about you at my aunt's dinner last Sunday."

Bobby couldn't help it either. "Was I the only one in town that didn't go to the dinner?"

Sofia didn't understand, but she smiled anyway.

Bobby had a serious look on his face and in his tone. "Yes, ma'am. I am the proud uncle of Jason, better know as the Jetty Man, for his knowledge and his ability to sit on rocks. I'm Bobby Merritt." His Elvis voice returned. "But you can call me Uncle Bobby."

Sofia and Peggy didn't want Bobby to leave. It was fun having him in the store with them. The entertainment was over, however, and he had to get home.

Jason stepped off the shuttle and onto the dock. His first stop would be the store, too. He waved to a busy Mr. Leek and was out the door of the fish house. Jake sat under the dock, eating his cheese-bologna roll. Jason didn't stop to stare; he kept moving toward his Sofia destination. The familiar bell sounded as he entered the store.

"Jason! I was just thinking about you. I can't believe you walked through the door." She did say the right things.

"Hey, Sofia. Hey, Peggy."

Peggy smiled and said, "hey." Sofia took over.

"Your uncle was just here. He's so nice. And he's so funny. He can talk just like Elvis, but you probably already know that. Oh, I almost forgot. Good afternoon, may I help you with something?"

Jason was surprised by her change in subject matter. Peggy was too.

"Sofia, sometimes you are so silly."

"Well, Mama said to do it with every customer."

"Not after you've had a full conversation with them." Sofia didn't care about anything but Jason. "Can I get you something?"

"I'd like a grape Nehi."

Sofia's beautiful eyes lit up. "Uncle Bobby, he told me I could call him Uncle Bobby, had an orange Nehi. Y'all must think alike. Both of y'all had a Nehi."

Peggy couldn't take it. "Sofia, you are talking a hundred miles an hour and saying very little. Slow down and think before you talk."

Sofia looked at Peggy with an interesting smile on her face. "Thank you very much for that rather embarrassing moment. Now that you have put me in my place, may I continue to serve this customer?"

Peggy smiled again. "Sofia, you are so silly." Jason liked the way they treated each other. He liked being with them.

"One cold grape Nehi coming up." Sofia went to the cold drink box and pulled the drink out of the ice and handed it to Jason. "There you go."

"Thank you."

They both walked to the counter, where Peggy stood at the cash register. He paid for the drink. Sofia didn't want him to go.

"How was your job today? I'll bet it's hard out there."

"It was fine. It's hard sometimes."

"Your uncle called you 'Jetty Man'."

"Some of the workers are calling me that. Mr. Hawkins gave me that name last night at Bill's Hideaway."

Sofia's eyes lit up again. Peggy's did too.

"You were at Bill's Hideaway last night, too?"

"Yeah. With Uncle Bobby and my mama."

"Did you see Margie there?"

Jason's heart went crazy inside his chest. He knew the feeling well.

"Yeah, I saw her. She was with two other girls. She sat at our table."

"Oh, that's right. Your mother told us Margie sat with y'all."

"You talked to my mama?"

"Yes, this morning. She came in for a few things and told us she saw Margie at that place. We can't believe she went there. We can't wait to talk to her when she gets back. We want to hear all about it. Mama will kill her if she finds out she went out there."

Jason popped the top off his Nehi with the opener, hanging on a string, at the front counter. He didn't want to leave, but he didn't like the direction of the conversation. His memory flashes of Margie's topless turtle ride kept his attention divided between Sofia's questions and Margie's hard naked body. The battle in his head was too much. He needed to retreat.

"Well, I need to get home and get me a shower. I've got barge dirt all over me. Thank you for the drink."

Sofia knew she couldn't keep him there. "You're welcome."

Jason looked at Peggy. "Nice to see you too, Peggy."

"You too, Jason."

He was out the door and around the corner of the building. He heard a noise behind him and turned to see Sofia running around the corner, after him.

"Jason, wait." She ran right into his arms, kissed him on the lips in broad daylight, with Mr. King sitting on his porch. The shock of the kiss was nothing to Jason compared to the shock of her words when the kiss was over.

"I wish I could go home with you and take a shower too. I love you." She turned and ran back around the corner and was out of his sight. Jason was in a state of pure mental shock. He wanted to go back and get her. His thoughts were crazy.

"Mama, this is Sofia. She came home to take a shower with me. Could you get us some towels?" Jason smiled at his thoughts. He waved to Mr. King and went home.

Mary C. and Uncle Bobby were discussing the sheriff's death, when Jason walked in the front door, still reeling from Sofia's last words.

"Hey Jetty Man. Did ya hear me today?"

Jason smiled. "Everybody heard you."

"Good. That was the idea. How was work?"

"It was fine."

"Can't you ever say anything, but 'fine'?. Everything's always just fine with you. 'Just fine', 'I'm fine', 'Fine, fine, fine.'" Jason had to smile at his uncle. He did love him.

"Hell, I'd be fine too, if I was twenty-one years old and all four of Miss Margaret's daughters were after me. Them's some pretty girls and they all want some of the Jetty Man."

Jason tried not to, but he had to smile again.

"Hell, boy. I'd be grinnin' too. You couldn't knock the smile off my face, if them four was after me."

Mary C. had heard enough. "Now, y'all stop that foolish talk. Those are nice girls. That Margie might be feelin' her oats a little bit, but she's just tryin' to show her independence. It's her time to do that. The other girls seem to be way behind her, but they'll have their time to fly too."

Margie's naked body flashed in Jason's head. Thoughts of her were becoming common with him. Her body was similar to Jessie's.

"Well, listen to your mama, giving us her 'let the girl feel her oats' philosophy. My, my, how we have grown. All I know is, every time I see one of those girls, they ask me about Jason. Hell, boy, what did you do at that dinner? And how come I wasn't there? And that young one with those deep blue eyes, God, I wish I was young again. Me and Jason could take 'em out on the town. One at a time, two at a time, or all four at once. It wouldn't make no difference to me."

"I said stop talkin' like that. You need to respect those girls."

"We heard ya."

Jason looked at his mother while she was talking, but he was more interested in the vision he had of him, Uncle Bobby and the four sisters crammed into Mary C.'s Falcon, going out on the town. He smiled at his funny fantasy date and sat down in the living room. Uncle Bobby stopped talking.

"Jason, did you hear about the sheriff?"

He shook his head "no" at the question.

"He's dead. They think somebody killed him and threw his body in the ocean. His body washed up on the beach at the pier in Atlantic Beach. I just can't believe it."

Jason was surprised at the news. He was sorry when anyone died, but he really didn't like Sheriff McIntosh at all. He wouldn't miss him and probably wouldn't think about him again.

Mary C. walked out onto the porch and sat in the swing. Bobby started reading the Journal newspaper and Jason went to take the shower he needed. A "shower with Sofia" fantasy began as soon as he pulled the shower curtain closed. His ability to fantasize had become an art form. Mary C. couldn't relax or sit still. She was up and down, in and out of the house. Bobby couldn't handle all the movement.

"What the hell's wrong with you? This thing with the sheriff bothered you that much?"

"He told me he loved me."

"What?"

"He said he had been in love with me for years and that he wanted to take care of me."

"God, girl, what do you do to these damn men around here? It's a family curse, ain't it? We can't help it. It's out of our control. First me, then you and now Jason. They want us all. It's a curse. I tell ya. It's a damn curse."

Mary C. hated Bobby's way of expressing himself at times, but he was funny. "Can you ever be serious?"

"Why? It won't change nothin'."

Mary C. knew that in his own twisted way, Bobby was right.

"The man said he loved ya?"

"Right here on this porch."

"If that don't beat all. You just don't never know what people are thinkin' sometimes. Folks have somethin' on their minds to say and they just can't do it. People are crazy, plumb crazy."

"Oh, Bobby! And another thing. That big sailor who got beat up so bad at the Fish Bowl, he's dead too."

"Who told you that?"

"I called the hospital to see if he was still there. I thought maybe he was out and he killed the sheriff. They told me he was dead."

"Well, Miss Perry Mason, you better leave that stuff alone. You got no business askin' any questions. You've already said you didn't see anything and don't know anything. Leave it at that. It can only bring you trouble."

"I need to get out of here for a little while."

"I do agree with you wholeheartedly. Let me find your keys." Bobby handed the keys to Mary C., as she walked out the door. "Be careful. I'm sorry about Mac."

Mary C. started the Falcon and was gone again.

The sun was going down, as Jason walked out onto the front porch and joined Uncle Bobby, who was relaxing in the porch swing.

"Nothin' like gettin' dirt of the workday off ya, is it? Damn, boy, you do look squeaky clean."

"I am."

"But, are ya fine?"

"I'm fine, too."

"Boy, you have created the shortest, full sentences, known to man. If you were ever to say more than four words at a time, I'd mark it on my calendar. Hell, I ain't got no calendar. Well, if I had a calendar, I'd mark it."

Jason did love Uncle Bobby.

"I was goin' to bed, but I can't sleep for some reason. Sometimes you can be too tired to sleep." Uncle Bobby shared his philosophical gems of wisdom with Jason. Jason thought he had an answer for Uncle Bobby's restlessness. "You want to take a walk?"

Uncle Bobby's eyes lit up. "A walk? Hell, no! I just told you I was too tired to sleep and you want me to take a damn walk. If I'm too tired to sleep, don't you think I just might be too tired to walk? What the hell's wrong with all y'all?"

Jason held back a smile. But it was hard.

"Besides, them four sisters would go wild as bats, if they seen us both at the same time. The curse would have 'em for good. They'd be tearin' our clothes off right there in the street, for everybody to see. Mr. King would have a damn heart attack. No, we can't do that to those poor love-starved girls. I'll stay here and fall asleep in this swing, you go on and take on those four vixens. Just take notes and read 'em back to me in my old age."

Jason wasn't sure what the word vixen meant, but he knew it sounded like something wild. He began his walk.

Mary C. drove past the little jetties, on her way out of the small town. She had no particular destination, but had to be on the move. A blue truck passed her, going in the other direction back into Mayport. The sound of the truck, as it went by, sent a rush of cold blood through her veins. She knew that sound. It was the sound she heard the night she was blindfolded and stood naked at the lighthouse. It was the sound of the vehicle when it left her there and drove away. It was the truck she had been held captive in, deep in the woods. She began to tremble and she was sick to her stomach. All her muscles contracted and she felt every bruise again. Mary C. pulled the car off the road and stopped to get control of her body and thoughts. She had to see who was driving that blue truck. She turned the Falcon back toward Mayport.

Jason was near the store again. He wanted to see Sofia, but he didn't want to talk about Margie's big coming-out night. He knew Sofia would have more questions about that night and he had already had too many visions of Margie on that loggerhead. He couldn't take anymore. He looked around the corner of the building and stayed hidden at the same time. He just wanted to see if Sofia was there. She was there alright, but she was leaving. Miss Margaret and Sofia were getting into their station wagon.

"Peggy, you stay for one more hour and then Susan will be here and you can go home."

"Yes, ma'am." They drove away, and Peggy walked back into

the store.

Jason turned to head toward the ferry slip. A rusty, blue truck went past. Jason had to jump back when the truck came close to him. It stopped in front of the store. Jason recognized James when he jumped out of the truck.

"Damn, Jason. I almost hit ya. I didn't even see ya, at all. I coulda hit ya and never knew it. Sorry 'bout that."

"That's alright, James. How ya been?"

"I'm good. I heard 'bout you savin' that man and all. What the hell made you jump in that water? You coulda' got killed ya'self."

"I don't know why. It just happened so fast."

"Well, good to see ya. Tell that pretty mama of yours, I said, 'hey'."

Jason nodded as James went into the store. For some reason Jason didn't want Peggy to be in the store alone with James. He didn't go inside, but he didn't leave either. He waved to Mr. King and sat down at the edge of the building.

"Good evening. May I help you with something?" The formal greeting changed with the time of day.

"Damn, ain't you a looker."

Peggy put her head down and smiled.

"Don't look down, darlin'. Don't you dare hide those eyes. Those kinda eyes make a man do crazy things."

She looked up at him.

"What's ya name?"

"Peggy."

"Well, Peggy, I'm James. It is a real pleasure to meet you. You ain't one of Miss Margaret's little daughters, are ya?"

"I believe so."

"Damn, I heard y'all was all grown up and pretty now, but I didn't think they meant this grown up and this pretty. I'm gonna spend more time shoppin' here, from now on." He handed Peggy a few items he had been picking up as he talked. "Maybe, some time you would like to do something with me. Your choice."

"Maybe."

"Damn, maybe's good enough for now. I wish I didn't have to run. I believe we would get along real good. Peggy, darlin', I will be back, and real soon." He paid for his things and left. Peggy didn't like James very much, but the attention and possibility of adventure excited her.

Jason watched James pull away from the store in the blue truck. He drove to the front of Strickland's Restaurant, got out of the truck and walked in. Jason felt Peggy was safe now, so he went onto the ferry slip, his original destination. He didn't see his mother's car pass by Strickland's and the blue truck.

Mary C. drove by once and then circled back. She stopped and parked the Falcon about fifty yards away and walked to the truck. She had not seen the driver yet. Mary C. found herself standing at the side window of the blue truck. It didn't take but a few seconds for her to be sick to her stomach again. The first thing she saw was her torn, blood-stained panties, hanging from the mirror. Her body was riddled with muscle spasms of anger. She reached through the window and pulled her panties off the hanger. She squeezed them in her hand and held them tight as she ran back to her car, where she would sit and wait for the driver of the truck to show himself.

Jason sat on his favorite pylon at the ferry slip. He hadn't watched the fiddler crabs run all week. His new job and all the happenings had taken all his time. He was glad to be a workingman, but he did miss his moments alone and to himself. The Buccaneer was pulling into the slip on the other side of the river. Jason planned to sit and wait for the carrier's return to Mayport. Mary C. waited too.

While the ferry docked and loaded, James sat and ate. Jason had the crabs to occupy his wait time. Mary C. had her panties, faded bruises, and thoughts of revenge to occupy her wait time.

The ferry horn blasted and Jason watched the Buccaneer leave the other side, headed for Mayport.

Mary C. watched James walk out the front door of Strickland's. Her blood ran cold again, when she saw him and realized he had been the one who hurt her and scared her so badly. James had not crossed her mind, until that moment. She would have never thought he was the one that night. She hated him for what he did and what he was. She knew she would be the one to punish him for that awful night in the woods.

The sound of the truck's engine sent more fearful and angry chills through her body, as James drove past her and on down the road. He was gone. Mary C. went home with her panties and her thoughts of revenge. James wouldn't notice his missing trophy for some time.

Jason watched the ferry until it stopped to rest against the Mayport side. The cars drove off and down the road. It was near dark and Jason knew he needed to get on home. Six A.M. came early and the big red rocks would probably be there in the morning. A cool breeze touched his face, as he stood up off the pylon. The air took his breath for a brief second. It was the oak tree. Jason would not go, yet.

Bobby had left the swing and gone to bed, by the time Mary C. got home. She was glad to have the time to herself. She needed to think and decide what she could and would do. The swing seemed the perfect place.

Mary C. had a hard roughness to her, more so than other women. It was a personality trait she acquired during her less than ideal life. She was a true victim. Not only last Saturday night, but many times before. Mary C. had weak moral fiber. She was selfish and truly cared about few others. She had sold her body and favors for money. Her vices and own pleasure came first and she had moments of pure mean-ness. When a woman like Mary C. turns to revenge, God help us all.

Jason ignored the call of the tree and headed home. Even with the Jetty Man within, he was still not ready to face the tree. He knew the tree had given him courage at one time and it had introduced him to Jessie. But, it had also taken away his humanity and, for a while, his sanity. He was not ready to face either side of the oak.

Jason liked the time of day when the sun had just disappeared and light and dark seemed to criss-cross each other. It gave Mayport and the river the look of Jason's dreams. The ferry horn added to the pleasures of his walk.

Jason had too many things to think about. His job, Sofia, the other sisters, his family, living up to his new name. All manner of thought ran through his mind. He was preoccupied with all that had transpired, until a moving shadow, a phantom, a vampire appeared. Like a black cat, Jake crossed Jason's path. The moving shadow scared Jason at first, but he left caution behind and he followed the black trench coat into the approaching night.

He could see the shadow moving ahead, with the black cape flowing behind, as a symbol of the chase. Jason had no idea what made him continue his pursuit. Jake went deeper into the black section of the small town and Jason followed. He had been there before when he looked for Jessie. It seemed darker there to Jason; there were less lights than the rest of the town. Jake passed the Blue Moon and Jason heard music from the tavern as he went by. Jake turned a corner and for a second Jason had lost him. Jason stopped and realized he was too far away from home and the safety of the ferry slip. He had made a mistake and he was afraid. He walked slowly toward the corner where Jake had gone. He was standing at the corner edge of a small cinder block house. He listened again and heard a man talking. His mouth went dry, but then his nostrils flared. The familiar aroma of peanuts boiling filled his nose. He loved that smell. His curiosity gave him the courage to look around the corner. Jason's heart jumped when he saw the back of the black trench coat, only a few feet from him. Someone was talking, but Jason couldn't see who it was because Jake blocked his view.

"I don't believe I almost let y'all burn. I forgot all 'bout you, little darlin'."

It didn't take but a few seconds for Jason to realize that no one was talking to Jake. Jake was talking to the peanuts boiling in the pot he was stirring. The phantom of the night had been running to save the peanuts from burning or boiling over. Jason had never heard Jake's voice. It was strange to Jason that the skinny black man would talk to peanuts and not to people. Jason's heart jumped again, when, without turning around, Jake greeted his new friend of the night.

"Why would the Jetty Man follow Jake?"

The question stunned Jason and as usual he had no answer. Even a man who only talked to peanuts had to carry the conversation to Jason.

"Ya ought not be down here at night. This ain't your place." Jake turned to face the Jetty Man. His white eyes seemed to jump out of his head at Jason. Jake looked back at the pot.

"You like the boiled ones, don't ya?"

Jason liked his voice, it was deep and new to Jason's ears. It fit him.

"Any time you made your pick, you picked the boiled ones."

Jason was confused by Jake's words and knowledge of his favorite selection when it came to choosing the peanut bags. It was true, he always picked the boiled ones over the roasted.

"I know lots 'bout you, Jason. It's time for us to talk. And what better place than right here in the middle of Nigger Town, eatin' boiled peanuts. I know what the white folk call this place."

Jason hated that word; he always did. "People don't say that no more."

"You don't say it. But they still say it. You never said it. You'll probably go to heaven for that one thing. You never said it." Jake dipped out a mesh spoon full of hot peanuts. The hot water ran out the bottom of the big spoon and back into the pot, leaving the steaming hot brown nuts on top. He dumped them into bowl and handed them to Jason. Jason held the bowl with two hands.

"Thank ya, Mr. Jake. I don't know your proper name, sir. Everybody knows you as Jake."

Jake did the same with a bowlful of nuts for himself. He sat down on a bucket that was upside down. Jason sat on the ground.

"My name is Jake Green."

Jason's eyes lit up and his heart raced in his chest.

"That's right, boy. Jake Green. Tom Green's my brother."

Jason couldn't believe what he had just heard. He knew it had to be one of his dreams. Jake and Tom Green? It was too much. He allowed the dream to continue.

"I know all about ya. Tom told me everything. He loves you like you was his own. He told me that."

Jason wanted to hear about his dead friend and he wanted to know the things he had said. "Tell me, things. Please. Tell me what you know."

"If you eat the boiled ones with me, I'll tell you everything and more. Tom would like us eatin' 'em together. This time has been coming. You decided it was tonight."

Jason broke open the first of many boiled peanuts he would eat, while Jake talked.

"I know you saved Tom that night at Floyd's. Tom told me before he left."

Jason had to interrupt. "What do you mean, before he left?"

"Before he run off. He couldn't stay here. A black man killin' the white sheriff in self-defense? They'd a hung him that very night. He had to go and never come back. We all knew that. It had to be that way. You were just a little boy, but you saved him. That Floyd woulda killed him before the night was over."

Jason tried to absorb Jake's words. "You're talkin' like Tom Green is alive and didn't die that night."

Jake smiled. "That's just what I'm sayin'. He is alive. He's been livin' in a little town called Ruskin, near Tampa. He grows tomatoes. I been to see him a few times, but he can't ever come here. People remember things 'til everybody's dead. It's best he stays in Ruskin. He asked me about you two Christmases ago. I told him I always see ya. I told him 'bout the game y'all crazy fools played and what it done to ya. We prayed for ya, together, that night."

Jason had thought Tom Green had died fourteen years ago and now he finds out his best friend grows tomatoes in a town called Ruskin. "Maybe, I'll go to Ruskin one day," he thought.

Jake wanted to fill his overflowing brain with more. "I know 'bout you and Jessie and the oak."

Jason's heart raced, when the black man mentioned them both.

"Eat them peanuts, boy. Tom showed me how to fix 'em. It'll be a taste you remember."

"I know. I tasted it in the first one. I'm glad about Tom Green. I'm just surprised and confused. I get confused sometimes. I hope this is real."

"It's real, alright. The tree can end your confusion. Ya just too scared to go."

A chill ran through Jason's body. He didn't like talking about the tree, but he did want to know about Jessie. "Tell me 'bout Jessie."

Jake stood up and stirred the pot again.

"You need to know 'bout Miss Bell first." Jason hadn't thought of the big black woman in years. A vision of Miss Bell, standing at the heading tables on the dock, holding her big stick, flashed in Jason's head.

"You were the instrument of Miss Bell's revenge. You and Jessie. That mean boy took Bell's life. He killed her for that money. He had to die, like Bell did, facedown in the sand at the tree. You made that happen."

Jason listened to Jake's reasons for the bloody game. "What about the other boys?"

"They were like Willis and would have brought misery upon the world. They needed to die."

Jason was trying to accept Jake's words. "What about Eddie?"

"I don't have all the answers 'bout that game. I do know that some folks don't have much to offer and some give all they have early. There are those who leave little behind. Maybe, your friend gave all he had that day."

It was difficult for Jason to believe the actions of that day were created to avenge Miss Bell's death. It was hard enough to believe he was sitting with a talkative Jake, eating boiled peanuts, much less believe he was an instrument of revenge.

The conversation had taken a twist that scared Jason. It was obvious Jake was a believer in the tree. He wanted to leave, but he still wanted to know about Jessie.

"You've been talkin' like Jessie's here."

"She should be here with you. You both have to finish what you started. The confusion must leave your head before you go to the tree. You must be aware. That's why you struggle and can't go yet. Jessie will be with you when you stand at the tree."

Jason knew the sacrifice would be too great if he was to see Jessie. He didn't like the fact that Jake was making a deal with him on behalf of the oak. He was afraid. "I gotta get home. I don't know what to say to you. Why don't you talk to people?"

Jake stood up and moved away from the pot. "I talk. I just don't talk to white people. I'll walk with you, so nobody throws ya in a pot and boils ya too."

Jason never thought he would be happy to be walking with Jake, the vampire, at night. There was no more conversation during the walk out of the black section of Mayport. Jason liked the music coming from the Blue Moon when they passed by. He knew Uncle Bobby would like it too. They walked to the old closed down icehouse that stood as the dividing line between the white and black neighborhoods. Some of the boys hid there the day they played the game. Jake broke the silence.

"I'll head on back now. Don't talk to me, just 'cause ya see me."

Jason couldn't help himself. "Why do you roll the meat and cheese like that, to eat it?"

Jake smiled. "It's from when I was a little boy, kinda like you and how you still dunk your toast in the coffee."

Jason's eyes widened at what Jake knew about him.

"Like I said, I know lots 'bout you, Jason. I know when you breed with Jessie at the tree, the power will return tenfold."

Jason's blood ran cold at Jake's final words of the unusual encounter. He made no response and quickly walked away. He wanted to run, but he didn't want to show his fear so openly. He looked back to see if Jake's white eyes were on him, but the phantom was gone.

CHAPTER EIGHT

MARY C. HAD BEEN SITTING IN THE SWING FOR AN HOUR. SHE HATED JAMES and the silent rage inside her had given her the visions of her revenge. The images, of what was to come, flashed on a big movie screen in her head. It would be Saturday night, the same as her night of abuse.

Jason's mind was reeling with Jake's information and prediction. The truth of Tom Green was the blessing of the night and he was grateful to Jake for telling him. He would keep Tom Green's secret. And one day, maybe go to Ruskin. He saw Mr. Leek's truck leaving the fish house and he saw Mr. King leave his perch on his front porch and go in for the night. The store lights caught his eyes next, as the thought of Sofia cleared his mind.

As Jason approached the store, he could see there were a number of evening customers, more so than usual. Miss Margaret and the oldest, Margie, were helping the customers. Jason wasn't sure what a meeting with Margie would be like. He had not seen her since the wild night at Bill's and on the beach, in the red Star Chief. His decision was to head on home.

Jason was about fifty yards down the road, when he saw car lights moving toward him. He stepped off the road, so the car had plenty of room to pass. It was obvious the car was slowing down and it was going to stop near him. He was nervous at first, due to all

Jake's strange talk. The car stopped before it got to him. The glare of the headlights kept the driver's identity a secret for a moment. It just so happened, the driver wanted to be known. The driver side door opened and someone stepped out onto the road.

"Would you like a ride?" Jason couldn't believe his eyes when sister number three, Peggy, offered him a ride in the family station wagon. He walked toward the passenger side, as Peggy jumped back in behind the wheel. They sat together, across from each other. She was as brave as the other.

"I'm off work. I've got the car. I don't want to go home. And I've been looking for you. Would you like to ride out to the little jetties?"

Jason liked her hair. "That'll be fine."

Peggy wasn't looking for any conversation. She would create it if she needed it. They were off. Jason thought she had probably talked to her cousin, the other Peggy.

Jake stood next to the huge trunk of the oak tree. He had made the climb through the soft sand. He took the hard path Miss Bell had used, when she would cleanse herself with her own sweat. He heard no babies crying and the sand did not move beneath his feet. He wanted to be a true believer, like Miss Bell, but the tree gave him no signs and no directions. It offered him nothing. He did want to be part of the tree, so badly. He hoped he had the answer that would prove him worthy.

Peggy was a chip off the older Peggy. She was the wildest of the three sisters he had encountered. Jason worked his magic, but Peggy had magic of her own and it centered around pleasing Jason. She was no beginner and Jason had no doubt she had parked at the little jetties before. Her confidence level was higher than her sister's and Jason liked the way she demonstrated her experience. She was the quiet sister, with secrets screaming inside. Someone had taught her to please her partner first. Jason knew cousin Peggy had a hand in her style, but someone else must have refined her techniques. Perhaps it was just natural for her to please. She finished a rough, passionate kiss and moved her head to his lap. Her long raven hair covered his lower body, as Jason sat up in the front seat. Jason knew he was in her mouth. He laid his head on the back of the seat. She worked her magic for a long time and then remained through his explosion. Someone had taught her that. Peggy kept her head in his lap, as if she was fatigued from her hard work. She got more pleasure from his pleasure. That was new for Jason; he liked it. She lifted her head.

"I really love doing that. I've been wanting to do that since I saw you at Aunt Margie's. Did you like it?"

Jason didn't want to talk at all, but he felt he should express something. "I loved it. It was great." That was enough talk for them both. She put her head back down. They rested.

Mary C. stood on her front porch, looking into the night. She didn't think about Jason, or Hawk, or Mac. James and her ordeal of fear and humiliation were the only thoughts running through her hateful mind. He would be punished and she would orchestrate his ordeal. He had three days.

Her mind cleared for a moment, as car lights appeared on the road leading to the front yard. The car stopped at the edge of their property. She wasn't concerned at first, but it was strange how the car stopped that far away. She thought it was just turning around, but she realized that was not the case, when the car lights went out and the car sat there in the dark. She watched the car and knew she could get into the house and alert Bobby if she needed to. There was enough moonlight to see someone, if they were out in the open. Whoever it was watched her from inside the car. A light flashed in the car when the driver lit a cigarette.

The light went out, but left Mary C. with more awful feelings. She didn't believe what the flash of light told her. If she had faith in her night vision, she would know Charlie Klim sat in the dark car. She saw the Derby on his head, but didn't want to believe it. Mary C. refused to accept that the evil one was actually sitting in her front yard and watching her. As disbelief and a state of shock kept her standing there, the car door opened and Charlie Klim stepped out onto the ground. She knew it was him.

"That you, Mary C.?"

His voice and question made her quake inside.

"That is you. Woman, you never do change, do ya? Now, of course I can't see no wrinkles from here in the dark, but that body of yours still looks like a rock from here."

She took a deep breath. "Why'd ya come here, Charlie? It ain't right for you to be here."

"Well, you know better than most that I ain't been too good at right and wrong. I get 'em mixed up sometimes. Don't be so mean to me. I just wanted to see ya. I've always been crazy 'bout ya. You know that. I never meant to hurt ya that night. You always did make me crazy. I had too much Jack at the rocks. You let me come home with ya. It just got outta hand. If that boy of yours hada left us alone, you woulda calmed me. You always did before. Hell, woman, you liked it rough sometimes. You've hurt me before too. I've had scratches and bite marks on me for weeks 'cause of you. I know ya didn't want the boy to cut me, like he did. It was hard for me to take what happened that night. Time takes a little away each day. I'm back Mary C. and I'm back for one of two things. You or the boy. We can live happily ever after, or somebody can die. Either way, I'm back."

Mary C. was frozen with fear and hate. Charlie's last words were pounding in her head as the car lights came on and the car drove off. Another set of car lights appeared coming toward Mary C. again. Peggy was bringing Jason home after she had given him a few lessons. They passed Charlie and Jason saw the Derby hat he had seen at Bill's Hideaway. He looked toward the house as they pulled up to the porch. Mary C. had not moved. Jason left Peggy before the car stopped.

"Mama, you alright?"

"Yes, I'm alright."

"Mama, that was Charlie Klim. I saw him last night too. Did he try to hurt you? What did he want?"

"He just wanted to talk to me, but I told him to leave."

"I don't like him bein' back. I don't want him to hurt you."

"He ain't gonna hurt nobody. Who's that in the car?"

"Hey, Miss Mary C. It's me, Peggy. I gave Jason a ride home."

Mary C. looked at Jason's wrinkled shirt, but talked to Peggy. "That sure was nice of ya. Did you run over him before you picked him up?"

Peggy wasn't sure about the answer or the question. "Why, no, ma'am. He was walking on the road."

"Never mind, I was just foolin' with ya. Thanks for gettin' him home. He never does know when to get home."

"Well, good night Jason, Miss Mary C."

"Good night, Peggy."

"Good night." Mary C. looked at Jason, as Peggy pulled the station wagon out of the yard. "Your Uncle Bobby's right, it is a curse."

Uncle Bobby was the only member of the family to sleep much that night. Jason tried to think about the pleasures he had with the sisters, but the ugly thoughts of Charlie Klim interfered throughout the night. Mary C. thought of Charlie's threatening words, but her plan of revenge on James overshadowed Charlie's words. She would deal with James first and then turn her attention to the other evil one.

After another restless night, Jason was up for his morning ritual. He opened his mother's bedroom door slowly to check on her and to see if she was alright. He was worried about her, but he was also out the door of the house, when the first of six clock chimes sounded. He hurried to the store to continue his morning ritual, with milk, honey bun and, he hoped, a look at Sofia, or who else might be minding the store. It was Margie. Jason had not talked to her since their wild sea turtle ride.

"Jason, good morning! I was hoping you'd come by this morning. I haven't seen you since the other night. I really had a great time. I've been wanting to tell you. It seems everybody in my family has seen you, but me."

Jason's heart beat a little faster at her last comment. He wondered if the other two had shared any information with Margie. He felt strange and as usual Margie didn't wait for him to join the conversation.

"Everybody's talking about you and how you saved that man. He's a famous man too. And about that sheriff getting killed. There's lots of excitement around here. And I waited on that Jake, already this morning, alone in here. He just left. He gives me the creeps. Can't he talk?"

Margie had Jason's head spinning like a top. He guessed she really thought they were having a conversation, when in reality, she was the only one who had said a word up to that point. Jason was going to be late and he wanted to tell her she hadn't even asked if she could help him. Miss Margaret wouldn't like that. "I gotta get to the shuttle." Jason walked to the shelf and picked up a honey bun.

"You want milk too?" She finally treated him like a customer.

"Yes, please." Jason met her at the register, paid and turned toward the door.

"It was great seeing you, Jason. I want to see you again. Maybe I'll see you this weekend. I miss you."

Jason was out the door.

The activity and the dock and the shuttle ride were the same as before. The ferry horn and the honey bun added to the consistency of his ritual. Jason liked the order to his actions. It eased the confusion in his head. Jake had broken the order Jason had established. He was glad to be going to work. No other thoughts took his mind when he worked. He did love being a workingman.

Even though Mary C. had a restless night, too, she was up early. She would need all three days to prepare herself for Saturday night. She sat at the kitchen table and wrote down what she would need, and steps she had to take to succeed. Bobby had left that morning, before Jason. She was alone and she would plan and carry out her plans alone.

As the shuttle turned into the mouth of the St. Johns River, all the workers stood at the sight before them. Jason was in awe as his mouth dropped open at what he saw. Two huge barges had docked overnight with the red cargo they had been waiting for. The first load of red mountain rocks had arrived.

Some of the rocks were as big as cars, some even bigger. One was almost a perfect ten foot cube. Jason thought it would be a good lunch rock, if when it fell, it landed in the right position. Jason thought it was, no doubt, the mother rock of this first load and probably any other load. He really liked that rock. He prepared himself for an exciting day. His preoccupation with the rocks had taken his mind away from the tree. The shuttle had passed it and Jason didn't even think of looking in that direction.

The work would be hard and steady that day and the big machines would be in high gear, moving the rocks and placing them strategically into the water, in front of the older rocks. They would be stacked on top of each other, until the top rock on the pile broke the water level above, and became visible. It was a long, dangerous process and every worker had to be alert and safety conscious. Mr. Hawkins gave his morning speech and warning of the dangers ahead. The roar of the big engines, the rocks moving and the water splashing that day made the barge the most exciting place for Jason to be, or for anyone to be, especially the Jetty Man.

Mary C. finished her coffee, her revenge checklist, and she was dressed and out the door. The Ford Falcon was on the move. Her first stop was a wooded area, in East Mayport near the marsh, behind where the Big House used to stand. She drove into the woods on a hunting trail. She had hunted for Indian arrowheads there when she lived nearby, as a teenager. Her first sexual encounter with Charlie Klim had taken place where she stood at that moment. Jason's father had died in those same woods and Mary C.'s mother had disappeared and been presumed dead after she wandered into the marsh, after Daddy Bob's untimely death. Mary C. looked around and thought of the history she shared with her surroundings. It was the perfect place. The onetime Indian burial ground would be her battleground. Perhaps the ghosts of the mounds and the ghosts of her past would be with her when she met the devil, James. She had left her mark there before; she would mark her territory one more time, Saturday night. The Falcon rolled.

The work time on the barge raced along. Lunchtime found Jason and his followers sitting all over the rocks. His lunch rock was filled to capacity; he could have used the new big mother rock, if they would drop it where he wanted. Mr. Hawkins watched the multitude again, as they moved to be near the Jetty Man.

Mary C.'s next stop was to visit an old trusted friend. She knew she would not be questioned or judged when she made her request. She drove up to a small shack located at the end of Seminole Road, just before you entered Atlantic Beach. Her old friend, Skinny, sat in front of the shack in a poorly-wound beach chair. His eyes lit up, the best they could, when Mary C. stepped out of the Falcon.

"Lord have mercy on my sinful soul. I know these old eyes are playin' tricks on me." He looked to the heavens. "Lord leave this vision with me forever."

Mary C. smiled at his praise and compliment. "You ain't dreamin'. It's me. How are ya?" She moved closer and he stood up for the embrace they both knew was coming. It was a meaningful hug they both enjoyed. He held her at arm's length, for a closer look.

"God has blessed you, Mary C. He allows you to stay the same. He doesn't do that for the rest of us. Why does he do such a wonderful thing for you?"

"You are still crazy. But it is good to see ya."

Skinny had helped Mary C. many times throughout her life. He had gotten her out of trouble on a number of occasions and had rescued her from the clutches of late night admirers. He worked with her when she used to wait tables at the old Fish Bowl. He had many opportunities to assist her when she was in distress. Skinny praised the Lord each day and knew his Bible from cover to cover, but he could still be the toughest man alive, in the name of the Lord. An eye for an eye was his favorite concept, from the Old Testament. The Old Testament did give Skinny a great deal of leeway for self-interpretation.

Mary C. respected the rough one, because he always respected her. They were never intimate, because he said she was too pretty for a man like him. He would always want more and he couldn't have it. He even told her one time that he never was very good with women and anything more than a friendship with her would probably ruin things. Sometimes Mary C. wished she would have given her favors to Skinny. If anyone deserved her abilities to please, it was Skinny. He knew her visit had substance.

"It's really good to see ya, woman, but what brings you to me at this stage of your life?"

"Why don't you just get right to the heart of the matter. Can't we say hello, first?"

"Me and you ain't never not got right to business. The best thing 'bout you is how you 'cut to the chase'."

"A man hurt me, bad. And another wants to. I have to do this myself. When it's done there will be a new Mary C. rise from the ashes. I have to wash myself clean of all that has gone before; then and only then, will I be able to change."

Skinny's eyes were filled with her words. "Damn woman, that sounded like it came right from the Scriptures. You are embarking on a quest of biblical proportions. Tell me what I need to do to be part of this revelation and your renaissance. Praise the Lord, give me my direction."

Mary C. knew his words were no joke or laughing matter to him. He meant what he said and her response would be on the same level.

"I need to be able to knock a man out, with one hit, with my strength. Whatever I use, I must be able to hide it on me or somewhere easy to reach, before I use it. Is there something you know of that will cause that kinda damage?"

Skinny gave serious thought to her request and question. Not once did he act surprised or like he wouldn't assist her. "I do have something I created years ago. I used to put it up the long sleeve of my shirt. It laid flat against my forearm. If and when I needed it, it was close at hand, literally. I think I know where it is." Skinny walked into his shack and left Mary C. outside. He was gone less than a minute.

"Here it is. I call it the Skinny Blackjack. It's like a regular blackjack, just not as thick. It's skinny, see. Get it? Skinny." He handed the black object to her. It was made of black leather. It had weight and she could feel the hardness of the metal under the leather. It bent back and forth in the middle, but both ends were the same so you could hold either end in your hand. The entire object was about a foot long and three inches wide. It didn't look like much to Mary C.

"This thing will do what I need?" She had a doubtful look as she held the weapon in her hand.

"Well, it ain't gonna do it alone, but with me showin' ya the right way to use it, I promise it will do what you want. Step this way, please." Skinny led Mary C. to an area behind the shack where a hard-packed canvas bag was hanging on a rope from a tree. He took the Skinny Blackjack from Mary C.'s hand and hit the bag, sending it swinging, and scaring Mary C. enough to make her scream.

"My God, Skinny! Ya 'bout gave me a stroke. Tell me when you're gonna do somethin' like that."

Skinny shook his head. "That's the point, ain't it? Ya not 'spose to know when it's comin'. Now, you try it."

The weapon was back in Mary C.'s hand. She hit the bag.

"Not bad. Now come from this angle and use your wrist a little more."

She hit it again.

"Good. Now add speed and those pretty shoulders as you turn into the bag."

It was her hardest hit so far. It sounded like a cannon going off. That particular blow would have taken any man down. She knew if she could duplicate that swing James would fall at her feet, the exact place she wanted him. She would spend the majority of the day practicing her swing and talking old times with Skinny.

The deck of one of the big barges was empty. Every rock was in the water. The other barge would be emptied tomorrow and they would both leave, making room for two more. The day was filled with nonstop action and Jason loved the pace they had to keep to make it all happen. He actually didn't want it to end as the shuttles pulled up for the trip back to Mayport.

Jason sat in his usual seat on the shuttle. He thought about getting home and making sure his mother was alright. He wanted

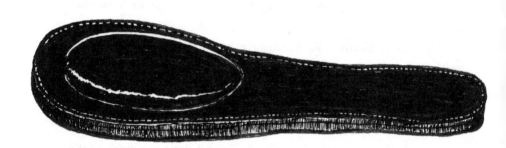

SKINNY BLACK JACK

to see Sofia too. The sound of Elvis cut into his thoughts, as the *Mary C.* pulled alongside of the shuttle. Uncle Bobby had the King blaring and a megaphone at his mouth, singing along with "Don't Be Cruel."

"I don't want no other love. Baby it's just you I'm thinkin' of . . . a don't be cruel . . ."

Jason looked up as the big shrimp boat passed the shuttle, headed for Mr. Leek's. Jason did love Uncle Bobby.

Mary C.'s training was over. She thanked her friend. The Falcon rolled back to Mayport. The family threesome were all on roads headed home. Bobby would have to unload his catch and Jason would stop at the store, for his usual seek and find mission. Mary C. would be the first of the trio to reach home. She would surprise her two men with dinner. She felt good about her future.

Jason didn't linger at the dock. He waved good-bye to Mr. Leek, popped Uncle Bobby on the butt as he passed him and went straight to the store, in search of Sofia. When he entered the store, and the bell on the door announced his arrival, he found much more than he ever bargained for.

All four sisters were standing somewhere in the store. They were everywhere. It could have very well been one of his dreams, that's how wild it looked to him. His mouth and throat went dry when all four sets of loving eyes fell on him. It was as if the mother of all red rocks was swinging above his head, waiting to drive his body into the floor of the store, like a human nail. Sofia was counting stock on a shelf toward the back of the store. Peggy was at the register. Margie was filling the icebox with drinks and Susan was cleaning the glass on the counters. His head was on a swivel and if he didn't get out of there, he would surely throw up. He knew Sofia would never speak to him first with the others there. He thought she was the only one who could keep a secret. As usual, the others waited for Margie.

"Good evening, Jason. Back from a hard day on the jetties?"

Even if Jason wanted to answer, he knew if he hesitated a second Margie would continue. She didn't disappoint him.

"Listen to this. We're all going to the haunted house tonight to hear Mr. King tell his ghost stories. Why don't you come and sit with us?"

Sofia joined in. "We need someone with us, who has been before and knows what to do. We don't want to look like fools."

Peggy was next. "I'm not sure I'm going. Is it real scary?"

Then Susan. "Do you believe there's ghosts in his house?"

Jason wanted it all to be a dream, but he knew it wasn't. Margie had more.

"We would really like you to go with us, so if you can, we'll be there at eight o'clock."

Jason was mentally beaten into the floor. He had not responded to any of the comments or questions, but none of the girls seemed to notice that fact or care. They all went back to their work, none wanting to show any interest in Jason to the others. The three younger girls gave way to Margie, as if they knew she had designs on Jason. But all three of them kept their secrets about Jason from Margie and each other. It may have been the most tangled web in the history of weaving. Jason walked to the cold drink box and stood next to Margie.

"Is there a strawberry Nehi in there?"

Margie reached into the box. "One left. Aren't you the lucky one."

Jason begged to differ with her lucky remark, but he didn't. She handed him the drink.

"Thank you." He paid Peggy at the register.

Sofia had to speak up. "Try to come tonight if you're not too tired."

Jason smiled and was out the door. Home would be the safest place for him that night. He rounded the corner of the store and ran into his Uncle Bobby.

"Well, well, well! This is insane. It is definitely, insane. I just watched four of the most beautiful women in this world, all look at you with want in their eight eyes. Ain't it wonderful what havin' a new name means sometimes? I couldn't walk in the store with all them lookin' at you like that. I feel for ya, son. It's been happenin' to me all my life and now it's started on you. It's a curse, I tell ya, a damn curse." Uncle Bobby put his arm around Jason's shoulder and they headed home.

"And all four want you at Mr. King's tonight. You gotta big decision to make before eight o'clock. I wish I had your problems."

Mary C. had country fried steaks coming out of the pan when they walked through the front door.

"Jason, do you smell somethin' good cookin'? And do you see what I see? Your mother, my sister, at the stove for the first time in weeks. Tell me it ain't just me that sees it."

Mary C. shook her head at Bobby's foolishness again. "Okay, that's enough. Don't push your luck. Both of you go wash up and eat now, while it's hot. You can take a full shower later. I think I judged your arrival pretty good, don't you?" They both followed her instructions and came back to the table where Mary C. added rice, peas and creamed corn to the country fried. The iced tea hit the spot, and started a nice family meal, the kind Jason wanted.

The trio was silent as they ate at first. All three of then had their own type of tiring day. Mary C. knew they were enjoying the fruits of her labor and she didn't mind the quiet time. Even Bobby had no pressing subject to ignite the usual conversation. He noticed the silence around them.

"Boy, are we a lively group tonight. Y'all must be as tired as me. We're all pretty pitiful sittin' here tonight. I know I haven't had much sleep lately, so I know you two haven't had any. You two don't sleep at all. The meal's great, little sis."

"Thanks. And you're right. We are all so tired all the time. Especially you two. Y'all are workin' all day, stayin' up late and gettin' up early. Your body can't take that kinda beatin'."

"Well, you don't have to worry 'bout me this night, 'cause when I finish this plate, I'm takin' a hot shower and I'm in the bed. I ain't settin' no alarm. I'm gonna wake up, when I wake up." He looked at Jason.

"The one you have to worry about is this one right here. There's a ghost storm brewin' at Mr. King's tonight and there's four true witches waiting to boil and eat your son, the Jetty Man."

Mary C. looked at her son and then back to her brother. "What the hell is your fool uncle talkin' 'bout now?"

"Nothin', Mama. Mr. King's tellin' his stories tonight, that's all."

Uncle Bobby stood up. "Yeah, right." It was time for Bobby's shower.

Jason helped his mother clear the table and wash the dishes. He liked working with and being near her. He thought about the dinner at Miss Margie's when they were all cleaning up. It was a real family thing to do. He liked it. He didn't think about Mr. King's until the clock began chiming the eight count. He took his shower and thought it would be better for him to stay home and not face all four sisters at one time. It was hard enough dealing with one at a time.

All four sisters sat in Mr. King's living room. There were ten other young people sitting around the room. Mr. King sat in a big blood-red velvet chair. A young pretty blonde-haired girl sat in a green rocking chair directly across from Mr. King. It was a special chair and spot in the room. It was reserved for the guest of honor at the event. Her name was Sara and it was Sara's birthday. It was her choice to be in that green chair. Mr. King would direct all his attention to her as if she was the only one in the room with him. He would ignore the others as if they were ghosts themselves and invisible to him and Sara. It was a great technique to generate the fearful atmosphere they were all there to experience. Only candles lit the room, causing any movement among the spectators to be exaggerated and bounced off the walls that surrounded them. The four newcomers were scared already. They sat close together, hoping sheer numbers would keep the spirits away. Mr. King began.

"Hello, Sara. Are you okay with all this?" Mr. King wanted his guests to be uncomfortable in a comfortable way.

"Yes, sir. Don't you remember me, Mr. King? I sat here last year on my seventeenth birthday. It was great and I wanted to do it again."

Mr. King did not change his expression. "I'm flattered and impressed with you, Sara. I usually don't get someone for a second time."

Sara smiled and waited for Mr. King to go on.

"I've been told, Sara, you have requested that I tell you about the oak tree and the oak babies. I haven't had that request in many years. Why are you interested in that story?"

"I have a friend from school. We both graduated from Fletcher High this past year. She told me her older brother Billy was killed while he played in a game at the tree. Do you know if that is true or not? She's my friend, but the story is very hard to believe. If it's true, I'd like to know what happened and I'd like to know about the game."

"You have put me in an interesting situation here tonight, Sara. I want to please my special guests, but folks around Mayport haven't talked about the tree since those boys died up there."

Her eyes lit up, adding to the candles. "Then Billy did die there."

"I think one of the boy's was named Billy. He was new in town and the family moved after his death." Mr. King looked around the room in his dramatic fashion. "I think perhaps it is time to tell the 'unknowing' about the oak tree. You cannot hold me responsible if after you learn about the tree, you become a 'believer.' If you do not want to hear of the tree, you need to leave now." He looked at each person.

The four sisters were too scared to leave. They whispered to each other that their Aunt Margie had mentioned the tree and the game when they were talking about Jason. They were all four intrigued and wanted to know more. No one was leaving that candlelit room.

"For some strange reason, years ago, nobody knows when, the big oak tree on the sand hill became a contradiction in nature. It was a true symbol of good and evil. Stories ran wild about the tree and the powers it possessed. Many became believers of the stories and thus believed in the tree. It was said that each time lightning hit the tree it absorbed the power and became stronger each time. For years, people kept track of when the tree was hit by lightning. They also kept track of the shrimping. Someone, no one knew who, came up with the information that the more lightning strikes to the tree the better the shrimp season. Shrimpers would pray for the lightning to rip into the tree. The good and evil concept came about because of the tree and the sand hill. It is very strange for a tree of that size and weight to be able to stand in the soft white sand of the sand hill. It is a contradiction in nature. Another interesting and strange thing about the tree is it has two completely different sides to it, north and south. On the north side nothing grows, there is only soft white sand. On the south side there is growth. Palmetto fans, prickly bushes and a few cabbage trees grow in the sand. There is even a fruitbearing grape arbor on the south side. Folks said the two sides showed good and evil."

"Then out of the blue someone said they heard babies crying at night, when they were near the tree. Folks started saying there were 'oak babies' walking around Mayport. The tale had it that if a man and woman would make love in the sand beneath the tree after midnight, they would be given a son with the power of the tree. The child would be part of the tree. As a man planted his seed, the oak planted its seed. They called it the 'Breeding.' The lovers could not tell of their act, or the child would lose all the power he had been given. If a boy grew strong, or was handsome, or had a talent, people would suspect that his parents did the Breeding. This privilege was only for the males, but there was talk of a girl who was half white. People thought she was an oak baby, or belonged to the tree in some way."

"Then a group of boys started playing a chase and capture game. They called it Duckin'. Like most things about this, no one seems to know why they gave it such a name. It was a wild game. After one group had captured members of another group they were placed in an area below the tree. They would only go free if other members of their team would climb up into the tree, swing down on a rope and tag them, before they were knocked off the swing by the opposing team waiting below. The collisions during the swing-downs caused many injuries to both teams. Again, someone said each time there was an injury during the game, the shrimp were plentiful. Playing the game became an annual tradition. The more blood and broken bones, the more shrimp were caught. The injured boys became heroes for making the sacrifices. This went on for years. The rougher the game, the better the shrimp. Folks went so far as to say that the tree absorbed the blood from the sand, like it absorbed the lightning, and it grew stronger. As long as the boys played the game, all were satisfied, along with the tree.

"Then there was the year when no blood fell on the sand during the game. No player broke a bone. Not one boy was brave enough to take a collision. They were not serious about the game and did not honor the past. The act of playing the game with courage was to be a moment for a boy to cross over into manhood. It would make him worthy. None of those boys that day had been given any character or honor. They had little worth at all. After that game the shrimp season was the worst ever recorded. Mayport's shrimping families almost starved. The believers blamed the boys and marked them as cowards. Some called it, and pardon my French, 'the pussy game.'

"One of the boys lived with a father who tormented him each day about the game. Willis took the mental and verbal and physical abuse from his father for a full year. At the end of the shameful year Willis gathered new players for Duckin'. He planned to make that game the roughest, meanest game ever played. He made sure blood fell on the sand."

"Willis created a day of pain and death, to be sure his father would be satisfied. Sara, your friend's brother, Billy, died at the hand of Willis during that game. It was about five years ago. No one knows what made Billy play that day. It was unusual for newcomers to play. They say five boys died that day, but I think there was more. Some boys got scared and didn't go to the tree. They lived, but couldn't tell what actually happened at the tree. There was only one survivor at the tree and he has never talked about what happened that day. He could put the strange puzzle of that day together. The believers say the tree will not allow him to tell what happened because he is a true oak baby."

The room remained silent as Mr. King ended his story. The four sisters were all dazed by the tale they had heard. The guest of honor,

Sara, broke the silence.

"Do the people here still believe in the power of the tree?"

"There are still plenty of folks who worship the tree. You pass them each day if you work the streets here. They're in your store every day." He looked in the direction of the four sisters. It was the first time that night he acknowledged anyone but Sara. His attention sent chills through all four of them.

"Do you believe in the tree, Mr. King?"

"Sara, I'm Catholic. I can't worship a tree."

The tour of the house began and Mr. King took his guests upstairs, hoping to find a few ghosts. The four sisters would leave that night more in love with Jason than before. He was a great lover, the Jetty Man and now he could be an oak baby. It was a curse.

CHAPTER NINE

FRIDAY MORNING WAS JASON'S FIFTH DAY ON THE JOB. THE FIRST FIVE DAYS were exciting and he gained experience each day. His social life had taken a drastic turn, adding even more excitement. Uncle Bobby and Mary C. were both sleeping like rocks when he left for work. He didn't want to face any of the sisters, but the milk and honey bun had become an important part of his workday ritual. Sofia was alone that morning.

"Good morning, Jason. I really missed you last night. I kept looking for you to walk in the door."

"I fell asleep. I was just too tired."

"It was great. We talked about it all night. I can't believe I got up and made it here. I'm so sleepy now. I'll get your milk."

She was the greatest. Jason picked up the honey bun.

"That house is haunted. I believe it now. We didn't see any ghosts, but you could just tell they were there." She wasn't sure about mentioning the oak baby story, so she didn't. She thought it was better he wasn't there. Mr. King would not have told the story if Jason was there. She had a surprise for Jason.

"I think I can get away to see you tonight. Are you interested in spending some time with me?"

Jason's heart raced, as usual.

"If you can't or don't want to, it's fine. It's up to you. Will you be too tired after work tonight?"

He had to say something. He wanted to be with her. And she was asking him. "I'd like to go with you tonight."

She smiled. "I don't have a time or know where yet, but I'll have all the details when you get back from work. I'll let you know then. Just plan on it, okay?"

Jason nodded in agreement and was off to the shuttle. He needed a busy workday to keep Sofia off his mind. The two shuttle boats left the dock at the same time. The ferry horn greeted the workers as Jason took his first bite of the honey bun. Sofia would be on his mind until he got to the barge. It started out as another pleasant ride to work. It was short-lived.

Jason's blood changed directions in his veins and ran cold when the other shuttle passed his shuttle. The black Derby hat of Charlie Klim caught his attention as the little boat went by. Charlie Klim stood at the wheel, steering the boat to the work site. He was the new captain of the shuttle. Jason hated that hat and the devil wearing it. The honey bun lost its taste; he fed the fish with it. He would be on the barge soon and his work would clear his head.

Mary C. woke up with the second phase of her plan as the priority of the day. Her coffee cup was empty and she was ready to continue the preparation for her meeting with the devil. She had Friday and Saturday to complete her list of things to do. The Falcon was moving again.

Uncle Bobby looked out his bedroom window and saw the dust from the dirt road, as the Falcon drove away. He would not shrimp that day, but he had a number of things to do on the boat and he needed fuel and supplies for his next trip to sea. His coffee cup was empty and he was ready to face his day. His list of things to do did not compare to Mary C.'s list and his workload and worries would not be that of Jason's. He was, however, getting ready to face the devil; he just didn't know it. He was not prepared for such an encounter. He left his truck in the yard and walked toward Mr. Leek's. He stopped at the store. He liked seeing the sisters and was interested to see who was minding the store. Sofia was still there and greeted him when the bell on the door alerted her.

"Good morning, Uncle Bobby. May I help you with something?"

He loved looking at those girls. He thought Sofia was the most beautiful, but she really was the baby of the group. The other three had a woman's look to them and they were all actually of age and were old enough to do what they pleased. He loved Jason, but envied him for his youth.

"Good mornin' to you, Miss Sofia. How are ya, on this Friday mornin'?"

"Jason was here this morning. I'm great." She was excited to share her information with Jason's uncle.

"You really like Jason, don't ya?"

"I love him."

Uncle Bobby was taken aback by her quick, open comment. "You love 'im?"

"Yes, sir, I love him. I've never been in love before and I really like the way it makes me feel. I know my sister Margie loves him too and she will most likely win his heart, but I still love him. No one ever takes me very seriously and I know they think I'm a baby, but I'm not. I just thought I would tell you that."

Bobby was struck with the Jason Syndrome. He had no answer or reply for Sofia. She talked so fast and it was like she was reading it off a page or she had rehearsed it hours before she said it. He walked to the cold drink box and pulled out a grape Nehi. He really didn't want anything, but didn't want to enter the store and not buy something. He walked to the register, where Sofia waited.

"I'm sure you think I'm too young for Jason, too. I'm not sure what that has to do with anything. Everyone's so concerned about age when it comes to relationships. History has seen many teenage brides."

Bobby had heard enough and he was not ready for a history lesson. He handed her the money for the drink. "I always have a grape Nehi after my mornin' coffee." He headed to the dock. He knew Jason didn't have a prayer when it came to the covey of sisters.

It was another hectic day on the barge, but it was exciting and everybody stayed on the move. Horns, whistles, men yelling instructions, and the sound of big red rocks splashing in the water filled the air. Jason was helping Big Jim direct the placement of the rocks and he was learning about how to signal the crane operators as to their position. He had worth and substance and had never been so happy with himself and what he was doing. There was no confusion in his head, when he stood on the barge.

Mary C. drove the Falcon through the black section of Mayport. She hadn't been there in years. She stopped the car next to a wooden fence used to keep pigs penned up. The smell of the animals took her breath away for a moment. A black woman approached her from in front of a small wooden house.

"Who's out there with my pigs?" She held a stick in her hand.

"It's me, Miss Ida Mae, Mary C., Bob Merritt's daughter."

The old lady squinted her eyes. "Who?"

"I used to come here when I was little. My daddy would buy a pig now and then. It's been a long time. I didn't think you would remember me."

"You come to buy a pig? I ain't sold a pig in years. What ya wanna buy a pig for? Folks don't butcher hogs no mo'."

"I really don't want to buy a pig, but I do need your help and I'll pay you for it. Can I talk to you for a minute?"

Uncle Bobby was working on the stern of the *Mary C.* when one of the shuttle boats floated up carrying a group of men who had been out to the work site. After the men left the boat it stayed tied to the dock for about twenty minutes. The shuttles made runs back and forth all day and since the accident with Steve "the Crane" Robertson, they kept a shuttle at the barge at all times. Bobby sat on a small wooden stool as he spliced two ropes together. The shadow of a man showed on the deck in front of him. He knew someone stood above and behind on the dock. He waited for the owner of the shadow to say something, but the shadow stayed in place. Bobby didn't turn around.

"Okay, I give up. I can't guess who you are."

The shadow stayed the same. It was obvious the intruder was waiting for Bobby to get nervous or curious enough to turn. Bobby did.

He didn't like what he saw: the sight of Charlie Klim standing above him, under his trademark black Derby hat.

"I sure wish I hadn't turned around. I was havin' a real good day." He was at a distance, but he was still eye-to-eye with the devil.

Charlie smiled. "You can go on with your good day, Bobby Boy. Don't let me mess it up." He turned and started walking away.

"Tell your sister I said, 'hey'."

The men on the barge wanted to work through lunch, but Mr. Hawkins made them all take the forty-five minutes to eat, rest and relax mentally and physically. He said he appreciated their offer, but they deserved the time down. There were too many who wanted to sit with Jason on his rock. Jason and his followers walked onto the beach and sat under Bill's Hideaway in the shade. It wasn't far from the rocks and they wouldn't do it every day. Mr. Hawkins watched the men from his usual perch on the barge. The sight of those men walking, talking and sitting with Jason bewildered him. He was amazed at the spirit and substance in the young man. He thought about Mary C.

Mary C. was thinking about one thing as she took four empty, white, five-gallon paint buckets from the trunk of her car and carried them to Ida Mae's house. Her list of things to do was getting shorter.

Bobby was finishing his work on the *Mary C*. He was still uneasy about his unexpected visit from Charlie Klim. He knew Charlie's return would only mean trouble for his family. Bobby had other things to do away from the dock and boat, but he would be there to meet Jason when he returned on the shuttle. Mr. Leek passed, as he was walking on the dock.

"Hey, Bobby. You need anything?"

Bobby looked up as his blood boiled in his veins. "I need to know what Charlie Klim's doin' here."

"He got a job on the shuttle. You know he's so crippled up, he can't do much of any real work."

"I thought we were rid of him. Ain't he 'spose to be in jail?"

"Bobby, I don't think he was in jail very long. He was hurt so bad, they didn't keep him."

"Well, I don't like him bein' here, with Jason workin' out there. He's gonna run into him sometime, if it ain't already happened. I don't know what will happen if Jason sees Charlie. It's a scary thought. I want to save Jason the shock, if I can."

"I didn't think about that when I saw Charlie. You think he'd hurt the boy?"

"I think he'd hurt 'em both, Jason and Mary C., if he gets the chance. An evil man like him don't forget nothin', or forgive nothin'. And he's got a lot of reasons to hate them both. Devils like him don't forget, they just get worse. Charlie Klim is walkin' misery, or in his case limpin' misery." Neither one smiled at Bobby's analogy.

Mary C. carried the white buckets back to her car one at a time. They were heavier now, because they were no longer empty. She placed each covered container into the trunk of the Falcon, paid Ida Mae twenty dollars and was off to the next destination on her list. She touched the Skinny Blackjack lying beside her on the front seat of the car.

Jason saw the other shuttle leave the barge twice during the day. Each time he couldn't see if the evil one was at the wheel, but just the thought of it made Jason uneasy. The red rocks continued to splash in the water and Jason continued his work pace. In one week he had become a real workingman, a hero, was given an important name, skyrocketed socially, had been compared to Jesus, and Charlie Klim was back. His cup did runneth over.

The bell on the door rang as Mary C. walked into Miss Margaret's store. Margie was behind the counter with the register and Susan was putting stock on the shelves.

"Hello, Miss Mary C. May I help you with something?"

"Yes, Margie. Do y'all have any of that heavy thick tape?"

"We have some black electrical tape in our hardware section on the wall where the tools are. Is that what you're talking about?"

"I was looking for somethin' thicker." She scanned the area with different kinds of tape.

"I got this kind that they use on the shrimp boats." Margie held up a roll of three-inch-wide silver electrical tape.

Mary C.'s eyes lit up. "That's perfect. That's just what I was looking for." Her list was now even shorter, as she walked to the register to pay for the tape.

Margie was her usual brazen self. "Miss Mary, why do people think Jason's an oak baby?"

Susan looked at her sister in disbelief after her forward question. Mary C. was surprised too, but didn't show it on her face. "Margie, what kinda question is that? Who told you that?"

"Mr. King was telling us about the oak tree and the sand hill and the game. He said Jason was the only one to live after the game." Mary C. shook her head.

"Ol' man King must be runnin' out of ghost stories if he needs to tell those stupid oak tree tales. He just wants to shock y'all, that's what he does best. Scare and shock young people."

Margie wanted more and knew the way to get it. "Then you didn't make love under the tree and have Jason?"

Mary C. couldn't hold back her surprise at that question. Susan had to say something to her older sister.

"Margie, I can't believe you. Have you gone crazy, asking her that?"

Margie didn't seem to care. "I think it's the bravest, most romantic thing I've ever heard. Just in case the legend is true and the power of the tree could be put into your baby, it would be worth the effort, just in case it was true. If it wasn't true, then, no harm done. A mother would be a fool not to try it. I'm doing it one day."

Mary C. was still speechless, but Margie's sister Susan wasn't.

"Stop talking like that! You're embarrassing me and being very rude to Miss Mary C."

"I don't mean to be rude to you, Miss Mary C. I really don't. I hope you did it and Jason is an oak baby. I think it's a wonderful thing if you did it. I just want to know about it."

Mary C. was ready to join the conversation. "First of all, the tree has no power at all. That is the most ridiculous superstition we've ever had around here. And we've had some real doozies."

"You don't believe in the tree at all?"

"Not a little bit. It has no powers. It makes no babies. And I wish I would have stopped Jason from playin' that stupid game. He didn't want to play and I could see it in his face, but I let him go anyway. I've done a lot a foolish and bad things in my life, but that was the one mistake that haunts me the most."

The two sisters were silent as they listened to Mary C. Margie was hungry for any information about Jason and the tree.

"Don't you think it's strange that Jason was the survivor that day of the game? It's like the tree took care of him, don't you think?"

"It wasn't Jason's time to die. He has other things to do. Jason fits into a plan, I think. Just like this week when he saved that man in the water. He saved me one night. He stopped that awful boy, Willis, that day, so he wouldn't hurt anyone else. He is very special, but it ain't from no oak tree. I don't know where it comes from, but it ain't that stupid tree."

Margie knew it was time to end her questions and allow Mary C. to go about her business. "Miss Mary C., I didn't mean to be so nosey. I just didn't know anything about the tree and it was really interesting and different to me. I'm sorry if I said anything to upset you."

"Margie, you didn't upset me. I know people like those wild stories about the tree. I just wish they didn't have to add Jason to the story. That awful day will be with him from now on, but I wish folks didn't have to remind him about it all the time. I'm glad he didn't go to Mr. King's last night."

"I'm sure Mr. King would not have told the story about the tree if Jason was there. He wouldn't do that."

"Well, girls, thanks for the tape and the conversation."

The bell sounded on the door as Mary C. left. Susan walked to Margie.

"Are you crazy? What's wrong with you? Why did you say that stuff to her?" Susan was a three question sister.

Margie didn't hear or care about Susan's reprimand. She thought about the tree. "I think she's lying. I think she laid under that oak tree and made Jason. She just can't talk about it or admit it, because the tree will take his power away, and she knows it."

Susan remained in shock at her older sister's interest in the tree. "She didn't sound like she was lying to me. She said the tree was stupid and just a superstition."

"She has to act like that. You heard Mr. King. People who did the Breeding can't tell they did it. I know she did it. You know how wild people say she is. She did it, I tell you. And the reason these things happen to Jason is the tree is watching over him and protecting him. I think it's cool and I want to know all about it."

"You think it's cool? You have lost your mind. You never say 'cool'."

"I say cool all the time."

"Well, I never heard you say it before. It doesn't fit you, Margie, I'm sorry. Try not to say it too much. Or better yet, find another word. One night at Bill's Hideaway and she talks like Uncle Bobby. I guess the Elvis records will be next."

Jason's fifth day on the job was ending. Mr. Hawkins walked to him as he was preparing to climb down the rope ladder to the shuttle.

"Hey, wait a second, Jason. We're goin' to work a crew overtime tomorrow. It's not required, but if you would like to make the extra money you can work. I know this is short notice, so you don't have to do it. We'd like to have ya, if you don't have Saturday plans."

Jason's heart was racing at its usual excited pace. "I'll work."

"The shuttle will leave the dock at eight in the morning. We'll let y'all sleep a little later."

Jason was down the ladder and onto the shuttle. He didn't pay any attention to the other shuttle as it pulled away and headed toward Mayport. He was thinking about working tomorrow and about Sofia for that night.

Uncle Bobby and Mr. Leek stood on the dock as the two shuttle boats pulled in. Jason didn't see them at first. Bobby looked to see if Charlie was behind the wheel of either boat. He didn't see him on the shuttle Jason was on. Mr. Leek tied one of the boats to a dock pylon as another dockworker tied the other. Jason jumped to the dock and joined Uncle Bobby.

"Hey there, Jetty Man. You alright?"

"I'm fine. I'm workin' overtime tomorrow."

"Damn, boy. That's time and a half. Damn, boy."

Jason smiled at his uncle's comment. He didn't realize Uncle Bobby was making sure they moved away from the shuttles and into the fish house.

"Let's get on home, boy, and see if that mother of yours is still in a cookin' mood. But, don't expect it."

Jason had Sofia on his mind. "I need to get a drink from the store."

"Yeah, right. A drink." Uncle Bobby knew there was more to Jason's store visits than a Nehi.

"I'll meet you at the house."

"Hell, boy, I'd much rather go with you. I never realized how much fun it was to go to the store."

Jason smiled. Bobby wanted to stay near Jason until they made it home, but a stop by the store, with a possibility of seeing even one of the pretty sisters, was a good reason to tag along with his nephew. They left the fish house and walked to the main street. As they passed Strickland's, their walk was interrupted by a sweet voice. It was Sofia, standing on the side of the building.

"Jason, over here."

Jason and Uncle Bobby turned toward the voice.

"I didn't want to talk at the store. I didn't want my sisters to see us. Hey, Uncle Bobby."

Bobby saluted her, but just shook his head at Jason's luck with women, especially any of the sisters.

"I'd like to see you tonight, I just don't know where and how. Can you get a car?"

Jason looked at Uncle Bobby. His uncle had no choice. He nodded "yes."

"Great! How about we meet right here at seven? Let's make sure

it's dark. It would be much better for me if it's dark. I'll see you then."
She kissed Jason on his cheek, turned toward the store and walked
away.

Jason had not said one word. Bobby had not said one word. Sofia
said it all. Jason had a date with a beautiful girl and never opened his
mouth. Uncle Bobby was amazed at his nephew's success rate with
the opposite sex.

"I don't think I've ever witnessed anything like that before. I'm
not sure exactly what happened here, but I am glad I was here."

Jason smiled, but said nothing.

Uncle Bobby couldn't help it. "I'm sure you're 'fine' so I won't
even ask." They headed home.

Mary C. was ready again for her two workingmen. The table was
set and she was filling the plates as they walked in the front door.
Bobby was pleased and surprised.

"Mary C., you are a changed woman. This house has smelled of
good groceries two days runnin'. You're gonna spoil us, woman. Is it
somebody's birthday?"

"Get washed up, you two." She didn't have to tell them twice.
They cleaned up and sat down to fried mullet, lima beans, rice and
coleslaw. All three at the dinner table knew Charlie Klim was back in
Mayport. Each was hesitant to tell the others. No one knew how the
others would react to the information. Uncle Bobby started the family
conversation.

"Jason needs a 'ride' tonight. Is the Falcon available?"

Jason looked at Uncle Bobby's surprising statement and question.

Mary C. reacted quickly. "No it's not. I've got plans tonight."

"Really? Well, Jetty Man, it's the ol' truck or feet do your stuff."
Jason smiled.

Mary C. was intrigued. "Why does he need a car so bad?"

Jason looked at Uncle Bobby.

"Don't look at me. I don't need a car. You do."

Mary C. was looking at Jason. "Well, what's the big deal?"

Jason was embarrased and wanted Uncle Bobby's help. It didn't come.

"You're on your own. You got women lined up four deep and you need me to tell your mother about why you need a car. Too bad."

Mary C. was still looking at Jason. "You need it for a girl? Can't you take the truck?"

"Yes, ma'am, that's fine."

Uncle Bobby shook his head again. "He's fine, as usual and I'm on foot. This romance thing is really getting me down."

Mary C. wanted details. "Is it that wild one, Margie? She's somethin', that one. I saw her in the store today and she is as forward as they come. She wants to breed under the oak tree."

Jason and Uncle Bobby looked at each other with eyes opened wide, then at Mary C.

"What? She wants to breed? She told you that?"

"That's right. And if you're goin' out with her, don't go to the tree. She wants to birth an oak baby."

Jason sat there with a vision of himself and Jessie under the tree. Uncle Bobby had his own vision of him and Margie under the tree. They were both shocked by Mary C.'s information, but they were both pleased with their fantasy visions. Especially Uncle Bobby.

"She wanted to know all about the tree. Mr. King told them all about it at his house last night and the girl's gone wild about it. Don't you go near that tree with her."

Jason had no intentions of going to the tree. He remembered Jessie's words about breeding, and Jake's, too.

He would stay clear of the sand hill. Uncle Bobby's fantasy with Margie ended when Mary C. added more to the conversation.

"That Margie's after you and she might be too wild for you."

Margie, sitting on the loggerhead, flashed in Jason's head.

"Be careful with that one."

"Mama, it ain't Margie."

"Oh, that's good! That's good! . . . It ain't?"

"No, ma'am."

Mary C. had a bewildered look on her face. "Who the hell is it?"

"Sofia."

"What?? The baby?? Jason, you're too old for her. Her mama'll be mad 'bout this."

Bobby joined in. "I don't think her mama's gonna know. Sofia asked Jason to meet her. I was there, I heard it. He really can't say 'no' and he shouldn't. He didn't say anything to her and I mean not one word."

"Well, he better think about this thing. Three other sisters closer to your age and you pick the baby of the group."

Bobby jumped in again. "Now, Mary C., none of 'em are babies. And she picked him, he didn't pick her. You say don't go with the older one 'cause she wants to make an oak baby. Then when you find out it's another sister, you find something wrong with that too. Besides, that baby, as you call her, is more woman than the other three. And I don't think she'll take him to the tree. Let's look at the good side of this."

Mary C. took a deep breath. "You're right. I like her too. She is beautiful and, Jason, you are so handsome. Y'all will look great together."

"Oh God, Mary C.! Let's all throw up together. Can your handsome boy have the car?"

"No. I told ya no, already. The truck will have to do."

"You heard her, boy. After you eat, you need to clean that seat out. It's a mess in there."

The conversation about Jason's possible date had taken their minds off Charlie Klim. Mary C. had also stopped thinking about her revenge on James. For the first time, Jason's love life was a family issue. The first of six chimes rang out from the clock in the living room. Jason had an hour to clean the truck out and prepare himself for Sofia. Uncle Bobby was the greatest.

"Okay, Jetty Man, you go get squeaky clean and I'll clean the truck. I just want to be some part of this romantic evening."

Mary C. shook her head. "You are a fool."

"Hell, I'd like to see if Margie would like to swing in that tree, but everybody's so hung up on this age thing."

"Bobby Merritt, you oughta be ashamed of yourself."

"Well, you made me be ashamed at Bill's last week when those two pretty young things tried to dance me to death. Now I have to be ashamed 'cause Margie wants to be an oak mama. Is shamin' me your reason for livin'?"

"You want the last of this coleslaw?"

"Later, leave it out." Uncle Bobby went to clean the truck. Jason was an hour away from Sofia.

Jason was in the shower, Mary C. finished the kitchen clean-up and Bobby was cleaning the truck. She didn't mind the others not helping. It felt good to see Bobby helping Jason and she felt good about herself. Her life was changing and she would complete the needed changes within the next two days. She walked to the truck.

"Bobby, talk to me before Jason comes out here."

Bobby knew Mary C. needed his full attention. He stopped his cleaning and listened.

"Charlie Klim's back. He was here the other night."

"I know he's back. I saw him. What do you mean he was here?"

"Here, at the house. Out there." She pointed where Charlie had sat in his car. "He said he was here for me. He wanted me and if he couldn't have me, he'd kill Jason."

Bobby's eyes caught fire. "He tried to scare me today, too. That's why I waited for Jason. I didn't want him to run into Charlie alone."

"What are we goin' to do?"

Bobby still had the fire. "He ain't gonna hurt us, none of us. I promise."

"I'm just worried 'bout Jason. He's still driftin' off now and then. He might not see Charlie comin'. That really scares me."

"I wasn't sure how Jason would take it, but maybe we should let him know so he'll be careful and on the lookout. I hate all this crap with Charlie. Jason's doin' so good and I hate somethin' messin' it up. I'm worried too."

Jason was splashing his face with Old Spice. It would be part of his ritual. His jukin' ritual. Jason heard the Falcon engine fire up.

He looked out the window and saw the car pulling out of the yard. Mary C. was gone again.

Uncle Bobby walked into the house. "Well, if that ain't clean enough, I can't help it."

Jason walked into the front room.

"Ahoy, captain. Did you fall in the Old Spice bottle, or what?"

Jason smiled. "Thank you for cleaning the truck."

"You're welcome. Just be careful." Uncle Bobby wanted to mention Charlie Klim, but he didn't want to ruin Jason's night out. He would talk to him later. Jason and the clean truck headed to meet Sofia. Their first meeting place was less than a half mile away.

Mary C. drove the Falcon down the dirt road in the woods at East Mayport, toward the Indian graveyard mounds she knew so well. She wasn't comfortable with being there in the dark, but her mission needed the cover of night. The car headlights would show her the way on the road and a flashlight would guide her when she had to leave the car. The mounds were ahead and she would take the chance of being alone. She hoped the animals of the night would not be on the move so early. She stopped the car, but left the lights on and the motor running, for visibility and a quick getaway. Her heart raced when she opened the car door and stepped out into the woods. The flashlight showed her the perfect place for battle.

Jason pulled up next to Strickland's at the same place he had stood with Sofia earlier that evening. The second the truck stopped, Sofia came running out of the dark corner of the building and, with one leap, she was in the seat next to Jason. In one smooth motion she slid across the seat and kissed his cheek again.

"Let's go!! Go!!" They were on the move, but didn't know where.

Mary C. took the white buckets out of the trunk of the car, one at a time, and carried them to her chosen spot. They were heavy and she was careful to keep the lids on tightly. She placed a bag of her revenge equipment behind a tree and covered it with leaves. She looked around the area after she had strategically placed the items she had collected. It would be her battleground. It was so appropriate for her to choose that place for her rebirth. It was one day away. She was back in the Falcon and leaving East Mayport. She headed home to begin the second phase of the Friday night part of her preparation.

Jason drove the truck past the little jetties. He would not take Sofia there, because he had been there with her sister, Peggy. It wouldn't be right. Sofia had been sitting close to him since she jumped into the truck. It was obvious she was nervous, because she was very quiet. Jason knew it was the first time she had ever done anything like that. She was going against things she had been taught. She was doing something that was wrong to her, but she didn't care. Her feelings for Jason made the decision for her.

"Where can we go, so nobody sees us?" She leaned her head on Jason. His heart raced again. He knew where he wanted to go.

"I know a place where no one will bother us, but you might not like it."

She was excited and willing to go anywhere that they wouldn't get caught. "Let's go. As long as nobody sees us. We can't let anybody see us."

Jason headed the truck toward the best spot to be alone.

Sofia's eyes popped open when Jason turned the truck into the entrance to the Mayport cemetery.

"Here? Oh my! I don't know if I can be here. I'm nervous enough without worrying about having graves around me. Some of my relatives are out here. Oh my!"

Jason knew it would be the best place. "Sofia, listen. It's dark and you can't really see the graves unless you look for them. We'll stay in the truck. No one will come out here and that means no one will see us. You wanted to be alone and this is the best place."

She wanted to stay with him and people do crazy things when love is involved. "If I get scared, we can go?"

Jason smiled. She was beautiful with her eyes sparkling in the dark. "Let's stay for five minutes. If you don't like it we'll leave."

She smiled at the possible five-minute limit, then grabbed Jason and kissed him, as if the five-minute limit was her limit. He allowed her to kiss him and she did most of the movement and work. The first kiss, of many more to come, ended.

"I'm so glad to be with you. I've been thinking about it ever since we had coffee at the store." Jason returned her kiss just in case he only had four minutes. She pushed her body through his and pinned him to the seat. The passion reminded him of their first kiss upstairs at Miss Margie's. There was something different and special about how she moved and how she touched his face, hair and neck. She seemed to melt into his arms like she had done before. Again, it was as if she could pour herself and feeling all over him. He wanted to kiss her again and again. And then some more. Each one was better than the one before. They moved all over the seat while they kissed. They laid down and pressed their bodies together.

"I've never been with anyone like this before. I was saving these kisses for you. I didn't want to give them to just anybody. We both need these kisses."

Jason loved the way she talked. Her movements excited them both and Jason put his hand under her blouse to touch her breast. She didn't move his hand physically, but her words did.

"I know you have been with other girls and you are very experienced. I really want to do more with you and I think I will, but I'm very nervous and scared, so don't think I'm a baby if I ask you to let me tell you when it's okay I know you can teach me, but right now I'm rather nervous about the whole thing. I'm not teasing you and I do want to do more."

Jason liked the idea of being the teacher. He had been the student and learned his lessons well. He thought he would be a good teacher. The kiss after her words was the best so far. They were the perfect fit, as if God, or the oak, had matched their lips. Jason was aroused and excited, yet there was a calmness she generated in him. He would lie there and kiss her as long as she would stay. They had gone way past five minutes.

Uncle Bobby sat on the front porch swing as the Falcon drove up to the house.

"Damn, woman, I didn't think I'd see you so early."

"I came to save you from borin' ya'self to death. I'm goin' over to the Fish Bowl and I thought I'd give you a ride to Bill's or wherever you want to go, unless you want to go to the Bowl with me."

"No, thanks. I'd rather be bored here alone than sit at the Fish Bowl. Why you wanna go back there anyway, after all that crap last week?"

"I like it there." She changed the subject. "I really felt bad about you bein' here alone and the way you helped Jason was really nice of ya. So I thought you deserved a ride."

Bobby stood up and smiled. "Mary C., you're scarin' me. Are you feelin' okay?"

"Shut up, and get ready if you want to go. I'm gonna change, but it won't take me long. The Falcon express will be rollin' shortly."

Bobby shook his head at Mary C.'s attitude change and went to his bedroom to change.

Jason had pulled Sofia's shirt up and he was touching her breast freely as they kissed. She was firm and a perfect fit for his magic hands. Her nipples told him that she was excited. Her kisses got even better. They were addicting and he wanted more. Jason worked his magic on her breast with his lips, tongue and mouth. He loved the way she touched the back of his head while he buried it into her chest. She raised her upper body and pushed against his face. She was pushing her body through his. It was like being soldered together. It was a different feeling for Jason, one he had not experienced. He liked it.

Mary C. and Uncle Bobby walked out into the living room at the same time. He looked good and she looked better. They knew how to get ready and go. The Falcon rolled out of the yard.

"Take me to Bill's and I'll get a ride home."

"I ain't leavin' you there and you try to find a ride back home. I'll come back and get you, just don't run off with some woman. Stay there and I'll be back. I'm gonna go over there for a while and maybe I'll come back and stay here with you. Either way, I'll come get ya."

Jason and Sofia had settled in and the kisses were still raging. He touched her on the outside of her pants during a wild kiss and she didn't stop him. On the next kiss he unsnapped and unzipped her pants. He moved his hand into the position he wanted and touched her. Her lower body raised up and pushed against his hand as if the seat under her was assisting their pleasure. She held herself against his hand and fingers. He had to kiss her again; she allowed his hand to stay. Jason took a deep breath and lifted his head. A nightmare vision ripped his guts out when he came eye-to-eye with Charlie Klim's face pressed against the window of the truck. He was too scared to scream as Charlie smiled and held a flashlight to his evil face. Jason's eyes were locked with Charlie's. Sofia could feel his body quake as he faced the evil in the graveyard. He wanted to close his eyes, hoping it was a dream, but he dare not take his eyes off the evil face. Charlie slowly dropped his head down past the window until the face and vision were gone. Jason was frozen in place with fear. Sharp pains ripped through his heart. He had no idea what to do. Sofia entered his dilemma.

"Jason, are you alright? I know I'm not very good at this. I'm just scared, that's all." She reached up to pull Jason to her. He was stiff as a board and quivering, with chills of fear.

"Jason, what's wrong?" She sat up quickly with Jason's trembling body next to her. Jason's glazed look scared her and she knew something was seriously wrong. Jason found the strength and added to her fear.

"We need to go," he whispered. "We need to go now."

"Jason, you're scaring me. What is it?"

Jason slid past her slowly to the steering wheel. A muffled voice from outside the truck mimicked Sofia's words and sent an electric shock of fear through her body and added to Jason's pain.

"Jason, you're scarin' me. What is it?" Sofia's body shook uncontrollably. Jason's heart hurt worse when he saw the fear in her eyes.

"Oh God, Jason!! Who is that out there? Oh, God!!" The muffled voice cut through the night air once more.

"Leave her with me, Jason, and you can go back to your mama."

Sofia looked at Jason.

"He knows who you are, Jason. Oh God, who is that. I'm really scared. Don't let him get me. Please, let's go."

Jason turned the ignition key with his trembling hand. As the engine fired up Charlie jumped out of the darkness and pressed his face against the same window as before. This time he was eye-to-eye with Sofia. She went crazy with fear. She had never dreamed of being that scared. A bloodcurdling scream came from deep in Sofia's soul. It woke the residents of the cemetery and deafened Jason in the truck. She thought they were both going to die. The panic took away any reason she had within her. She was hysterical as Jason shoved the clutch into gear and hit the gas pedal. The moving truck leveled three headstones as Jason turned the truck toward the entrance. The noise of the breaking stones added to the nightmare. Charlie wasn't finished as he jumped into the back bed of the moving truck and screamed into the back window as Sofia screamed back at him. Jason kept the truck moving, Sofia continued screaming, with her head buried in the seat, and Charlie was gone.

Jason drove the truck onto the main road and Sofia lay, crying, in the front seat. Jason hated Charlie Klim, he always had. He worried that Sofia would never be the same. He knew what fear could do to a person. He touched her head as he drove back to Mayport. She trembled with fear, he trembled with hate. Jason pulled the truck into the little jetties. He had to see if Sofia was able to talk. He couldn't take her home in the condition she was in at the time. He stopped the truck. She didn't like it. She sat up.

"Why are we stopping? We have to get home and tell somebody."

Jason held her to his chest. "Tell 'em what? That we were in the cemetery together and somebody scared us, while we were layin' down in the front seat of the truck?"

"We have to tell about that crazy man out there."

"People been parkin' out at the cemetery forever and other people have been scarin' em for just as long."

"Do you really think that's all this was? Someone tryin' to scare us because we were parked there? Jason, it's more than that and you

MAYPORT CEMETERY

know it. He knew you and said ugly things. He followed us there, because of you. Now, I'm sorry about how I fell apart. I don't think I'll ever get over what just happened to us. That wasn't being a little scared, that was being almost scared to death. I know now that you can be scared to death. This was awful and someone should be told, so he won't do it again. Jason, that man was crazy and he wasn't some boy playing a graveyard ghost joke on us. He wanted to scare us to death."

Jason knew she was right and she had suffered through an awful ordeal, because of him. She had a right to know the truth.

"Okay, you need to know."

Sofia was still shaking, but listened the best she could. "That was a man named Charlie Klim."

Sofia remembered what her Aunt Margie had said about a man named Charlie Klim. "He's the man you cut up because he was hurting your mother."

Jason nodded his head. "He's come back to Mayport and he's working on the shuttle boats. He likes to scare people and he's mean. I think he's here to do something to me because he's been crippled since that night."

Sofia was sick to her stomach. "Oh Jason! What are you going to do? This is really awful. I've never been in anything like this before. He could kill us both."

At that moment car light blinded them both and Sofia screamed again. A car drove up behind the truck and blocked them in. There was no exit at all. Sofia fell down in the seat and buried her head again. Jason was frozen again with fear as someone got out of the car and walked toward the truck. The silhouette of a man walked up to the back of the truck. Sofia was praying and Jason was shaking. The man reached into the back of the truck and picked something up, then walked to the window where Jason sat behind the wheel. He stood there looking at Jason. Jason slowly turned toward the man and the darkness. Again he was eye-to-eye with the evil Charlie Klim. Charlie held up his black Derby hat to the window.

"I left my hat in the back of the truck. Tell ya mama, I said 'hey'."

Charlie was gone and Jason stared out of the window as if Charlie was still talking to him. He could feel Sofia shaking. She was in a state of shock and seemed to be sleeping. The car lights behind them were gone. Jason was too scared to do anything; he just sat there with his hand on Sofia's head. He didn't know what to do or any better, so he let her sleep.

CHAPTER TEN

MARY C. DROPPED BOBBY OFF AT THE WOODEN STEPS AT BILL'S HIDEAWAY.

"I'll probably be back to sit with you. Don't run off with none of your floozies."

Bobby waved her on and headed up the steps. The jukebox music was like a magnet to him. He needed change for a dollar. The sound of Elvis would soon fill the room. Bobby was in his environment. It was strange for him to be there on a Friday night, but he would get used to it. He stood at the jukebox. Kelly passed by, carrying food to a table.

"Hey, Bobby. I'll be right back. Where ya gonna sit?"

"At that back corner over there. There's a good view from over there. And ain't a bad view right here." Bobby looked Kelly up and down, then turned his attention to the jukebox as she walked away smiling at his attempt to flirt with her. He punched in a few Elvis tunes, but had to wait on the records before him. They were good, but not Elvis. He moved to the corner table he had pointed out to Kelly. She was at his service as soon as he sat down.

"You want something to drink first, or ya eatin' tonight?"

"Are you on the menu, tonight?"

She smiled. "Now, if you can't come up with anything better than that, you ain't gonna impress me at all. And I happen to be in a mood where I want to be impressed. So with that information, I'm gonna get you a glass of water and I'll be back to take your order and you can be thinkin' of a real way to impress me."

Bobby didn't know why Kelly was talking the way she was, but he sure liked it. He couldn't wait for her to return with his water.

James turned around to greet his customer and found himself eye to eye with Mary C. sitting at the bar. She saw the surprise in his evil eyes. She understood his hesitation to speak to her.

"Hey, James. You look like you've just seen a ghost. My makeup must be awful tonight, or is it the lights in here?"

His head cleared momentarily. "No, it ain't that. You look good. I was just surprised to see you here. It is Friday night and, well, you just caught me by surprise, that's all. What can I get for ya?"

"An easy Jack Black. And I'm only drinkin' that one tonight, so help me with that, will ya?"

James nodded "One drink, that's it?"

"Well, I just needed to get out of the house and one drink might help me sleep better."

"Why can't ya sleep?"

Mary C. looked around the room, making sure James would be the only one to hear her. She leaned over the bar, exposing her healed breasts for him to see if he wanted. "I can't sleep because of you."

James' eyes widened. "Me? Why me?"

She was whispering now. "You know why, James."

His heart ran like Jason's as she whispered more.

"Let me tell you somethin'. Life is crazy and people are crazy. Hell, I'm crazy. And I have been looking all my life for someone to do the things you did to me that night. I love the pain, but nobody has ever come close to what I needed until now. I know we can't be no item or go out on a date. Your mama would kill me. But, I want you to know that whenever you want to be like that again, please let me be the one."

James was shocked by what Mary C. said to him. He didn't know what to say. She had more.

"You don't have to say anything. You can deny it if you think that's best. I'm just here to tell you I know the truth and I want more and I think you do, too. If I hadn't been so drunk I would have enjoyed it even more and so would you. I would have joined in better than I did. I want you like that whenever you have the urge."

James took a deep breath. "I'm not gonna talk about that night. I am interested in your secret proposition."

Mary C. smiled. "Good, that's fine. I won't mention that night again. But, I'll remember it forever."

James smiled too. "Me too."

She hated him as she smiled and showed him her breasts across the bar. She sipped her easy Jack Black.

Sofia was awake and sitting up in the seat next to Jason.

"Oh God! Jason, I was really hoping this night was a dream, but it all is happening, isn't it?"

"Yes, but he's gone. We've been here for about a half hour and he's gone."

"What did he say to you, or was I dreaming?"

"No, he was here. He dropped his hat in the back of the truck and came to get it."

"Oh God! Jason, this is all too crazy."

"Well, he could have hurt us and he didn't. He really likes to scare people. And he did what he wanted tonight."

"Jason, we should tell somebody, but you're right, we really can't. If any of my family found out I don't know what would happen. They'd probably send me away somewhere."

"We're not gonna tell anybody. I might tell Uncle Bobby that Charlie tried to scare us so someone will know. He won't tell."

"That's a good idea. Tell Uncle Bobby and maybe he can make him leave you alone."

"It ain't that easy when you're dealin' with a man like Charlie. You see, Charlie don't have no rules to live by. You can't get the best of someone who has no rules. They wake up in the mornin' thinkin' 'bout what they can do to take from the world that day."

Sofia had never heard Jason talk like that. It was as if he was a father giving his child a lesson about the evil men in the world. "What an awful way to live your life. He is crazy, isn't he?"

"He's more than crazy, he's the devil himself."

"Take me home, Jason. I want to go home."

Kelly stood next to Bobby's table with her order pad in her hand. "Have you decide what you want yet?"

"First, I would like to say I'm sorry for that stupid comment earlier. I like you and don't want you to ever have a reason to think poorly of me."

"You're impressin' me already. That was nice and I accept the apology. I like a fresh start. What can I get for you?"

"That ain't you on the menu." They both laughed.

"I have to agree with Mary C. about you, you are a fool."

"But you like me, don't ya?"

"I wouldn't tell now if I did."

"You do, I can tell. The same way you can tell about me."

She smiled again. "I can't wait on you to decide if we like each other or not. I got people needing to eat and they all think I'm their mama."

"Well, I'll take the fried shrimp special again with iced tea and I don't want you to be my mama. But, I do want ya."

She left to serve her other customers.

Mary C. finished her easy Jack Black. She had watched James serve the other customers. He liked her looking at him. He moved closer to her.

"What are you doing tonight?"

"I've got to go get Bobby. He's stranded and I should have already picked him up. I have to take him to get his truck and I'm not sure when I'll be back."

"What about tomorrow night, your regular night out? Any plans?"

She gave him the best smile of all. "You tell me. Do I?"

"Yes, ma'am, you do. You come in whenever you want and I'll see that I can get off early."

"I have a lot of fantasies that have not been fulfilled. Do you do fantasies?"

"If last Saturday night was one of your fantasies, yes, ma'am, I am definitely your fantasy man."

"I thought we weren't gonna talk about that night."

"We ain't." He moved to the other end of the bar to serve another customer. She stood up, but he didn't want her to go.

"You leavin'?"

"I told you, one easy one so I could sleep, but I have a feeling I'm still gonna have a hard time fallin' asleep this night."

"Me too." She had created an inner rage inside his black soul. He wanted her again right then. He would not sleep either, with the anticipation of his sexual methods of cruelty. He watched her walk through the restaurant and out the door. He would be on fire for her by Saturday night. Her plan was falling into place. The Falcon moved in the direction of Bill's Hideaway.

Jason drove up to the side of Strickland's where he had picked Sofia up earlier.

"I don't want to just leave you here. Why don't I take you home and you can say you got a ride from me?"

She didn't want to be left alone to walk. "How can we do it?"

"Where are you supposed to be, anyway?"

"Well, I'm really supposed to be home. Daddy's out of town, Mama's at Aunt Margie's until real late. I was more worried about my sisters. If they went home and I wasn't there, they would know something's up. They were all working at the store, but with my luck one of them probably went home and they're all looking for me now."

"Let's ride by the store and see if they're all still workin'. You might be wrong and they don't know you're gone."

She agreed and she ducked down in the seat of the truck as Jason drove by the store. Sofia had spent most of the night in the position she was in at that moment. "I see all three of 'em. They're in there, alright."

"Really? Oh God! Get me home and let's pray Mama didn't come home early." The truck was moving again.

Uncle Bobby was enjoying his shrimp special and watching Kelly move around the tables as she worked. His Elvis songs were playing and he was relaxed and enjoying his dinner alone and his brief visions of he and Kelly in intimate positions. He looked up from the table and saw Mary C. walk through the swinging doors at the entrance. He caught her eye and motioned for her to sit with him. She moved toward the table. She was hoping to see Hawk, but she didn't. Bobby stood up and pulled a chair out for her. A first, for her.

"Who are you trying to impress? Me, or someone else in the room?"

"Can't I show my sister some respect in public? Besides, Kelly needs someone to impress her and I'm plannin' on bein' that someone. You gonna eat or what?"

"I'm starvin' and would like to sit here and watch my brother act a fool over a woman, who is workin' him for a tip, again."

"No, that ain't true, this time. It's different, this time. You see, and tell me if it's my imagination. Nothin' kickin' at the Bowl?"

Mary C. found another smile. "No, but it will be kickin' tomorrow night."

"The only way that place will ever be kickin' is if they have a ten-for-one night and give away free lobster tail dinners. Now, that might add a little excitement over there. Then I'd go. Oh! Here she comes."

Kelly greeted Mary C. "Hey, Mary C. Can I get ya somethin'?"

"Hey, Kelly. Yeah please, I want a combination fried shrimp and deviled crab dinner, with the all the extras."

"Comin' right up. Sweet tea, okay?"

"Perfect."

Bobby couldn't stand it. "What the hell has gotten into you? You ain't never been this happy and polite in your life. This is really scarin' me. I want the truth right now. Are you a born-again Christian?"

Mary C. couldn't help it either, she had to laugh at Bobby's question and serious facial expression. "You are the craziest man on this earth. Can't I just be happy without you makin' a big deal of it?"

"Are you an oak mama or oak baby? 'Cause that can make ya happy too."

"Ya better stop. Just let me be and we can enjoy our dinner."

Bobby watched Kelly. Mary C. watched for Hawk.

Jason pulled the truck up to the front of Sofia's house. There was a porch light on and the light she had left on in her room.

"No one has been home. They won't know I was gone. Thank the Lord. I'm going in so I can make sure it looks like I've been home all this time. You need to go talk to Uncle Bobby. And please be careful. I really do love you."

Jason's heart raced at her words.

"I'll do better next time, but I won't go back to the cemetery." She gave him another Sofia Special, making him want more. She went into the house. He was alone in the truck. He hated Charlie Klim and wished he had killed him when he had the chance. He wanted to find the evil one and kill him for what he had done to Sofia. He would not run into Charlie Klim again that night.

Kelly brought Mary C.'s meal to the table. Bobby was almost finished with his.

"Here ya go. Can I get you anything else?"

"No, I think this'll do it."

Kelly made Bobby's night. "Mary C., I'd like to take this boy off your hands tonight. If he ain't all talk."

Mary C. and Bobby were both surprised with Kelly's bold declaration. Bobby looked at Mary C. as he said, "See, I told ya she wanted me."

"Well, the way I see it, you two been makin' goo-goo eyes at each other every time he's in here. Maybe it's time to see what's behind the goo-goo."

Bobby couldn't believe the nature of the conversation around him. "Damn, Mary C., you do have a way with words. And you, Miss, you need to talk to me. My little sister ain't got nothin' to say about what I do. You kinda threw me a curveball for a second there and I had to take a moment to recover for the next pitch. Now, will that pitch come from me or you?"

"Well, I started this thing tonight. I have to finish this table and two others, then I'm off. I would like to go home and take a hot bath and get this fried food smell out of my hair. You can help me do that if you are so inclined."

Bobby looked at Mary C. "Thanks for comin' by, but I don't need a ride home."

Mary C. smiled and shook her head as Kelly went to her other tables. Bobby was grinning at Mary C., like a pit bull before he bites you.

Mary C. gave him the respect he wanted at that moment. "It is definitely a family curse."

Bobby moved his Elvis lip. Mary C. ignored him and ate her dinner.

Jason's mind was raging with fear and anger as he drove alone in the truck. He wanted Charlie Klim dead. He wanted to kill the evil one himself. Jason hated the fear he felt in the cemetery, when he was eye-to-eye with Charlie. Being the Jetty Man didn't make a difference and he was disappointed and ashamed of himself, at his lack of action.

The ferry horn sounded as the Buccaneer left the Fort George side of the river for its final ride of the night. He drove to the ferry slip and prepared to watch the big carrier dock until morning. The lights of the ferry were visible as he stopped the truck near the bulkhead. Jason had to get his thoughts together. It was a mistake not telling the others about Charlie Klim; he didn't know they were keeping it a secret, too.

Jason sat in the truck as the ferry floated toward him. The sight of the big boat had always given him pleasure and he needed a good moment. The moment was short-lived when he saw movement behind the truck, through the driver's side-view mirror. His heart jumped in its usual fashion and the thought of Charlie Klim flashed in his head. He jumped from the truck to face his enemy.

"I didn't mean to scare ya, Jetty Man."

Jason's raging eyes cleared when he realized the night phantom, Jake, was the cause of the movement he saw in the mirror. He didn't want to see the skinny black man, but he was relieved it wasn't the evil one.

"A man with your gift don't need to be scared of nothin'. Nothin' can hurt ya, less ya let it."

Jason didn't want to hear the old man's words of praise. He knew it had to do with the tree and Jason had enough confusion around him without the tree. "Please, sir, just let me be. I can't add you to this night." Jason was surprised and scared with Jake's response.

"You defeated evil as a boy. Now, defeat it as a man. You know how and you know where the power comes from. As soon as you admit to ya'self about what you are, then and only then will you defeat this evil that plagues your soul. It is your destiny and it cannot be changed."

Jake's crazy words pounded Jason like the waves pounded the red rocks. His head hurt as he fought the visions of that day at the oak. Jake knew his torment.

"True evil has returned and you must use what you are and what you have to save us all. The chosen ones never know they have been chosen, until their deed is done. And sometimes they don't know then."

Jake's words continued to add confusion to Jason's awful night. He jumped back into the truck, started the motor and hit the gas, spinning the tires in the white lime rock packed at the bulkhead. The white smoke from the lime rock surrounded Jake, like a vampire's fog. As the truck moved away, Jason looked into his rearview mirror, but Jake was gone.

Mary C. had finished her dinner and was preparing to leave for home. Kelly was checking out at the register so she could go home for the shower she had invited Bobby to participate in. Bobby was at the jukebox listening to one more Elvis tune for the road.

"Well, brother dear, are you sure you don't want to go home with me? Or take me home and come back with my car? You might wish you had a way home, later."

"You may have a good point there, sis."

Kelly joined them. "I'm ready for that shower. What about you? Have you decided yet?"

Bobby looked at Mary C. with his best smile.

"Drive carefully."

Mary C. knew he was hooked. "Y'all have a good time. I'll see ya in the mornin'."

They all walked out onto the deck that surrounded Bill's. Bobby and Kelly were down the steps and into her car in record time. Bobby waved to Mary C., as Kelly hit the gas and they were off. Mary C. walked to the Falcon and she was rolling down the beach too. She saw Kelly's car taillights disappear in front of her as the car turned up the ramp leaving the beach. The ramp would also be Mary C.'s exit. She turned the Falcon onto the wooden ramp.

A car was parked in the road, blocking her from driving onto Seminole Road. She had to slam on the brakes, or run into the car. The Falcon slid on the dirt and stopped only inches from the car blockade. She braced herself with her arms so her head would not hit the steering wheel. She was shaken for only a few seconds. When the dust began to clear around the two cars, she saw Charlie Klim standing next to her car.

"Evenin', Mary C."

The pounding of her heart was almost too much for her to take. She was scared.

"Where was brother Bobby goin' in such a hurry? I ain't sure, but I think that sexy waitress was drivin'. They were sure in a hurry."

Mary C. didn't respond. She was really scared.

"Would ya like to go have a drink with me? We can have a date. I need to start takin' ya out, so folks can see we're together again, for good. I ain't changed much since the last time we laid together. A few more scars maybe. You ain't seen my scars yet, have ya? You like scars, don't ya? Well, you oughta be crazy 'bout me when we're both naked again."

Mary C. was sick to her stomach and felt she would throw up at any second.

"I tried to explain the other night, how this thing with us is gonna go. I don't think you listened and I don't think you took it very seriously. I'd like to take this opportunity to explain it one last time with your complete attention."

Mary C. knew he was crazy and she had no idea what she was

going to do.

The evil one continued. "You and me are gonna be together. You are gonna forgive me for my past sins against you and I, in return, will forgive you and that boy for y'all's sins against me. We'll be the happy family you and me never had." Charlie moved closer to the window of the Falcon, bent over and smiled at Mary C. The wild look on his face scared her even more, as his voice changed and he spoke slowly and deliberately.

"And you, Miss Mary C. will open those pretty legs of yours, whenever I want them opened. Just like you used to."

She wanted to fight back with words, but she was too afraid. His next words added even more to her anguish.

"Oh, by the way, I saw Jason tonight."

She hated him telling her that.

"Your little man was parkin' in the cemetery with a girl. A girl with real pretty tits. Your little man was playin' a tune on 'em 'til he saw me."

She tried to be calm and not make him crazier then he was. "Did ya give him a good scare?"

Charlie liked Mary C.'s first words of their meeting.

"Yeah, I think I did. That little whore did some screamin' and Jason ran over some headstones when he was haulin' ass outta there. That's sacrilegious, ain't it?"

Mary C. knew she had to be careful with her words, but she was relieved that Jason got out of the cemetery. "I didn't know young people still parked in the cemetery."

"Well, yours does. Then he took her to the little jetties to suck on her some more. Where these little whores come from?"

Mary C. was worried, but she had to know what happened. "Did ya scare 'em away from there too?"

"No. I had to get my hat. It fell off my head when Jason took off and I fell out the back of the truck. I was pissed at first, but I'd a done the same thing if I'd been that scared. I got my hat out of the truck and left him to his little whore. I told him to tell ya, 'hey,' but he probably won't."

Mary C. didn't want to stay there, but she would do nothing to make him angry. She was happy he had not physically harmed Jason. As long as Charlie was talking to her, Jason was safe.

Charlie added to her discomfort when he reached his arm through the window and rubbed the outside of her shirt, touching her breast. She reached to stop him and held his wrist. His big hand still touched her as she held on.

"Hold still now and don't be contrary. I just want a walk down memory lane. You have always felt good to the touch, woman."

She stared at him with no emotion in her eyes. He moved his hand and rubbed her between her legs. She held her stare and her eyes were empty. She hated him. She hated James. She hated Sheriff Floyd. She hated all men.

"I'm gonna put that sparkle back into those eyes of yours if it kills us both."

Mary C. knew he was right about somebody dying.

"I'm gonna go have a late drink at Bill's, so if ya want more rubbin', turn this baby around and we'll have a date. Who was that with Bobby?"

"It was Kelly, that nice waitress. They were goin' to take a shower."

Charlie smiled. "Did we ever take a shower together? I don't think we have. I don't think I've ever took no shower with a woman. Let's go join 'em. We can all be fuckin' clean."

"I'm not goin' and bother them. Besides, I have no idea where they went."

"I know where she lives. It's just up the road. I've seen her washin' her car in the front yard. We could surprise 'em and we could tell Bobby we're back together."

She had to think fast. "You gotta let me tell Bobby about us. You can't expect me to just spring it on him. He's not gonna like it too much, so please let me do it. I need to tell Jason too, so don't be tellin' him about it if you see him again."

"Ya think Bobby'll be against it?"

Mary C. was dealing with the insane and she knew it. "Well, you gotta understand, there's been a lot of bad blood here for a long time. But, I'm sure he will come around."

"I'm sorry I said I'd kill the boy. I didn't know you still loved me like this. Ya think Bobby'll let me move in with y'all? I ain't got no place for all of us."

She was amazed at the drift the conversation had taken. "Well, it is his house and I'm a guest there, too. We'll just have to see. I need to get on home now."

He looked to be in deep thought. "Yeah, you need to go. I can't see ya tomorrow, but I'll stop by Sunday morning. You wanna go to church?"

Mary C.'s eyes widened at his question.

He smiled an evil smile. "I was just foolin' 'bout church."

She backed the car out of the trap and drove around Charlie's car. Mary C. was on Seminole Road and headed home. She wanted to see Jason, make sure he was alright and talk to him about his scare in the cemetery. She knew Sofia was the girl Charlie saw in the truck with Jason. The Falcon flew toward Mayport.

The water from Kelly's shower was bouncing off Bobby's back, as he lathered up her shoulders, back and backside. He rubbed her backside area longer than the other spots.

"Could you leave me a little flesh back there, big boy?"

"You peeked already?" They both laughed at Bobby's joke. He pushed what he considered his manhood against her.

"Be careful, you could put somebody's eye out with that thing." She was funny to Bobby and they were relaxed with each other. He turned her around and they faced each other. She reached down and held him in her hand, gripping it like she was preparing to sword fight.

"You gonna leave a little flesh on there, big girl?"

She held on and smiled. "You peeked already too, huh?" She turned back around and put both her hands on the wall, leaned forward, pushing her huge breasts against the wall and stood up on her tiptoes, elevating her backside that Bobby had just cleaned so thoroughly. It was an incredibly sexy sight for Bobby to behold.

She knew he was enjoying what he saw and would soon have. She moved her legs wider apart and went up on her toes again. It was the last invitation Bobby needed. He entered her body from behind as the water bounced off them both. It was wild and exciting, and Bobby was glad to be with her. Their introductory shower of ecstasy and pleasure ended when the white shower curtain that protected them was ripped away from its metal ring hangers. Bobby and Kelly both screamed as the curtain was pulled away from around the bathtub.

A shotgun blast roared in the little bathroom, shaking the whole house. Bobby took the entire spray of pellets that flew from one of the barrels of the doubled-barreled gun. The force slammed Bobby into Kelly, who stood between him and the wall. The one hundred metal BBs tore open his chest and stomach. He was already dead when he looked at Charlie Klim, standing there. He fell over the edge of the tub and then onto the floor. Kelly stood there trembling in shock, splattered with Bobby's blood. She screamed again when Charlie stepped over Bobby's body and grabbed her with his free hand, by her hair, pulling her out of the tub, over Bobby and onto the floor. He pulled her to her bedroom and threw her naked body onto the bed.

"Where do these guys find all these whores?"

Kelly was being scared to death. She knew she was going to die and had no power to stop it. Charlie put the gun down and started taking off his clothes.

"I can't believe you handle people's food and then go home and hold somebody's dick in the same hands. My food, his dick: I don't think I like that." He stood naked next to to the bed. The sight of his scars added to Kelly's already fatal shock.

"I'm sorry about your new boyfriend, but he had to go. Ya see, I'm movin' in with Mary C. and Jason and ol' brother Bobby probably would have given me a bad time about that. I really don't need no more bad times. Now, as for you. You can either die right now, this very second, or you can live as long as it takes for me to get tired of ya. The length of time for me to tire of a woman depends strictly on the woman. And I have to admit I think you could keep me happy and busy for a long time if you wanted to. And you do look very creative. Why don't you keep my attention as long as you can?"

Kelly got up on her knees and held up her trembling arms, inviting Charlie to her. Her only goal was to stay alive, no matter what she had to do.

"Now, that's excellent. I think we're gonna be good friends here tonight, don't you?"

She nodded "yes," as Charlie crawled toward her.

After Jason left Jake, he drove past Sofia's house to make sure she was safe. He could tell other members of her family were home now and he felt better, knowing someone was there with her. With Sofia at home with her family, Jason went home to wait for his.

Mary C. drove the Falcon into their yard at the same time Jason pulled up in Uncle Bobby's truck. She was glad to see him and she was glad to be home. She needed to tell Jason about Charlie, but she knew she had to stay focused on James and their meeting Saturday night. They were both out of their vehicles at the same time.

"Jason, are you alright? I was so worried about you."

"Mama, what's wrong?"

"I saw Charlie tonight. He told me about you and him in the cemetery and the little jetties."

Jason was too surprised at what his mother was saying. He had to get his thoughts in order.

"Why did you take her out there? What were you thinkin'?"

"Mama, where did you see him at?"

"At the ramp on the beach. He told me he didn't hurt you, but I wanted to be sure. He lies so much. Is Sofia alright?"

"Mama, I hate him. I wished I'd a killed him that night."

"Oh, Jason! I know he's an evil man, but I'm still glad his death ain't been on your hands all these years. You've had too much death around you. You don't need no more."

"Mama, the man's crazy and he's gonna hurt us all."

"No, he won't hurt any of us anymore. He promised me."

Jason was a man now and he understood more about his mother.

"What did you have to promise him?"

She looked at her son after his question cut deep into her dark soul. She had no words.

Jason did. "I will kill him for sure, this time, if he ever comes near any of us. That's my promise."

Mary C. walked into the house. Jason sat on the porch swing. He couldn't hear the second shotgun blast that shook Kelly's house and ended her torture.

It was getting late, as Jason looked out into the night toward the oak tree. He couldn't see it from his house, but he knew it was out there. The shuttle boat would leave for the dredge at eight o'clock and he wanted to be there on time. He thought Uncle Bobby was in his bed and he saw his mother's bedroom light go out. The moonlight lit up a small area at the end of the dirt road, leading to the house. For a moment Jason thought he saw Jake, black trench coat and all, standing in the light at the end of the road. An eye-clearing second look gave him no vision of the phantom. The tree would call to Jason, in his dreams, throughout that night.

Chapter Eleven

Jason opened his eyes and looked at the clock next to his bed. The shuttle would leave Mr. Leek's dock in an hour. He was exausted from his night of dreams, but excited about working. It would take his mind off the evil turmoil around him. He checked to see if his family were still with him. He loved the sight of his mother safe in her bed and he figured Uncle Bobby had left before Jason woke up. He dressed, fixed his lunch and hurried to the store for his ritual breakfast and, he hoped, a moment with Sofia. Jason was disappointed when he entered the store and heard the creator of the "Greeting" demonstating her superior technique.

"Well, good morning, Jason. May I help you with something?"

He wanted to tell Miss Margaret the girls were not always following the greeting procedures and that her greeting was excellent and he felt extremely welcomed. But, as usual he kept his thoughts to himself.

"Wait a minute. A honey bun and a carton of milk, right?"

Jason looked at the fortune-teller.

"Sofia told me that's your good luck breakfast."

Jason smiled at the thought of Sofia talking about him to her mother. "Yes, ma'am."

"Well, I think it's nice to have a good luck charm of some kind, don't you? Something that makes us feel good and gets us through the day." Even though she was older, she was still very pretty and Jason could see her four daughters in her.

"Yes, ma'am."

"My girls are really taken by you. Sofia talks about you and how y'all have had coffee here in the store and you stayed while Jake was here. He is strange, you know. I'm nervous myself when I'm here alone with him. Can he talk?"

Jason wanted to tell her "yes," but he knew she wouldn't believe him. Besides, she was like her daughter Margie, and really wasn't interested in an answer to her question.

"Sofia's not feeling too good this morning. She was up all night, so I let her sleep late this morning."

Jason's heart raced when he heard Sofia was sick. He knew it was because of their encounter with Charlie. Miss Margaret kept talking.

"And Margie tells me you helped her one night on the beach when they got her friend Stephanie's car stuck in the sand."

Jason realized he was part of Margie's lie about that night on the beach and he had another flash vision of her, in panties only, riding that big turtle toward the water. Miss Margaret ended his flashback.

"Then, Peggy said you helped her when the station wagon ran out of gas near the little jetties. She was lucky you came along and not some stranger."

Jason had not been aware that he was an intregal part of a number of falsehoods. She had one more.

"And then Susan told me you helped her that night she was so upset and left the store. You said some very nice things to her and I appreciate it. You seem to be a good luck charm for my family."

Jason thought he had heard enough about his ficticious good deeds and he really didn't know what to say. He had to get to the dock, but he wanted to see Sofia. He found a strange courage as he moved toward the door.

"If it's okay, I'd like to stop by after work today and see how Sofia's feeling." His mouth was dry after he made his request and waited for her response.

"I was just thinking about that. Let's do this. How about you being our guest for dinner tonight and we can all properly thank you for the kindness you have shown my girls? I'll look for you at six-thirty."

Jason could only say one thing. "Yes, ma'am."

"Good, we'll see you then." Jason was out the door and headed to the dock.

Mary C. was up and her first cup of coffee was almost gone. She had so much to think about and she was glad she would be alone all day to put the finishing touches on her plans. She realized Bobby hadn't made it home and she hoped his night had been better than hers. Mary C. had wanted Bobby to settle down with a good woman. She knew he liked Kelly and she hoped last night was the beginning of something good for him. She fixed her second cup and started dressing.

Once again she looked at her naked body in the full-length oval mirror in her bedroom. Her physical pain and injuries had almost healed and her mental injuries would be healed before the day ended. She turned from side to side, admiring what she had to offer at age forty-one. She liked what she saw in the mirror; she was not going to allow anyone to ever hurt her or her family again. She would rid the world of the devil, James, and then the evil one, Charlie. There was no doubt in her mind that it would happen as she was planning. They would all be safe.

Jason entered the fish house as the diesel engine of the shuttle fired up. There was only one shuttle running that morning because the overtime workers were just a skeleton crew and there were only twenty workers who had been given the opportunity to work the extra time. Jason patted Mr. Leek on the back as he hurried to the shuttle. Jason was happy as he jumped on the boat and found his normal seat empty. He didn't think about it, but the workers had left his seat for him out of respect. He sat down, nodded to the other workers and tore the wrapper off the honey bun. The shuttle was moving away from the dock; he was happy to be headed to the barge. The ride to the barge was the same as during the regular workdays, except Jason looked at the great oak tree as the shuttle went by it. He held the rope ladder for his fellow workers and, as usual, he was the last to make the climb to the barge above them. He stepped on the first wooden board of the ladder.

"Let me steady that thing for ya."

Jason turned toward the voice and the helper. He found himself eye-to-eye with Charlie Klim once more. Jason was alone on the shuttle with his evil enemy. He was frozen again with fear. Like a dog, Charlie sensed Jason's fear. He was a master at intimidation and fear. Jason had faced fear and Charlie before, but he was still petrified.

"That's a long way up, ain't it?" Charlie looked up at the barge.

Jason couldn't say anything.

"After I saw you last night, I saw the rest of your family. I talked to ya mama on the beach. I got a date with her Sunday. Then I saw Bobby at a friend's house. He was just gettin' out of the shower and was still drippin' wet, when I saw him. He's always been a clean one, that Bobby."

Jason's eyes were locked on Charlie, but he couldn't hear all his words. He wanted to get to the top of the barge and be safe as the Jetty Man with Big Jim and Mr. Hawkins. Charlie still held the rope and Jason still had one foot on the ladder, when a voice from above was his salvation.

"Jason, you havin' trouble? You need some help?"

The evil one had an answer for Big Jim. "No trouble down here. I'll steady the rope and he'll be right up."

"Well, get on up here. Mr. Hawkins is waitin' on you."

Charlie wasn't through with his weak prey. "You sure made a lotta friends this week, ain't ya? And your little whore has really got pretty titties. I won't be so nice on her the next time I catch y'all in the wrong place."

Jason was up the ladder and didn't look back at Charlie. Big Jim was waiting for him and didn't notice the fear in Jason's eyes as he escorted him to where Mr. Hawkins and three other men were standing. Mr. Hawkins announced Jason's arrival.

"Here he is now, gentlemen." Mr. Hawkins stepped to Jason. "Jason, this is Mr. English, Mr. Reynolds and, of course, this is Mr.

Robertson." Jason shook all three of their hands and it took him a second to recognize Mr. Robertson, the man he had saved only five days ago. Steve "the Crane" Robertson hugged Jason, like they were father and son. Jason returned the kind gesture.

"I want to thank you, young man, for what you did here that day. I don't remember much of it, but I've been told of your unselfish act and bravery. That, my friend, is a rare quality today and I'm glad you were here when I went into the drink down there."

Big Jim, Mr. Hawkins and Mr. Robertson's companions were all smiling and seemed so proud of Jason. Mr. Robertson had more praise for the young hero.

"When you get off today, Mr. Hawkins will give you a savings account book from the Ocean State Bank in Atlantic Beach. The account is in your name and it has one thousand dollars in it. It's just something I want to do to show you how grateful I am to you. It's easy to say thank you. I needed to do more, so please accept it as my thank you."

Jason was once again speechless. No one had ever done such a thing for him. Mr. Robertson was understanding about Jason's silence.

"I know you're not much of a talker. I do like a quiet man. If you ever need anything, don't hesitate to ask me. I'll always be there for you, remember that." Jason wanted to tell him about Charlie in the shuttle below, but he didn't. He did, however, find a few words. "Thank you, Mr. Robertson. I do appreciate it."

"I know you do, son, and call me Crane."

Mr. Hawkins put his arm around Jason. Jason was grateful to him too.

"And thank you, Mr. Hawkins."

"You're welcome, Jason and call me Hawk." Jason's heart went wild in his chest and his hair stood up on his arms. He was excited about the money, but the privilege of calling Mr. Hawkins "Hawk" at his request had much more meaning in his life. He would most likely never call him anything but Mr. Hawkins, but he could if he ever wanted to. That's what mattered to Jason.

Mary C. waited for Bobby to come home, but she had to take care of a few more things before the night was on her. She would take James to task first and then turn her attention to Charlie, for his turn. The Falcon hit the road again.

Mary C. thought about driving to Kelly's house to see if Bobby needed a ride home, but she decided to go on into Jacksonville Beach first for a few items she needed for that night. She would look for Kelly's house on her way back. If his night with Kelly was good enough to keep him away this long, she didn't want to disturb him and his new lady friend. He deserves a good time, she thought. The Falcon passed the little jetties and left Mayport, headed for a store in Jacksonville Beach.

Most of the work on the barge that morning was cleanup and preparing the machines for Monday morning. The foremen planned where certain rocks would be dropped, while the workers serviced the machines and cleaned the deck of the barge. Lunchtime came quickly. Mr. Hawkins watched the majority of the workers move down to the rocks to sit with Jason on his lunch rock. Big Jim went too. Mr. Hawkins counted only five workers remaining on the barge during the lunch break. Big Jim was the only pelican who saw the Hawk move down to the rocks.

When Mr. Hawkins came near the lunch rock, he maneuvered himself where he could listen to the lunch conversations but would not be seen. He leaned against his own rock and listened to what was said during the forty-five-minute break.

It didn't take the Hawk long to realize why the men flocked to Jason each day. It wasn't because he gave them words of wisdom or creeds to live by, or spiritual revelations, or even just good advice. It was because he listened to them and was genuinely interested in what they said. Most of the workers told about themselves, while Jason and the others listened. Jason's few comments were always of a positive and encouraging nature. Each worker would add his experiences to the story. Each man listened to their fellow workers' stories and took time to respect each other as Jason respected them. It was obvious that each man felt good about himself, because people were interested in what they had to say. Jason was the perfect psychiatrist and he was holding group therapy sessions on the big red jetty rocks. Mr. Hawkins shook his head, smiled and returned to the barge. He had to blow his whistle and bring lunch to an end. They would work until three that day.

Kelly was scheduled to work the Saturday lunch shift at Bill's Hideaway. She was seldom late for work and always called if she was sick or going to be late. After she didn't answer her phone, they waited an hour for her. Bill, the owner, decided to send his son to see if she was at home. The front door of Kelly's house was wide open when the young man pulled up on his moped. He called out for Kelly from the open front door, but there was no answer. He walked slowly into the living room and called for Kelly again.

"Kelly, it's me, Little Billy. Dad sent me over to see if you're okay I didn't want to scare ya by just walkin' in. The door was wide open. Kelly!" He didn't like the silence around him. He felt something was wrong; he just didn't know how wrong.

Little Billy continued his slow, cautious walk. He could see the open door ahead was to a bedroom. He was afraid and sorry he was there. His fear could not prepare him for what he saw when he looked into Kelly's bedroom and torture chamber. His stomach went sour instantly, as a hot liquid filled his throat when he saw Kelly's bloody, naked body on the bed. Her eyes were wide open and screaming at him with fear and pain. He ran from the house and jumped on his moped. His confused and terrified mind thought only of getting back to the restaurant and letting someone else return to Kelly's house. He only saw one victim. Someone else would have to find Bobby's lifeless body on the bathroom floor.

Mary C. walked out of the store and threw two bags on the front seat of her car. On her way home she would stop at Skinny's place in Atlantic Beach, and practice a few more hard swings with the black-jack on the heavy bag hanging in his backyard. She had everything on the revenge list and now she would wait for the proper time to dress for the fight.

The shuttle floated below the barge as the workers prepared to make the climb down to their ride back to Mayport and Mr. Leek's dock. Jason didn't see him, but he knew Charlie was still at the wheel of the shuttle. Jason made sure he was not the first one to go down the ladder. If he sat in his regular seat, he would have his back to the wheelhouse and he wanted to be able to see Charlie if he made an appearance. Jason stood at the stern of the boat, where he could see both sides of the wheelhouse. He would be able to see Charlie no matter what side he came from. Jason didn't know Charlie would have to stay at the wheel during the ride back to the dock.

Jason looked up at the oak tree. A strong gust of wind took his breath and moved his hair from in front of his eyes. His heart pounded and he wanted to drive that bowie knife deep into Charlie's body. He thought about Charlie saying he had a date with his mother when they were alone on the shuttle that morning. He knew it was a lie and he would kill Charlie if he even tried to see his mother. Jason could see Mr. Leek's dock ahead. He also saw the *Mary C.* still tied to the dock. It was strange for Uncle Bobby to take two days off in a row.

Jason jumped off the shuttle and he was glad to be on the dock and walking through the fish house. Mr. Leek greeted him as he walked by.

"Hey, Jason. How was Saturday on the barge?"

"It was fine." Jason looked back at the shuttle. He had Charlie Klim on his mind.

"I heard Steve Robertson was out there to see you and thank you for savin' his life."

"Yes, sir, he was. He was real nice to me."

"I also heard he really thanked you, in what they call a monetary way."

Jason held up his new blue savings account book. "Oh, you mean this?"

"My, my, Jason. Good things are ahead for you. You make us all proud."

"Thank you, Mr. Leek." Jason wanted to tell his friend he could call Mr. Hawkins "Hawk," but he didn't.

"What ya got planned for tonight to celebrate?" Jason hadn't thought about celebrating, but he knew what he was going to do that night. "I'm havin' supper at Miss Margaret's house. She invited me this morning."

"Well, then, make that your celebration." Mr. Leek patted Jason on the back. Jason liked him. He was out of the fish house and headed toward the store and home.

Jason passed Strickland's and was turning onto the street leading to the store when he saw Jake standing in an open field on the other side of the street. Jason stopped when he saw the skinny black man. He wondered if Jake was near his house last night when Jason thought he saw him in the moonlight. He wanted to walk away, but Jake got his attention.

"Jetty Man, it is time. You hear me? It is time."

Jason stared at his strange new friend and heard the strange words he was yelling from across the street.

"I said, it is time. Jessie is here and she knows it's time. Why don't you? It's all around you, Jetty Man. The true evil of the world has come to Mayport and it has come for you. You are the only one who can stop it. You can't do that without Jessie and the tree. It is time to please the tree again. This evil will chew you up and spit you out if you are alone. You've seen it already and you cannot face it alone. But you will have to face it. It is your destiny."

Jason had heard enough of Jake's ravings. He started walking away and toward the store. Jake was not finished yet.

"When you need me tonight, I'll be at the tree. It is a safe place. If you come, Jessie will have to come too. She will know you are there. She waits for you to decide both y'alls' fate."

Jason didn't believe Jessie was in Mayport and he thought Jake was just trying to make him go to the tree. He didn't want to do that.

He could still hear Jake talking as he walked away and went into Miss Margaret's store. The bell on the door announced his arrival once more.

"Hello, Jason. May I help you with something?"

He was surprised when he saw the oldest of the sisters, Margie, was in charge of the store. He wanted to find out about Sofia, so he tried to create a conversation with his turtle riding sidekick.

"It's nice to see ya. Where ya been lately?"

"Where have I been? I should ask you the same question. You're the one who can't be found. I've been looking for you almost every day. You're either at work or home sleeping. Jason, you even worked today. You need some time off."

Jason smiled at her concern. He liked the fact she cared. "I've only been workin' a week. I don't need any time off yet. I'm just gettin' started." Margie liked Jason talking to her. It made her feel he was interested and she wanted him to be interested. That night on the beach had left a mark on her heart and had ignited her sense of adventure. She wanted more and she hoped it would be with him.

"Mama said she invited you to dinner tonight. Are you coming?"

"Yes, I think so. It was real nice of her to ask me." He could see Margie's excitement.

"It's going to be neat sitting at the table with you and knowing what we shared. We'll be sitting right there with my sisters and mother and we will have a secret together. I think that is so cool, don't you?"

Jason wasn't sure how to answer her question. He wanted to say, "I'll have more than one secret at that table," but he kept that thought to himself. As usual, she really didn't want to hear his answer.

"I can't stop thinking about that night we were together. I can't help it, I just can't. Believe me, I've tried. I know we can't be a steady thing, but whenever you want to be with me, I'll be there." She continued her forward ways.

"I hope I won't crowd y'all tonight. Your family's so big and I don't want to be in the way."

"No, it won't be a problem at all. My father's still out of town. And Sofia's been in bed all day. She may not eat at all."

He didn't like hearing about Sofia's day in bed. "What's wrong with her?" He knew Margie would have the information.

"She just seems worn out to me. Mama says it could be the flu, but I just think she's tired. She stays up late at night, comes here to work early in the mornings. That catches up to you after a while. Sleeping all day is probably the best thing for her."

Jason liked Margie's explanation, but he knew there was more to her condition. He would always blame himself for that awful night at the mercy of Charlie Klim. Even if he was to rid them all of the evil one, that night could not be undone. He hoped Sofia would be able to recover from the ordeal. He knew how fear could change a person and he wanted her to be the same as she was before that night. He wanted to go see Sofia, but he was too dirty and he didn't know who was home with her.

"I need to get home and get this work dirt off me."

Margie was having the longest conversation she ever had with Jason and it was a special moment for her. She didn't want it to end.

"Jason, I'm off tonight, so if you think about it and you're interested, we could do something later, after dinner. We can't talk about it at the house, but we could meet somewhere. I'd really like it if we did."

"That would be nice. We'll have to see what happens."

Margie had an interesting and frightening thought. "I would love to meet you at the oak tree."

A chill ran through Jason, as a vision of the tree slammed into his mind. Then Jessie, Sofia and Margie all rolled in the sand beneath the big oak. He hadn't had such an intense head flash all week. He shook it out of his head. He had no words. She didn't care.

"I'm sorry if that surprises you, but I'm serious about it. I'm not saying we have to do the Breeding. I'm saying I'd like to be with you there. I'm not afraid and I know you're not either. I know you will protect me if we go there. I trust you and I know the tree will not hurt its own."

Jason was lost in her words and he still had no words of his own.

"Just remember, when you want to go there, please take me with you. Now, you better get on home because Mama will be looking for you at six-thirty sharp."

Jason walked out the door in a Margie-induced daze. He wanted to go home.

Mary C. practiced her blackjack swing. Skinny was home, but did not accompany her to his backyard. He gave her the privacy she needed to prepare herself alone and get her body and mind ready for whatever she was compelled to do. He had asked no questions to that point and would ask none later. He could hear the blackjack as it slapped the bag with each of her swings. He knew someone was going to feel the wrath of a woman who had been seriously wronged. It had a biblical ring to it. Two Atlantic Beach police cars went screaming passed Skinny's house. Mary C. heard them, but she could not see them from the backyard.

Jason walked up on the porch of his house. Uncle Bobby's truck was still where Jason had left it last night. The *Mary C.* was still at the dock and a look inside the house told him Uncle Bobby was not home and there was no indication he had been there at all. A hot shower would clear his head and he would be able to think about what he should do. He didn't like being alone. They had all been together each night that week, until last night. He felt better about things when his family was with him. He hoped the shower would help.

Kelly's front yard was full of police cars and two ambulances. The inside of the house was full of police officials and paramedics. Evidence technicians were taking pictures of the two dead victims and the rooms where they were found.

Mary C. had worked up a sweat perfecting her blackjack swing in Skinny's backyard. She practiced longer than she had planned and the day was getting away from her. Skinny liked the wild look she had when she joined him at the front of the shack, where he sat in his beach chair.

"Lord have mercy on my poor soul, woman. You do have a certain look about you that stirs my insides."

She wiped the sweat from her forehead with her shirtsleeve.

"You just love me. You'd say good things about me no matter

how I looked."

"Maybe so, but I do know pretty when I see it."

She smiled and accepted his compliment. He offered her his assistance.

"Remember, if you need me, I'll help ya. Just tell me what I have to do."

"I have to do this alone. It really has to be that way. I can't explain it . . ."

Skinny stopped her. "Ya got nothin' to explain. I just wanted you to know, I'm with ya if ya need me."

She nodded her head. "I know, Skinny. I know."

The Falcon was twenty minutes from Mayport. Mary C. thought only of James and what she had to do. Her plan to stop at Kelly's and see if Bobby needed a ride faded, and she didn't think about it until she was almost home. She hoped she would find him at the house.

Jason was splashing Old Spice on his face. Uncle Bobby had taught him that. He wrote a note to his mother telling her where he was and for her to tell Uncle Bobby he had the truck. Jason wanted to leave his thoughts of Charlie, the oak tree, Jake and Jessie, all behind, and concentrate on Sofia and the evening with her family. He wanted to be with her, hoping to ease her mind of the fear she was feeling. The clock in the living room chimed the first of six. He would rather be early, so it was time to go. He couldn't wait any longer for Uncle Bobby or his mother to show up. The Falcon was passing the little jetties as Jason drove the truck out of the front yard. He would arrive at Miss Margaret's house at the same time Mary C. would be driving into the front yard. Neither one had any idea they had lost Uncle Bobby and they were entering into a night that would change both their lives forever.

Mary C. took the two bags off the front seat of the car and went into the house. She saw Jason's note right away and read it while she walked to her bedroom, throwing the two bags onto her bed. She was pleased he would be with Miss Margaret and her girls. She knew he would be safe and she could go about her business without worrying about him. She thought Bobby must have really fallen for Kelly and she would like to talk to him about his new romance. She felt it was all falling into place and the time was right for all their lives to change. She would start the rebirth by getting rid of one of her devils.

Jason knocked on Miss Margaret's door. He had butterflies in his stomach and his mouth was dry when the door opened and Peggy, the wild one from the little jetties, welcomed him.

"Good evening, Jason. Welcome to our home."

Jason loved the way they all talked. It was so proper and had substance. "Thank you." He walked in, with her leading him into the living room. Susan and Margie were rushing down the staircase together. Miss Margaret entered the room as the girls made it to the bottom of the steps.

"Girls, girls! You sound like a herd of horses coming down those stairs. You're going to scare our guest away. What will he think of us, running in the house like wild Indians." She turned to Jason.

"Jason, I'm so glad you decided to join us. With their father out of town, it's nice to have a man in the house at dinnertime. I hope you don't mind being the man of the house tonight."

Jason liked the way Miss Margaret talked to him. Her three daughters steadied themselves and smiled at the new temporary man of the house, as their mother continued her formal greeting.

"We all want to thank you for all your kindness toward our family and we hope you will consider our home a place where you are always welcome." The girls continued smiling at their guest. Miss Margaret knew Jason would not have much to say, so she assisted him.

"Since you're here a little early, we can go ahead and eat. Evertything's ready, and I know if you worked all day you're a hungry man."

Jason found a few words. "Yes, ma'am."

She took Jason's arm, escorted him to the dining room and directed him to sit in the chair at the head of a six-seat table.

Margie moved quickly to claim the chair to Jason's right and Peggy did the same on his left. Susan sat next to Margie and the other chair was empty. Miss Margaret walked toward the kitchen. "Let me get the main dish." She left the room. Margie was in charge.

"Jason, do you like pork roast?"

It didn't surprise Jason when she was the first of the girls to speak. "Yes, I do."

Miss Margaret returned with the roast. "I hope you like pork roast, Jason. I'd like to think my pork roast is as good as my sister's pot roast."

Jason smiled and found some courage. "I'm sure it is. It sure smells good." Miss Margaret returned his smile and she liked the confidence he had building inside as he became comfortable with his surroundings. She continued. "This is a special night for two reasons. The first is because you are our guest and the second is the fact that this is our community meal. Each one of us cooked something for this dinner. The pork roast is mine, the mashed potatoes are from Susan, Peggy's specialty is the macaroni and cheese and Margie made the desert. Sofia usually takes care of the vegetable and the iced tea, but we let her sleep. She's been pretty sick today. I was hoping she would join us and eat a little something."

Jason's heart raced when Miss Margaret mentioned Sofia. He was the only one at that table who knew why she was so sick that day. He hated Charlie Klim. Miss Margaret cleared his head of his Charlie thought.

"Jason, how's your family?"

Jason was surprised at her change in the subject matter. As usual he was caught off guard, but the question was easy enough. "They're fine."

Miss Margaret nodded her approval. "Let's bow our heads for the blessing."

Mary C. stepped out of her bathtub, wrapped herself in a towel and walked into her bedroom. She took her battle uniform from the two bags on the bed. Her makeup would be more like war paint, as she made herself as beautiful and desirable as she could. A look in the mirror when she removed the towel met with her approval. She was proud of her body and liked what she saw in the mirror. She would use her body as a vehicle for her revenge. It seemed only fitting that she would use her body as part of her rebirth.

Jason was sorry Sofia had not joined the dinner, but he was enjoying the food and the attention directed toward him. Margie was rubbing his right leg with her foot, while Peggy did the same to his left leg. He hoped their toes didn't touch. Susan couldn't reach him under the table, but if she could have, she would have been rubbing with the others. Miss Margaret directed most of the conversation to Jason.

"Jason, you have had an interesting and exciting week at your new job. Now that the week has ended, how do you like working out there?"

Jason was ready to add his few words to the conversation. "It's fine. I like it."

Margie couldn't help herself. "Mama, they call Jason the Jetty Man, because he saved that famous man."

Miss Margaret didn't know. "I knew you had saved a man from sure death, but I didn't know they had given you a name. Jetty Man, is it? Those workers are always ready to give somebody a new name. It really is an honor when your fellow man gives you the respect of calling you by a name that has meaning. You should be very proud to be called Jetty Man."

Jason liked the way she talked. She reminded him of her sister, Miss Margie.

Mary C. thought about Bobby and wondered if he was alright. She wasn't too worried, because she knew he could take care of himself. She had to stay focused on her plan and she would allow nothing to pull her away from the situation at hand. She was ready to begin her journey. The Falcon rolled toward the Fish Bowl.

It was time for dessert at the dinner and Margie was the star of the moment. She cut a big piece of cheesecake for Jason and smothered it with strawberries. It was the perfect ending to a perfect meal. He wished Sofia was there, but the dinner was still perfect. Margie's smile couldn't have been any bigger. She was proud when she handed Jason the plate.

"I hope you like cheesecake."

Jason's eyes answered for him. She knew he was pleased. She served her mother next and then her sisters. Jason understood being proud of something. He felt the same way about his work on the barge. He found another bond with Margie. He began eating his dessert.

CHAPTER TWELVE

MARY C. STOPPED THE FALCON IN THE PARKING LOT OF THE FISH BOWL. She sat in the car, looking at James' blue truck. Her preparation was flawless. She knew what she had to do, how to do it and had confidence in the outcome. She had to get her mind and body ready. Like the Spanish matador, her attire was dazzling and she would wave the red cape of sexual pleasure at her horned enemy and victim. When she stepped out of the Falcon and her heels touched the ground, she felt her calf muscles bulge as she stood up. Each step she took flexed her leg muscles and moved her closer to her prey. She entered the front door of the restuarant.

Mary C. never looked more beautiful or inviting than at that moment. She wore black leather short-shorts, exposing a small area of her butt cheeks on each side. Her white long-sleeved half blouse was tied in front, showing her stomach muscles. As usual she was braless and certain movements would expose her breasts. Under the long white sleeve, strapped to her forearm, was the Skinny Blackjack, the most important part of the uniform.

All eyes in the room were on her. She could feel each one, but she was only interested in two eyes in the head of the devil. Mary C. didn't realize James had been watching the door for her arrival. He saw her the moment she walked through the front door. The devil was already excited and hungry for her. She made her way to the bar. James tried to act as if she had little effect on him, but he wanted her that very moment when she stepped to the bar. She owned him already, she just didn't know it yet.

"Hey, James. How are ya?"

"I'm good, now that you're here."

She smiled and sat on the bar stool near one end of the bar. She wanted privacy when she talked to James. He made drinks for the other customers, but couldn't keep his eyes off Mary C.

"When you get a chance, fix me Jack Black on a little ice."

James stepped toward her. "An easy one?"

Mary C. smiled again. "I don't want anything easy tonight."

Her statement excited James even more than he was already. He was beside himself. He had plans to get off early, but he didn't want to wait.

Mary C. moved her drink to her lips. She could see the lustful rage in his eyes. She knew the fatal game had started.

After dessert, the dinner party moved into the living room. Jason was listening, as usual, as Miss Margaret and her daughters talked about a number of different subjects. Miss Margaret created the subjects for the conversation. Jason drifted at times with visions of his moments with the three sisters sitting near him and looking at him. He knew all eyes were on him. He had felt that before. Miss Margaret did not know it but she stopped his sexual visions.

"Jason, the weather is supposed to be terrible late tonight. I heard a Northeaster was coming in, and that usually means at least three bad days of wind and rain. I don't think you will be able to work on that barge if that storm comes in, do you?"

Jason knew nothing about a Northeaster and, as usual, was caught off guard by another question directed at him. Margie wanted to join in and doing so saved him for the moment, giving him more time to find his reply.

"Now, those rocks are scary when those storm waves start crashing on them. Remember that time we all rode to the beach before that hurricane? That was scary. You won't be able to work out there if a storm comes in."

Jason had time to collect his thoughts. "I didn't hear about the storm. Maybe it'll pass before Monday."

A hard knock on the door interrupted Jason's contribution to the conversation and startled the four ladies in the living room and their guest, Jason. They all looked toward the door, as Margie moved to see who was there. Miss Margaret wanted caution.

"Don't just open that door. See who it is first."

Magrie looked out the side window. "It's Mr. Leek, I think."

Margie opened the door. Miss Margaret didn't like it, but the door was already open. Mr. Leek stood on the porch, a few feet back from the door.

"Good evenin', Margie. I'm sorry to bother y'all at home. I need to talk to your father if he's here, please."

"Daddy's not here right now, but my mother's here."

"Could I speak to her, please?"

"Yes, just a second." She turned to the group in the living room.

Miss Margaret had heard Mr. Leek's request, so she joined Margie at the door. "Come in, Al, don't stand out there. What brings you here this evening?"

Mr. Leek stayed on the porch. "I don't need to come in. I've been workin' all day and I smell like a mullet. I'll stay out here. I do need to talk to you."

Miss Margaret stepped out onto the porch with Mr. Leek and closed the door, leaving Jason and her daughters in the house. The girls were quiet because it was unusual for Mr. Leek to be there talking to their mother privately. Jason knew it was strange too.

"What is it, Al?" She knew something was very wrong.

"It's Bobby Merritt, Jason's uncle. He's been killed."

"Oh no!" Miss Margaret's heart sank into her stomach.

"Jason told me he was comin' here tonight for dinner. They've been tryin' to find his mother, but no tellin' where she is on a

Saturday night."

"What happened?"

"Somebody shot him and a waitress from Bill's, at her house. Her name was Kelly. They think maybe it was a jealous boyfriend. The police are looking for the boyfriend now."

Miss Margaret shook her head in sadness. "That Bobby was a lady's man. This is awful. That poor boy in there. How much more can he take?"

Mr. Leek agreed. "I know. I was thinkin' about that on the way over here. His life has been full of tragedies and things were really gettin' better for him. He's come a long way, but somethin' like this could undo all the good and send him back to the wordless, emotionless child. That was a strange time for all of us who knew him."

Miss Margaret nodded her agreement. They both knew what Jason had endured during his young life.

"I'll send him out so you can tell him he needs to go with you and find his mother." Miss Margaret walked back into the living room.

"Jason, Mr. Leek needs to talk to you."

The three girl's looked at their mother and then at Jason. They knew something was wrong. He knew it, too.

"Yes, ma'am." Jason walked out onto the front porch. Mr. Leek closed the door. Jason's eyes were wide open.

"Yes sir."

Mr. Leek's throat went dry. He hated being the messenger. "Jason, it's your Uncle Bobby."

Jason's eyes widened even more and his stomach went sour. Mr. Leek's next words ripped him open.

"He's been killed."

Jason knew it was only one of his dreams. The cemetery, the dinner, Mr. Leek on that porch, it was all just a dream. He just needed to wake up. None of it could be real. Mr. Leek knew Jason was somewhere else at that moment. Jason's empty eyes told Mr. Leek he was no longer on the porch. He had to bring the young man back.

"Jason! Jason! We've got to find your mother. She needs to know what has happened. Do you know where she is?"

Jason returned to the porch. "You know for sure he's dead?"

"Yes, son. I'm so sorry."

"How?"

"Somebody shot him and a waitress named Kelly at her house near the beach."

Charlie Klim's face flashed in Jason's head. "Where did they find 'em?"

"At her house."

"No. I mean, where in the house?"

"I'm not sure about all the details."

"Where are the police now? Where is Uncle Bobby?"

"They're waiting for me at the dock and I think another policeman is waiting at your house in case your mother comes home."

"I need to go home first. Then I'll look for Mama. Thank Miss Margaret for me."

Mr. Leek didn't know what to say. He was surprised at Jason's calm reaction to the news. Perhaps he had been dulled to the effects of death or he was so deep in shock and would explode at another time. Either way it was a sad moment for them both.

Jason walked past Mr. Leek and climbed into Uncle Bobby's truck. As he started the motor, Sofia looked out her bedroom window. She watched him drive away and had no idea what was happening. She laid her head on her pillow. Mr. Leek gave Jason's "thank you" message to Miss Margaret.

James served Mary C. her second hard Jack Black on ice. She wanted to add to his rage.

"When can you get out of here? You're drivin' me crazy. I've been thinkin' 'bout this since we talked."

"Me too." She had the devil by his tail.

"You said you'd be my fantasy man and I've been thinkin' 'bout that."

"Yeah, so what's your pleasure?"

"I have a favorite spot in the woods. I've been there before, but never with a man who could satisfy my needs or please me. I know you don't mind bein' in the woods, so I thought we could go there. No one would bother us."

James's blood was boiling inside his perverted body. "Whatever you want. And it don't matter where."

She smiled and sipped on her drink. James called his replacement to come in earlier than planned. He wanted to be with Mary C. as soon as possible.

"I'm gettin' off earlier than I expected. When he gets here, we can go."

"Good, but we can't leave together. When he gets here, I'll leave and then you follow in a few minutes. I'll wait at the monument and you can follow me from there."

James nodded his approval of the plan. He was excited.

A young police officer was waiting on Jason's porch when he drove Uncle Bobby's truck into the yard. Jason jumped from the truck and the young man met him at the steps of the front porch.

"Sir, I'm Officer Johnston. I've been waiting for someone to return home. Are you Jason?"

"Yes."

"Do you know where your mother is at this time?"

"No."

The young officer hesitated.

Jason took the words from him. "I know 'bout my uncle."

"I'm sorry, sir."

Jason wanted to know more. "Do you know what happened?"

"Yes, sir. He was shot at a friend's house. She's dead too. Both shot, sir."

"Did ya see 'em?"

"Yes, sir. I was the first one to enter the house after it was reported."

"Can you tell me where you found them in the house?"

"I guess that'll be alright. The woman was in her bed and your uncle was in the bathroom. It looked like he was in the shower when it happened."

Jason entered a deep dark place in his dreamworld. He was

no longer with the young Officer Johnston. Charlie's words on the shuttle, about Uncle Bobby coming out of the shower, beat Jason like the blackjack his mother would soon swing. He saw the tree and Jessie, then Jake and Uncle Bobby dancing. Charlie's evil smile filled the dream, then a dead squirrel fell from a tree. The four sisters, like naked witches, beckoned him to the oak. Charlie's face pushed against the window of the truck. Sofia sceamed. The young police-man knew Jason had mentally left him.

"Sir! Mr. Jason! Are you alright, sir?"

Charlie's evil eyes faded and became Officer Johnston's eyes, as Jason returned from his visit to the darkness.

"I'm so sorry, sir. I know this is an awful shock to you."

Jason shook the young man's hand and walked past him into the house.

The first of eight chimes began on the living room clock. The police car drove away, but Jason didn't hear it or see it. The wind began to blow outside as the eighth chime sounded. The Northeaster Miss Margaret had mentioned was moving into Mayport. Jake's words of the tree, Jessie and Jason's destiny, filled his head. He knew Jake waited for him at the oak.

James's replacement behind the bar arrived and James was pre-paring to leave. Mary C. had already made her sex-walk through the main dining room and she was at her car in the back parking lot. The Falcon headed to the monument to wait for her abuser.

The monument was located about a mile from the Fish Bowl. It was a tall white concrete pillar with a metal shield-shaped insignia in the middle of the pillar. It was to honor the landing of the explorer Jean Ribault, near the St. Johns River. It was interesting how the little town of East Mayport was the resting place of such a beautiful monument.

Mary C. parked the Falcon next to the pillar and waited for James. She was there only a few minutes when the lights of James's rusty blue truck flashed on the dark road, coming straight at her. The truck slowed down when it approached the pillar. She didn't want James to stop because she knew how excited he was and he might not want to wait on his pleasure if he got his hands on her. As the truck began to stop Mary C. pressed the gas pedal on the Falcon and drove off with James following close behind. They headed toward the woods and Mary C.'s Indian burial grounds. She would not hunt for arrowheads that night. They were less than a mile from the turnoff that would take them into the woods and to Mary C.'s favorite place.

Jason's fragile mind was being bombarded with visions of the past and the present. He wanted to hide somewhere deep in the corners of his mind and never be found. He was an expert at doing just that. The moment had become desperate in his attempt to control his emotions and his sanity. He saw himself driving the big bowie knife into Charlie's heart as Charlie screamed in pain. The noise and the movement of the porch swing ended his vision. He stood on the porch with the bowie knife in his hand. He didn't remember getting the knife from his room, but it was there with him. The wind moved the swing again, announcing the arrival of the Northeaster. The air took Jason's breath and he thought about the tree. He could feel the strength of the wind increasing each time it touched him. A distant flash of lightning, far across the river, lit up the sky and caught his eye. A distant thunder rolled after the flash. The wind, lightning and thunder reminded Jason of the great oak tree.

He joined the wind and stood there with the familiar weapon and wanted Charlie Klim dead. It was only fitting that the knife did the honors and finished the job it started. Jason wanted to look into Charlie's eyes when it happened. He wanted Charlie to see him and know it was Jason. He wanted Charlie to know who was cutting his heart out. Jason was in the truck and driving out of the front yard. As if it was his partner, the big knife sat on the front seat next to Jason. He would find Charlie Klim.

Mary C. turned off the main road and onto the narrow hunter's trail leading to the Indian burial grounds. James was only a few feet behind her. The mounds were only a hundred yards away after the turn. She stopped in the area she knew well. Mary C. knew she would have to strike before James began his abuse. If he got his hands on her, she might not have the opportunity to deliver the blow she needed. She didn't want him to touch her at all.

Mary C.'s heart was racing as her hate for James filled her with courage. There was no turning back. She asked the Indian spirits to swing the weapon with her. The first swing had to do the job. She pulled the strap off the blackjack and slid it down into her hand and gripped it as she had been taught. James was out of his truck and walking toward her car door. She took her high heels off so she would have better balance and traction, or in case she had to run. She took a deep breath and stepped out of the car to meet the devil.

"Damn, Mary C., I didn't think we'd ever get here. I didn't know it was way out here." She stepped toward James as he moved toward her. His momentum carried him directly into the path of the moving blackjack. It was a perfect swing and connection. It sounded like a cannon going off in the quiet woods when it hit his head. The leather-covered metal hit James on his left temple, exactly where Skinny told her to strike. It opened up a huge horseshoe-shaped cut around his left eye. James fell against the side of the Falcon and stared at his attacker.

Mary C. was shaking with fear as she looked into his blank eyes. She wanted him on the ground. The second swing of her weapon hit James in the back of the head. Again, the cannon sound broke the silence surrounding them. She got her wish. He was on the ground.

Mary C. began working to complete her task. She picked up his heavy legs and placed one of his feet under each of her arms, so she could drag him in front of the Falcon. The car lights showed her the way into the woods. It was dark and she didn't want to be in the woods too long. She knew she had to hurry.

Jason drifted in and out of his dreamworld as he drove Uncle Bobby's truck. He had no idea where he was going, he was just going. His rage burned inside and the evil visions continued beating him like his mother had beaten James. His head cleared for a moment and he stopped the truck, hoping to find his bearings and remain in the world of reality. The pull was strong and he didn't know if he could beat it. He touched the big knife on the front seat next to him, making sure it was real. It was.

Mary C. sat James up against a tree. He made a painful noise in his throat. She wanted him to be alive. She collected the items she had placed in the woods the day before. Then she took a rope and tied him to the tree by wrapping the rope around his chest and stomach. She used the three-inch silver electrical tape to bind his legs together. She used the same tape and technique for his hands and head. Mary C. wrapped the tape around his forehead, pinning his head against the tree. The same was done to his throat and then she forced an object into his mouth, leaving only his eyes and nose uncovered. She wanted him to come to, and face her. He had to know it was her.

Mary C. gathered the rest of her revenge tools. She placed the four white paint buckets she had filled at Miss Ida Mae's on the ground next to him, along with the four Winn-Dixie grocery bags. She took the top off one of the white paint buckets. The smell was horrible, as she dumped the three-day-old pig swill on James's taped and bleeding head. The wet swill splattered all over him and the ground around him. The awful odor and the cold liquid hitting him all at once shocked James into consciousness. She loved it when he opened his eyes.

"Well, welcome back. I was afraid you wouldn't wake up and be able to see firsthand what was happenin'." James focused in on Mary C. and when he realized he was tied down, he panicked and struggled to free himself. He could not move at all. He could hardly breathe for the odor and he was choking on the object in his mouth. Mary C. moved closer to him so she would be eye-to-eye with the devil.

"You oughta like that pig slop drippin' off ya. I got plenty more for ya. And that thing you got stuck in your throat: that's my panties you hung in your truck, you son of a bitch. I just might hang yours on the mirror in my Falcon and ride around showin' em off like a blue ribbon. Here, let me cool ya off again."

His eyes widened as Mary C. poured another bucket of the pig swill in his face. He could do nothing to stop her.

Mary C. wanted to linger with her victim but she knew the woods

TURKEY BUZZARD

were too dangerous as the night moved on. James made noises as she dumped the other two buckets of swill on him. Then, she poured the contents on the grocery bags on him too. They were full of all kinds of food she had allowed to spoil and become rotten. The last bag was full of corn. She dumped it between his legs. He shook his body and continued his noises.

Mary C. knew she had to go. The smell and the food would get the attention of the creatures that came out at night, looking for a meal. The car lights were the only thing keeping them away at the moment. She knew it wouldn't be long before they came calling. She walked toward the car, stopped and walked back to tell James one more thing. They were eye-to-eye for the last time. She could see and feel the fear, hate and horror in his eyes.

"This is what knocked the shit out of you." She patted the leather black jack against the palm of her hand. "It's called a blackjack, if ya didn't know. That name kinda fits ya, don't it?"

James tried to beg her with his eyes, to stop, as she turned and walked to the Falcon. The woods went dark around him as the Falcon backed away and Mary C. turned the car around. He watched the red taillights disappear down the narrow hunter's trail.

It was pitch dark around him at first. Then his eyes adjusted to the small amount of moonlight coming through the clouds and tree limbs above him. His attempts to free himself were useless; only Mary C. could save him and she was at the wheel of the Falcon headed back to Mayport.

James's left eye was closing from the swelling, but he opened both eyes as wide as he could. He also knew the creatures of the night would smell him from miles away. He was worried about the bigger animals and he had no idea the smaller animals would be dropping in first.

It took only a few stinging bites for James to realize he had fire ants all over him. He had no way to brush away the tiny insects. They bit him, wherever and whenever they wanted. His next visitor was one of the bigger animals he feared would be appearing.

A small bobcat walked slowly toward him, sniffing the ground,

MONSTER PIG

as it made its way closer to his feet. The small cat started eating some fish that had fallen from Mary C.'s grocery bags, then moved to James, licking and biting his left boot. The cat continued eating the food off the ground around him.

Every kind of bug in the woods was crawling on James in a matter of minutes. He was numb to the ants, but they continued to bite him. He heard an owl call above him in the tree, but he couldn't move his head to see it.

He saw a shadow of something, as it flew down from the trees around him. At first he thought it was the owl. He tried to see where it had landed, but again he was unable to move his head. He could see only the creatures directly in front of him. Two big opossums and a small one began fighting over pieces of lettuce near his leg. Their fight carried the two big ones onto his body and the claws on their feet and paws scratched his neck, as the two climbed over him.

The shadows he had seen from above were black buzzards. The scavenger birds hopped toward him and started eating something near the tree behind him. One jumped on his chest and picked at the blood on his face. He couldn't move his head, so he closed his eyes as the black bird's sharp beak penetrated his closed eyelid. He could feel the skin being pulled away and it was only a matter of seconds before his eye was picked out of his head. He cried and asked God to save him and forgive him his sins.

The buzzard was gone. The bobcat was gone. The other animals were gone. The insects continued eating him, but the disturbing silence had his shaky and broken attention. He saw movement in the woods directly in front of him. He thought Mary C. had tortured him enough and she was satisfied with the lesson she had given him. There was hope in his evil heart, until he saw the first of six huge wild boars, sniffing the ground and charging to the dinner table. The first wild pig that reached James was a true monster with a crooked and broken tusk. The monster drove his big nose and tusk into the pile of corn between James's legs. The other wild boars joined their leader. Their hunger and the corn made them crazy. They would eat, fight and tear James to peices. Only the creatures of the night and the Indian spirits would hear his muffled screams.

Mary C. had not noticed the wind while she was deep in the woods. She would never know her revenge was not only for her, but it was also for her new friend, Sheriff McIntosh. The Falcon rounded the curve at the little jetties. She had to find Bobby and Jason.

Jason was still sitting in the truck and his visions ended the moment he stopped the truck and pulled off the road. He had no idea where he was and the wind and fog coming across the river didn't help his situation. The wind blew white sand against the windshield. Jason stepped out of the truck so he would have some idea where he was. He knew as soon as his feet hit the ground, he was standing at the bottom of the sand hill and the oak tree was above him in all its glory, waiting for a bolt of lightning to cut a few notches in its limbs.

Jason's legs seemed to go against his will, as he began his slow climb to stand next to the tree. He didn't remember picking the bowie knife up off the front seat, but it was in his hand as he made his walk. Jason was no stranger to the surroundings. More visions from the past flashed in his head as he came closer to the oak. He saw his friend Eddie with blood and sand on his face. He had seen that vision many times. Willis called for Jason to swing down. The ferry horn started the race. His trip into the past had taken him to the tree; he stood on solid ground. The tree was only a few feet away. He had not stood there in five years and he didn't want to be there then.

He touched the tree with his hand and walked around its huge trunk, never breaking contact, as he had done the first time he was introduced to the tree. On his first circle the wind stopped blowing under the tree. On his second complete circle he saw Jake standing below the sand hill near the grape arbor. At the completion of his third circle he found himself staring into Jessie's green eyes. He had not done that wonderful thing in five years. He had no fear; it was his destiny. She was only there to fulfill the Breeding with Jason; it was her destiny. He knew there would be no words. He had none anyway and Jessie never had any. They were perfect for the secrets of the oak.

Jessie wore a white nightgown-type covering that revealed her naked body when she dropped it off her shoulders to the ground beneath the tree. She moved to Jason, as she had done before, and pressed her body to his. She worked her magic and his pants and shirt were on the sand with her gown. She wasted little motion as she lay down in the sand and pulled Jason down on top of her. Jessie reached down and placed Jason inside her and like before she did all the work. She moved and pushed until he was deep inside her body.

Jessie rolled them both over and sat on top of Jason, driving him even deeper. He had seen her in that position before. She was like a wild animal as she moved, made her noises and worked for deeper penetration. Jason was again on familiar ground. He loved it, but could not control himself. Jessie screamed an unnatural scream as they both exploded at the same time. Jason looked up at Jessie when she screamed and saw a flash of lightning in the sky behind and above her. They were perfect. The Breeding was done.

Jason was on his knees trying to recover some sense of reality. He knew this dream well. He looked at Jessie's naked body lying in the white sand. The imprints of their bodies filled the sand around her. He touched his forehead to the trunk of the tree, hoping it was all the same dream that had haunted his nights. A noise turned him away from the tree and back to Jessie. She was gone from the sand. At first his dream theory seemed true, but a second look told him it was all real, as he saw Jake moving down the other side of the sand hill. The skinny black man had wrapped his black trench coat around Jessie's naked body and she was moving away with him.

Jason stood alone at the tree. The wind began to blow and wiped the white sand off his naked body. He saw his shirt and pants where they had been dropped. Her gown was there too. He put his clothes on and left Jessie's Breeding gown in the sand. He wanted to make the walk back down to Uncle Bobby's truck and get away from the tree. Another lightning bolt cracked in the sky above the tree, causing Jason to turn quickly to see if it hit the mighty oak.

He saw no fireball from above hit the tree, but what he did see caused his blood flow to change directions and he felt as if his heart would beat its way out of his chest. The bowie knife was sticking into the trunk of the oak tree. Jason was afraid, yet he found himself stepping to the knife. The entire blade was stuck into the wood, with only the handle visible. It was deep into the bark. Jason gripped the handle and pulled. It was too deep. He pulled harder, but the tree would not let go of the steel blade. The tree challenged Jason again. He wanted his knife.

He grabbed the handle with both hands and put his foot on the tree for more leverage. For the first few seconds of Jason's effort the tree held the knife. Jason used all his strength and yelled in dispair when he lost his grip and fell to the sand. He looked up at the limbs above him. He wished it all to be a dream. The tree had given him his knife back. It was in his hand. He knew he needed it to complete his victory over the evil one.

Mary C. began the battle; her son would finish it. He left the tree and walked back to the truck. He had to find Charlie Klim. No one on the sand hill that night knew the Breeding, and Jason's struggle with the knife had a one-woman audience.

Margie, the oldest, had left the house when her mother told them about Uncle Bobby, hoping to comfort Jason. She saw the truck and knew he was at the tree. She was in shock at what she had seen and afraid when she found herself standing near the huge trunk of the oak tree. She didn't remember making the climb up the sand hill. She touched the oak with her trembling hand and moved around it, as Jason had done. She made one complete circle, then she picked up Jessie's gown from the sand. She felt a weight on her shoulders and she was on her knees. She was light-headed as she lay back in the sand looking up into the limbs and branches above her. A cool breeze touched her body and she realized for the first time she was naked. It felt like the sand was rubbing her back. She rolled over and over, joining her body prints with the prints of the true Breeders.

Margie got what she wanted: her formal introduction to the oak tree. After that night, she would visit the oak many times and become a true believer. She would remember it all but never tell anyone, not even her sisters. She loved Jason even more and hoped to one day fulfill the Breeding with him. Jason pulled away in the truck while the oak played with its new disciple.

Mary C. was home and worried about her two men. She stood on the porch looking into the darkness and the Northeaster. A set of car lights flashed on the road leading to her house. She hoped it was Bobby's truck, but it didn't look like his lights. When she realized it wasn't Bobby's truck, she thought of Charlie Klim and she walked to the Falcon to get the blackjack. In a way she hoped it was the evil one. It wasn't. Mr. Leek's truck drove up to her porch and he stepped out into her yard.

"Mary C., we've been lookin' all over for you."

She could see the concern on his face. She knew something was wrong. "Why? What is it?"

Mr. Leek took a deep breath. He hated being the messenger again. "It's Bobby, Mary C. It's Bobby. He's been killed."

She didn't want to hear it again, but she asked anyway. "What did you say?"

"Bobby's been killed. He's dead, Mary C." Her legs went weak and Mr. Leek grabbed her as she sat down on the floor of the porch.

"I hate to be the one with such awful news. We couldn't find ya. I've been checkin' here 'bout every hour since I talked to Jason."

"You told Jason? When?"

"Earlier tonight, over at Margaret's. I think he came back here first, looking for you. Then he left."

Bobby being dead had no place in her mind. "Are you sure 'bout Bobby?"

"Mary C., the police found him and that waitress both shot to death at her house."

"Oh God! Kelly too?"

Mr. Leek nodded his head. "The police think her old boyfriend caught 'em together."

Charlie's evil face flashed in her head. She remembered him saying he wanted to take a shower there and he knew where Kelly lived. She had to know more. "Do you know any details about what happened? Where's Bobby now?"

"He's at the police station and they're waiting for you. I've already identified him, but they need a relative for the paperwork."

"You saw Bobby?"

"I saw 'em."

"Did they tell you what happened?"

"The only thing they know is the woman was killed in the bedroom and Bobby was in the shower when he was shot."

Mary C.'s heart raced like Jason's and she knew the boyfriend was not the killer. It was the evil one who had taken her brother, so he could be with her, with no interference. She knew he would take Jason next.

Mary C. had no idea Jason was parking Uncle Bobby's truck next to Charlie Klim's car, outside at Bill's Hideaway. The weather kept most of the regular customers home that night, so there were only a few cars parked on the sand.

Jason stepped out of the truck and onto the beach sand. He took his partner off the front seat and stuck the bowie knife down into the back of his pants, covering the handle with his shirt. The big blade lay flat against the crack of his butt. He walked up the steps to the deck above. He looked toward the tree, as the wind from the Northeaster moved his hair from his eyes. He walked through the swinging doors that opened into the honky tonk.

The main room was empty, except for one couple at a corner table. The jukebox was silent and there was no life to the room at all. Jason reached in his pocket and took out a five-dollar bill. He walked to the bar and requested five dollars in quarters. He heard the cue ball crack and pool balls rolling on the table in the game room, as he walked to the quiet juke box. He filled the coin slot with the quaters and punched in every Elvis song on the song list. He walked toward the game room.

Mary C. wanted to find Jason. Mr. Leek had a suggestion.

"He may have gone to see Bobby. The police talked to him and he may be waiting for you there."

She agreed. "That's true. I need to go there first. I need to be with

Bobby. Where do I go?"

"Get a jacket and I'll take ya. You don't need to be drivin' by ya'self."

Mary C. went into the house for her coat and then left with Mr. Leek for the police station. Her own act of murder would not cross her mind again that night. She considered it an act of justice and the defeat of an evil presence.

Jason saw Charlie's black Derby hat first, before he saw Charlie. It was sitting in a chair near the pool table. Charlie and another man were in the middle of a game of Eight Ball when Jason stepped into the light. Charlie was setting up a shot when he looked up and saw Jason standing at the end of the table. Charlie smiled, that smile Jason hated, and looked back down at the cue ball and made his shot. His heart was too cold to be disturbed by Jason.

"Hey, boy. What brings you out on a stormy night? Did ya mama send you to get me?"

Jason hated Charlie and he could only stare at the evil one.

"Ya kinda eyeballin' me, boy. I don't like nobody lookin' at me like they wanna do somethin' to me. You wanna do somethin' to me, boy?"

Charlie's friend wanted to play. "Charlie, can't ya see the fool's either crazy or drunk? Make ya damn shot."

Charlie tossed some money on the table. "It's your game. I need to take this boy outside and talk to him. I'm gonna be his stepdaddy, ya know. He needs to show me a little more respect than I seem to be gettin' here tonight."

The man took the money and went to sit at the bar. Charlie took the hat from the chair and put it on his head, then turned to Jason. Jason did hate that hat.

"Come on outside with me. We'll greet the Northeaster and discuss our problems and possible future."

Jason didn't let Charlie get close to him, but he did follow behind his enemy, as they walked through the main room and out the swinging doors onto the top deck outside.

Charlie stood at the railing. Jason kept his distance and was ready to defend himself or run, whichever he needed. The Northeaster was blowing the white foam off the waves and it was rolling up under the building. Other waves were crashing against the big red jetty rocks.

"You don't talk much, do ya, boy? That's good, I guess. I want ya to see my scars one day and when I'm married to ya mama, I want ya to say ya sorry 'bout what ya did to me. That'll be ya weddin' present to me."

Jason wanted to scream and cut Charlie's head off with the knife. He knew the time was not right, but he also knew it was his destiny.

"What are ya doin' here tonight, boy? Why ya look so mad at me? I really don't like that look you give me." Charlie was surprised when Jason's voice joined the wind from the storm.

"My mama did send me to get ya. Somebody killed Uncle Bobby and she told me to see if you'd come be with her." Jason could see Charlie's insane evil heart fill with a crazy pride.

"Did she now?"

Jason nodded.

"Well, why didn't ya tell me she needed me, boy?"

Jason looked down and humbled himself to the evil one. "I was scared of ya. 'Cause of what I done to ya."

"So somebody killed Bobby?"

Jason put his head down again. "Yes, sir."

"Damn, I always liked Bobby. He was funny and damn if he didn't sound just like Elvis."

Jason hated him.

"Where's ya mama now, boy?"

"She's at the house waitin' for us."

"Well, hell, let's go. We oughta not keep ya mama waitin'."

Charlie turned toward the steps and put his hand on the railing. With one motion Jason pulled the bowie knife from his pants, chopped off two of Charlie's fingers as they held onto the wooden railing, and grabbed Charlie's Derby hat off his head. Jason moved halfway down the steps after his attack. He stood there and bathed in Charlie's pain. Charlie looked down at Jason with pain and hate in his eyes, holding his bloody hand against his chest with his other hand.

"You are crazy, boy." Charlie grimaced in pain as he watched Jason put on his Derby hat. "You are the craziest son of a bitch around. But you're a dead son of a bitch. I'm gonna kill ya, just like I killed Bobby. Then I'm gonna go eat ya mama and stick this hand up her ass." Charlie held up his bloody three-fingered hand. Jason wanted to run back up to him and cut him some more. Charlie took that thought away when he started moving down the steps.

Jason moved onto the beach. He hated Charlie's words about his mother, but he knew he couldn't get careless with a man like Charlie. One foolish mistake would be too costly. Jason backed away as Charlie stumbled down the steps. He almost fell, but managed to keep his balance. Jason could see his enemy was in great pain. He had seen that look on Charlie's face before. Jason was prepared for Charlie to come after him. He was not prepared for Charlie to move to his car. Jason stepped further away, as Charlie used his good hand to open his car door. He reached into the car and pulled out his shotgun from the front seat. Charlie turned and fired the gun at Jason, spraying the small metal pellets all around Jason. Most of the pellets hit the wooden steps, while others kicked up the sand. The distance between Charlie and Jason, the wind and Charlie's state of pain caused Charlie's aim to be less than accurate. Jason was, however, hit by a number of pellets. They entered his right thigh and left side, right under his rib cage. He knew he had been hit.

Jason ran under the building to the wooden pylons. Charlie's second shot tore wood off one of the pylons near Jason and a pellet pierced the top of Jason's ear. He was hit again and bleeding from three different spots on his body. Jason watched Charlie walk toward the pylons and reload his gun. Jason left the pylons and ran to the big red jetty rocks. Charlie had two shells left in the gun, but Jason didn't know that. The evil one would wait for the right moment to kill Jason and get his hat back. Charlie knew he would catch him at the rocks. Jason would be trapped and have nowhere to go. He could take his time as he limped toward the rocks.

Jason reached the rocks and looked back to see if Charlie was still coming. Charlie's pain and hate were driving him on as he made his way to the jetties. Jason had to move up into the rocks as Charlie drew closer. He was insane enough to chase Jason all night and Jason knew it.

The rocks were wet and slippery and Jason figured Charlie would have a hard time getting to him in his condition. Jason jumped down between two rocks as Charlie reached the first rock Jason had stood on earlier. Charlie took a breather.

"Come on, boy. Be a damn man for a change. You always hit 'n' run. Stick that head of yours up one time from them rocks, so I can blow it into the river. Ya gonna make good crab bait, boy."

Jason could see Charlie through the rocks and he knew the pellets could reach him if Charlie shot at him again.

"After I shoot ya, boy, I'm gonna take that big knife of yours and cut ya head off. Ya mama ain't never gonna see ya again. Everybody's gonna say, 'What the hell happened to Jason? He musta went crazy after Uncle Bobby died.' But the crabs'll know where ya went."

As Charlie talked he moved up onto a higher rock, hoping for a better vantage point. Jason knew Charlie was closer, but he didn't move. Charlie wasn't high enough to see him. If Charlie moved again, Jason would have to run, but not yet. Charlie wanted to torment Jason even more.

"I like this weather. It's good for killin'. It's gloomy and shit. Ya need gloomy weather when ya cut somebody's head off. Killin's gloomy, ain't it? It was gettin' gloomy when I caught Bobby in that shower. His little weenie was hard when I shot it off. Hell, I almost missed it. And that big tittied woman he was with, she didn't keep my attention for more than an hour. She just didn't have any imagination."

Jason was sick to his stomach from Charlie's words, fear and pain. He looked into the darkness in the direction of the oak tree. He couldn't see it, but he knew it was there. A wave from the ocean side of the jetties slammed into the rocks near Jason and splashed him and Charlie with salt water.

Jason didn't know why, but when the water from the wave had

passed, he stood up and faced the evil one. Charlie saw Jason standing on a rock above him. He was within the range of the shotgun.
Charlie was insane and was happy to see Jason.

"Hey, boy! Bein' the Jetty Man sure ain't made ya no smarter,
has it? Damn, boy, ya bleedin' a bunch, ain't ya?" Charlie stepped
closer.

"I want my hat back, damn it. I'm gonna put it on ya mama's
head when she's suckin' on me. I'll think of you. Like ya right there
with us."

Jason knew Jake was right. It was time. Time for Jessie, the oak
and the evil one.

Charlie fired the gun again, spraying Jason and the rocks around
him. Jason fell into the rocks below him and he knew he had been hit
again. He was bleeding from his neck and the side of his face.

"Damn, boy, ya dead yet? Show ya'self one more time and I
won't have to climb up into these damn rocks to finish ya off. There
better not be no holes in my hat."

Jason was hurt and he knew he couldn't take any more pellets
hitting him. Charlie had shot at him three times and hit him each
time. He was soaked in salt water and blood.

Another big wave crashed into the rocks, covering Jason with
water. The salt water burned each small hole the pellets had made
on his body. He didn't realize Charlie had moved closer to him.
He looked up and the evil one stood on the rock directly over him.
Charlie held the gun up and aimed it at Jason's head. Charlie was
truly insane.

"I thought I hit ya with that last shot. Hell, I ain't missed ya yet.
Do me a favor since we're gonna be family and shit. Move my hat out
of the way."

The Derby was next to Jason on the rock. He picked it up and put
it on his head. Charlie smiled and shook his head.

"Ya know, I never thought ya was as crazy as everybody said,
but tonight you have made a believer of me. Ya don't really think
that'll save ya head, do ya?"

Charlie pulled the trigger of the shotgun at the same time the third and biggest wave crashed into the rocks. Most of the pellets bounced off the rocks and hit both Jason's legs. He screamed in pain as the water from the wave covered him and tossed him over another rock. Charlie was knocked off his rock and slammed into another. The empty shotgun fell from his hand and was lost in the water and rocks. The water carried Charlie from one rock to another, and like Jason, he was completely covered with water for a few seconds.

Jason couldn't see Charlie at first. He knew the pellets had hit him again. Jason was in pain as he crawled over two rocks, trying to find the evil one. He reached for the bowie knife, but the water and rocks had taken it too. Jason saw the barge above him, through the fog. He realized he was on his lunch rock. He laid back on the flat surface and for a moment felt safe. He closed his eyes, hoping it was another bad nightmare. A painful noise told him it was real.

Jason crawled to the edge of his lunch rock, in the direction of the noise. Jason looked over the edge into the rocks below him and saw Charlie. He was bleeding from the side of his head and he was wedged between two rocks. Each time a wave hit the rocks the area around Charlie would fill with water. The tide was coming in and most of the rocks would be underwater within the hour. Charlie would be covered sooner than that. Jason stared at the evil one from his special rock. Charlie looked up and smiled. He was the most insane of them all.

"Hey, boy, you dyin' too?"

Jason watched another wave cover Charlie. He was covered with water for a long time. Charlie shook his head as the water went down.

"I hope you're dyin' with me. Tell me ya are. Say somethin', damn it. If ya not gonna talk to me, do me a favor and throw my hat down here."

Jason smiled and joined the conversation. "No!"

Jason lay on his rock through the night, all day Sunday and Sunday night. With no one fishing on the rocks during the storm, he would not be found until Monday morning when the barge workers arrived.

The storm was over, as strong hands moved Jason's torn and bloody body from the lunch rock. Big Jim and Mr. Hawkins carried their young friend to an ambulance, waiting on the beach. Jason had entered his dreamworld again, with no doorway back to reality.

A young man dressed in white pushed his silent wheelchair patient through the courtyard at the Chattahoochee Mental Hospital.

"I wish you could stay outside longer, Mr. Jason, but you know the rules."

A cool breeze touched the patient's face and moved his hair, igniting a small flame in a dark and forgotten section of his mind. His thoughts were shaky and broken, but they brought to his ears a voice from the past:

"Pea-nuts! Pea-nuts! Boiled and roasted."